ــ ــ ــ

## *666*
## *+666*
## *1998*

# *The Year Of The*
# *Beast*

**Book Number:** _1125_/10,000

_____
**Author Autograph**

Other books by Chris Cawood

*Legacy Of The Swamp Rat*

*Tennessee's Coal Creek War*

*How To Live To 100 (and enjoy it)*

*Carp* (To be published in 1997)

This book is the first in a series of mystery and general fiction by Chris Cawood. A selected number of each edition are autographed and numbered. If your book is autographed and numbered and you would like to receive the next in the series with the same number and also autographed, please phone the publisher and reserve your copy: 1-800-946-1967.

# 666
# 666
# +666
# 1998
# The Year Of The Beast

By Chris Cawood
Magnolia Hill Press
Kingston, Tennessee

Cover design by Chris Cawood and Hartgraphics of Knoxville, Tennessee. Author photo by Cindy Holmes.  Back cover photo by Grant L. Robertson and used by permission.

Printed in United States.

Library of Congress Catalog Card Number 96-94050

ISBN 0-9642231-9-8

5 4 3 2 1

*This is dedicated to all the women in my life who have supported and encouraged me during this project: Sara, Gaynell, Sandra, Suzanne, and Ruthie.*

### Revelation 13:18

*"Here is wisdom. Let him that hath understanding count the number of the beast: for it is the number of a man; and his number is Six Hundred Threescore and Six."*

### The Twenty-fifth Amendment
### To The United States Constitution

Section 1:  *In case of the removal of the President from office or of his death or resignation, the Vice President shall become President.*

Section 2:  *Whenever there is a vacancy in the office of the Vice President, the President shall nominate a Vice President who shall take office upon confirmation by a majority vote of both Houses of Congress.*

### Moammar Gadhafi—January, 1996.

*"Our confrontation with America used to be like confronting a fortress from outside. Today we have found a loophole to enter the fortress and to confront it from within."*

# One

The crowd waiting in Jackson Square counted down in unison as the seconds of 1997 melted away to the New Year of 1998. Hopes of new lives, dreams of rekindled loves, and desires for untold riches mingled throughout this assemblage of humanity. It was the hour of resolution, the day of inspiration, and it would be the year of the beast.

Brad Yeary's ambitions were narrower. His most immediate craving was just to make it through the night. And, if possible, to do that in the arms of the woman he held—Jill Crenshaw. His mind rushed ahead. His yearnings often outgaited his persuasive abilities.

New Orleans, though, brought out the romantic in everyone. The Quarter, from its wrought-iron balconies, overlooked a sea of all manner of humankind. Tourists, criminals, politicians, hookers, addicts, the homeless, the depressed, the down, the up, the religious, the cultish—they all populated this undulating sea. Blaring, somewhat melodious, music from brass instruments filled the night. Anyone who had ever been near a sax came out on New Year's Eve. For what seemed like the hundredth time that evening, Brad Yeary and Jill Crenshaw listened to a lyrical rendition of "When the Saints Go Marching In." That, mixed with "Old Lang Syne," set the tone for this hour.

A river of bodies flowed thickly through the narrow streets off Bourbon and toward Jackson Square. It was New Year's Eve in Party City. New York had its Apple, but New Orleans had its sax—and its sex too, for that matter.

New Orleans was the sexiest city in America. Brad's mind would wander to almost stream of consciousness thinking after he had two drinks. That's why he rarely drank. He was an anomaly in his profession—a reporter who seldom lifted the bottle.

"Are you one of those boozing reporters?" his first landlady had asked, as though there could be no other kind. And it was with a great degree of skepticism that she allowed him to rent the apartment—to which even a drunk would have had a difficult time doing additional damage. Today, a squadron of city departments with a phalanx of bureaucratic enforcers would have condemned it, but then—twenty years ago—it was an advantage not to be sober in order to live there.

Now, here in this close area that spanned the distance between the ghostly, water-colored St. Louis Cathedral and the levee of the Mississippi, the greatest congregating of bodies in New Orleans pushed and shoved. Eyes watched the white ball of light on the Jackson Brewing Company building across the way as though the stroke of midnight held some magical powers.

The city had magic—black magic, white magic, witchcraft, and all of the occult—in its history. But what was so special about New Year's Eve and the stroke of midnight when 1997 became 1998? It was already 1998 in New York and the rest of the East Coast that cloaked itself in Eastern Standard time.

"Let's go to bed at eleven and celebrate the new year with the Easterners and get a head start on all these crazy people," he had told Jill earlier.

But she wouldn't buy it. Just like a politician. But at forty-four, Brad sought the comforts of bed and the promise of sleep more than the excitement of the hour. Maybe in four years when Jill arrived at forty she would feel the same way. Tonight he would appease her by holding her into 1998. Then they would retire to the loaned Governor's Suite of the St. Laurent Hotel.

The great throng of celebrants swayed—packed together so tightly that the weak fainted and the brave barely withstood the pushing and shoving in fear of their lives. Breath oozed from bodies as they crammed against each other, the walls, and wrought-iron fence of the public area. Brad's agoraphobia met and shook hands with his claustrophobia.

Horns sounded, firecrackers exploded, and in the distance the report of guns being fired into the sky built to a crescendo of ear-shattering decibels.

"It's dangerous here, Jill. Those bullets could come down and kill us. It's happened before."

Jill turned toward him, her long hair brushing against his face. "A former police reporter afraid of a little shooting? Come on. Loosen up and enjoy it." She turned back toward the Jackson Brewing Company where fireworks arched over its roof in premature celebration.

Brad braced his back and legs against the cold concrete wall that supported the fence and tried to make a little separation between them and the unmovable for safety's sake. Being pinned against the hard surface and crushed lifeless if the mass rocked too far in his direction did not appeal to him. He wrapped his arms around Jill and gently kissed her neck. To hell with the fireworks. His own flames were burning within. He squeezed her body to his and wondered how long it would take them to walk the two blocks to their hotel after the year arrived. The perfume of her neck echoed with expected joys.

"Behave now. What if someone saw the Speaker of the State Senate of Louisiana kissing and groping with a despised reporter in the French Quarter of New Orleans? Word would get back to Baton Rouge before the New Year did."

A state senator in line to be the next governor had to be careful. Politics is politics. "There's always someone watching," she had told him numerous times. "Conduct yourself in public as though you are on the six o'clock news," she had said. "Because if you don't, you probably will be."

"Five, four, three, two, one . . . HAPPY NEW YEAR!" the thousands shouted somewhat in unison, horns blaring. Old man 1997 slunk away with all his disappointments and forgotten resolutions, never again to be, and the proud Babe 1998 entered the heart of New Orleans on wings of highest expectation.

State Senator Jill Crenshaw and *Times-Gazette* reporter Brad Yeary turned toward each other and there kissed, groped, and fondled in the presence of all—none of whom noticed.

IT WAS ELEVEN O'CLOCK New Year's morning before Brad sat up on the edge of the bed and looked toward the thick drapes where the sun's slanting rays were barely drifting in. He rubbed his eyes and turned toward Jill who was lying the opposite direction facing the wall with the sheet pulled over her eyes. He stood, walked to the window, and, pulling the curtains back, peered down to where the survivors of New Year's Eve were beginning to populate the narrow street—already out and into the sleazy souvenir shops.

The predominant colors were red and green—not leftovers from the Christmas just past—but the colors of the University of Alabama and Notre Dame who would play that night in the Sugar Bowl at the Superdome for college football's national championship. Red far outnumbered green for two basic reasons. First, practically the whole state of Alabama had migrated over to New Orleans for the game. Secondly, Catholics drank more than Baptists—so, many of the followers of Notre Dame were still holed up in their hotels with pillows over their heads or else sipping black coffee and swallowing aspirin.

He sat back down on the bed and picked up the phone from the stand.

"Jill, I'm calling room service for breakfast. What do you want?"

She rolled over and pulled the sheet tighter around her. He

asked again and began dialing.

"Nothin'," she mumbled from under the cover.

"You sure?"

"Okay, arn jew n toes."

"What? What did you say?" He wrinkled his nose at her as he told room service to wait.

She sat straight up. "Dammit. Orange juice and toast. Can't you understand anything?" she shouted and lay back down. "It's too early to be bothered. You've got to enunciate perfectly for a reporter or else they'll misquote you every time." She scrunched her knees up toward her breasts and closed her eyes.

He ordered. The healthy breakfast for her, and for him scrambled eggs, sausage, grits, and hash brown potatoes. A pot of coffee, a large orange juice, and two beignets for good measure. He could stand it. He was in good shape. One hundred ninety pounds on a six-foot frame. He ran two miles three times a week, played tennis, and worked out with weights occasionally. For a reporter he didn't think he was all that bad.

He walked to the bathroom mirror and there was harshly reminded that he was no longer a youngster. He pushed back the gray strands of hair that began at his sideburns and ended just at ear level. Brushed straight back with only a hint of a part in the middle, his thick hair reached just below his collar. He had calculated that the gray was migrating up his head a quarter inch per year. At that rate of progression, it would be another fifteen years before he was totally gray. Then there would always be hair coloring, although he had not dipped into that bottle yet. He was thankful that he still had a full head of hair—mostly brown with just the maturing look of silver.

He splashed cold water on his face and brushed his hair back.

Room service knocked at the door. A dark-complected local youth wheeled in the cart. Beads of sweat dotted his forehead. The kitchen was hot work even if it was just going and coming. He uncovered the steaming food that Brad had ordered, arranged the plates, poured the coffee, smiled, took the tip from Brad, and walked toward the door.

"Rough night, Senator Crenshaw?" He grinned and glanced toward the prone politician. Then he was gone.

Brad smiled. There was no secrecy, no privacy, no hangovers when you were in the public eye. Jill just grunted.

She finally sat up on the edge of the bed and sipped from her orange juice. She brushed her more-blond-than-brown hair back out of her face, tied Brad's terry-cloth robe around her, and looked at him. He pulled his chair up to face her and scooted the cart between them.

"Don't look at me this early in the morning." She took a bite off the corner of one piece of toast. "I know I look awful. What time is it anyway?"

"Eleven-thirty."

"Why are we up so early?  We don't have to be to the dome until seven tonight."

"It's a new day, Jill. A new month. In fact, a new year. We've got to beat it to the punch."

"It can wait. Give me a drink of your coffee."

"Do you want some of my sausage and eggs? Or a beignet?"

"No. It's not good for me. It'll make me fat, and I know you don't like fat women." She raised her eyebrows toward him.

"I love you, though," he said and took a big bite of the beignet. He wiped the powdered sugar from his face with the back of his hand.

"Were you talking to me or the beignet?"

"You. The beignet already knows." He reached over and patted her under the chin. "You were wonderful last night."

She looked up. "I was? What did we do?"

"Everything." He smiled, stood, and took his coffee to the window.

"Aren't you going to finish all this food?" She reached over and broke off a piece of the sweet pastry without him seeing and hurried it to her mouth while she watched him at the window. "It'll go to waste if you let it get cold."

"In a minute. Look at all these people out walking around—enjoying themselves. They have the day off, but you and I have to work today. It's not fair."

"The waiter that brought our food had to work. What we're going to do wouldn't be considered work by most folks. The people with service jobs are the ones treated unfairly. You and I have it made."

"There you go talking like a Democrat again." He returned to the chair, picked up the beignet and noticed the missing corner. "You have to be in the official state party delegation for the game, and I have to cover the activities for the paper. I even have to interview the dumb-ass Vice President at half-time."

"Vice President Harrot isn't a dumb-ass. Just because he's from Alabama, you've labeled him a dumb-ass. That's not fair."

"No, I labeled him a dumb-ass because he agreed to be Vice President. He was a good senator. He had some modern, progressive, and even original thoughts when he was serving as senator. But he's wasting away as Vice President. He should have listened to the advice of John Nance Garner."

"Who was John Nance Garner, and what was his advice, may I ask?" She took a long drink of her juice.

"Garner was one of the Vice Presidents under Franklin Roosevelt. He said the Vice Presidency isn't worth a jar of warm spit."

Jill swallowed hard. "Oh, please, Brad. It's too early for your earthy recollections of politicians long departed." She looked up. "Are you sure he said 'spit'?"

Jill moved the cart away and joined Brad at the table near the window where they both could look down on the ever-increasing crowd of milling people. Brad turned the television to the local news at noon. They showed a clip of Vice President Samuel Harrot arriving the day before with his wife and an entourage of Secret Service and press.

"Have you ever interviewed Harrot before?" Jill asked, looking at the screen.

"Once, during the campaign. He was passing through Baton Rouge."

"What did you ask him?"

"Why is a bright man like you running for Vice President?"

"What did he say?"

"Some bull like he always wanted to be Vice President. Wanted to preside over the Senate. The President was going to give him an important role in the administration. I almost bust a gut laughing. That's what they've been saying as far back as I can remember. Kennedy told LBJ that. LBJ told Humphrey. Nixon told Agnew and Ford. Carter told whoever that guy was that he had."

"Mondale."

"Yeah, I guess. Anyway, you get the point."

"What did he say? Was he upset that you took the Vice Presidency so lightly?"

"No. Actually, he was a good sport about it. He got me aside and told me off the record that it meant he was just one heartbeat from being President. That's what he was after and is after. But he was willing to serve and bide his time until he could run for the big job."

"Oh, the *big job*. I wished I had a big job. If he thinks being Vice President isn't a big job, I wonder what he thinks a state senator is?"

"Well, Jill, I guess the term *big job* was more mine than his. You have a big job, but you could have a bigger one. You need to be a little more ambitious. What are you going to do next?"

"I don't know."

"You could run for the U.S. Senate. Senator Ashford is up for re-election. You could beat him." Brad turned from the television to measure Jill's reaction.

"Are you kidding? I couldn't run against Senator Benjamin Edward Ashford. He'd beat my ass. He's in tight with the President. You know he helped pass the energy and tax legislation this time when the President was about to go under. Ashford could get all the help and money he wanted from the President's friends if anyone even dared to run against him."

"Well, maybe and maybe not. You'll never know till you try."

"Besides, Brad, you know my first love is the state. I want to do my job here. Maybe governor in two years, but not the U.S. Senate," she said. They looked back at the image of Vice President Harrot on the television with the announcer mentioning that Harrot would be at the Sugar Bowl that evening.

Brad raised his eyebrows and wrinkled his forehead, "I thought I was your first love. And you mean to tell me that the state of Louisiana is ahead of me? Well, well."

"You are my first love. That's why I want to stay here and not go off to that barbaric town of Washington." She reached over and took his hand.

"I think you could beat him, Jill. It would be a great opportunity. Ashford's too ambitious. I think he wants to be President."

"You do? Surprise, surprise. You know what they say. Every senator looks in the mirror each morning and sees a future President."

"Yeah, maybe so. That's what you could be—senator, then the first President of your gender."

"Governor is good enough for me." She stood, walked past him, and patted his rear end as she headed to the shower.

"That's sexual harassment, Senator Crenshaw!" he yelled after her.

"No, it's not. Because you were asking for it and wanted the attention!" she shouted over the sound of splashing water.

# Two

T hey walked the mile and a half to the Superdome with the already celebrating throngs. Alabama fans were on the march early. Brad and Jill made their way to the special credentials reception area. Jill was a favorite of Louisiana Governor Hugh Johnson. He had even made the Governor's Suite at the St. Laurent Hotel available to her and Brad as a special favor. He was waiting for her when she walked in.

"Madame Speaker! Get your pass and join us at the reception room. Vice President Harrot is going to drop by before the game. He said he wanted to meet you." The governor joyously shook her hand and gave her a grandfatherly hug. She would have been offended if it had been anyone other than Papa Hugh, as the governor was affectionately known. But she counted him as one of her mentors and benefactors. Papa Hugh had taken her on as his chief legislative sponsor of bills when she was first elected and brought her along ever since. He had warned her about political pitfalls and nurtured her like a daughter.

"What about Brad?" she asked and turned to her companion.

"Naw. We don't allow none of the Fourth Estate at this reception. Never know what they're going to overhear and print," he said. He gave Brad Yeary a hefty slap on the back. "Besides, he has an interview set up with Harrot for ten minutes at half-time anyway."

"Ten minutes? I thought I got the whole half-time with him."

"Nope. The V-P has to accept an award at mid-field at the end of half-time. But, hell, Brad, ten minutes with a 'jar of warm spit' is all you can stand, ain't it?" The governor laughed loudly and everybody around joined in except for Brad.

"I see someone else has heard the John Nance Garner story," Jill said. "See you at half-time." Jill waved to Brad and walked off with the governor.

Brad filled out the papers at the reception desk and received his picture I D and red-tag pass that allowed him on-field coverage. They gave him a pass for the Vice President's special room for his half-time interview. He began to think about the questions he would ask. He wandered toward the working sports reporters' hospitality room where there would be mounds of sandwiches, coffee, donuts, and the official press guides for latecomers.

AT SEVEN, THREE MEN met in a second-level bathroom. One carried a plastic walking stick. One had a pair of binoculars. The third held a fancy thirty-five millimeter camera with detachable flash. Two wore Alabama sweaters beneath long overcoats. The other wore a satin green and gold Notre Dame jacket.

The room was deserted except for the three, two of whom entered a stall. The short one stood on the commode and faced the other. The third man kept watch near the door to the room. Inside the stall, the man standing on the commode snapped the flash off his camera and also detached the side of the camera that contained the shutter button. Meanwhile, the man on the floor unscrewed the tip of the plastic walking cane. Then he took the crook of the handle off and put both pieces in his pocket.

The short man with the Notre Dame jacket took the shaft of the cane from the other and held it to his right eye. "It's clear," he said softly. He snapped the shutter button part of the camera onto the larger end of the hard plastic shaft. He held that end near his ear and pushed the button and listened. "It worked," he said even softer. He raised up to where he could look over the wall of the stall. "George, bring me the binoculars."

The man near the door of the room turned and walked the ten paces to the corner stall and handed the binoculars over the partition. The small man grabbed them. He took a plastic covered cable from his jacket pocket and screwed one end into an opening on the side of the binoculars and the other end into a port on the portion of the camera that had been attached to the big end of the walking stick. He held the binoculars to his eyes and looked straight ahead. He aimed the walking cane down toward the shoe of his companion in the stall. He closed his left eye and saw the shoe in the right side of the binoculars. He moved the cane slightly and aligned the cross-hair directly over the big toe area of his friend's shoe.

"Bang," he whispered. "If it was loaded, you wouldn't have a foot."

He handed the apparatus to his friend to hold. "Now, remember, keep your four fingers up and just use your thumb for the trigger. There's only one bullet, so it has to be perfect. Is that about right?" he asked as he slid the triggering button attached to a cable down the shaft of the cane to where it would fit his hand.

The taller man took off his coat and from inside the lining pulled out a belt-like harness which the shorter one helped him put around his waist and slid up to just beneath his armpit. He took a broad metal hinge from the overcoat pocket and attached it to the harness and then to the thicker part of the cane just beneath the shutter button mechanism. The shorter man then helped the other back on with his overcoat with the right sleeve fitting over and hiding the now-modified deadly cane. They left the stall and went to the mirror. All adjusted and with the binoculars slung around the taller Alabama fan, the three made their way to their seats—two on the second level and one on the third level.

The Alabama band marched onto the field as the teams finished their warmups.

IT WASN'T THAT BRAD Yeary didn't like football games. He did. But he mainly followed LSU football and had little energy or concern about other teams. Yet, here he was on the sidelines, fifteen minutes until game time, intrigued with all the pageantry. The cheerleaders, the bands, the flashing scoreboard with the built-in television screens that allowed instant replays of all important plays just reaffirmed to him that in America entertainment was king.

Millions of dollars were being spent to see which group of young men could move a small oval-shaped spheroid made of cowhide across a field of artificial grass to the goal of the opponent. The farthest a team would ever have to go would be a little less than three hundred feet. Usually they only had to travel eighty yards or less. In Las Vegas and throughout the betting world, other millions of dollars would change hands, depending on many unknown factors in this game. Who was leading at a particular point, total yards gained, sacks of the quarterbacks, even the number of time-outs taken would be bet on.

He shook his head as he pivoted a full three-hundred-sixty degree turn on his heels. There was an exact demarcation between the Alabama fans and those of Notre Dame. Red then green. But then he would notice blotches of crimson scattered throughout the stadium where the Tide fans had bought other blocks of tickets.

If ever a group lived up to the definition of "fans," it was the delegation from Alabama. They were fanatics. Brad looked for the two men he had seen pictured in the paper. They had traveled to every Alabama game for the past twenty years, it said. They carried an old broomstick with an empty super-size box of Tide detergent impaled thereon, topped by a roll of toilet tissue. They would hold it up and yell, "Roll Tide." Cute, he thought, and then noticed them on the third level. He was surprised that security let them in the stadium with a broomstick.

He walked over to the box seats near the twenty-yard-line where Jill was sitting with the rest of the state and federal dignitaries. Security kept him ten yards away, but she saw him and waved. She sat beside Governor Johnson who was turned around talking to someone from his staff. Vice President Harrot was not in his seat yet. He looked for Senator Ashford, but didn't see him either. Perhaps Democrat Johnson had left Republican Ashford off his guest list. Maybe the Republican Vice President was all that Papa Johnson could stomach at one time.

ALABAMA LED 14-10 WITH two minutes left in the first half. Brad began his walk around the field to rendezvous with the Vice President for his scheduled ten-minute interview. He noticed that Harrot had not left his seat yet. "I'm going to be upset if that 'jar of warm spit' keeps me waiting," he mumbled to himself as he departed the field into the bowels of the Superdome.

Security and Secret Service officers led him into a small room with two tables, the same number of telephones, and some refreshments. There were two others in the room already. More Secret Service, he thought. The one escorting him told him to wait and the Vice President's press secretary would be right in. He sat. Shortly, a stout, young, dark-haired woman whom Brad recognized from photos to be Liz Arzenhoff—the V P's press secretary—bounded through the doorway with two others.

"Brad Yeary, it's great to meet you." She extended her hand. Brad shook. "I've heard a lot about you. A tough questioner I'm told. The V P thinks highly of you. That's why he wanted to give you this exclusive interview."

Brad nodded. It was the same old bullshit. It didn't matter if it came from a man or woman. The politician's mouthpiece tried to flatter and honor the lowly reporters so that they would get an easy and favorable interview. He never had bought it, and he wasn't now.

"When's Sam going to be here?" He enjoyed the expression on Liz Arzenhoff's face when he called her honorable boss by his first name. He looked at his watch. "I'm a busy man, Ms. Arzenhoff. I'd hate to have to say in my column that the V P stood me up because he couldn't find his way in here or had too much to drink."

"Oh, no, Brad. He's on his way now. Just had to shake a few hands," she said. A little nervous laughter followed.

The door burst open with two agents in front and two behind the Vice President. Samuel Harrot could have played Presidents in movies. His wavy, silvery hair, sparkling blue eyes, and smile were disarming—even to the cynical reporter. His handshake was firm but not bone shattering. Brad released his hand and smiled into the face of the man who was a heartbeat away from being President.

"Sit down, Brad. Do you need anything? These folks will get you whatever you want."

"No. No, thank you, Mr. Vice President. I'm fine." Brad wondered why he was being so formal. Then, he realized that Samuel

Harrot was a presence. He appeared intelligent and alert. From following his career, Brad knew he cared about his country. He was a little awed for a moment.

They both sat on the same side of one of the tables with the Secret Service at the door and on the other side. Liz Arzenhoff sat beside Harrot. Brad put his small tape recorder between him and the Vice President so that he would know this was "on the record." Liz Arzenhoff put hers beside his.

"Mr. Vice President, what will the administration do if Iraq, Iran, Saudi Arabia, and the other oil-producing countries follow through with their threats to cut back on their supply of oil to us if we don't meet their demands?"

The Vice President smiled. "Brad, ask me about the ballgame. Alabama's ahead and you don't even ask me one loosen-up question."

"Okay. Who do you think is ahead, Mr. Vice President?"

"Who's ahead? Alabama. And they're going to stay ahead. Though, I must hasten to add that the fine team that Notre Dame has is one that could pull a lot of surprises." Liz Arzenhoff laughed at her boss's attempt at bi-partisan sportsmanship.

"Now, about the Mid-East problem. I believe the President is doing the correct thing. We need the oil, and if necessary, we may have to send some troops over to protect our national interests."

"Is that what you think, or is that what the President thinks?"

"Both," Samuel Harrot said and looked down at the table.

Brad made some notes while the Vice President shifted in his chair. He had preached conservation, exploration, and use of alternative energy sources for years. He was a team player though.

"Are you going to run for President, Mr. Harrot?"

"No. My plans are to support the President and, if he wants me on the ticket, to run again for Vice President. I've enjoyed my job. The President has found many projects to occupy my time. I'm continuing to grow and learn."

Brad continued the questioning for nine and a half minutes until Liz Arzenhoff looked at her watch and interrupted. The V P had to be back on the field for a presentation. He was to receive an award for the President who couldn't be present.

"After the game, Brad. We'll finish this conversation after the game. I would like to go off the record with you and tell you some things to watch for over the next several months," he whispered to Brad after the tape recorders were off and he stood to go back to the field. "I'll leave word that it's okay for you to come to our suite. Can you make it?"

"Sure," Brad said. He watched the Vice President go through the door toward the field escorted by Secret Service and Sugar Bowl officials. What did Harrot want to tell him? Hm! Off the record. This

could be good. He began forming a game plan to tell Jill that he had
to go to the Vice President's suite instead of back to the St. Laurent
Hotel with her.

By the time he got back to the field of the Superdome, the band
had parted into an inverted V to make space for the dignitaries and
the awards. The Vice President was just taking his place in the center
next to Governor Johnson and the Sugar Bowl president.    Jill
Crenshaw stood to the governor's right. Brad walked up and joined
Liz Arzenhoff. They stood on the sideline directly in front of her boss
but twenty-five yards away. Brad waved to Jill who acknowledged it
with a slight nod. She looked elegant standing there in a cream-col-
ored suit, holding a bouquet of roses, and smiling for the whole world
to see. He was glad they were friends—and lovers.

The public address announcer began the presentation ceremony
as all of the officials stared straight ahead. At least twenty Secret
Service agents scanned the crowd from the sidelines. A wave of applause built with the award ceremony. The crowd stood as one.

ON THE SECOND LEVEL in the middle of the stadium about
thirty feet above the field, the man with the Alabama sweater and the
overcoat stood next to the man with the Notre Dame jacket on his
right. Hundreds and thousands were still making their way to and
from the concession areas and the bathrooms, unconcerned with the
half-time ceremony. But these two were highly interested as well as
the other man with the Alabama sweater on the third level.

The man with the Notre Dame jacket pointed to the dignitaries. With that signal, the man in the overcoat raised the binoculars to
his eyes, lifted his right arm as though he also was pointing. The end
of the hard plastic cane was barely visible beneath the sleeve of his
coat. The plastic was still cool against his palm. He extended the four
fingers of his right hand, almost in the style of a Nazi salute, and felt
for the trigger button with his thumb. Through the right side of his
binoculars he saw the Vice President. He aligned the cross-hairs on
Samuel Harrot's chest, braced himself, and gently squeezed the button.
His arm jerked less than an inch. The sound was inaudible.

Brad Yeary was staring straight at Vice President Harrot. A
slight look of puzzlement spread across the Vice President's face. That
was all. Then his knees buckled and he fell in a lump to the artificial
turf.

# Three

For a split second, for a fragment of time that seemed like an eternity, no one noticed that the Vice President of the United States lay prostrate on the fifty-yard line of the Sugar Bowl field in the Superdome. At the lip of the Sugar Bowl logo painted on the artificial grass, an eerie stillness enveloped his body.

Paralysis momentarily gripped Brad Yeary, who had been staring directly into the eyes of Samuel Harrot. The Vice President fell with his head almost touching the left foot of Jill. She stood with Governor Johnson looking peacefully at the crowd, still smiling and waving.

Then it seemed like everyone was aware. The crowd quieted, and in Brad's eyes the scene began to move as though in slow motion. Jill was the first of the official delegation to notice the felled V P. She dropped her bouquet of red roses and kneeled down beside him, placing a hand on his chest and taking his left hand in hers.

She spoke to him but drew no response. She pushed on his chest, as though in automatic response to a person whose heart had stopped beating.

His mouth stood agape and his eyes stared into the reaches of eternity. He did not respond when she spoke to him. At that point, a man she recognized as being with the Secret Service pushed her aside.

Brad and Liz Arzenhoff ran almost in stride toward the commotion but were intercepted five yards from mid-field by other Secret Service agents and local police. Despite the protestations of Liz that she was the Vice President's press secretary and chief assistant in attendance, she was held back. Nor did it help Brad to wave his red "on-the-field" pass in an effort to look closer.

The V of the band parted to either end, and the other dignitaries wandered toward the sidelines. They gathered in little knots facing toward the middle of the field where Samuel Harrot had not moved since falling. There, Secret Service Agent-In-Charge Al Shanker worked furiously over the Vice President and simultaneously spoke into his Walkie-Talkie. He waved for the ambulance and paramedics to join him.

Jill walked dazedly toward the sideline and collapsed into the arms of Brad. She steadied herself and looked back toward Harrot.

"I think he had a heart attack. He was unconscious." Her body trembled.

Brad put his left arm around her shoulders and took her right hand in his. They both continued their gaze toward the center of attention. Her hand felt warm and wet, almost a greasy wet. They both noticed the dampness at the same time and looked at their interlocked fingers that were now red with blood.

Jill blanched white and passed out in Brad's arms. He gently laid her down and motioned for some help. He took a handkerchief from his pocket and wiped the blood from her hand and then his. She recovered almost as fast as she had fainted.

She looked at her hand again. "Brad, was that blood on me? It must have come from Harrot. I touched his suit coat at his chest. But I didn't notice any blood then. Was that what it was? Brad? Do you know?"

He was afraid to say. He didn't want to think that. A heart attack would be better. Maybe even food poisoning. Not a murder. Not an assassination. Not in the middle of the Superdome. Not in front of seventy thousand witnesses. He looked down. The blood was gone from her hand and his. It was just a hallucination. Then he looked again at the crimson and white handkerchief.

"I don't know, Jill," he told her. What he did know bothered him. He was now endued with the information, the knowledge, the evidence, that only he and Agent Shanker shared at this moment in history.

And for the time being, Shanker was doing his best to see that it was kept confidential. As soon as he opened the suit coat of the Vice President, he saw the neat circle of blood which had spread in size to the circumference of a grapefruit. He felt for a pulse but found none. He looked into non-responsive and dilating eyes. Samuel Harrot was no longer with them. For the Vice President, the score would always be Alabama 14, Notre Dame 10.

But this knowledge, he determined, would not go any further at the moment. The assassins would not know that they were superbly successful. Make them wonder. Let them wait like everyone else for an official report from the hospital. He could control that. But at this instant his main concern was in being able to handle the local paramedics who, he knew, would want to do everything they could to stabilize the Vice President before putting him into the ambulance.

They had to load him now. Not work on him on the field and give others a chance to know the Vice President was dead. He gestured wildly for the paramedics to take Harrot immediately, showed them his badge, and began to reach for his sidearm to persuade them. They obliged. He jumped in after them.

As soon as the ambulance cleared the tunnel leading from the floor of the arena toward the outside, Shanker ordered the driver to stop, and squatting next to the Vice President, he talked into his hand-held radio.

"Man, we can't stop," one of the paramedics protested. "We gotta get this dude to the hospital. We have no vital signs. If he has a chance, it will be at the hospital." He pressed the chest of Harrot with his latex-gloved hands.

"Listen. I'm going to tell you just once," Shanker said. He opened his suit coat, flashed his badge, and put his hand on his gun, "I'm in charge here, and if I say stop, I mean stop. And if I say shit, you better start reaching for the Charmin." All four of the medical response team eyed the badge and gun and nodded assent.

Shanker opened the door and jumped out. He motioned for the chief of security of the Superdome and a captain of the police who had been trotting along behind the ambulance to come to him. He kept his hand on the door but pushed it nearly closed to where no one could see inside.

"I'm going to the hospital with the Vice President. This is to go no farther than your ears, understand?" They nodded. "He's been shot. I don't know how bad. But don't let anyone leave until I call you from the hospital."

"Shot?" the captain whispered.

"Yes. Don't say it again."

"Al, we have seventy-two thousand people. We can't keep them all here. People leave all the time. It would create a panic if we announced that no one was to leave. Five hundred have probably left since the Vice President fell to the ground. We can't stop them," Harry Winstead, the chief of security, said.

"Well, hell, Harry. The guy who shot him is here. We can't just let him walk out."

"Who is he?"

"Shit, Harry, I can't tell you that. But the Vice President was shot from inside the Superdome. So, it has to be someone here."

"So, we have seventy-two thousand suspects, give or take a few dozen."

"Listen. I have to go on to the hospital. If you can't stop them from leaving, at least search everyone." Shanker knew how absurd and crazy his last request was before it had fully left his lips. "I'll tell you what. Get all the metal detectors you can locate—from the court-houses—from the airport—wherever—and set them up at as many exits as you can cover. Look for a rifle. But any kind of gun, if you find any kind of gun, detain that person as long as you can. Keep the gun and take as much information as you can. We can't let the killer or killers just walk out."

"Did you say killer? Is he dead?" the police captain asked.

"No, he's not dead until the doctor says he's dead," Shanker said. A mob of cameramen and news reporters was surging toward the ambulance.

"Announce that the Vice President fainted and is being taken to the hospital for observation. That's all. Got it? Get the damn metal detectors set up. And don't clean the stadium up or sweep or anything that might lose any evidence. We'll be back later with a team to check everything." He swung the door open to the ambulance and jumped in.

"Go," he shouted to the obedient driver. The rear wheels of the ambulance burned rubber on the concrete floor, and people scattered from in front as it careened toward the exit with lights flashing and sirens blaring.

At the exit onto the street, they picked up a two-car police escort. Shanker took a card from his inside pocket and studied it. Bellevue Hospital was the nearest. All of that was written on the card. The hospital, the most direct route, and other routine information was typed out in case of a medical emergency. This was standard for all Presidential or Vice Presidential visits to every city. He sat back against the wall of the van as he shook his head from side to side and looked once again at the man he was supposed to have guarded.

The paramedics still worked over the Vice President, but their motions had slowed considerably as their sense of desperation had settled into an acknowledgement of reality. There was nothing they could do for him. There was nothing the team of surgeons and the squadron of waiting medical support people at the hospital could do for him. This wild ride through the wet streets of New Orleans on New Year's night was totally useless—a farce.

"I want to see each one of your I.D. tags," Shanker shouted to the paramedics. They handed them to him. "I'm writing your names down here," he explained as he put his pen to a page of a small pad he carried. "You are the only ones who know that the Vice President has been shot and is probably dead. No one else is to know that at this time. You understand?"

They nodded.

"What about you in the front? You hear me?"

"Yes, sir."

"You understand?"

"Yes, sir."

"If word gets out before I release it, I'm going to be sure the culprit who spreads it is arrested for interfering with a federal investigation. Understand? Not a word. Not a word to anyone. All reports and paperwork have to be seen by me. If you don't believe me, check with your boss. But that's it. This investigation is not going to be fucked up."

He got back on his radio. "I'm with the Gray Fox. Bob, are you there?"

"I'm here, Al," the voice crackled through the receiver. "How's it going?"

"Bob, get me a secure land-line to headquarters as soon as you get to Bellevue. I'm sure they're calling now. But we have to be secure. I'll meet you there. Be sure we have enough of our people and locals to keep everyone out of the E R at the hospital. 'No comment' is the only message for now. More to follow. Understand?"

"Affirmative."

The next three minutes seemed like forever. Shanker ordered that there be no communications between the ambulance and the hospital, afraid that it might be picked up by someone who would figure out the real condition of the Vice President.

He rubbed his wet forehead and leaned back against the wall to brace himself. The reality that he had lost the one he was to protect was beginning to set in. He was a failure.

He thought back to when he first decided to be in the Secret Service, back to 1963, when he had watched in wonderment the replay after replay of President Kennedy's assassination. As a high school senior then, he had told himself if he had been there in Dallas that day, it would not have happened. There, over thirty-four years ago, he vowed to become an agent and protector of the highest officials of the United States.

He joined the agency straight out of law school twenty-seven years ago and worked himself into the position of having guarded three different Presidents and four Vice Presidents. As one of the agency's most trustworthy and dependable men, he had received letters of commendation from everyone he had been assigned to guard. He had put his own body between a would-be assassin and a former President. He would have given up his body as a shield for his country.

Now, five years from the time when he planned to retire, he let one slip through his fingers. Defeat, failure, catastrophe, and assassination rang in his head and spread a deep sickness to his stomach. No one in the agency who was called upon to protect those in power ever approved of putting their men before great crowds in open areas. It was to invite someone to try their luck—to take a shot. There were enough mad men and women in the country who wanted their moment of glory—regardless if that moment was as a murderer.

Usually assigned to the President's detail, he had volunteered for this duty when the President didn't need him. He was to have a few days off when the Vice President went to his home in Alabama where he wouldn't need as big a contingent of guardians.

He had planned a week's visit with his aging parents in the hills of East Tennessee. He was sure they were watching on television. They were so proud of him.

"Our son guards the President of the United States," they would remind anyone who would listen. "And the President asks our son for advice on how to run the country very often," they would add. Now they would see the Vice President carried out of the Superdome followed by their son and hear the announcement that Mr. Harrot had fainted. He wished that his lie were true.

The siren was silenced as the ambulance pulled into the semi-circular receiving area of the emergency room at Bellevue Hospital. The police kept the curious behind a barricade they were just putting into place.

"Don't let anyone see any blood as you take him in. And act like he is alive," Shanker ordered as the doors of the emergency room swung open in simultaneous harmony with the doors of the ambulance.

AS SOON AS THE public address announcer had made the announcement that Vice President Harrot had fainted and was being taken to the hospital for observation, Brad Yeary left Jill Crenshaw in the care of Governor Johnson and his staff and sprinted toward the tunnel that would take him to an exit. He had to follow. He was a newsman. That was his job.

"Don't tell anyone about the blood. I will call you as soon as I know anything. Stay with the governor and his guards," he whispered to her before sprinting off.

Jill was weak from fright. The governor was too, but he didn't know to be as frightened as Jill. She asked and the governor agreed that they should await word about the Vice President out of the crowd of people. They were escorted to the room where they had partaken of the reception for the Vice President before the game began.

National television had not shown the collapse and fall of Harrot as they were on a commercial break at the time. The network was scheduled to show just a cameo appearance of the Vice President accepting the award for the President. The television higher-ups were still leery of showing too many politicians, even those who had been elected, for too long a time for fear of having to give the other party an equal or near-equal amount of time.

Their fourteen cameras had been running and recording, just not on the air. So when the commercial break ended, the sports-trained announcers turned into news broadcasters as they showed a rerun of the Vice President collapsing. They broadcast another angle, another, and another. But there was nothing on tape to dispute the official story that Harrot had merely fainted, except for the suddenness of the fall and the stillness of the body.

The game was delayed several minutes as some semblance of order was restored. Always suspicious of the "official story," every news organization that was present with more than one staff member dispatched someone to Bellevue Hospital to see if there was more to the drama than just that Harrot had fainted from bad food or something. Other television networks immediately sought permission to use the feeds of the network broadcasting the game to show their audiences.

THE ALABAMA-CLAD MAN with the long overcoat and the shorter Notre Dame attired roundish gentleman met again in the bathroom five minutes after the fall of Harrot. Once again the room became practically deserted as the curious filed back into the arena to see what the commotion was with the stricken Vice President.

The shorter man assumed his position inside a stall and stood on the commode. He squatted to where he could not be seen over the door. He helped slip the overcoat off his taller companion and detached the plastic rod from the supporting brace and hinge. Unsnapping the firing mechanism from the bigger end of the cane, he repositioned it onto the thirty-five millimeter camera. Both cables, one to the trigger and the other to the pair of binoculars, were taken loose, rolled up, and placed in the Alabama fan's pants pocket. He then raised his Alabama sweater, slipped the support harness from beneath it, and pulled the sweater back down.

The third companion, who also sported a Crimson Tide sweater beneath an overcoat, joined them as lookout and handed a small bottle containing a clear liquid over the wall of the stall. The shorter man took the bottle, poured its contents into the larger end of the plastic staff after re-attaching the screw-on tip to the smaller end.

Once the cane filled with the transparent fluid, he placed the smaller end into the water in the commode, took a cigarette lighter from his pocket, and struck a flame to the large end that was already smoking from the contents of the bottle. With a great whoosh, the cane melted away into the water of the toilet leaving it a thick green. The short man pulled a latex glove from his pocket, slipped it onto his hand, and retrieved the metal tip of the cane from the murky water. Then, he flushed.

With their mission accomplished, the three walked back toward their areas of seating. They deposited the overcoat of the Alabama fan who had fired the shot in the trash can on the way out the door.

THE CAPTAIN AND HARRY Winstead had alerted the chief-of-police to Al Shanker's request for the metal detectors at all exits from the Superdome. The chief finally extracted from them that Harrot had been shot and detection devices were needed. With that knowledge, he ordered trucks dispatched to the airport warehouse and the courthouse to bring all available units to the stadium. Trucks rolled out through the dark night. The teams began to prepare for the second half kick-off. With luck, the units would be in place and ready to use before the game ended.

BRAD YEARY DID NOT have to worry about passing through one of the units as he dashed out the exit and into the cold night air. He was cooled and heated at the same time and by the same thought. He was the only newsman in the world with the information that the Vice President had been shot. He knew where the closest trauma hospital was, and as he hailed the nearest cab, he spat into the open window, "To Bellevue Hospital. Like a bat out of hell." He handed the driver a twenty to get his attention.

"Man, if you hurt, you oughtta call an ambulance," the swarthy cabby smiled back at Brad. "But I have to admit that I can sho' nuff get you there quicker," he continued as his cab's tires wailed against the damp pavement. "May I ax what the hurry be?"

"Hell, no. Just put your foot through the floorboard. Take me to the emergency room."

# Four

T he platoon of highly paid physicians, thoracic specialists, neurosurgeons, and cardiologists stood looking at each other as they each in turn mumbled a grave prognosis for Samuel Harrot. After the first five minutes—if not before—they knew there was no hope. They shook their heads in a collective acknowledgment of the inevitable truth. He was beyond their help.

Shanker sat to the side, a good six feet from the gurney where his charge lay, with a phone nestled between his knees as he held the receiver to his ear.

"Bob, when Lenora gets here, I want to see her before anyone else. I'm going to stay here with him. I need you to patch me through to Washington, and dammit, we'll need the agent-in-charge of the FBI down here too."

WHEN HE WAS BEEPED, John Dobson, the Agent-in-charge of the FBI office in New Orleans, was already aware of Vice President Harrot's collapse. Dobson was sitting in the tenth row of the second level at the Superdome. Catholic by birth, he had always followed Notre Dame football and attended games when the opportunity arose. He was just returning to his seat next to his wife at the time of Harrot's fall. He had no official function at the game, and like the other twenty-five thousand Notre Dame fans, was hoping for a second half comeback.

A little chunky to be picked out as an agent by the casual observer, Dobson enjoyed the opportunity to wear the green and gold satin jacket that usually hung in his closet at his home just ten miles away. He had pushed his dark-framed glasses back farther up his nose and looked on with concern as the Vice President had been taken from the stadium. He was not reassured by the announcement that Harrot had merely fainted. He knew that they would not announce anything else in fear of creating a panic and stampede. This time he hoped the official version was true. Three years from retirement, he wanted to finish out his career in the agency in the state of his birth. The less excitement the better.

He handed his wife his binoculars and brushed back his silver-gray hair. "Darling, if this is business, I'll call you later from the office. You have our car keys don't you?"

"Yes, Dear. Please try to get back. The children do so want to spend some time with you."

"You know I'll be back or home as soon as possible."

He leaned down, and she kissed him bye. "I'll pray for you," she said. The teams were lined up for the second half kick-off.

He looked toward the field. "You better pray for Notre Dame. Those Alabama boys are kicking their butts."

THE MEN AND WOMEN of the press had been allowed only into a hallway connecting the emergency room of Bellevue Hospital with the main section. There they mingled about, shouting questions toward anyone who looked official. A bank of phones was being hastily strung along the wall of the corridor. Liz Arzenhoff tried desperately to break through the line of police that separated them from the light green doors which opened to the trauma unit of the emergency room. As the doors would occasionally swing open for the passage of a doctor or a nurse, she could only glimpse men in suitcoats standing guard a ways farther down where she knew her Vice President was being treated.

"Why the trauma unit if he just passed out?" the more astute reporters would shout to Liz and anyone else who would listen. She didn't know and felt helpless herself. She had absolutely no information to impart to the questions thrown at her. In this time of crisis, she was as completely shutout as any woman on the street would have been.

Brad Yeary was nowhere to be seen among the clamoring horde of reporters in the hallway. He disdained an appearance there. He knew Bellevue Hospital from his first ten years as a reporter when he worked the police beat. Often he would go to Bellevue to followup on a shooting, a beating, a plane crash, or any other catastrophe. The hospital was known for its trauma response team. And Brad Yeary had built up a network of sources at the hospital who had not forgotten him over the last ten years despite his now being the chief political reporter for the largest newspaper in the state. If he ever needed to use those sources, it was now. That was why he had sought out a nurse in the quiet of an ante-room just a little removed from all the hubbub.

"Darla, I need it. You can trust me. I would never disclose my source without permission. Just tell me, is he alive or dead? I know he was shot." He pulled the blood-covered handkerchief from his pocket.

Darla Puckett sat across the small green desk with her arms folded across her chest. Her lips were pursed tightly until she saw the red rag and then her mouth dropped open. She and Brad went back a long way. They had known each other for fifteen years. Very closely for his last five years on the police beat, more sporadically during the last ten, and hardly at all since he had taken up with Jill Crenshaw.

"Brad, you're only here because he's a big shot. If it was some kid who'd been shot, you'd still be partying with Ms. Priss or what's her name—Crenshaw—at the Superdome with all the other bigwigs and socialites. Why should I risk my job for you?"

It was a good question. For two of the ten years that he worked the police beat he would wind up at Bellevue almost every night at the time Darla was finishing her shift. She had been his friend and lover when his marriage had ended prematurely. They had commiserated about how difficult it was to keep a marriage together with the odd hours they worked and the pressures and stresses of both the news business of Brad and the trauma business of Darla.

On dark spring nights they would lie together in Darla's bed in an upstairs French Quarter apartment. With the window open, they told time by watching the moon make its slow arc across the Mississippi leaving a sheen like sparks from fireworks on the barely flowing muddy river.

They were both younger then, but Darla still had the dark hair and languid eyes that always said, "I'm ready. Come and get me." She had put on a few pounds, and now her eyes appeared more tired than slow.

"Will you come back and see me, Brad? Or is this just a 'one nighter' with you going back to the hoity-toity society?"

"Darla, you know I cared for you. I still do. Things change though. My job took me away from you just like it did from my marriage. We knew it would happen eventually. But I need this bad." He looked pleadingly into her eyes.

She gave in—as she always had to the guy with the Rasputin eyes. She nodded.

"He's dead?"

She nodded just slightly, but it was acknowledgment enough for Brad.

Brad buried his head in his hands.

"Oh, shit. He's dead, and I'm the only newsman in the world that knows it." He reached across the desk and took both of Darla's hands in his right hand and softly stroked the right side of her face with his left.

# Five

L enora Harrot was a lady of unusual dignity. She could not be described as elegant, but as with many women who had married young and subjugated their own private ambitions to those of their husbands, she carried herself with a grace and air that had been steeled by long years in the shadow of her ambitious spouse. With a muted calm, she neared the door of the room in Bellevue Hospital where her husband lay dead.

Bob Clary of the Secret Service met her and asked her to wait. "Mrs. Harrot, you know Agent Shanker. He's with your husband and wants to speak with you before you see the Vice President."

"Yes, of course," she said. She took a tissue from her purse and dabbed briefly at the corners of her eyes. "Is he okay?" She looked away.

"Mrs. Harrot, agent Shanker's been with your husband and will be able to explain his condition better than I." Clary turned away and pushed the button on his Walkie-Talkie.

Shanker listened to the short message from Clary who was less than thirty feet away, just past the double doors. Now alone with the expired Vice President except for one nurse and one doctor whom he had asked to stay, he prepared himself for the most difficult task he had ever performed in his professional life. He would be the bearer of black news to his friend's wife that she became a widow without ever having the opportunity to tell her husband goodbye.

He had guarded Samuel Harrot more often than any other Vice President. He had hunted quail with him in Alabama, had ridden on his power boat, and had played poker with him long into many distant nights. Lenora was always the gracious host, treating the ever-present agents as part of the family—not just hired help. How had he failed his friend—and made Lenora a widow at age fifty-four?

He stood, rubbed his eyes, swept his fingers back through his still-thick hair, and straightened his suit coat. He went to the gurney where the body of Samuel Harrot lay, still warm, with the shirt torn aside so that the paramedics and doctors could use all the heroic efforts known to them to restore life. He brought the sheet up to cover the Vice President's face until he learned if Lenora wanted to see him in that condition.

At the door, he brought her quietly in, taking her right hand in his and grasping her elbow with his other.

"Al, did he have a heart attack? Is he okay? Where is he? I want to see him." She sank her head onto his chest and sobbed as though she already knew the answers to all the questions. She looked up at Shanker, "Is that him on the table? Why aren't the doctors and nurses doing anything?" She dropped her head back down.

"Lenora, I'm sorry. Sam's gone. He died. There was nothing anyone could do." He squeezed her to him and felt a tremor strike through her body. She slumped toward him as her knees buckled.

"No, no, no, he's not dead! Sam has so much to give to the country—to me—to our family. He's not dead, Al. He can't be. He's in good health. He has no heart problem. They're wrong. Tell them to work on him. Al, you must. Sam's all I have."

Shanker eased her into a chair and sat beside her. He called the doctor and nurse over to see if she needed anything. He had to let her work through the first few minutes of denial before he told her the other shocking news that her husband had been shot —assassinated— while she watched from the stands.

BRAD PRACTICALLY BROKE THE forefinger on his right hand punching in the numbers on the telephone to reach his publisher. He dialed five different numbers before tracking him down at a party where news of the Vice President's collapse at the Sugar Bowl had just been received. There was a long silence on the other end of the line when Brad told the publisher and the owner of a television station that not only was the Vice President dead, but that he had been shot.

"Are you sure? Dead? Shot?" was the stunned reply that finally came weakly through the line. "I thought they said he'd just fainted."

"Listen, Ed, he's dead. He was shot in the chest. I have a blood-soaked hanky to prove it. That's just their temporary cover story that he fainted. What do you want me to do?" Here he was with the biggest scoop of his career but didn't know where to run with it. It was only on rare occasions that he could get away with calling the publisher, Edward E. Pinthater, by his given name. This was one of them. He was an equal with the financial genius of modern publishing because of his knowledge. He might even be more than equal—a bit above—considering the news he was holding. He waited for the big boss to think through the situation. Would they put it on the air and in the paper now or wait?

Brad did not think himself good at ethical dilemmas. On the one hand, they had information that would be anxiously received by millions throughout the country. On the other, would they jeopardize the safety of anyone or the investigation that was sure to follow if they went with the news before it was announced officially?

Finally, Pinthater started to organize the scenario in his mind. "Brad, what sources do you have to say he's dead, and that he was shot? Do you have two confirming sources?"

Brad thought. His editors and publishers always told him to avoid libel suits with two bona-fide sources. Accuracy, accuracy, accuracy was the one and only principle written in stone for those who came up through the old journalism school. What would be the consequences if he were wrong? What if Darla had some pent-up rage and saw this as a way to get back at a lover who had deserted her in her time of need after their torrid relationship in the French Quarter? What if the Vice President was still alive and recovering from a mild bout of food poisoning, and he wrote that he was dead?

No libel. They couldn't sue. He was a public figure. Sorry, a little error. No, he realized it would be the end of his career as a serious journalist. He would always be the butt of the joke as to who greatly exaggerated the demise of the Vice President. And he was not humorous enough to go on a one-man Mark Twain tour.

"Yes, chief. I have my sources. I can't say who. Death was confirmed by a higher-up at the hospital. He was shot. I have a blood-soaked handkerchief in my pocket. I wiped blood off a person who bent down to help the Vice President. It was no heart attack. I don't have two sources for each of those facts, though. But a reliable one on each count."

There was more silence as both continued to think.

"Brad, if you're wrong, you know the consequences?"

"Yes." He knew them all too well.

"Okay, then. I want you to start writing the story in your mind. We go to press in two hours. We won't go with the TV yet until you do this," Edward Pinthater was talking in measured phrases, thinking aloud as he went. He, too, was aware his paper would be the laughing-stock of the country if this front page news was wrong. It wouldn't just be Brad Yeary who would go down the tubes.

"Go to the highest authorities there. Secret Service I guess, or maybe FBI. Shoot straight with them, in private. Tell them what you know. See if they will confirm it. See if they can give you a valid reason for withholding this news from the public. We'll have covered our asses a little that way.

"Call me back in fifteen minutes. If I don't hear from you, I'll assume they have killed you or are holding you. So, tell them I'm going on TV in twenty minutes with the story if we don't get an understanding. Got it?"

"Yes," Brad said before he thought. Confront and confirm. The old reliable technique. If they would not deny that Harrot had been shot, it was probably true. The same for his death. But Brad was short on knowing exactly what Pinthater expected as far as an "understanding."

He had played hardball many times in the past with political people who were trying to hide dirty little scandals. Nepotism. Bribes. You vote that way for me, I vote this way for you. Who's screwing whose secretary. But he had never played against the Secret Service or the FBI. They might not take kindly to any threats.

From his only year of law school, he remembered the term "obstruction of justice" was used quite frequently by police types when someone was going to hide or disclose information that could hinder an investigation. He decided he would push as hard as he could, pretend that he knew what he was talking about, and hope that he would not be spending the remainder of the night with the drunks at the city jail or handcuffed to a radiator in some obscure federal office.

He took out his spiral-bound notepad, retrieved a pen from a pocket, and sprinted off toward the barricade at the emergency room door looking as official and like a newsperson as he could muster after the hour he had just spent.

"Dammit, I have to talk to whoever's in charge here with the Secret Service or the FBI," he shouted. The two sullen-looking uniformed policemen brought him to a sudden stop with arms like cords of steel. His attempt to break through the line they had formed ten feet from Agent Clary failed miserably. Clary saw the commotion and stepped toward the reporter.

"What do you want?" Clary asked him from behind the broad shoulders of the policemen.

"Are you Secret Service or FBI?" Brad shot back, not backing off one inch.

"Secret Service. What do you want?"

"I'm Brad Yeary with the *Times-Gazette*. I just need thirty seconds with you, alone."

"We have no comment," Clary said, contempt dripping with his words. He clinched his teeth and glared at Brad.

"I think you should talk to me," Brad said as he leaned forward between the shoulders and arms of the uniforms who were holding him back.

Clary, too, leaned forward to where he was nose to nose with the pesky reporter. "Why the hell would I want to talk to you?" He almost spat at Brad.

"Because I know that Harrot is dead and that he was shot," Brad whispered. He took out the wadded up handkerchief from his pocket in his right fist and opened it just enough that Clary could glimpse it between their close faces. "And I'm going to broadcast that story in just ten minutes unless I can talk with your head man. I know it shit ain't you, or you wouldn't have your lard ass out here," Brad whispered again just loud enough to let Clary know he was not intimidated.

"Let him through," Clary told the police. It was damage control time. "Wait right here and I'll let you talk to Agent Shanker. He's in charge. What did you say your name was?"

"Brad Yeary. *Times-Gazette* chief political reporter." Brad threw in the last phrase just to let the Service know they weren't dealing with a lightweight.

# Six

S hanker talked on the phone with headquarters in Washington as Lenora Harrot walked to a secure and private lounge. Clary entered the room that was now Shanker's domain. The doctor and nurse sat forlornly in straight back chairs on the opposite side of the gurney from Shanker while the body of Harrot began to cool. Shanker wanted instructions or at least approval of his plan.

The body would remain in New Orleans until an autopsy was performed. He would not let it leave his sight until that procedure was completed. He would invite the FBI. They would work together if they could. This was not going to be a Dallas and Kennedy mess where thirty years later books would be written about how he screwed up the investigation, about body parts missing, or about bullet fragments unaccounted for.

He was in New Orleans, and he wasn't anxious for some local attorney general with a wild-hair up his ass to start a conspiracy investigation. It would be done correctly from the start. He had failed in protecting the Vice President, but he would not fail in doing all that he could to see to it that the culprits were brought to justice and that the evidence would be preserved to allow a conviction.

He didn't notice Clary. "Hell, this is important. You've got to reach him. In the meantime patch me through to Grady at Camp David." He looked around, saw Clary, and motioned for him to sit beside him as he waited for the connection.

"What are you doing in here, Bob? You're supposed to keep guard outside."

"Trouble, Al. Big trouble. Word's leaked out. There's a reporter who wants to talk to you, or else he's going on television live in ten minutes with the story."

Shanker looked at him and shook his head. He kept one ear to the phone listening to the static.

"Does he have the goods? Does he know anything?"

"Yes, the basics. Harrot was shot. Harrot is dead."

"Shit!" Shanker closed his eyes in pain. "Bring him in but keep him by the door till I get through with this call. Who is he?"

"Brad Yeary. *Times-Gazette.*"

"Hey, he's the guy that had an interview with Sam at half-time. I might can talk some sense into him. Bring him in." Shanker focused his attention on the telephone again as Clary left.

"Grady? This is Al with the Vice President. You heard about his collapse? Bad news. He's dead. Shot. Assassinated." He waited for it to sink in with his friend Grady Williams who was in charge of the President's detail. Then he heard his friend's voice quaver on the line.

"Al, I know you wouldn't joke about something like that. But I can't believe it. What's the deal?"

"I don't know. We need to go to the alert phase. More security for the President. Military option for the grounds. I can't locate the chief yet. We're trying to keep the cover on it down here temporarily till the game is over. We have a fucking seventy thousand possible suspects, and they're all going to walk when the game is over. I feel helpless.

"We need to put a detail on the Speaker of the House and the Speaker Pro Tem of the Senate. No one would kill a Vice President unless they intended to get the real power too, would they?"

He was just beginning to wonder what they were in for on New Year's night. Never in the history of the republic had a Vice President been assassinated. He could not even remember an attempt. A few nasty letters sometimes, a few bomb threats, a few loonies, but no Vice President had ever come under fire. So, it must be a broader-based attack on the American system of executive power and succession that the assassins were after. At least it wouldn't hurt to be prepared.

Clary and Yeary stood at the door. Shanker finished his short talk with Grady Williams. He reached out to shake Brad's hand.

"Bob, why don't you wait outside while Mr. Yeary and I discuss the situation we have here. We need to talk in private." Shanker motioned toward the door.

"What about the doc and nurse? You want me to get rid of them for a while?" Clary asked.

"Naw, they don't have ears. They don't even know why they're here. We'll be okay. Just the four of us." He motioned Brad toward the chair near the phone where Clary had sat a few moments earlier.

It had been a while since Brad had been in a room with a recently dead man. But there was little secret that the sheet-covered mound lying on the gurney that ended with well-polished shoes was the late Vice President. He breathed a mental sigh of relief that Darla had not

been leading him astray. He was glad that the news was now confirmed by him. But even he, a hardened and cynical reporter, felt his
throat contract at the sight. A living, breathing, human being, apparently well-intentioned and loved by many, had been taken away at the
whim of someone who, obviously, did not have the same qualities. And
he, the cursed reporter, was here to tell the guardians that he was
going with this to the nation so that he could be credited, along with
his newspaper, with the biggest scoop of the last several years.

"Mr. Yeary—"

"You can call me Brad, Agent Shanker."

"Very well. And you can call me Al, Brad, just like we were
friends, which I think we can be. We both have similar goals, I'm sure.
The question may be how we each can achieve our objectives without
doing harm to the other's.

"Now, I know it wouldn't do any good to ask you how you were
able to tell us that Harrot was shot and is now dead. It may have
been just a lucky guess . . . and a very good bluff. Or you might have
had the goods from the start."

Brad listened and tried to size up Al Shanker. He guessed him
to be nearly ten years older than he. The Service did not hire dimwits
or allow them to progress to the point where they were guarding Vice
Presidents and Presidents. Most were usually law or accounting grad-
uates who had undergone rigorous training and education in the agency itself. They were good at psychological bullshit too.

"That's the Vice President, right there," Shanker continued as
he swept an arm toward the gurney and a frown crossed his face.
Brad saw the agent's eyes moisten when he looked over toward the
body.

"I didn't do my job . . . or do it right, or he wouldn't be there.
He was shot in the Superdome in front of seventy thousand witnesses
and at least one assassin, and I'm sitting here waiting for the local FBI
head so that we can devise a plan of how to respond."

He looked directly into the reporter's eyes.

"Brad, I have a serious problem. But what is more important
is that the country has a serious problem. You understand? What
about the President? You ever recall a Vice President getting knocked
off before?"

Brad shook his head.

"That's right. Never. Must be someone looking higher up. So
what do I do to protect our republic and keep order in our democracy?"
Then he got knee to knee with Brad and lowered his voice even more,
"And what about the crowd at the Superdome. What kind of reaction
would we receive if we announce that the Vice President was shot and
is dead? Would there be a stampede? Would it create a panic? Would
more people be killed?"

"I don't know," Brad answered, not even knowing if the agent wanted an answer.

"I don't know either, Brad. That's why I've determined to wait until fifteen minutes after the game to announce in a news conference what we know. I want to give those people a chance to get out without having to worry if the guy next to them is carrying a gun, a bomb, or whatever. Can you see my point?"

"Yes," Brad answered.

"Can you help me on this, Brad?"

The reporter sat back, put his pen and pad away, and cast a glance toward the Vice President's body while he pondered the question for a full minute. The air chilled him. He rubbed his hands together. He loved his country. He loved his profession. He wanted to protect and promote both. This story and how he handled it could make or break his career, his reputation, his credibility.

"Al, I'm sure that some people believe that reporters don't care about anything. Whether people get killed in a stampede or whether someone else gets shot. Or whether the country goes to hell in a handbasket as long as we get first dibs on reporting it. But I've withheld stories before, waiting on the right timing. Now, understand, not this big a story. But I see your point." He looked at the floor and then back up into Shanker's eyes. "Can we deal a little bit?" Brad asked, his eyes widening.

Shanker's mouth dropped open a bit, and he glanced once again toward the gurney.

"Perhaps. What do you want?"

"Three things," Brad began. He spoke very low and slowly, illustrating each point with an extended finger. "First, I want you as an off-the-record source for followups. I don't want to be pushed aside in the investigation of what happened if I hold up with this story. You can trust me to act responsibly. Second, I want to see the chest wound on Harrot. And, if I get those two requests, I will hold off with my story until fifteen minutes after the game . . . and last, you delay your news conference to twenty minutes after. I'll be five minutes ahead of you, but you'll have accomplished what you wanted—to get the majority of the crowd out of the Superdome before the news breaks. How about it?"

Brad didn't really care to look at the mortal wound of Harrot. But it was something tangible to assure him that Shanker would live up to the remainder of the bargain.

Shanker sat stone-faced and silent. Shanker could hold him temporarily—as a potential witness or something—until after the news was released, but that could create serious problems down the line about interfering with the freedom of the press. It could lead to agency embarrassment and to Shanker's dismissal. Brad figured that

Shanker didn't know whether he could trust the reporter. Maybe Shanker would find a spark of integrity in Brad's eyes. Or had he felt confidence in his handshake?

"You've got me by the balls on this one, Brad. I'm going to trust you. It's a deal. I'll let you know what I can—always off-the-record and channeled and written in a way where it never could be attributed to me. You understand?"

Brad nodded.

"Where're you from, Brad?"

"Louisiana, Al, and you?"

"East Tennessee."

"Is that different from the rest of Tennessee?"

"It sure the hell is. We keep our word, and kill anybody who lies to us or messes with our dogs or our women. In that order. Let's shake on it."

The two Southern gentlemen stood, shook hands, and walked the five steps to the gurney. Brad was shown the single entry hole that had penetrated the Vice President just below the breast bone. Otherwise, Harrot looked in amazingly good health and physical condition for a dead man of fifty-six.

He had at least an hour before he broke the news to the nation on Pinthater's television station. Brad was already writing the story in his head as he was shown another exit from the room where the deal was made. He walked to the main lobby of the hospital and down the hallway to another friend's office. There he borrowed a laptop computer, plugged it into the telephone jack, and got on line with the newspaper's processor so that the story would be ready for the first edition. While typing away, he called up the publisher and told him the deal. They had a confirmed story that would be broadcast five minutes before the official announcement. He had seen the body.

Pinthater was delighted—except he wanted to go with it earlier.

"No way, Ed. I gave my word. It's the right thing to do. Besides, it will give us time to get a full crew together. We need team work to follow up on this. Give me all the reporters you can spare." He hung up. He had convinced him.

His next call was to try to locate Jill. After four futile attempts, he got through to the governor's suite where Hugh Johnson and his entourage had decided to go after leaving the reception area in the bowels of the stadium.

"Jill, is everything all right there?" He leaned against the receiver and continued to type out the story that would run in the morning edition beneath the banner headline:

VICE PRESIDENT HARROT ASSASSINATED

"Yeah, Brad, everything's fine here. What's happening? How's the Vice President?" she asked from the crowded room where about twenty men and women were milling around, standing in little knots watching the remainder of the Sugar Bowl, and awaiting word on Harrot.

"Listen. I can't say anything now. But turn to Channel Five ten minutes after the game. You be sure to stay there until I can get back. You won't hear any news on his condition until then. Don't leave. You hear me?" He couldn't tell her more. Someone in the room or even at the hotel desk might be listening.

"Brad, can't you tell me anything? Some good word that I can pass on to the governor?" She was sitting now. Her hands began to tremble.

"No. I have to go. But I'll be up there before too long. Just watch Channel Five. Bye." He hung up, looked at a few notes he had made on his pad, and again began to type away furiously. He had to make this deadline, but he wanted to write the story in a way that would give him credit and would bring out the emotions involved in the death of a statesman.

AS THE FOURTH QUARTER got underway, the two Alabama fans and the one with the Notre Dame jacket lost interest in the game and began their slow walk down the ramps of the Superdome. The walkway wrapped around in walled circles forever. Very few were leaving now, and they didn't have to press through large crowds. Their job was done. They would read the final score in the *Times-Gazette* in the morning.

As they neared street level, they slowed. The metal detectors were set up and the few early leavers had to pass through. They looked at each other and then at the uniformed police. Smiling, they walked through without a hint of a problem once they had handed their binoculars and camera to one of the guards. Outside, they hailed a cab for the ride to the warehouse near the Mississippi—about a mile from the French Market at the corner of Jackson Square—where they were to receive another part of their million dollar fee.

# Seven

Alabama and Notre Dame each scored only a field goal in the third quarter to leave the score at 17 to 13 in Alabama's favor entering the final quarter of the game that would decide the national championship for the just completed football year of 1997. Both coaches continued to play it close to the vest through the fourth quarter.

With a minute left in the game, Alabama's All-American punter launched a beautiful spiral that boomed like a cannon from his foot down to the ten yard line of the Irish. The only problem was that he out-kicked his coverage team by ten yards.

The smallest player on the field, a black youth from Florida who had forsaken the warmth of the South for the chance to play with Notre Dame, cradled the ball into his chest, put it under his right arm, and started a rather slow and deliberate return for the first five yards until he passed the first wave of defenders. He then sidestepped toward the right sideline and ran like a deer two yards from and parallel with the side boundary. He ran, protected only by the thin white line from all the Alabama players standing in front of their bench, toward the far end.

Crimson Tide players on the sideline watched in horror as he sprinted within spitting distance of their coach who viewed only the backside of the green-shirted speedster. He raced untouched into the endzone. With the extra point, Notre Dame won by an eventual score of 20 to 17.

Many Alabama fans cursed the coach. Some wished they were dead. Alabama failed in its bid for a second national championship in five years.

FBI AGENT JOHN DOBSON arrived just after Shanker and Yeary made their little deal. Dobson, who was still attired in his Notre Dame jacket, was quickly brought up to speed on the situation by Shanker. Dobson tried in vain to reach the Director of the FBI. He looked at Harrot's body and agreed that Shanker should stay with it until the autopsy was performed.

Dobson directed a pair of agents to witness the procedure. Both Shanker and Dobson worked together to prevent any foul ups that could compromise the investigation. In addition to Louisiana's best pathologist, Dobson called in world-renowned forensic pathologists from Tennessee and Ohio to be part of the autopsy team. They both would be there within hours.

Shanker marveled to himself that Dobson of the FBI also agreed with the steps that he had taken to have the metal detectors set up at the Superdome and the instructions concerning the clean-up of the stadium following the game. So often in the past, petty jealousies and turf wars created discord between the agencies. Shanker hoped Dobson would be a person he could continue to work with. The Secret Service would not be in charge of the investigation of the murder of Harrot, but with Dobson he would at least be informed.

Dobson sat in the now often used straight back chair near the phone awaiting a return call from the director as he and Shanker considered who else needed to be notified.

"We'd better call in the U.S. Attorney and the state and local district attorneys. They'll be pissed off if they learn this from the television," Dobson suggested and Shanker nodded.

"Call them in and tell them a few minutes before we announce it, but don't tell them over the phone. You agree, John?" Shanker asked.

"Right."

They decided to let Dobson and Harrot's press secretary do the news conference. Shanker had not been out of the presence of the body of Harrot since he fell, and he wasn't about to change that.

Dobson looked down at his jacket. "This won't do, Al. I can't do an announcement wearing this outfit. He slipped off the Notre Dame jacket and draped it onto the back of the chair. "Can I borrow yours?" There in the presence of the doctor and nurse, Shanker of the Secret Service loaned Dobson of the FBI his tie and suit jacket. They both managed a slight smile. It was probably a first in the history of both agencies. The coat was a bit long and a little snug for Dobson, but it would do.

Al Shanker finally called in Liz Arzenhoff. As Harrot's press secretary, she needed to know. At the game's end, he and Dobson prepared for the announcement. For the first ten minutes the stout young Arzenhoff paced along the wall in shock.

"I can't do this. I can't face the nation in ten minutes. Harrot is dead? I can't believe it."

Shanker expected such a reaction and knew that it would eventually fall to Dobson to handle. Arzenhoff didn't have enough details and wouldn't be able to assimilate them rapidly enough to do justice to the conference in a mere twenty minutes from learning of Harrot's death.

By now, though, the President knew, and all other top officials were apprised. Secret Service and military guards swept in almost instantaneous phalanges to the homes of all of the men and women in line of Constitutional succession to the President—all the way to the tenth in line. The Director of the FBI was located and called back in. The plan was going forward. By morning there would be at least a hundred agents in New Orleans tracking down the assassins.

Armored personnel carriers stood guard at all the entrances to Camp David. Marines in camouflage and with night-vision goggles swept the grounds, not only of Camp David but of the White House. In Georgia with the Speaker of the House and in Kansas with the Speaker Pro Tem of the Senate, squadrons of arms-toting military and agency personnel suddenly made the ones they were protecting feel important—more important than they had felt in their lives.

Brad pushed the button on his watch that gave him the exact time from the end of the game. At precisely ten minutes after the last whistle, he closed up his laptop computer and walked the fifty yards down a crowded hallway. Past the conference room where Liz Arzenhoff and John Dobson would hold forth in ten minutes, he stepped single-mindedly into another room just beyond where his television crew waited. He had told the producer what to have—pirate video from the network which had broadcast the game where they had shown Harrot falling at the half-time ceremony. "Try to get a shot showing Jill Crenshaw reaching down to help the Vice President," he had told them.

For him the tragedy in Dallas in 1963 had forever been etched into the retina of his memory by the scene of Jackie Kennedy reaching for the Secret Service officer at the rear of the open limousine when she knew there was nothing more she could do for John. The scene here, too, would have to show a respected lady reaching down to help. It would be a human touch that no one could resist once they knew what happened. He would be way ahead of the other television networks with tape and story. The falling of Harrot would now take on a whole new significance—a frightening one to him. He had to convey that emotion.

"With the story concerning the collapse of Vice President Samuel Harrot, here is Brad Yeary, chief political correspondent for the *Times-Gazette*, live from the emergency room area of Bellevue Hospital," the news anchor of Channel Five said solemnly for the lead-in for Brad.

Dressed in jeans, a dark blue, almost black shirt, and a soft brown tweed sportscoat, Brad stood in the stark room holding only his spiral-bound note pad. His facial expression was somber and tired, but alert. He looked directly into the camera.

"Samuel Harrot, Vice President of the United States, is dead. He was the victim of an assassin's bullet at half-time of the Sugar Bowl game where he was scheduled to accept an award for the President. Harrot's family and the President have been given the news.

"From what I have learned, he was dead almost immediately

when he fell to the turf. At that time no one knew he had been shot by a sniper positioned somewhere in the Superdome. In about five minutes, the official announcement will be made just down the hallway here at Bellevue Hospital in an adjoining room. The Vice President was killed by a single gunshot to the chest."

As Brad broadcast the terrible news to the nation, the production crew of the station showed a clip of the Vice President falling and Jill Crenshaw kneeling down to comfort him. In the adjoining room where monitors were set up in anticipation of an official announcement on Harrot's condition, men and women of the media looked on in awe and shock at the screen showing Channel Five's broadcast. In a sudden swing of news-crowd hysteria, they ran from the room where the official announcement would shortly be made next door to where Brad Yeary was holding forth with the news of the year.

Like BB's falling into a bucket of water, the news spread in concentric circles to those at the hospital like Shanker who was watching on a set in the room where Harrot's body lay, to the hotel suite where Jill Crenshaw and Governor Johnson studied the screen with a score of others, and thence to the state and nation. Even at 1 a.m. Eastern Time, the number who were watching Brad Yeary was the largest audience ever for him.

Ed Pinthater had reached a hurried agreement with CNN to carry Channel Five's broadcast live. He told them they would not regret it. As the circles spread, so did the intensity until it became more like rifle shot, pinballs, and then cannon balls that were being dropped into the bucket of water. The news of the assassination of its second ranking official splattered the nation.

Brad Yeary quickly became news himself. That was a violation of a standard and basic precept of journalists that he held to—report the news; don't become the news. He told most of what he knew in the five-minute interval he had between the time he was to begin and the time that Dobson and Arzenhoff were to deliver the official version. He was prepared to switch to their announcement once he was cued. But as Dobson and Arzenhoff ran at least three minutes late, Brad was forced to continue. Once he paused, the gathered newspeople started popping questions to him. Instantaneously, he was on all the major networks and was being photographed by the flashing cameras of numerous print media.

He ignored the questions. His competitors should not have invaded his space. He kicked himself for being short-sighted by not having security present to keep the others out. Finally, he was cued that Dobson and Arzenhoff were ready. With that, the fifty or so media, their camera crews and sound people, rushed back to the adjoining room for the official version.

# Eight

At the Marriot Hotel, State Senator Jill Crenshaw sat in stunned silence. She was sad, shocked, grieving, and hurt all at the same time. Sad, shocked, and grieving because of the death of Harrot, and a bit hurt because Brad had not forewarned her and had used, or at least allowed his publisher's station to use, the footage of her kneeling down beside the fallen Vice President.

She sat and sobbed quietly to herself. That was part of the rules that she and Brad played by. Neither would let their feelings for the other interfere with doing their jobs. He would report what he had to report, and she would vote, sponsor, and support legislation and programs that she wanted to without regard to Brad's desires or Ed Pinthater's wishes. But why couldn't he at least have said that Harrot was dead?

Twenty minutes after the game the exit tunnels at the Superdome were still clogged with thousands of people trying to leave and being bottlenecked into and between the metal detectors. Word spread quickly through the lines that the police were looking for guns.

People began getting nasty. Many had been drinking. Alabama fans were upset at losing. A few mouthy Notre Dame stalwarts were rubbing in the victory by singing their fight song with some homemade lyrics that reverberated through the catacombs of the tunnels. Bottles were thrown; fistfights broke out; some people turned back toward the stands; and chaos reigned over the last thirty-thousand struggling fans.

The police, for safety's sake, removed the detectors and let the hordes pass through.

AROUND A CARD TABLE upon which sat two feebly burning candles, the three assassins huddled with the money man at the New Orleans warehouse. They stood in the aisle between rows of metal barrels stacked three-high.

The dark-skinned man with a neat mustache sat impassively. He opened three envelopes and flipped through what he told each man was eighty thousand dollars in hundred dollar bills. He closed them back up with string and handed one to each of the two Alabama-clad men and to the man with the Notre Dame jacket.

"There's a boat waiting for you. Ali will guide you. The boat will take you to a Saudi tanker in the Gulf where you will receive a like amount. Then to Paraguay where you will be met by another agent with your final payment." He stood and shook each of their hands.

"Congratulations, you were successful." He barely came to the shoulder of the shortest of the other three. It was a scant hundred yards from the door of the warehouse to the speedboat that was waiting on the Mississippi already aimed toward the Gulf. They met Ali at the door and trotted down the parking area toward the dark water.

"What a waste of money," the short olive-skinned man said as he watched the boat speed off. He closed the door to the warehouse and slowly walked toward the French Quarter to prepare for his Friday prayers.

DOBSON AND ARZENHOFF COULD not offer any more real news than Brad had already announced to the nation. But Brad went to the briefing just in case. They disclosed even less than Brad already knew. Neither Dobson nor Arzenhoff answered any question that was shouted to them at the end of the three-minute statement that was bringing shock to the nation.

Who did it? Why? How with all the security? Had they found a gun? Had anyone been arrested? Were there any suspects? What were they doing at this moment in the investigation? Was there just one shot as Brad Yeary reported? How did Brad Yeary know?

To all of these, Dobson told them there would be information forthcoming, but he had nothing for now. There were no suspects. At this early stage no one was sure how the assassination was accomplished. But, he assured the nation, the FBI would not rest "until the assassin or assassins are brought to justice."

Shanker watched the announcement from his position in the room with Harrot's body. The monitor was small but he could see all too well. The one question that he answered aloud when it was shouted to Dobson by a reporter was, "Is this the first time that a Vice President has been assassinated?"

"Yes, hell yes!" He mouthed the words and clinched his fists in the otherwise silent room.

The story was too big to put to bed. Brad called and asked Jill to stay at the Marriott.

"Don't try to go back to the St. Laurent. I've got to stay with the story a little longer." He didn't tell her that he had already been contacted by NBC, ABC, and CBS to come on their early morning news shows to tell what he knew. His celebrity status was growing, but he declined the offers. He would rise and fall on the printing presses of the *Times-Gazette* and make an occasional television appearance on Pinthater's Channel Five in New Orleans.

His stories would be copyrighted, and anyone quoting from them would have to identify him and his paper as the sources. In addition, he held in one pocket of his tweed coat a mini-cassette tape of his ten-minute interview with Harrot. Pinthater wanted him to turn that interview into a five-part series over the next week. In the other pocket he possessed the handkerchief that was soaked with the blood of the late Vice President.

He didn't have much, but what he had was more than anyone else. He was the last to interview Harrot. He would have had a longer conversation if Harrot had lived until after the game and returned to his hotel. Sometimes the illusion of having all knowledge was more powerful than actually having it. People would be waiting to read his stories.

His immediate problem was that he had only asked Harrot about five real questions in the ten minutes time. From that, he would have to construct a story around each of them as though Harrot were Moses bringing the tablets of stone down from the mount. The questions hadn't amounted to much. It was not his best interview. If he had known that Harrot was going to be shot ten minutes after his last statement, he would have framed queries that would have had significance for the ages.

He was afraid that the contents of the other pocket would soon be subpoenaed as evidence although he could not conceive of any reason that the FBI, or whoever, would want the bloody piece of cloth. In any event, he would hide it and think about what to do with it later.

He immediately started his first follow-up story. The details weren't there yet, but he would fill them in later in the day. His account would center as a theme on the Vice President's last interview but would have to include any new developments on the investigation, funeral plans, and perhaps comments from friends, family, and associates of Harrot. He would like to interview the President but was certain that would be blocked for the time being while the Secret Service kept the chief executive under wraps.

Already ten reporters from the *Times-Gazette* had been assigned to the story, and to Pinthater's credit, they all would be working under Brad. He had to see and approve each story before it reached the printing presses.

He made a few notes, headed from the hospital, and hailed a cab to take him to the newspaper.

LOUISIANA'S SENIOR SENATOR, BENJAMIN Edward Ashford, did not attend the Sugar Bowl where many of the other political bigwigs were on New Year's night. Instead he spent a quiet evening at his ancestral plantation house just outside of Lafayette. It had turned off cool and breezy during the day with a smattering of rain.

He had retired to his library that occupied the larger part of the second floor of the white-columned house. From that vantage point, he could look out the window eastwardly toward Baton Rouge where he had served as governor before leaving for the U.S. Senate ten years before.

He loved the power of government. He did not love the process of being elected that seemed to be such a part of the Louisiana tradition. He was not and never would be a glad-handing Huey or Earl Long type. He didn't really care much for sports, and that was why he was not at the Superdome on New Year's night. Besides that, he could barely suffer the political types when he had to, and he certainly wasn't going to mix with them when it was not necessary. It was two years until his reelection, and there would be plenty of time to go through the embarrassing routine and run the gauntlet of political handshaking, backslapping, smiling, and baby kissing. He would rather be in his library overlooking the two hundred acres that were left of the Ashford Plantation.

Although the estate had shrunk in size, the power of its owner had not. Benjamin Edward Ashford was the first in six generations of very prominent Ashfords to ever occupy a state-wide office. His father and grandfather before him had served in the state legislature and took their turns as local judges, but no one had risen in government as far as he.

Unfortunately for him, there was no one left in the family to enjoy it with him. His wife had died five years before. They were childless. There were not even any close cousins, nephews, or nieces. He was an only child. So, near the end of the Twentieth Century and the beginning of a new millennium, Benjamin Edward Ashford was the last—the last in a long line of the Ashford landed gentry. He would have to enjoy his achievements alone.

A senator of wealth could have afforded several servants to look after his needs, but Senator Ashford retained only two on the plantation. Amelia Tadford served as his cook, maid, and keeper of the books for the farm. Her son, B.J., did the majority of the work around the estate. Ashford hired some seasonal help only when necessary because, in reality, the plantation was one in name only. Fewer than fifty head of beef cattle were the sole occupants of the vast fields except for the wildlife—deer, foxes, muskrats, and others—that used the acreage for passage from one safe haven to another.

In the Southern tradition, Ashford's servants were black, descendants from their slave forbearers who served other Ashfords in the time before the unfortunate conflict that forever freed them to barter their services rather than be owned.

Amelia Tadford, now in her forties, had been a beautiful young lady. Most of her charms were still there. Predominantly of African-

American ancestry, she also had blood that if it had been DNA-tested would have shown a mixture of French, American Indian, and Cajun. Even now her steely blue eyes, which would flash from time to time with a temper that she always battled to keep under control, sat in a face of character as though chiseled from black marble. Her nose and lips showed more of her Indian and French heritage than African. Because of her physical characteristics, she had not been well accepted into the black community to which she felt she rightfully belonged. Early in life, she decided to stay on at the "master's" plantation if he would allow. She had married another servant, but they divorced. She was as much sixth-generation servant as Senator Ashford was squire.

She and B.J. had watched the Alabama–Notre Dame game while the senator wandered about in the library looking at old and obscure books of world history and anthropology. They could hear him occasionally as he would move the ladder along the built-in rail above the last shelf in the twelve-foot high wall of books. The scratchy, shrill screaks of the steel ladder against the guides added a haunting aura to the lone, dark house. He would maneuver until he could climb and take down a volume for perhaps a ten-minute perusal and then begin the same task again.

She believed the senator spent more time in looking for books and moving the ladder than in reading. Like all other viewers, Amelia Tadford was shocked to learn that the Vice President of the United States had been assassinated. She knew that the senator had always warned her not to disturb him while he was in the library, but surely he would want to know this news. One of his colleagues, the presiding officer of Ashford's Senate was dead. She looked at her son.

"B.J., should I tell the Senator?"

"Huh, uh. Not me. When he say he don't wanta be disturbed, that's what the old man means." He shook his head and looked straight into the television screen. "If he's in that library when Jesus comes back, Mr. Gabriel's gonna hafta wait and blow that trumpet a second time for Mr. Senator. He won't come out of there for nobody. He's meditatin'." He laughed at his last phrase. "He's probably just up there jackin' off. But I guess meditatin' is meditatin'."

"B.J., don't say such a thing about the Senator," his mother said. "He loves his books. He don't have no family. Just us. Be a little kinder. He's taken care of us when no one else would. Mr. Ashford's a gentleman. I believe I'll go up and tell him. This is important news."

B.J. cast his eyes upward. "Might as well, Mom. I don't hear him screeching around with that ladder anymore. He's probably gone to sleep."

Amelia turned away from her son and walked quietly up the

wooden staircase that swept in a semi-circle to the landing on the second floor. The library doors were closed. She knocked softly but received no response. She rapped again a bit louder. Still no answer. Deciding to risk a severe scolding, she gently turned the door knob and pushed one of the oak entryways open just enough so she could squeeze her thin body into the darkened room.

"Mr. Ashford. Senator Ashford," she called out just above a whisper. He didn't answer. She looked where the ladder hung along the dark wood shelving, then toward his desk, but could not see the senator. Then as she turned to her right she saw him near the window that looked out toward Baton Rouge.

Senator Ashford, with his back toward Amelia, sat Indian-style on the floor. He was barefooted with his legs crossed in front of him. He wore only a white silk robe that wrapped him like a cocoon, pulled up in back to where it blended with his hair and tied in front. He sat with his head bowed—chin on chest, his eyes closed—at the edge of where the expensive Persian rug ended. The hardwood floor extended beyond to the window that was opened a bit. All the lights were off. The only illumination was from two old oil lamps that had been placed at the base of the window. The light shimmered off the side of his robe, making the cloth appear alive although he sat perfectly still.

She was afraid to say anything more. She was frightened to leave. He really was meditating. Oh, if B.J. could only see this, she thought, then pinched herself for having such a silly notion. Or, maybe he was also dead like the Vice President. He was motionless as though in a trance. For what seemed like several minutes she stood there mute.

Finally, without moving, opening his eyes, or lifting his head, Senator Benjamin Edward Ashford said in a whispery voice, almost a rasp, "What is so important, Amelia, that you would disobey a standing order and interrupt my meditation?"

Her hands were like ice—her mouth dry. She reached back and grabbed the door knob so she wouldn't fall.

"Sir. Senator Ashford. I thought . . . I thought you would want to know . . ." She could barely speak. Fear stole her tongue.

"Yes, Amelia?" he said  without any change in his position. "Spit it out."

"Sir, they just said on the television that Mr. Harrot—Vice President of these United States—was shot dead at the Superdome just a couple hours ago."

There was another period of silence with Ashford remaining perfectly stone-like.

"Yes, Amelia. Ball games are mindless, dangerous things. It is enough." He fell into silence again. Amelia turned and departed the library, leaving the Senator to his meditation.

AGENT SHANKER AND FBI Agent Dobson met in a small room adjoining the one where Harrot's body had been autopsied. No matter how many times they had seen a body cut apart and examined, there was no getting used to it. Neither had witnessed one in several years until now. It was dehumanizing. The doctors, pathologists, and attendants were matter-of-fact in their job. Brain size in circumference and weight. All the organs the same way. They dictated into their little recorders, more like they were talking about the dissection of a frog in high school biology than about the body of the late Vice President. An autopsy was a total invasion of the human body that couldn't be undone no matter how prettily they tried to sew the gutted and de-brained hulk back together.

They knew what had killed Harrot before the first cut was made. Everything else was just extra that had to be done. Now what was left could be released to his family for proper disposal. He had been killed by a single gunshot wound. That was true. It was strange, though. There was a lone entrance wound but no exit wound. The solitary shot had pierced the skin and muscle tissue directly beneath the sternum to a depth of two inches and then exploded like a Roman candle at its zenith into ten pieces that erupted into a starburst pattern. Every vital organ was penetrated by a piece of the bullet no larger than a pellet. The heart, liver, kidneys, lungs, spleen, and intestines were all ripped open.

"It didn't make any difference where that bullet hit. If they got him any place in the torso, he was going to be dead," Dobson said as they reviewed the preliminary notes.

"At least we have the bullet," Shanker said.

"Yeah, in ten parts. It'll be tough for ballistics to match up the rifling with that. He didn't have a chance. Dead by the time he hit the turf."

"Have you ever seen or heard of a bullet like that, John?" Shanker asked and shook his head. "Yeah, I know a bullet can fragment. But into ten pieces with a perfect pattern? They knew what they were doing."

There was a knock at the door. Agent Clary came in.

"Dobson, your people at the Dome want you to call. They finished the preliminary sweep of the place."

Dobson was gone less than five minutes when he returned and sat down with Shanker and Clary.

"Your metal detectors worked, Al."

"Great! What did they find?"

"Well, let's see. They confiscated twenty-eight handguns from people as they were leaving." He looked up at Shanker.

"Twenty-eight?" Shanker shook his head.

"Yeah. They got those folks' names and addresses for follow-up if we want to interview them. But that's not all," he looked at Shanker and then at his pad. "They found another sixty in different trash cans all over the stadium. Seems like when the people learned the cops were looking for guns, everyone who had one, except for the twenty-eight brave souls who turned them in at the metal detectors, stashed them in garbage containers."

"Sixty? I can't believe that, John. You mean at any given ball game there's a possibility of that many handguns being present?"

"Well, you gotta remember, Al, that forty thousand of those folks were from Alabama. And the crime rate in New Orleans is high. I'm surprised there weren't more." He smiled and zipped up his Notre Dame jacket that he had retrieved after the news conference. "No rifles. And I don't think a handgun could've done this."

"No."


AT SIX O'CLOCK ON the morning of January Second, a lone fisherman pushed his small skiff away from the bank of the Mississippi River near Venice, Louisiana, south of New Orleans. There the river cuts through its alluvial plain and begins to fan out into four fingers to greet the Gulf of Mexico.

He had fished for a mere half hour when he heard the roar of a speed boat approaching from the direction of New Orleans.

The old fisherman looked out at the strange sight. So early in the morning for a boat to be in such a hurry. He could see only the red and green running lights and the two bright white strobes at the stern. No occupants were visible in the darkness, and no voices could be heard over the roar of the engine.

A half mile past the fisherman in the middle of the river, the speeding boat exploded into a thousand pieces, sending a fireball a hundred feet into the air. Shock waves from the blast rocked the boat of the fisherman just a few seconds later. He pulled to the bank and watched. By the time he coaxed his twenty-horsepower engine back to life and toward the sparkling debris, all the bigger parts of the boat had sunk. With only a flashlight to guide him, he looked for survivors. He found none.

He searched by feel more than sight. He finally located a piece of cloth that he fished from the river into his boat. It was no more than a foot square. He shined his poor little light on it and looked at the crimson scrap. Attached to the cloth was most of a letter—a big block A.

# Nine

S leep eluded Brad Yeary in the days following Harrot's death. In constant motion, he interviewed, wrote, telephoned, reviewed, answered, asked—everything that he knew to do to get the complete account. Having shown he had the goods on the initial story, he developed a wide audience and following for every word he wrote or spoke over the next several days.

At the paper, his associates treated him with great deference. Even Pinthater, who had always remained distant and aloof, dropped by Brad's office to check on the progress of the continuing series and to be sure he had everything he needed in the way of resources and staff. Brad finally had to put a stop to taking calls if he had not requested information from the person.

People from all over the country phoned him. Every weird and far-out theory as to what the death of the Vice President meant and who did it gravitated to him like he was a magnet. The Klan, Jews, Catholics, Notre Dame fans, the CIA, the FBI, the Secret Service, the unknown son of Lee Harvey Oswald, a seed of Charles Manson, the governor, the Arabs, the Russians, the president of the Orange Bowl were all put forth, with numerous others, as the plotters who succeeded in their assassination attempt.

Shanker's concern that other attempts might be forthcoming had not materialized. Not a single out-of-the-way incident occurred near the President or other ranking officials. Most of those claiming responsibility for the killing were checked out and quickly discounted. All was quiet.

With Pinthater's permission, and with a payment to Brad, his columns were picked up for national syndication. A readership of many millions developed where the week before he was lucky to be read by fifty thousand. His picture splashed across newspapers and television news shows throughout the nation. With this notoriety, which he secretly relished at first, came the inevitable inability to go anywhere without being recognized. Having always traveled in anonymity, he was now beset at restaurants, airports, and even walking to his apartment in the French Quarter by people wanting his picture or an autograph.

By Tuesday, January Sixth, he had begun to grow tired of it all. He had to travel to Montgomery, Alabama, for Harrot's funeral, and he didn't want to be a sideshow and detract from the service. He bought some sunglasses and a baseball cap—a type which he had never worn before—and attempted a slightly disguised trip through the airports of New Orleans and Montgomery.

For the past two days his attempts to contact Shanker for his first follow-up since the Thursday shooting had gone unanswered. He couldn't get through to him, but he knew Shanker was still in New Orleans. The President had announced that a special team made up of the top people in the FBI would handle the investigation, with Shanker to be the liaison to the Secret Service and directly to the President himself.

Shanker must have some clout with the Prez's people. It was all to his good. If Shanker kept his word, Brad, once again, would be the first newsperson to know. Of course, all the major television news departments were also trying to buy their sources within the investigative team to have the jump on their competitors.

Every senator except for the senior senator from Pennsylvania, who was hospitalized, and the junior senator from California, who was under indictment for fraud, came to the funeral. The small church could barely squeeze two hundred mourners into its clapboard-covered sanctuary. The building stood on a windswept hill just off Highway 331, south of Montgomery. This was where Samuel Harrot attended as a child and later a little sporadically as an adult. He could have been buried in Arlington, but he would be laid to rest there in the church cemetery where his ancestors' bones waited beneath the red clay soil of his native Alabama.

The President didn't attend, it was announced, because of fear of another assassination attempt from the still unknown source. However, in the audience were both Shanker and Dobson.

Shanker tugged on Brad's coat sleeve when Brad walked down the aisle toward the assigned place for the few members of the press who were allowed in.

Brad leaned down. Shanker cupped his hand to his mouth. "I got your calls, Brad. I couldn't return them yet. I'll talk to you when I get back. We have some interesting film," he said in a low whisper. Brad nodded, walked to the press area, and took his seat.

Family, staff, senators, the Speaker of the House, and a few ranking cabinet members filled the room with faces of somber sobriety. Flowers enveloped the entire front, and their sweet perfume thickened the air with the reminder of death, pushing any hint of other fragrance from the building. An elderly African-American lady, entirely clothed in black down to a black lace veil, sat at the organ and played soulful dirges as the mourners made their way down the aisles to their seats.

Outside, a score of FBI agents watched those who entered and the hundreds of others who stood out in the cold to listen to the service through loudspeakers. Two vans filled with agents secretly videotaped every arrival. Perhaps the assassin would attend the funeral in order to gain some morbid satisfaction. It had happened before, just as pyromaniacs returned to their arsons.

Brad turned and gazed at all the assembled politicians. "Where the carcass is shall the eagles be gathered together," he quoted to himself, his eyes sweeping over the mass of power or supposed power. Was he facing the person who would be the next Vice President of the United States?

Since 1967, the Twenty-fifth Amendment to the Constitution allowed the President to nominate a successor in the event of the removal, resignation, death of the Vice President, or elevation of the Vice President to the Presidency.

It had only been exercised twice in the past thirty years. Once when Nixon nominated Ford to serve after the resignation of Agnew, and then when Ford chose Rockefeller as Vice President following Nixon's resignation in 1974. Brad knew his political trivia. Who was the only person to serve as Vice President and President without being elected to either? Ford. It was a good question at parties, especially after a few drinks when no one could think anyway.

Decorum prevented a public discussion of who would be the probable successor to Harrot since his death the previous week. That had to wait "until at least after the funeral," politicians said. But Brad knew, as did all others who followed the maneuvering of politics, that there had been talk, and not only talk, but promotion of prospective candidates for the job from the time it was announced that Harrot was dead. Before the body was autopsied or even cold, there had been backroom discussions.

If consideration was delayed too long, a candidate would be on the outside looking in. The great turnout of senators and representatives at the funeral mirrored as much. Each of them, at least of the President's party, saw himself or herself as the next Vice President. Except for being a heartbeat away from the Presidency, Brad still thought the assessment of John Nance Garner was pretty well on target.

Tears spilled from many during the service. No reporter cried, just the politicians.

The mass then assembled around the little cemetery which lay on the hillside facing the direction of the rising sun as more words were said about Samuel Harrot—father, husband, Vice President of the United States, former senator from Alabama, patriot, and favorite son.

WHEN IT WAS OVER, Brad flew back to New Orleans. He put the story to bed with the final in his five-part series on Harrot's last interview. What did Harrot want to tell him when he invited him back to the hotel? That question still haunted him. He determined to take two days off and spend those in Baton Rouge with Jill. He hadn't seen her since the day after the assassination.

As soon as he had safely sent the story from his terminal at his desk to the print-point, Brad switched off the keyboard, processor, and monitor and turned toward the window that looked toward the Mississippi. The view was partly blocked by taller and newer buildings.

He could barely glimpse the slow-moving brown river. But he could feel it. The river always soothed him. She was his ever-waiting lady. She massaged the nerves and smoothed the harried edges. The solace of the river had calmed him over the years as few things or people could. He looked forward to Jill's apartment in Baton Rouge which snuggled peacefully near the levee. There they could walk, sit, talk, and all the while be stroked by the lovely lady they called "Big Muddy."

"Brad." His peaceful thoughts were interrupted by the hoarse voice of Pinthater who came through the door and put an arm around him like he always did when he wanted something. "What are you doing?"

"Closing down, sir. I haven't had a day off in the last two weeks. I'm going to take a couple of days and go up to Baton Rouge." Why did he feel a need to explain? For the sake of peace, he tried to be polite to the publisher.

"That's good. Take a few days. You've worked hard. You deserve it." He patted Brad on the back and sat down in the cubicle they called an office. He leaned back in the overstuffed chair that faced the window, interlaced his fingers behind his head, and smiled up at Brad. "We're going big, Brad. We can't let it stop. Gotta stay on top. Press forward and take advantage."

Brad just stared at his boss. What was he getting at? He didn't need a pep talk, and the way Pinthater talked in short, staccato sentences irritated him. For the past five years, he had been able to avoid much contact with the publisher, but now, with this story, the boss wanted to stay on top of every move—wanted to read every word—know every detail before it was published.

"Yes, sir. I'll stay on top of it. But right now I'm going up to Baton Rouge for some R and R."

"Sure. And, Brad, when you get back, I want you to go up to Washington and interview the President." Pinthater smiled.

Brad crossed his arms. "Sir, I have never interviewed a President. I've interviewed them before they became Presidents and after they left office. I've even shouted a few questions in a group news conference like Sam Donaldson taught me, but there's no chance of me getting in to talk with the President. He's too busy with selecting a new V P and running the country," Brad said and stepped nearer the publisher.

"Oh, yes, there is." Pinthater's smile did not diminish as he looked up at his ace reporter. "His office called today. They want the President to talk with you. It's going to be an exclusive." The portly old man bounded out of his chair and pounded the dazed Brad on the back.

"They called? They want me? When? Who called?" Brad rubbed both hands back through his long hair and then pressed the palms to his eyes, pacing the room in small circles, surprised that the President knew he was alive.

"The Prez has been reading your stories. He likes your style, your thoroughness, your accuracy. They've selected you for the first in-depth interview about his reaction and feelings concerning Harrot's death," Pinthater said.

"His press secretary called me an hour ago. You were busy. So I took the call. Didn't want to disturb your writing. So go off and have a good time. You'll fly up on Sunday for the interview on Monday. And I want you to hit him hard on who the new V P is going to be. See if we can get another scoop. And when you come back from Washington, I want you to go interview Senator Ashford. He's being mentioned, you know, for the V P."

"Yeah, him and every other Republican who holds office, has held office, or aspires to office. I don't see Ashford as V P. He's too ambitious. There's talk that he might run for President himself in two years."

"What better way to get rid of a possible adversary than give him the Vice Presidency where he can cool his heels for six years? Remember, the President was a politician before he became a statesman." Pinthater walked toward the door.

"When did he become a statesman?" Brad shouted after him. He wheeled around and dialed Jill's home number and—when there was no answer—her number at the state capitol.

"Is Senator Crenshaw in? Yes, this is Brad Yeary. I'd like to speak to her a minute if she has time." He was put on hold where he was able to listen to country music while he waited. It was brief. Jill was on the line.

"Is this Brad Yeary? I thought you were dead. Anybody alive

would have called long before now or would have been here."

Brad listened and knew it was going to take him a while to renew this relationship. He was ready to apologize.

"Jill, I'm sorry. I've been so busy. But I talked the old weasel into letting me off for a couple of days. Thought I'd come up. How about it? When will you be home?"

"You're sorry all right," he heard her say but could tell that he was already breaking through. His contriteness paid off. "Well, okay. Come on up. But I have to work late tonight. A big committee meeting. Just let yourself in. I should be home by midnight. We'll talk then."

"Okay, Jill. I'm really, really sorry. I'll cook up something for us for a late dinner and bring a bottle of wine. How's that?"

"Okay. What kind of wine?"

"Does it matter?" Brad asked. "And, Jill, I got some great news."

"What?"

"I'll tell you when I get there. See you around midnight."

# Ten

**M**idnight. He glanced at his watch. It was just five. Less than two hours to Baton Rouge. He would take his five-year-old Ford Crown Vic the long way, stay off I-10, and enjoy a midwinter's leisurely drive along the rural roads that parallel the river and its levees. He'd stop and buy some shrimp, brown rice, and wine. He might pick up some gumbo that he could heat at Jill's. He'd have a head start on the dinner he promised to cook. With a Cajun mother who taught him what real food tastes like, he relished the times he could relax and cook up something hot.

In the late afternoon traffic, he snaked out of the downtown bottleneck onto the route that had grown overly familiar to him during the past five years. New Orleans to Baton Rouge, where the seat of Louisiana government resided and where deals were made and sealed with a drink, was roughly eighty miles of scenic beauty for someone who loved bayous and swampland.

As he drove, he began to think ahead to his interview with the President, to his next series of stories, to talking with Shanker. What had Shanker meant by *some interesting film*? Why had the President requested an interview with him? The miles flowed beneath the car as his mind wandered further. How soon would the FBI find the assassin, and would he be the first to have the news? This must be the top priority of every law enforcement agency in the nation and, perhaps, beyond.

On Highway 1 on the west side of the Mississippi as he neared Bayou Goula, he eased his old Ford onto a side road for a mile. He followed it to a dirt road where a half mile farther stood a small grayish-white building that had not seen a coat of paint since the Depression. Above the doorway a hand-lettered sign, itself faded to bare visibility, proclaimed the establishment to be Broussard's Cafe and Shrimp Seller. The small building squatted on wooden stilts over a creek where three shrimp boats were docked for the night. With darkness, yellowish-orange light flickered through the windows with a hint of blue neon beyond.

Inside, Brad relaxed with a beer. Others who also professed Cajun blood to be the reason for their rowdiness filled the small bar area. Whatever coursed through their veins, it was already loud and getting more boisterous.

This was the edge of Cajun country that lay mainly to the west and southwest. From the mid-1700s, Acadians had been displaced from their homes in what later became Nova Scotia when they were caught in the middle of the tug-of-war between England and France. Then in French Louisiana they found a home and intermingled with other French and some Indian blood. The Acadians became 'Cadiens and then Cajuns as the tongue slowed and they became less concerned with perfect enunciation.

The Cajun influence was greater than their numbers. It permeated everything. It was hot. Hot sauce, hot cooking, loud music, and a love of life that Brad would have adopted even if his mother had not been Cajun. She had taught his dad to cook, and Brad learned from him.

He finished his beer and put his gumbo, shrimp, sauce, and brown rice into a brown bag. Brad was provisioned for his chef's job at Jill's. The Ford was still warm in the dusty parking lot where he had left it. As he walked back out into the cool night air, the screen door slammed behind him, but the loud music followed him to his car and onto the dirt road.

Back on Highway 1, nearing Baton Rouge, he turned onto a larger highway that would take him downtown and beyond to Jill's apartment. There he first heard the ominous thunking sound of a tire gone bad. Flat. It was confirmed to him when the car began to list a bit to its left rear.

"Just what I need," he said aloud, scanning the road ahead for a sign of a service station that might be open and have someone who could change a tire. He knew by experience that "service" in service stations passed with the Beatles of the sixties. Elvis might not be dead, but service was. The stretch was deserted except for an occasional liquor store, convenience depots, tanning salons, and video rental shops sprinkled among hulks of buildings that had been closed, boarded up, or burned down. Baton Rouge definitely was not moving in this direction.

To his right, in the middle of three acres of vacant pavement that had been at one time a parking lot for a thriving shopping center, stood a giant, sparkling white circus tent illuminated with spotlights without and within. The canvas stretched to three stories high. What circus or rock star had borrowed the vacant lot for a show?

He hated the tax laws that made it more financially rewarding for companies to depreciate-out a building, desert it, and build at another location—leaving the old neighborhood deprived of stores and services and with buildings that became dilapidated and finally fell in on themselves. It had been a subject of a three-part series he had done three years ago. It didn't help though, and this was just one prime example.

No help was near as he pulled into the parking lot where at least two hundred cars already surrounded the tent. Lined up at the back of the white centerpiece were three buses of the type that country music stars use to tour. They were sometimes owned by those who fancied themselves musicians just because they were able to grate on the nerves of their elders by scratching their fingers over electrical contrivances called musical instruments. As a child he had made a similar noise with fingernails on squeaky chalkboards to agitate his teachers. Parked behind the buses were two giant, gleaming white tractor-trailer trucks with printing he could not read at that distance and light.

He parked the limping Ford and examined the damage. The tire was warped off the rim of the left rear. The trunk disclosed his lack of proper maintenance as the spare was also flat.

"A flat tire at a rock concert," he mouthed angrily to himself. He imagined being mugged by kids in leather vests and spiked hair. He could picture them eating his shrimp, rice, and gumbo over his bloody, prone body.

But as he looked closer, he noticed the occupants of the cars still pulling in and parking near the tent were mature men and women—families, young couples, and singles. It must be a circus instead of a rock concert. Then his eye caught the sign at the entranceway a little farther down the street. Emblazoned on a theater-type marquee that he could read even from this distance was the announcement:

THE REVEREND WILLIAM HUTTETH
UNVEILS THE MYSTERY
OF THE SEVEN SEALS
OF REVELATION
JANUARY 8-14

It *was* a circus.

He remembered David Koresh and the Branch Davidians of five years earlier. At Waco he had watched as the prophet and seventy or so of his followers were consumed in an inferno as the FBI and ATF moved in after a three-month standoff. He remembered Jamestown and Jim Jones when the charismatic leader persuaded hundreds to commit suicide in the jungles of Guayana by drinking arsenic-laced grape Kool Aid. He was afraid, cynical, and mistrustful of all who claimed to have the answers or *revealed* spiritual secrets that only they could see.

He believed in a God who would speak to him in plain terms that he could understand. The Ten Commandments he could fathom, though not always obey. Those, along with the first and second commandments of Christ to love God and neighbor, had always provided an ethical and moral standard for him.

He aspired to them in some sense or form, but the terrible difficulty of the simple had worn on him through his forty-four years. From the time of his assignment at Waco, he had not abided those who developed a cult-like following by perpetrating upon their followers an unending study of the book of Revelation. He usually wrote them off as charlatans and would-be shamans who deceived by beknighting themselves as ones able to divine the thoughts and actions of good and evil spirits.

As for Revelation, he had read it once, at the insistence of a Baptist girl at LSU of whom he was fond. As a Catholic youth, he had left all scripture reading and interpretation to the priests who his mother had told him were in the line of hierarchy to the bishops, cardinals, Pope, and God. His mother insisted that he attend mass, finger his rosary beads as he said his Hail Mary's, and go regularly to confession, whether he thought he needed it or not.

His Baptist girlfriend, though, had pointed out to him an otherwise obscure passage in the book of James that implored Christians to "confess your faults one to another." She had put it to him this way: "When you go to confession, does the priest reciprocate and confess his faults to you through the partition?"

Of course, his answer had been "No." That was during the time when he thought that priests did no wrong. But after that, he became a non-practicing Catholic. His study of Revelation had been short and uninspired. He understood less than one percent of it. It was then that he reverted to the basics. He had decided that it was difficult enough to follow the things that he did understand from the Bible without taking on the mysteries that he could never grasp.

Now, he had driven his broken-down Ford into the parking lot of the Reverend Hutteth who possessed the key to the seven seals of Revelation. From him or his helpers he would have to ask aid for a flat tire or else risk harm in this worn down neighborhood. Perhaps Hutteth was a healer as well as a diviner, and if he could heal cancer or a broken arm, surely he could speak a few words in the direction of his flat. The tire would reinflate, and he would be able to go on his way toward Jill's.

He walked toward a uniformed guard at one of the tent's entrances from where he heard the sound of smooth, soft hymns. He glanced at his watch. It was only seven-thirty. He could still make it to the riverside apartment in plenty of time if he could only get some assistance.

The man who identified himself as chief of security for the Reverend Hutteth looked down on Brad with sympathetic eyes. He shook his head. "I'm sorry, son. We can't help you now. The show . . . I mean the service is about ready to start. But I'll check around, and I'm sure we can aid you afterwards. It'll only last a couple of hours. Or else you can take your chances walking down the highway." He nodded toward the forsaken avenue and its borders of ramshackle buildings.

That was an option that Brad didn't want to exercise. "What about a phone? Do you have a phone around here?"

"No. There's plenty of communications in the Reverend's bus. But it's off limits and locked up until after the service." He nodded toward the buses. "Tell me your tire size, and I'll get you fixed up as soon as it's over. The best thing for you now is to go on in and enjoy the music and sermon. You might learn something about what's going to happen over the next few years. It might change your life. Who knows, maybe God let you have a flat tire in order to give you an opportunity to learn his will for you. There's no charge. There's still some good single seats down front. Then you come back out after the service and we'll take care of that old tire."

Brad gave him his tire size. He decided there was no real alternative to the invitation he had just received.

# Eleven

He walked through the tent entranceway just as a choir was taking stage. The recorded music was turned off. The purple-robed and radiant singers walked onto aluminum stands five tiers high.

Over the asphalt of the parking lot a thick layer of wood shavings had been spread which lent a circus smell to the scene. Wooden folding chairs were arranged in a semi-circle facing the stage. He looked around the tent that was about two-thirds filled to what appeared to be its near thousand capacity. Except for the chairs and shavings, it was all very high tech.

In a triangle behind and on both sides of the platform were large video projection screens that were suspended from the roof beams of the tent by cables. Each was at least twenty feet by twenty feet. As the choir began, different images were projected behind and to the sides. Beautiful mountain scenery on one, then a swiftly running mountain stream on another, and eagles soaring through the air—wings spread to take the updrafts—on the third.

The lights were turned down and spotlights from the rear circled the robed singers who represented the melting pot of America. Black women, hispanic men, those with an oriental heritage, and one Brad believed probably to be a native American.

The masterful voices of these singers, who numbered at least a hundred, were amplified through microphones and a sound system that had been honed to perfection. The audience was surrounded by a rhythmic, stirring beat that not only could be heard but could be felt and almost became a part of the body as it reverberated off sternums and skulls, reaching inward to attain accord with seven hundred souls and beating hearts that filled the tent. It was definitely a production, Brad allowed—a well-defined warm up for the main production—the Reverend William Hutteth.

All those in the audience were ready for the message after they had been entertained, uplifted, and inspired by the trained voices of this choir that performed for a half hour—ending with an acappella version of "Amazing Grace" that brought the crowd to its feet in thunderous applause. That signaled the entrance of the exalted Reverend.

Just ten rows from the front and near the center aisle, Brad was able to look directly into the face of William Hutteth. No one had a better seat in the now almost packed tent. He was gazing up from the proper obeisance position as was everyone else present. The choir parted, and for the next hour and a half no one would be at a point of higher elevation and no one would upstage the Reverend Hutteth. The choreography had been arranged in deference to the exalting of the Reverend. The show had played in many cities before. Now it was Hutteth's turn to enthrall the audience.

He was a presence. Dressed in an off-white suit with the coat still buttoned near the waist, Hutteth was lean, tanned, and a container of energy that could barely be held back until the applause ended. He bowed. He raised his arms. He looked out over the sea of worshipers from behind dark glasses. He lifted the microphone to his lips.

"Thank you, thank you, thank you," he said softly. And then after a pause to allow the crowd to quiet somewhat, the tall preacher, who Brad guessed to be in his mid-thirties, wiped back a strand of his long dark hair that had fallen over his forehead. He stilled the adorers further with, "Praise the Lord, praise the Lord, praise the Lord. Wasn't that just the most beautiful and stirring song service that you ever heard?" He clapped his hands together as the last of the choir departed the stage and brought another standing ovation from his followers. Even Brad stood. He didn't need to offend anyone if he was going to get his tire fixed.

For the next half hour, Hutteth was a storm of activity as he walked from side to side of the stage. With his booming voice that was aided by decibelic amplification of unknown quantities, he recounted the history of God's people from Adam and creation through the time of the patriarchs to Moses, David, Daniel, and eventually to Christ. He had set the stage now for the main and cogent parts of what would be the future of God's people as told in Revelation.

This was why the people had come. They believed they knew the historic. The past was evident. The present was an enigma that might be explained by someone who could show what was behind the seven seals. This, the Reverend Hutteth was willing to do.

He left no doubt that the secrets and mysteries of the last book of the Bible had been given to him, and it was his duty to tell these poor souls so that they also could prepare for those dire times that would soon be upon them, and, in fact, had already begun. This was his sole mission in life. He had written, he had spoken, and he had explained in as many ways and forums as were possible that the inhabitants of the earth were in the midst of treacherous times which began in 1991.

The screens behind him now exploded with scenes of volcanos, floods, wars, earthquakes, and other pestilence. The lights again went down. Only Hutteth stood illuminated with a spotlight from high in the back as though it were coming down from God. He had their attention. When he paused, it was so quiet that Brad could hear the blood coursing through his head and feel his heart beating in chorus. If Hutteth had such an effect on him, a cynical non-practicing Catholic—almost agnostic—what were all the others feeling?    Fear and reverence?

"Friends, let me tell you. We are in the midst of a twelve-year period that began in 1991 and will end in 2002 which is like none other. Revelation predicts this if you study it. Study it like I have from my youth."

On the screens on either side of him flashed the numbers of the years in a size at least ten feet tall. The number "12" was projected on the screen behind him.

"Do you see anything unusual about both these years? 1991? And 2002? Well, first off, the span of these years including both 1991 on one end and 2002 on the other is twelve years. Twelve has always been an important number, an exalted number, a revered number with God and his people. How many tribes of Israel were there? Twelve. How many apostles did Jesus choose? Twelve."

In the dark of the tent, people nodded their heads in agreement.

"And what about the numerals that are arranged to make up 1991 and 2002? Well, I'll put it this way because some of you may have been like me—not good at numbers until I started studying Revelation. If you reverse the numbers in 1991, what do you get? And in 2002, what do you get? That's right, that's right, I see some lights coming on in your heads even though it's dark out there." He smiled broadly.

"You get the same numbers—1991 backwards or forwards is 1991. And 2002 backwards or forwards is 2002.

" 'I am alpha and omega, the beginning and the ending.' You see, these two years are of great significance from that standpoint. It is God's design to give us a clue to his great mystery. We have to see it." He paused, looked out over the hundreds of quiet worshipers, and walked slowly to another portion of the stage directly below one of the huge screens.

"Many great and mysterious things have already occurred during the first half of this twelve-year period that we just completed a little over a year ago. But I'm here to tell you tonight that the great and terrible things that are mentioned in Revelation will begin to be completed during the remaining five years of this numerical span of a dozen years. Already, in 1991, the Russian empire, that great Satan that thought itself to be an anti-Christ, crumbled into nothingness. In 1993, David Koresh would have given a warning of other things to come, but he was cut down before he could reveal the prophecies.

"The great Satan fights back. You have to know that. There's a war going on folks. Are you prepared? Are you ready?"

There was a muted sound of whispering. He turned on his heel and walked to the other side of the stage, and overhead the numbers on the screens changed to all colors of the rainbow and sparkled in brilliance like a starburst. No doubt Hutteth wanted his audience to remember the span from 1991 through 2002.

"What else will be included in this twelve-year period? The end of the century? Yes. But more than that, there will be the end of the second millennium and the beginning of the third. And then will the end of the earth come in 2002?

"Listen, and I will tell you. No one knows when the end of time will be except God. Right? Certainly. But, perhaps God is telling us.

"He is warning us. He is longsuffering and patient. However, at some point there has to be a reckoning. The harvest is coming. We are living in perilous times. Satan is at work. Are you ready to battle?"

They were. There was spontaneous applause that began in the back and sped forward in the near darkness until all were standing again and giving ovation to the handsome and lean Hutteth.

He looked into the lights so that his glasses reflected back a sparkle like diamonds and a halo appeared above and slightly behind his head with the aid of the spotlights.

He recounted all the major world disasters from 1991 to the present, aligning them with specific prophecy from Revelation. He could find David Koresh and Waco in Revelation along with the Mississippi flood, the California floods, earthquakes in South America and Japan, wars in Eastern Europe, the rise and fall of the dollar, and any other terrible thing that happened since 1991.

He noted the peace accord signed by the PLO and Israel in 1993 as being prophesied in Revelation. He pointed to the bombing in Oklahoma City and the subway gassings in Japan as being indicators of the end of time. They all led unmistakably to Hutteth's interpretation of the last book of the Bible.

His wealth was unknown. From where Brad sat, it was obvious that the rings on six of his ten fingers were filled with diamonds and rubies. Yet, Hutteth was able to project a homebody character of deep Southern roots with which his audience could identify.

Brad had read about him before the discovery this evening. Hutteth was an orphan reared in a religious group home as a youth. He had been in some serious trouble as a teenager but had overcome that to become a charismatic proclaimer in his twenties and now very successfully into his thirties. Unmarried, he was said to attract an endless string of young women who were religious groupies. But he was careful not to ever be seen sporting about in public with any of those women.

For the next half hour he continued to harangue the now-captured audience with Revelation. When he spoke of the red horse of the second seal, the screens erupted with ferocious appearing war-horses that glowed the red of a setting sun with flaring nostrils and faceless, hooded riders. Hutteth knew his subject and his audience; Brad would give him that. The newspaper man even began to take notes. He wondered why. What could a political writer do with a story on a religious zealot who claimed to know the secrets of the book that everyone else was afraid to read? Perhaps it could be used as a filler sometime. His attention was drawn back to the preacher.

" 'Here is wisdom. Let him that hath understanding count the number of the beast: for it is the number of a man; and his number is Six Hundred Three Score and Six.' That's what the last verse of Chapter Thirteen of Revelation says. Now that, of course, in our number system is six hundred sixty-six."

With those words the screen became ablaze with the numerals bursting forth like a volcano spewing forth red, liquid lava. Again, no one would miss the message. The number was important. If there was just one number that people remembered from the Bible, it was this one. Superstition with the three sixes of Revelation was as pronounced as the unlucky thirteen.

Brad grinned. He wrote in his pad *SIX SIX SIX* and then with a few strokes of his pen changed it to *SIX SAX SEX*. "Six saxophone players had sex," he said beneath his breath.

"The number of the beast is six hundred sixty-six." Hutteth paused while the screens flashed the Arabic numerals 666. "It is the number of a man." He waited again for it to sink in.

"And I tell you it is the number of the year in which that man—the Beast—appeared and will appear."

With that, he was off and giving a brief history of the world as to what was happening in the year 666. "Mohammed died in 632. But by 666 the Muslim Arabs were conquering all those who stood in their way. The Caliph Ali oversaw the conquering of North Africa during that time. He was the first appearance of the Beast—in the year 666.

"Now by 1332—which is the second appearance of 666, the doubling of it—it was time for the second appearance of the Beast in the form of the Ottoman Turks who swept everything out of their way in Turkey and Asia Minor. Where once it was Christian, it became Muslim.

"Read your history. It'll back me up. Christianity has suffered in both the appearances of the beast in 666 and 1332. From the seed of Abraham came forth both the Christ and the anti-Christ. Jesus and the Beast. Christianity and Islam." He paused. Quiet enveloped the crowd like a giant hand squeezing the breath from them one by one. Then he continued.

"But that is not the worst. The number three in the Bible has always represented God, as in the Trinity. Three in Revelation signifies the power of God. And when the Beast appears the third time, he will assume the power—the usurped power—of God for a short season to perform horrible deeds.

"My friends, the third appearance of six hundred sixty-six, where the Beast will burst forth with the power of God is upon us. It is 1998. Nineteen hundred and ninety-eight." The screens erupted with the numbers.

**666**

**666**

**<u>666</u>**

**1998**

"This is the Year of the Beast. I'll tell you more tomorrow night. You can also read about it in my books, or see and listen to it on my tapes." He pointed to the stacked tables. "I know there are some unbelievers. Even among us there are those who scoff and make fun. I hope you are not one of them, or else you may have to face the Beast on your own.

"If you have the imprint of Christ in your heart and on your forehead, you will have nothing to fear in this time or the hard time to come. But believe, believe, believe!" He fell to his knees and looked straight up as he raised his hands toward heaven. After a few minutes, he stood again.

"And I'll tell you another thing," Hutteth continued. He looked straight at Brad and wiped sweat from his face on the cool January night, "This year has started out as the Year of the Beast was destined. The death of our late Vice President Samuel Harrot is the work of Satan, the work of the anti-Christ, the work of the Beast. I am as sure of that as I am standing here.

"We have a reporter here tonight who was there when Harrot was shot. And I want to tell you, Brad Yeary," he said, pointing a bony index finger at the dazed reporter who sat stone-faced and dry-mouthed, "it was the work of the Beast, and 1998 is and will be the Year of the Beast."

# Twelve

B rad Yeary slowly stirred the shrimp and brown rice. There alone in Jill's kitchen, he could not exorcise the images and words of the Reverend Hutteth from his mind. Each time he looked down and gazed at the pinkish-white shrimp moving among the dark grains of rice, he would instead see the red horse of the second seal or the white horse of the first.

In this dark hour there erupted on his forehead a cold sweat, and he winced at every strange sound. A man of forty-four should not be frightened of the dark and unknown. He shook his head. He was to meet the President on Monday, and here he was almost shaking because of what a preacher had told him, and shown him, and moved in him. He was grateful that his tire was fixed. At least they did that for him.

But how did they know his name? He was easily recognized now, what with all of the publicity and his series of stories on Harrot, but when Hutteth stared him down with unblinking eyes and pointed that skinny index finger toward him and called him by name, he could have fallen to the woodchip-covered ground. If it wasn't his recognizable face, maybe it was his license plate that they had tracked down. A policeman could do that; why not Hutteth's security officer? Sure, that was it. They wanted to check out this wanderer before they fixed his tire. If he had been wanted, they might have turned him in.

It had turned out well, though. Hutteth's theory on 1998 being the Year of the Beast was interesting. How could you disprove it? Mathematically, it added up. Three times six hundred sixty-six is 1998.

He didn't want to believe there was anything supernatural involved in Harrot's death. That would be just one more thing for the conspiracy buffs to get into.  It would be better for the country if the assassin was just someone on the lunatic fringe who did it for some sense of receiving fame.  The assassin must be partly crazy to kill a Vice President who mattered very little in the great scheme of things.

Chills ran up his spine.  He remembered the visual effects that the preacher used to support his version that the twelve years bookended by 1991 and 2002 were of unearthly significance and this was just the beginning of the end.  Why did Hutteth want an interview?  He bent down and smelled the steaming mixture of rice and shrimp.  That's what the chief of security had told him on his way out.

How had he put it?  "The Reverend Hutteth wants to talk with you soon about Vice President Harrot's death."

Sure.  That would be fine.  "I'll call.  Or have the Reverend call me," he had told him, assuming that it would all be forgotten.  But now he really wanted to talk with Hutteth, not with all the flashing lights and screens present, but a real sit-down, face to face interview where he could talk to him as an equal instead of staring up at him as though he were some kind of god.

Through the kitchen window, he saw the headlights turn into Jill's driveway.  He walked to the blinds and separated them enough with two fingers to look at the car.  If it was Jill, fine, but he wasn't letting one of the four horsemen in.  The garage door opened with a slight grinding sound and the white Volvo eased in and out of his view. Ah!  Safe at last.  Another person to talk with.  He would not have to deal alone with the crazy thoughts fluttering around in his head.

It had been a long day.  Jill Crenshaw looked as though she were carrying the many burdens of the state on her shoulders.  She entered the kitchen door carrying a briefcase in one hand and her coat slung over her other arm.  "Brad, give me a hand."  He stepped to her side and took both the coat and briefcase.

"You're not going to be cranky, are you, Jill?"  He smiled.  He took the load into the adjoining room and laid it on a table.  By now, he knew his way around her apartment as well as she did.

"I have a right to be cranky, Mr. Hotshot Reporter.  I've been working with thirty cranky senators, a cranky governor, and a hundred and fifty cranky constituents since early this morning.  It rubbed off on me.  Everybody wants to know where we're going to put the next waste disposal plant.

"I'm getting burned out on this drivel.  If I knew I was going to be spending all of my time trying to reconcile all the forces of the trash industry, attempting to enforce government standards, and hoping to placate every neighborhood that wants to carry its trash to some other parish but doesn't want any foreign trash in its own backyard, I don't believe I would have run for this term of office.

"Then you have the nerve to be gone for a week without one

sighting and very few words. It's more than I can take." She sat down at the kitchen table and took off her shoes. Her hair fell around her face. She bent forward to rub her feet.

Even when she was cranky, she looked good to him. Brad stepped up behind her, and putting his hands on her stiff neck and shoulder muscles, began to massage them. "I'm sorry. Everything has happened so quickly that I didn't have time to breathe. Harrot's death has really pushed me. We'll find time, or make time, to be together more, like before."

"What's the great news you mentioned? Did you quit your job?"

"No, it's not that good. I have an exclusive interview set up with the President."

"The president of what?"

"Of the United States. They called the office and arranged it. Pinthater is really excited about it."

"What about you?"

"I'm more scared than excited. It's a first. Never been one on one with the top dog. I've got to do my homework and be ready. This is just one more step to making me have a great year. Unfortunately, my success has to be built on the tragedy of others. But that's the way it is with messengers. If it weren't for all of those crazies killing each other, who would have cared for Shakespeare's stories?"

Jill looked him in the eye. "Brad, I knew Shakespeare, and I can tell you, you are no Shakespeare."

She straightened back up and took off her dark blue suit coat, unbuttoned the first two buttons on her blouse, and pushed his hands away temporarily as she peeled it back and down to where her neck and shoulders were bare. "That's good, but do it a little slower and all the way from my neck to my shoulder." He began anew. She leaned her head forward again, draping her hair over her knees. "What are you cooking? It smells good."

"My brand of jambalaya. Not much in the way of vegetables. A little, but mainly shrimp and brown rice. And I made my own special sauce."

AFTER THEIR LATE DINNER, Brad and Jill walked the block to where a small park lay at the crest of the levee overlooking the Mississippi River. It was one of their favorite spots. From here in the spring and early summer, they would sit at sunset, watch the great ships come and go, and wave to tourists on the paddlewheelers. The sun would sink down in the southwest as though its orangish-red ball of fire were being extinguished by the muddy waters of the river.

When summer came in its fullness, heat and humidity drove them into her apartment. From her second-story balcony, they would enjoy a more modest view of the river.

Now the air was unusually warm for January. Jill wore a light jogging suit which appeared more like bedroom than street attire. She sat on the ground facing the river, and Brad sat behind her and resumed the slow kneading of the muscles in her neck, back, and shoulders. They sat in silence and gazed at the river while Brad continued his sensual massage.

Behind them the moon edged above the row of apartments, and on this clear night, the beams softly stroked their bodies. Jill felt the tenderness of Brad's hands. She wished it could always be like this. She wanted to stay in Louisiana and, perhaps, be governor some day. But what about the words Governor Johnson had whispered to her earlier in the day?

"Brad, can I tell you something? And you promise it won't go any farther?"

"Sure," he said. He stopped the massage, wrapped his arms about her, took her hands in his, and pulled her back to him. He nuzzled her neck and whispered into her ear. "You can trust me."

"I know I usually can. But I want to tell you what Hugh told me today, and I don't want to see it show up in some column a few days down the road. Got it?" She turned her head to where her right eye met his.

"If you want to tell me, Jill, it won't go any farther."

"Okay. Don't forget and accidentally put this in any story." She squeezed his hands in hers and looked back toward the river. "The governor said I could be the next U.S. Senator from Louisiana." She waited for that to sink in with Brad. He fidgeted a bit and then put his head on the other side of hers and rubbed his scruffy face against her neck.

"I told you that last week, and you didn't believe me. I said you could run against Senator Ashford and beat him. Remember?"

"Yes, you did, but that's not what Hugh's talking about."

"Well, what is he talking about?" Brad asked. He felt for the zipper on the top of her jogging suit with his thumb and began to ease it down ever so slightly from her neck.

"He wants to appoint me to fill Ashford's seat."

Brad had been more concerned with the zipper for the moment than her words. His thumb and forefinger were now working in harmony with his thumb finding the soft skin of Jill beneath the jacket. He blinked back to the conversation with the word "appointment."

"How can he appoint you to Ashford's seat? He's not dead and sure not going to resign unless you know something I don't. Has Ashford been caught fornicating with goats or something?"

"No. Hugh says Ashford is going to be the next Vice President. The President is going to appoint Ashford to take Harrot's place. That will leave a vacancy, and Hugh asked if I would consider it."

Brad laughed. Jill clamped her hand to where he had moved her zipper about half way to her breasts. "What's so funny about that? The television showed Ashford going into the White House to confer with the President about the Vice Presidency."

"Yeah, Jill. But every Republican who has ever put a razor to his face has been through the Oval Office during the last two days, all with hopes of being the next Vice President."

"Or, every Republican woman who has ever put a razor to her legs. I know that, Brad. But Hugh says he has it on good authority."

"How could he? He's a Democrat, like you. Are the Republicans running their decisions by Hugh Johnson for the benefit of his thoughts? I think not." He again started to tug with a little more earnestness on her zipper. He looked around to see if anyone was near.

"Just what if, Brad? What if I was offered an appointment as senator? Should I take it? And would you stay here or go with me?"

He leaned her back into his lap and looked at the moon's reflection off her pale green eyes. "Let me be the first to offer my congratulations. I definitely think you should take it if it's offered. I have my doubts that that scenario will ever come about. But I am certainly for you achieving that goal. May I kiss the next U.S. Senator from Louisiana?"

She smiled her consent.

# Thirteen

T he FBI investigation of Harrot's assassination had taken over a vacant floor of a downtown office building in New Orleans. Agent John Dobson thought they needed more room, but the third floor of the Annex Building which housed other federal offices, including the IRS on the first two floors, became home to this special task force. They still used the labs and technical facilities in Virginia, at headquarters, and in other parts of Louisiana. But the heart and nerve center were two floors above busy Poydras Street.

The disadvantages included the fact that hundreds of other people had access to the building. Phone and other communication lines ran through conduits in the building that some enterprising assassin or conspirator could perhaps intercept if they got their hands on blueprints of the building. Four of the five elevators that passed the third floor on their way to servicing all seventeen stories of the building had to be reprogrammed so that they would not stop on the third floor. The doors from the hallway on that floor to those four elevators were sealed. Only one elevator came to the third floor now, and that was the only place it went—from street level to the third floor. A highly paid agent was now playing elevator operator in order to assure no unauthorized access to the high priority mission. Guards at street level and at the third floor screened those who would enter and exit the lone conveyance.

The stairways were another problem. Fire codes prevented the locking of the two escape routes that served all the floors even though they were rarely used as long as the elevators worked. But someone wanting exercise and needing to go between the second and fourth floors could walk past the third floor entry. Deputy U.S. Marshals stood as sentries there to protect against a breach of security.

Agents, technical people, laboratory workers, computer visual production experts, secretaries, and all manner of others worked busily throughout the area except for one room that was off limits to everyone except four FBI agents and Al Shanker of the Secret Service. If the deputy director or director of the FBI came to town, they would be allowed inside, but no one else, except the President if he should dare want to know exactly what was going on.

The President had given the word. The director of the FBI had all authority in the investigation. He wanted a special team set up to solve this hideous crime as soon as possible. Through the intercession of the director of the Secret Service and Al Shanker himself, the President appointed him, along with John Dobson, as co-leaders of the team with the understanding that Dobson would make any final investigative decision but would confer with Shanker.

During the week since Harrot was shot, matters had proceeded at a hectic pace. The press, the citizens, the Congress, and the President wanted someone arrested. There was fear in the land as long as the assassin or assassins remained at large.

In the cases of the deaths of John Kennedy, Bobby Kennedy, and Martin Luther King someone was fingered and arrested, if not immediately, rather shortly after the fact. The would-be killers of George Wallace and Ronald Reagan were brought to ground quickly. The country had a lack of patience and wanted the culprit under control so that the citizenry could go on with its business without the prospect of uncertainty. John Dobson and Al Shanker felt these pressures along with the pure exhaustion of going practically non-stop since the Superdome shooting.

They were making progress though. From nothing, they had developed a rather gaudy collection of physical evidence and photographic displays that were beginning to show them how it was done—if not why and by whom.

First, the body that they buried in Montgomery was only the shell of Samuel Harrot. They had his brain, heart, kidneys, liver, and every other vital organ stored in a cooler now at headquarters. Harrot's family knew it and gave permission. There would be no missing part or missing bullet in this case.

Next, the final autopsy report varied little from the initial findings. Harrot died from a single gunshot wound to the lower chest—upper abdomen. The bullet exploded two inches into his chest in a burst of ten pieces that pierced every vital organ and produced almost instant death from loss of blood pressure and a perforated heart. They had recovered all ten pieces of the hard metal projectile and were in the process of assembling it like a jigsaw puzzle with the help of a computer.

One thing was noticed in the toxicology reports. The assassins were redundant. There was a toxin emitted by the exploding bullet that would have poisoned Harrot within a minute if the penetration of the metal explosion had not done its job. The chemists had not put an exact name to the poison but found it in an amount that would have been deadly.

Hundreds of people who were at the game had sent in copies of photos they had taken during halftime. Somewhere on the west side of the indoor stadium had sat or stood the assassin, and the agents hoped that person was caught on film. Video tapes from every camera angle of the official broadcast were being analyzed by agents with computer enhancement. A few home videos also surfaced, even though it was against Dome rules to bring in video equipment.

In addition to the network and fan tapes, the investigation also gained access to film and tapes made by the Sugar Bowl, the Southeastern Conference, the University of Alabama, and Notre Dame.

It wasn't that they didn't have any pictures; it was the problem of sifting through the haystack of thousands of feet of film and tape and hundreds of still photos that were made. It was exhausting work which had to be repeated by several separate teams in order to be sure that if one person overlooked something it was found by another.

Once the bullet had been reassembled to close proximity of what it looked like before exploding in Harrot's body, the hollow where the toxin had been injected was obvious. The bullet was found to be near the size of what is used in 30.06 rifles but not exactly. Of all the guns that were recovered in the Dome following the game, there were only three that the bullet could have fit. Tests of those three showed that none had been fired recently.

Despite their best efforts at finding the weapon with the metal detectors as fans exited, they had nothing. This left the investigators with the thought that the weapon could have been carried by someone in authority who would not have looked unusual toting a firearm—a policeman, a guard, even an FBI agent or Secret Service agent. They secured a list of all law enforcement people known to be there and started a slow procedure of checking weapons.

The videos proved to be of the most immediate help. By synchronizing tapes showing Harrot and the west side of the stadium at the time of the shooting, they were able to narrow their search for the shooter. The autopsy showed that the bullet penetrated only two inches before exploding. This small invasion had the effect of complicating the determination of the exact angle of entry.

But through a computerized process that took into account the angle of Harrot's torso at the time of impact and the information of the angle of the two-inch entry wound, the investigative team concluded that the shooter stood or sat in an area on the second level of the west side of the arena. Dobson and Shanker had to give up their original theory that the assassin must have stood behind a ledge or in a cubicle some place where he could rest his high-powered rifle on a firm support in order to attain so direct a hit into the exact center of Harrot's body.

The computer generated angle of shooting could not be exact

with the information at hand.  Just a slight movement by Harrot of the upper part of his body near or at the point of impact would change the line of fire by five to fifteen rows.  What they were able pretty plausibly to tie down was the area from which the bullet had been fired.  This area was thirty rows deep and fifty seats wide on the second level of the west side.  This narrowed the suspects to approximately fifteen hundred spectators or people who passed through that area at the time of the shooting.

For the past three hours, the four FBI agents and Al Shanker had been looking at this section of the fieldhouse crowd using five different tapes that showed that area.  They had looked at it days earlier and could not detect the shooter, but they knew he was there; he had to be.

Now they had divided the effort to where they were looking at enhanced tapes a row at a time, individual by individual, from ten seconds before Harrot was shot to ten seconds after he fell.  They examined a little over six hundred of the fifteen hundred spectators, ushers, and concession people selling Cokes, Cracker Jacks, and popcorn.  This was one of the better seating areas, near the fifty-yard line and not too high.  It was very good for viewing a football game or taking aim on a Vice President at half time.

A check of who had these tickets at their disposal had already begun.  It was an area that overlapped with travel agencies that bought blocks of tickets and then resold them to individuals or groups as a package with hotel rooms and transportation.  Other blocks of tickets were given to corporate sponsors and important politicians in the city and state.  Of the six hundred seats they were looking at, not a single one was purchased by an individual; they had all been parceled out in groups.

As much as tickets changed hands for a football game, it would be next to impossible to determine by ticket purchase who was sitting where.  If they were able to identify the shooter from these tapes, the best they could hope for would be to find the original purchaser or donee of the seats and go from there.  For these prime seats, scalpers may have raided the travel agencies or leaned on political friends to secure them for resale.

What was gained by the enlarging of the figures on the tape was lost in the lack of clarity and fuzziness of these same fans.  Shanker and Dobson sat side by side examining once again two rows on this second level of the west side.  Two monitors sat one on the other.  One rolled the figures of each individual while the other showed a close up of Harrot's face and upper body.

They were synchronized in a form of dark comedy.  The agents had to watch over and over Harrot's surprised expression and collapse in extreme slow motion as he was gunned down.  They also viewed the unbelieving and then startled look of each fan who was singled out for examination on the monitor.

Over and over both Shanker and Dobson stared into the flickering black and white screens as Harrot inevitably fell hundreds of times—dead before he hit the turf. The images on the fans' faces ranged from disbelief, to startled, to puzzlement, to nothing. Many did not know what they were seeing and therefore could not react. Others were looking away or talking to a friend or relative and missed the whole episode.

"Look at this one, John," Shanker pointed to his screen, "these two guys are a bit odd. Must be drinking buddies who bet with each other on the game. One is wearing a Notre Dame jacket, like the one you had on when I first saw you, and the other has an overcoat over an Alabama sweater."

He pushed a button that allowed the image to zoom out to where both men could be seen. Dobson and Shanker then saw the Notre Dame jacket clad man and the Alabama fan both point toward mid-field. It was obvious that the Notre Dame supporter had nothing in his hand. They rolled the tape through the time of Harrot's shooting.

"Wait, Al. Run that back. Did you see that?"

"No. What?"

"Zoom in on the right arm of the guy with the overcoat." Shanker pushed another button

"There, did you see that?"

"No, what?" Shanker asked louder. He rewound and played it a third time.

"There's a little puff of smoke that comes out of his overcoat arm where he's extending his right arm. Just barely a wisp. And just barely a little jerk, like the kick of a firearm. Almost indistinguishable. I think he's our shooter!"

Shanker sat transfixed looking at the scene over and over. He saw what Dobson did.

"But, John, that guy has binoculars to his eyes, and I can see his four fingers on his right hand extended. I can't see his thumb, but this tape with the enlargement is so distorted that the puff of smoke could be just a piece of lint or something that messed up the picture."

"But look at it with Harrot's tape on line and you see the puff of smoke and Harrot's fall are simultaneous," Dobson said. He stood and raised his arms toward the ceiling. "Hallelujah! Al, I'll say it again. We've found our shooter!" he shouted. The other three agents turned from their screens and stared at their boss who did a little jig on the tile floor.

# Fourteen

S unday afternoon when Brad returned to New Orleans and visited his office, his phone console looked as though it had been attacked by a swarm of pale Monarch butterflies. Light yellow Post-It notes papered every available square inch of plastic. They cascaded over onto his desk.

It was less than two hours until his plane left for Washington and his Monday interview with the President. He hurriedly scanned through the notes, wadding up and throwing into the waste paper can most of them, laying aside a few others, and finally jerking one close to his eyes as he read in the dim light.

"Call Papa Legba," was all it said. No telephone number. Brad knew why. Papa Legba had no phone. To call him meant to go and look him up deep in the backwaters of New Orleans near the cemetery where drug users openly met and others of questionable morals rendezvoused for social encounters.

If Papa Legba thought it was important enough to talk with him, Brad knew that the diviner of black magic had something impressive to say. Through the years, first on his police beat, and even later as a political reporter, he had never been led wrong by the old black man. With gnarled hands, he rolled the bones while looking into the soul of the observer for a hint of fear before delivering the verdict.

If people wanted to know their future or their past, Papa Legba, the high priest of voodoo, would oblige if the subject was worthy. It wasn't sport or a show with him. He took his religion seriously and lived in abject poverty. He was persuaded that he had a gift handed down through generations of forebears, both male and female, and this gift he treated with the greatest respect.

In times past, when it was important enough, he had provided Brad tips on crime suspects, not naming them, but identifying them closely enough that Brad could have a great story written before the police made an arrest. Politically, Papa Legba was privy to the great sewer of rumors that flowed through the back alleys and dark dead-ends of this town where spirit worship mixed with mainline religions as the blood had mingled over the centuries to create the living, breathing population that was New Orleans. He was held in high esteem. There were those who showed reverence through love and others through fear.

Brad checked his watch. He wouldn't have time to seek out Papa before his plane left. He folded the note and placed it in his wallet. As soon as he got back from interviewing the President, he would talk with the real shaman—Papa Legba.

MONDAY EVENING AT SIX, Brad was alone with his thoughts, except for two Secret Service men, as he awaited his time with the President. He sat near the Oval Office in a little room that had been dubbed the green room as though it were a waiting room for guests on a television show. In fact, it was the area of preparation for the biggest show in town—an audience with the most powerful single individual in the world. And here he was, Brad Yeary, ready to talk face to face with that man. He could hardly imagine it.

As he tried to relax, he pulled from his coat pocket a small kaleidoscope, held it to his right eye, and slowly turned the bigger end. The small pieces of glass sprung into intricate geometric designs in bright reds, greens, yellows, and blues. He leaned his head farther back and breathed deeply. It was an old relaxation trick of his. From the time of his first college exams, to airplane flights, to job interviews, and on toward other events that would create tension, he had found escape, comfort, and a soothing presence in the majesty and magic of these ever-changing images.

It had the same effect as the Mississippi River. Whenever he traveled away from the river, he carried one either on him or in his car. His collection exceeded two hundred from all around the world with some being over a hundred years old. In every city at junk shops, pawn palaces, or the local Dollar Store, he would search for a new kaleidoscope for his collection. They came in all shapes and designs—cars, airplanes, trains, animals, and buildings. They all served the same purpose—to smooth the ragged edges of his spirit. It was also, he knew, the story of his being. From many little broken pieces, he had formed a somewhat organized life, although the exact nature and structure of it seemed to change constantly.

Here he was with an exclusive interview with the President of the United States. It was a long way to come for a man who grew up along the banks of a bayou at Lafitte, Louisiana, the son of a Cajun mother and a shoe-salesman father of English heritage. Always encouraged by his mother to read, his first job at which he made any money was to deliver the *Times-Gazette* in his small backwater community on a bicycle built from parts he had scrounged. His father traveled in the shoe sales business throughout Louisiana and part of Texas. In his long absences, he left Brad as the man of the house.

He had loved those times of hunting and fishing. No fear of what lay hidden in the marshes and dark waters of the creeks and rivers. One small snakebite was his only injury during those learning years.

Especially sweet were the large family cookouts when his father was home and his mother's large extended family would gather for food, drink, song, and story-telling that lasted from Friday through Monday. The great tales enthralled him the most—hearing of hunting expeditions of the distant past, of relatives fighting in foreign wars, and of the history of the Acadians who settled that area. His reading and interest in relating the stories of the lifeblood of civilized society were what led him into journalism and then to law school.

He could not grasp the mundane and archaic precepts necessary for law school at LSU and left after his first year when he could make no sense of the "rule against perpetuities" or for more than five minutes comprehend the "rule in *Shelly's* case." It was all too obscure for a boy of the bayou. He wanted to be where life permeated every waking moment, not hidden away in a glass building, holed up in a musty library, or researching ancient manuscripts for some senior partner.

He appreciated what he had learned in his sole year of law study and found he was able to use some of that knowledge in his work as an on-the-street reporter. He had a leg up on other novice police beat reporters as he knew a little more about warrants, probable cause hearings, release on recognizance, and obstruction of justice. That little legal background also helped him to realize his initial goal of being a political reporter where real life's blood flowed daily just as surely as it did on the police beat.

As he continued to wait for the President, he realized that all those scattered pieces had fallen together to allow him this opportunity. The part that had fallen off was his marriage of five years. It was unfortunate, a result of his devoting the time to his job that he should have devoted to his wife and marriage.

It had not been a rancorous separation. There was really very little arguing between them after the first two years. He was not there enough to engage in little battles. He had made the police beat his home, his mistress, his life.

One day he had returned to their apartment to find his wife

gone with her share of their meager possessions and a note that said, "I've been here. You haven't. Now I'm gone. You have at it."

He knew it was the truth and didn't try to change her mind because he was not willing to change his life. He kept the note, though, as he thought it was quite poetic and summed up rather succinctly their failed marriage.

He had been "having at it" for the past fifteen years, mainly as a solitary figure who immersed himself in his work and the other small joys of an occasional trip back to Lafitte for hunting and fishing with boys he had grown up with and now away from. They had little in common. He was a journalist while they were shrimpers. Their hands smelled of saltwater and shellfish while his retained the odor of newsprint and ink.

As far as women, Darla Puckett probably had saved his life when he fell into despair and began to drink after his marriage ended. It was an odd depression, he thought, since he was with his wife so little during the last three years of their marriage that he wondered what he was missing. Perhaps it was just the stability of knowing that he could go home and she would be there—that she would always be there—because he was Brad Yeary, the hotshot police reporter, the boy-wonder of the *Times-Gazette*. The realization that a woman could walk away from him like his wife had done was what made him think, and think, and think, and dip into self-doubt and the depths of depression.

Darla had spent many nights restoring his view of himself. She found him attractive, masculine, sexy, and worldly. Their work hours were about the same, so for a hot two years, they were inseparable in the long nights of the French Quarter. That, too, had ended as he moved more into political reporting and away from the police beat and Bellevue Hospital. Very few politicians ended up at Bellevue—until Harrot. He spent more and more time in Baton Rouge and Washington and less and less in the Quarter or around Bellevue.

Now, fifteen years after his divorce, he had fallen for another woman—Jill Crenshaw. The ones between Darla and Jill did not even phase him. They were just bodies passing in the night. Jill was the one he wanted to spend time with. He cherished every moment and despised the time he had to spend in Washington away from her. He was duty-bound to do it though. He could not be the chief political writer for Pinthater and not go to the capital of all political maneuverings.

But he counted the hours until his return to Baton Rouge and the lady senator. With her he would consider marriage again, but they had avoided the subject, parrying around it as though they both were frightened by the prospect. She was a woman of power, intelligence, and beauty. Those bright stones of womanhood merged in her far better than any of the spectacular displays of color and light that he had ever seen in any cf his kaleidoscopes. But would all that come together for him, or just tumble away to be lost as a brief reflective moment of color and beauty in his memory?

The senator and the journalist enjoyed many of the same things, and their work took them to many of the same events. They both traveled to the jungle rhythm of politics, with her being the participant and he the observer-writer. Could they tolerate that much politics in one household?

He would go with her to dressy, formal affairs at the governor's mansion although he much preferred the softness of jeans and a cotton shirt to a tux and tight shoes. She enjoyed those parties where she could dress up and look every bit the princess, but she never seemed to relax as much in that company as she did when they were alone on the riverbank near her apartment. He believed she was a little self-conscious about her position, power, and wealth—being the only heir to her father's vast oil fortune. She never wanted people to think that she had accomplished what she had because of money—it was because of her talent, intelligence, and hard work. She wanted to be part of the "aristocracy of talent" that Jefferson had talked about rather than a scion of old money.

He knew he had not told the truth when she asked his blessing on the possibility of her becoming the next U.S. Senator from Louisiana if Ashford was appointed Vice President. He much preferred that they both remain in the Baton Rouge-New Orleans area. Year by year he cared less and less for Washington. It seemed as though the city was populated by those whose idea of government was to perpetuate themselves in office. Damn the Republic. Give them circuses and bread.

The time when a devoted citizen would come to the capital to watch out for the good of the democracy was long past, if it ever did exist. He knew that Jill would find the experience choking, devastating, and victimizing to such an extent that she might never recover from it. She could wallow around in the mire of this town for a lifetime and make no real difference. The system had devolved into one of a perpetual downward spiral toward the black hole of a bureaucratic purgatory where those with any virtue at all retired from the fray before they were drawn too far down to get out. It ate others.

It was also more personal than that. Their sharing time would be much different if she was a U.S. Senator rather than a state senator from Louisiana. He was to the stage in his life now that every day, every hour, every minute became more and more precious. In this somewhat selfish attitude, he prayed to the gods of politics and chance that the scene imagined by Governor Hugh Johnson and Jill Crenshaw would never come to pass. Benjamin Ashford, in his opinion, would not be the first choice of the President for appointment to the vacancy created by the death of Harrot. He wouldn't even be on Brad's ten most likely candidates for the job.

Ashford had never accomplished anything of note nor put forth any ideas of substance upon which to base a case that he deserved or needed to be a heartbeat away from the highest office in the land. However, over the past quarter century, the same thing could have been said about at least a half dozen others, including Agnew and Quayle. Stranger things had happened in Vice Presidential politics than Benjamin Edward Ashford being appointed to the second position in the land.

He would have to ask the President point blank the chances of Ashford in order to ease his mind and assure himself a future peaceful life with Jill in the bayou country rather than the sewer country of Washington.

When they were alone and out of sight of official observers, she enjoyed as much as he the roadside music barns, tapping her toes to Cajun music, and dancing in the loud and spirited crowd. They would go to oddball events too—like county fairs, tractor pulls, local horse shows where Jill could show off her knowledge of equine breeding, poetry readings that she so enjoyed, lectures by distinguished men and women of letters given at LSU or Tulane, or, as she had agreed on Friday and Saturday, to hear more from the Reverend William Hutteth.

It was there on Saturday evening that he had agreed with Hutteth's top assistant to meet with the Reverend for an interview on Monday next, the nineteenth of January, in New Orleans where Hutteth would be taking his tent show from Baton Rouge. Brad wasn't exactly sure why he had consented to it. In all probability it would be a waste of time that he could well use elsewhere, what with the interview with the President and the one that Pinthater wanted him to have with Senator Ashford later in the week. He needed time to write and everyone wanted to talk with him. He had to squeeze in Papa Legba as soon as he returned and balance all that with enough time to be with Jill. This story was pushing him to the brink.

He was fascinated with the clarity with which the preacher had continued the exposition on his theory of the importance of the twelve years they were now in the midst of as he and Jill listened to him on the two nights following his initiation to the orator. Jill had told him that the explanation that Hutteth gave of Revelation sent chills down her spine. It was frightening and at the same time hypnotic. Both could understand how the crowds had grown each night until there was standing room only.

It was unusual for such a show to compete with television and movies for entertainment, but thousands of people in Baton Rouge had flocked to the great white tent. They listened in rapt attention as the white, red, black, and pale horses pranced forth on the screens.

Reverend Hutteth peeled back each seal to give a peek at what he said would be the future. It scared Jill so that she refused to go while Brad was gone. He wanted her to attend and take notes for him to follow up on in the interview.

From the political realm, he was most interested in Hutteth's statement on the first night that Harrot's death was a result of the "work of the Beast." He could weave this into some future column as one theory on the assassination. Now, though, he readied himself for this interview where perhaps he would learn more about his immediate future. He put away the kaleidoscope, leaned his head back, and tumbled over in his mind the questions he would have for the President.

# Fifteen

Fifty feet away in the Oval Office, the President, his Chief of Staff Rob Steinheitz, and his chief political operative, George Garron, were finishing a discussion of the Vice Presidential possibilities. The President motioned them to retire to the outdoors toward the Rose Garden to continue their delicate talks. Outside and away from the office of supposed decision making, they walked slowly side by side in the unseasonably mild evening air they were enjoying in Washington.

"That damn Nixon ruined it for all of us," the chief executive of the United States said and grinned at his two trusted friends. "That taping system he installed in the Oval Office that got his ass thrown out haunts us all to where we're afraid to say anything around a piece of furniture. I don't think there's one in there now—not supposed to be—but how can you know for sure?

"The CIA or FBI may have put one in there before I ever took office just so they could keep tabs on us. Anyway, I feel more comfortable discussing sensitive matters out here unless I want to see them on the front page of the papers or hear them on the evening news. Even have to be careful of the Secret Service agents," he said, motioning toward the two men who were a discreet distance ahead and behind them. "Who knows how keen their ears are and who they report to?" His two associates nodded their agreement.

"Anyway, Rob and George," he continued, "we really did have a problem with Sam. He could have caused some real damage. As I told you a month ago, he had to go. One way or the other." He looked first to Steinheitz and then to Garron.

"We couldn't have gone into another year, and surely not an-

other term, with Harrot. I thought he would have gone along. I'm
sorry he ever found out. He was too much the patriot and it cost him.
I just wanted to let you both know that I will always back you up. You
did a good job on it. Apparently you did a splendid job. The FBI
doesn't have a clue yet.

"I'll keep up with the investigation, and if it ever starts pointing to anyone we know—" he winked, "I think I can keep it bottled up."
He put an arm around each of them. "We're all in this together, boys.
I won't do a Haldeman or Ehrlichman on you. You performed brilliant-
ly."

Both Steinheitz and Garron cast a quisitive eye at the other.
They continued their walk along the path under the outspread wings
of their boss who had just talked so casually on such a serious subject.

"Are we agreed on the choice for V P?" the President asked as
he took his arms down and faced one and then the other of his top
advisors. "We've interviewed twenty or so. Given each of them an
opportunity to have their pictures in their hometown papers and be on
the nightly news as a possible second in command. It's time to move
on now, isn't it? The people need to know we've made a selection.
Two weeks is enough time to mourn for Sam. The work of this great
country has to go on." He looked again at each of his confidants, his
trusted friends from high school and college who had climbed the ladder with him all the way to the highest office in the land.

"I think he's a safe choice," Garron said. "We should be able
to put him away to where he won't cause any problems, and he might
even be of some benefit in the Senate."

"Yes," Steinheitz plodded into the conversation, "he'll also help
to balance the geographical mix for the next election and keep us a
toehold in the South. He's safe. And easily confirmable by the Senate
and the House."

"Great. We'll announce it on Friday. I have this Brad Yeary
scheduled for an interview that I'm already late for," the President
commented and looked at his watch. "And, I'll float this possibility out
and let him run it in a story since he's from Louisiana. I'll say something like, 'Benjamin Ashford is one of the finalists whom I'm considering.' We'll see what kind of reaction that gets over the next couple of
days. If nothing disastrous shows up, we'll bring him up Friday, or
Monday at the latest, and do it."

BRAD WAS AS READY as he was going to be when the press
secretary to the President entered the green room and motioned him
to follow.

"Brad, I'm sorry the President was running a little late, but
he's had a lot on his mind the past ten days. He's trying to narrow his
choices for Mr. Harrot's replacement. It's really been tough. It's diffi-

cult to replace a man of Harrot's ability and strength."

He took Brad gently by the elbow as they neared the entrance to the Oval Office. In an almost whisper he told him how glad they were that he could come up and do this interview. "This is your first one on one with the President isn't it, Brad?"

Brad nodded.

"Well, I can tell you that the President is looking forward to it. He's read everything that you've written since the assassination and thinks you've done a wonderful job. You haven't gone to the extremes that some writers have or put out weird theories as to who was behind the shooting. You realize that it's unusual for a columnist who isn't from a large New York, Washington, or Los Angeles paper to pull off a face to face like this?"

"Thank you. I'm sure this will help me in my follow-up stories on the Harrot tragedy." Brad was barely able to mumble the rather formal response. The door opened and he was led inside.

The President stood and came around his desk. Garron and Steinheitz were exiting through another door. The press secretary did a very brief introduction. The President reached out his hand toward Brad and they shook. He looked larger on television to Brad. He looked into the pale blue eyes of the Chief Executive and felt his firm grasp. A couple of inches shorter than Brad, he appeared in control with dark blue suit, brilliant white shirt, and a striped red, white, and blue tie. His thinning blond hair had been styled and cut in a way so that only the close observer could see some scalp shining beneath. His broad smile and mouth full of teeth were what Brad remembered seeing in hundreds of commercials during the election in 1996.

He did not return behind his desk but sat with Brad in two similar chairs in front. The press secretary retired to a corner chair some distance removed where he unobtrusively remained.

"Mr. President, I want to thank you for allowing me this opportunity. With your permission, I would like to set my little tape recorder on the corner of your desk. Sometimes I'm unable to write down all the responses and like to have a back up to go to," he said and placed the micro-cassette on the edge of the desk equi-distance between him and the President. He looked for a nod of approval, which he received.

"Mr. Yeary, let me first say that I think you've done a very balanced job on the reporting of the great tragedy in New Orleans. I've followed your accounts closely. Would you care for anything to drink? This is very good public housing. They will bring us anything I ask for." He laughed and the press secretary joined in.

"No, I'm fine," Brad said and pushed the activate button on the recorder.

"Is this the first time you've been in the Oval Office?"

"It certainly is, Mr. President," Brad said. He looked around the room. "I've been to replicas of the Oval Office as it was during Johnson's and Truman's time at their libraries, but this is my first real visit. I hope it won't be the last."

"Me too, Mr. Yeary. Fire away. I'm ready when you are. I apologize that I kept you waiting for a half hour or so, but I've been so busy. I'll give you a full hour anyway," the President said and looked at his watch.

Brad had refined his interview style over the years to one that allowed him, somewhat like a good cross-examining lawyer, to soften up the subject with comfortable questions at the start. Then he would get more to the meat of the session as he went along. If he knew a person was likely to become offended at a particular line of questioning, he would delay that to the last. Then when it was time for the difficult questions, he would press hard. He would go as far as he could under the circumstances and time restraints.

If a person refused to answer the really touchy inquiries, at least he would have the bulk of the interview out of the way before the recalcitrance set in. Because of the ten-minute time limit with Harrot, he had changed his normal sequence of questions and had gone directly to the Mid-East situation as the focal point.

With the President, he would have a full hour and could do a great deal in that period. The touchy Mid-East would come last. He knew he had been called to Washington because of his coverage of Harrot's death and thought the President probably wanted to talk about that. He determined to keep that to the end also in order to show that he was in charge of the interview. He began the questioning with the domestic situation concerning the deficit and growing national debt.

The President appeared a bit surprised and looked fleetingly over to his press secretary. He recovered nicely by indicating how much he had depended on Harrot for guidance in some of those areas. He did that with each answer, working in Harrot's supposed role.

For a half hour, Brad trudged on through domestic policy, touching on conservation, disaster relief, and environmental restrictions on oil exploration along the Gulf coast. The President answered but with the slightest turn would try to direct the questioning toward the Vice Presidency.

Finally Brad relented. "Tell me a little about your relationship with the late Vice President." This gave the President the opening he needed to praise Samuel Harrot and extol him in words normally reserved for deities. The virtues of honesty, diligence, intelligence, and patriotism heaped upon him made it almost appear that Harrot should have been the President.

"Have you narrowed down your list of possible successors to Vice President Harrot, Mr. President?" Brad asked, hoping that Benjamin Ashford would not be among the finalists for the sake of his and Jill's relationship.

The President assumed a very solemn expression, bringing his clasped hands beneath his chin so that it almost appeared he was praying. "Yes, yes I have. My staff and I have looked at a number of very capable men and women each of whom I feel is qualified to be just a heartbeat away from the most difficult job on earth. Through a winnowing process we have narrowed our list down to three. We will be talking further with these three over the next few days and hope to announce our choice next week, probably Monday."

"Who are those three, Mr. President?"

The Chief Executive turned and looked at his press secretary as though silently asking, "Do I have to answer that question?"

Brad knew this was what he had been waiting for, the question for which he had agreed to have this interview.

The press secretary just gave a blank expression with a palms up gesture that signaled, "It's up to you."

"When will this be published, Mr. Yeary?" the President asked.

Brad looked at his watch. "Probably tomorrow if I stay and write the story in Washington."

"Okay, Mr. Yeary, you're a tough questioner, and I can see how you're being mentioned for a Pulitzer Prize for your reporting." The President smiled at Brad. "I'll tell you the three names before they even know they're finalists. We'll have to get busy and call the other seventeen before your paper comes out tomorrow," he said, more to his press secretary than to Brad.

Brad flipped a page in his notepad and looked at the recorder to be sure it was still taping before the President mentioned the three names. He would need verification on this one for Pinthater. The President was flattering him with mention of a possible Pulitzer Prize for his writing. He had not even thought about that until now. If that seed germinated and grew to harvest, he would not regret it. It would be a fitting crown to his career. The likelihood of it occurring though was less than his friend, Papa Legba, being nominated for mayor of New Orleans.

However, what the President was about to tell him would be another big scoop if the press secretary didn't turn around and call all his news friends as soon as Brad left. He might have to go with Pinthater's Channel Five for this one to get it first. He had told the President only when it would go to press, not when it would go to air. His distaste for the television medium might have to be overcome on this occasion in order to insure exclusivity.

The President first named a black woman senator from an industrial state, then a Jewish governor from a heavily populated eastern state. "The third one is your own senior senator from Louisiana.

Senator Benjamin Ashford."

Brad sat dazed. "Senator Ashford? Are you sure?" Brad saw his life passing before him. Jill may have been correct. And if she was right about that, she might be on target about her being the next U.S. Senator from Louisiana. For the first time, he acknowledged to himself that he was certain he did not want Jill to do that. He wanted her full time in Baton Rouge.

He sat silent for a full minute while he analyzed what the President had just told him. The three candidates would obviously give the President increased prestige among differing minority and female constituencies. In one fell swoop, by naming these three individuals as finalists for Vice President, the chief executive would ingratiate himself with women, blacks, Jews, and Southerners. He decided to press a bit.

"Could you narrow it down any further for me, Mr. President? Who's the leading choice at this time among the three?"

The President smiled, put the index fingers of both clasped hands to his lips, and appeared to be pondering the question. "No," he finally said, "that's as far as I can go at this time, although I would add that your senator weighs in very heavily with me and everyone I have consulted on the nomination."

Brad silently wrote those remarks onto his pad. He didn't show it, but he did not like the way that the President referred to Ashford as "your senator." He wasn't Brad's senator, and, in fact, he had very little use for him. He had never been able to pin it down exactly because Ashford's voting record wasn't all that much different from other Southern senators. It was more an attitude than anything else. The senator had always appeared a bit put off by the intrusion of the press or by requests for interviews, although he usually relented and allowed access in a way that it made the interviewer feel like a supplicant appearing before his king.

Brad then turned to his last questions—the thorny Mid-East questions concerning the oil producing countries banding together in a new coalition of previously unknown proportions. This was the line of questions that he had also put to Harrot.

"Mr. President, do you think it's going to be necessary to send troops to the Mid-East to insure that the United States will continue to have a constant and guaranteed supply of oil?"

The President turned and nodded to his press secretary. Brad could tell that the President didn't want to go too far with this line of questions.

"No. No, I don't think that will be necessary. I believe the leaders of those countries will react to reason and see that it's not in their best interests to restrict our oil supply or unduly increase the price."

"How would it not be in their best interests, Mr. President?"

"Well, I just don't believe that the nations of the world would be willing to trade with them if they started on a course such as this."

"A blockade, sir?"

"No. Just voluntary refraining from trade. And I believe that even if the leaders don't see it, all the millions of men and women over there would see it and bring pressure on their leaders."

"Are you countenancing a rebellion from within or a coup?"

For the first time the President frowned. "Certainly not, Mr. Yeary. That's illegal. It's just that the leaders over there and their people will be reasonable and not let this deteriorate to that point."

And then, as though on cue, there was a knock on the door. Chief of Staff Rob Steinheitz entered and informed the President that there was an urgent matter that needed his attention. The interview ended fifteen minutes early.

# Sixteen

A nd now, live from Washington is Channel Five's Brad Yeary with a late development on the replacement for Vice President Samuel Harrot—" the Ten O'Clock News anchor for Pinthater's television station led in. The camera zoomed to Brad with the illuminated White House over his shoulder.

Between his early exit from the interview and nine-thirty, Brad had put together his report. He had called the publisher and given him the news first hand, and as usual, Pinthater wanted to be sure to get the jump on all competitors with a live report on his late evening news show. For two hours Brad typed in his story on the word processor wired to New Orleans and practiced in his own mind the best way to handle the television broadcast at ten.

They were pasting into place the *Times-Gazette* story for the photography and then the presses when he met with the hired television broadcasting crew near the White House. For the second time in two weeks, he would be the first with the news concerning the second highest office in the land.

The producer cued him with the wave of a finger and instantaneously he was on the screens of all television viewers in New Orleans, Baton Rouge, Lafayette, and even little Lafitte, who had tuned in to Channel Five. Jill Crenshaw watched from her apartment in Baton Rouge. Brad had called her from Washington with the word that there would be important news on at ten. He didn't tell her that it would be him delivering it. So, as the camera framed him with the seat of power behind him, he pretended he was speaking only to Jill when he gave the essence of the President's statement.

"Louisiana's Senior Senator Benjamin Ashford was named today by the President as one of three finalists to fill the office of Vice President." He proceeded with a five-minute summary of his interview with the Chief Executive and named the other two finalists who shared this distinction with Ashford. He left the other parts of his interview untouched on television but told listeners that a more detailed story would follow in the morning edition of his newspaper.

With the broadcast completed, he walked immediately to the van where a mobile phone was available and dialed Jill's number. As soon as she answered, he could tell that she was excited. She could almost taste the U.S. Senate, he knew. "I'm on a flight back in an hour. Drive down to New Orleans and meet me. We have a lot to talk about."

She agreed.

His next call was to Pinthater, who told him that since they last spoke he had lined up an interview for Brad with Senator Ashford in Lafayette for the following afternoon. There went his plans to be with Jill for a relaxing Tuesday.

"What did you do that for, Ed? I'm supposed to be with Jill."

"Brad, this is hot. We've got to stay on top. No time to waste. There's time for play later on. You're on your way to a Pulitzer and the paper to a national reputation.

"I called Ashford, and although he said he'd have no comment tonight, he agreed to a three o'clock interview with you tomorrow. Keep going, Brad."

"Shit." Brad slammed the phone down. He wished he wasn't so fortunate as to be hot on this story. It was ruining his personal life. He could hear himself trying to explain this to Jill when he had just promised her all of his time for Tuesday. She was busy at that moment changing her schedule to accommodate their being together.

Before he could leave the van and while the television crew was packing, about ten men and women from the media came running from a wing of the White House asking where Brad Yeary was. At the speed of electricity, the other network affiliates in New Orleans had notified their Washington offices for follow-ups on what they had just seen on Pinthater's Channel Five, and from the White House Press Room, these had scampered to the point of the broadcast.

Brad threw up both hands as he left the van. "I can't tell you anything. Read the morning *Times-Gazette*," he said and ran for his rental car. He was gaining a new appreciation for those who found themselves the center of media attention.

EARLY THE NEXT MORNING in Fayette County, Kentucky, just outside Lexington, two men sat near each other in wooden slat-bottom chairs in a pure white block building. It was slightly removed from the barns and stables that quartered some of the best studs of Thoroughbred horseflesh.

Breeding season would not peak again for a couple of months.

Horse owners planned for their mares to foal in January, if possible, since the age of every horse was counted from January First of each year. If a colt was born on December fifteenth, it would be a yearling on the first day of the next month. So, it was advantageous to those breeding for racing to have the horses born as close after the first day of January as possible so that they would actually be near a year old by the following January birth date. There were only a scant few years to develop size, speed, and running ability. The Triple Crown was designed for three-year-olds.

Mid-January was busy in the Bluegrass-area stables for those who had mares birthing gangly young colts, but for the stud farm where these two men sat in the room overlooking the breeding stable, it was the slowest time of the year. They cut back on employees during the first three months of the year maintaining just enough to feed and care for the vast investment that they had in a dozen stallions, some of which had won various legs of the Triple Crown.

They boarded another twenty horses for absent owners who did not hesitate to charge from five to twenty-five thousand dollars for a single stud service. The men sat near a window that overlooked the area where the mares were brought during breeding season for their five minutes of passion with one of the thirty-two pampered horses. Now the studs lounged on this farm of two hundred handsome acres twelve miles from Rupp Arena and downtown Lexington.

The men longed for the same type of life enjoyed by the racehorses they owned and cared for. To be a stallion at stud was the zenith of equine life. They were fed all the fresh oats and grain that they desired along with vitamin supplements. They had the finest in health care and had their sparkling coats curried twice a day by attendants who also walked them and then allowed them to lope in the open fields. Or they could just stand and look over the picturesque white wood-plank fences that divided the acres off into green checkerboard squares.

Then during breeding season, distant owners would truck in attractive mares to the barn where they could enjoy a sensuous romp and then return to the green pastures of manicured grass.

The two dark-complected men, one much taller than the other who sported a neat mustache, watched the television that sat high in the corner of the sparsely furnished room. They both sipped aromatic tea from cups without handles that allowed little spirals of mist to rise in the coolness like slow-burning incense. They directed their attention to the early morning news shows that were following up on the President's announcement of the three finalists for Vice President.

"It's happening just as the Caliph said," the shorter man said to his younger and lankier associate. "Things are in motion." They nodded to each other.

"I miss Ali," the taller one said. "He so liked the fast horses. He could ride like he was a part of the horse. He liked all speed. Cars. And that beeg boat," he said.

The shorter man stood and looked out the opposite window toward the road that snaked through the now bare oak trees.

"Ali had to be sacrificed. The circle of knowledge was too broad. The three barbarians we had to hire for the job, Ali, you, me, and our friends in New York. Too many. Word would get out. People talk. Ali was a great warrior. He has gone to his reward."

"What about the youth who fashioned the firing stick? He is still alive. Does he need to be gone?"

The shorter man shook his head. "No. He has no knowledge. He did not know what the cane was to be used for. He only fabricated one part. The fiber optic cable for the binoculars and the firing sensor were both made other places. The three infidels assembled it and executed the plan, so they had to go."

The tall man stood. "I still miss Ali."

"Yes, that was a necessary waste. And the money," he looked up at his taller friend and smiled. "They thought two-hundred-forty thousand, but really just sixty thousand. No need to spread too much money along the Mississippi. I knew by the time they counted twenty thousand each they would have tipped the brown liquid Mr. Daniels too much to count further."

"So, we safe? No one knows but you and me and our New York brothers? What next?"

"And the White Caliph. So far I trust you not to talk." He nodded toward his friend with a slight scowl. "We await word for the next job. In the meantime we sit here and run our great American horse breeding farm that our family invested so heavily in. And seek ways to spend all their oil money," the short one said. He turned up the final drink from the cup.

# Seventeen

They were still in bed at Brad's apartment near the Quarter when Jill lazily turned over and looked at her watch. "Brad, it's already eleven. We better get up. You'll miss your interview with Ashford in Lafayette if you don't get a move on." She sat up in bed, turned and placed her two feet on Brad's buttocks, and began slowly pushing him.

He only mumbled. His sluggish pace toward the edge of the bed went unchecked. Finally he tried to catch himself as he began to tumble off, grabbing the sheets and pillow while descending to the floor.

"What are you doing?" he asked. He regained some sense of balance and stood beside the bed. Jill sat nude in the bed with her long, silky legs extended to where she had pushed him off. She smiled and didn't even try to cover up.

"I thought you might need a jump start."

He shook his head and stared at her. "You look good," he said and made a lunge for her. She avoided him by rolling out of the way and off the other side.

"No, no, no. No time to play this morning. You've got to get up to Ashford's."

Jill's reaction when Brad had arrived from Washington on the late flight home had been just the opposite from what he had expected. Instead of being upset that he could not spend the whole day with her, she was delighted that he was to interview the senator who had been mentioned by the President as possibly being the next Vice President.

She wanted to know more than Brad what Ashford's reaction was to that possibility. Would he accept if offered? Or would he advise the President to choose someone else and leave him in the Senate? She had bounced up and down in the car on their ride from the airport when Brad finally broached the subject of his having to interview Ashford. If Brad hadn't known better, he would have thought she had another man she wanted to get back to the following day instead of being with him. They had decided to spend the night in New Orleans at his place and then go to Baton Rouge where he would drop her off. He would then continue on I-10 to Lafayette to talk with Ashford.

She slept only briefly during the last few hours. Visions of the U.S. Senate flitted through her mind. She was already practicing her acceptance speech and mulling what would be her priorities on the national stage. If she were appointed, she would have almost two full years to get her feet on the ground and then be able to run for election as an incumbent.

If Brad did his job, she should know by tonight about Ashford's thoughts on accepting the position. Then her mentor, Governor Hugh "Papa" Johnson, would have to keep his word to her concerning the appointment to the Senate. She had been around long enough to know that there would be a hundred politicians lobbying for the job as soon as they thought there was a real possibility of a vacancy. She made a mental note to call the governor's office as soon as she arrived in Baton Rouge and arrange a long talk for tomorrow.

She stood, walked in front of where Brad was sitting on the edge of the bed rubbing his hair and eyes, and when she was sure he was looking, pirouetted in front of him holding her arms up like a ballerina and allowing her shoulder length hair to flow out and away. Once again she achieved the result of getting Brad's attention. He reached out and swatted her on the derriere. She continued her tight circles.

Then she slowed to a stop, took his hands, and brought him to his feet. There she embraced him as her cool skin met his warm. She pressed her breasts to his chest, wrapped her arms around his waist, allowed her hands to wander to his tight buttocks, and gave them a nail-etching squeeze. For a half minute they stood there in a still, wet clasping of body to body until she pushed him back just enough to part them and looked down his warm torso.

"Oh, my," she said, still staring downward. "We better go take a shower. I'll soap you up good and see if I can do anything about that. Then tell you what I'll do tonight," she said and led the political reporter toward the bath.

They were on their way by noon.

U. S. SENATOR BENJAMIN EDWARD Ashford wore his fifty-six years well. He was remarkably stout and broad-shouldered for a man who preferred the library to the sporting arena. He owed his musculature to his hobby of being around his cattle and walking over his two hundred-acre estate.

When home from Washington and not perusing his magnificent library, he would relax by helping maintain the fences on the farm by hand-digging post-holes the old-fashioned way. He disdained using the power-driven auger from his tractors. His appearance gave the hint of an old boxer built fireplug-like who wouldn't be knocked down easily. A slightly pugnose rested on a broad, jowly face. He owed his barely distorted nose not to pugilism, which he abhorred, but to an encounter as a youth when he was pulled along the ground and into a post by a young bull he had lassoed. He never turned loose of the rope despite the bovine dragging him over a hundred yards before attempting to scrape him off against a cedar post.

Once Benjamin Ashford took hold of something it was hell dislodging him from it. That was also the political history of this tenacious plantation owner whose white, curly hair had now receded to a point where a pinkish-white pate made up most of the crown.

As Brad drove up the gravel road to Ashford's Stratford Place Plantation, the senator talked in his first floor study to a middle-aged black lady of ample proportions and her neatly dressed son. They sat around a cherrywood table and sipped glasses of lemonade. Amelia Tadford, after serving the refreshments, retired to the parlor to await Brad Yeary's arrival.

"There it is, Senator Ashford," the lady said. She pushed a piece of well-worn paper across the table. Senator Ashford took it, put on his glasses, and began to read silently. The young man and his mother looked at each other and then back at the senator.

"Yes, yes, I see what you're talking about, Matilda. Jamal has done quite well. Nothing on this transcript except for A's for his junior and senior years." He handed the paper back to the mother and put his glasses back in his pocket.

He looked at the young black man. "Jamal, I'm proud of you. Like I told your mother three years ago when she told me you had a brain in that tall, lanky body of yours, I will be happy to help you to be able to go to college. You say you want to be a doctor and come back here to the community and serve the needs here?"

"Yes sir, Senator Ashford. I know it's going to be hard. But I've got it in my mind that I can do it. But you know Mamma's got seven other children she has to look out for. Even with the partial scholarship and grant that I can get, I couldn't make it without a loan."

"So you think you have it in you?"

"Yes, sir."

"There's a lot of chemistry, science, and many, many, long hours and nights before you get to your first patient. You know that, don't you?" the Senator asked. He stood and stepped to the window. He watched Brad walk to the front door.

The young man turned in his chair and faced the window where Ashford was standing. "Yes, sir. I know I can, Mr. Ashford. And my mother and me aren't asking for no handout. Just a loan. I'll pay it back as soon as I get out and on my feet."

"Your mother says you want to go to Tulane. Is that right?" Ashford asked and walked to a little desk. He leaned over, took out two pieces of paper, and began to write.

"Yes, sir. I want to go there. I've heard it's good. I've already visited and been accepted if I can get my finances in order."

Ashford was still writing when Amelia knocked on the door and stepped halfway through. "Senator Ashford, Brad Yeary of the *Times-Gazette* is here."

"Thank you, Amelia. Take him to the library, give him some lemonade, and tell him I'll be with him in a few minutes. I am in the midst of an important matter here."

Once the door was closed, Senator Ashford walked over and handed Jamal the two pieces of paper. The youth stood, read what was on each, and turned to the Senator. "Sir, thank you. But you forgot something."

"What's that, Jamal?"

"This check to Tulane. You forgot to put any numbers in it. It's just blank."

"That's right, Jamal. The little note to the registrar with that tells him to fill it in at the end of the year. It's for all your necessities that are not covered by anything else. I know the registrar. He'll have you sign a form to allow him to send me a copy of your grades each semester, and he'll take care of seeing to it that you have everything you need."

Ashford looked over at Jamal's mother. "What's wrong with you, Matilda?" The plump black lady sat dabbing at her eyes with a handkerchief, sniffing and blinking as she looked toward her oldest child who wanted to be a doctor.

"I'm just so happy, Senator. Praise the Lord. You don't know how much this means to Jamal and me. He couldn't have gone without your help. And, I'll see to it that he pays it back."

"Don't worry about that. This is my investment in the future. Now, I don't want you two telling anyone of this. It's just our little secret, okay? And Jamal, I'll make a little deal with you."

"What's that, Senator?"

"We'll allow you a B per semester with the others to be As and you don't have to pay any of that back." He took the free right hand of Jamal and gave it a firm grasp and shake. "Now sit down and tell me about what you're taking your final semester in high school. I have a few minutes," he said and looked at his watch.

BRAD STOOD IN THE foyer awaiting Ashford when he was rejoined by Amelia.

"Senator Ashford will be with you, Mr. Yeary, in just a few moments. If you will, follow me upstairs to the library. He'll meet you there shortly."

He paced along quietly behind the slim black lady. Brad was acquainted with most of the staff of Ashford's, both in Washington and Baton Rouge, but he had never before been to "the Farm" as he had heard staff members refer to it. And he had never seen Amelia Tadford at any function that he had attended where Ashford was present. Walking behind her, he was sure he would have remembered a lady of her beauty, grace, and elegance if he had seen her before.

As she swept up the stairway, barely lifting the long skirt of her dark blue floor-length dress that was festooned with white lily print, he could not help but eye her slender waist and the way that the dress clung to hips that would have befit a woman half her age. With her hair pulled back in a bun, crowned by a velvet ribbon, Amelia's neck and ears betrayed a woman whose beauty had apparently been hidden away in Stratford Place out of the view of those who could appreciate it.

He was so near her that when she stopped on the landing and opened the door to the library, her breasts, imprisoned beneath the navy bodice, brushed against his jacket when she turned to allow him to go into the library first. She put a hand to her lips where a wry smile arose as though by reflex, and her steel blue eyes gave a hint of times of flirtation in the recesses of her past. The moment passed. Somewhat flustered, Brad walked into the huge library that took most of the second floor of Ashford's ancestral plantation house.

He turned and tried to think of something to say to break the tension of the just past touching. "That's a beautiful dress you have on, Mrs . . . "

"Tadford. Amelia Tadford. And I am not a Mrs." She stepped closer to Brad than felt comfortable to him. "How do you say it? I'm a Ms. Not presently married." She smiled softly. She reached up and took an errant string from the lapel of Brad's coat and then, with both of her ebony hands, pressed the coat down against his chest. He could feel the heat and see her perfectly manicured nails painted a bright red. He hoped that she could not feel his heart pounding through the coat.

"I bet my friend, Jill, would look good in that dress," he said.

Amelia hesitated for a second; then she reached behind her and began to unzip the dress. She bent forward just enough to allow Brad a view of the prettiest brown cleavage that he had ever seen. "You want to take it to her and see?" she asked. She straightened back up and kept her hand midway of her back.

"No, no, no," Brad said as quietly, yet forcefully as possible, all the while looking toward the open door where he worried Senator Ashford would appear and think he was ravishing his maid. "It was just a figure of speech. It is a gorgeous dress, but you keep it on. Please, Ms. Tadford."

"You can call me Amelia," she said and stepped back a comfortable distance. "What does this Jill look like, Mr. Yeary?"

"You can call me Brad, Amelia. She's beautiful. A little bit taller than you. Nearly blond."

"Is she black or white?" she asked.

"White."

"You don't like black?" she asked. She lifted her chin and let a small pout draw up her sexy lips.

"No, I didn't say that. We've just known each other for a long time. We've sort of grown attached."

"I can imagine." She smiled at Brad. "Well if you and your white 'nearly blond' friend ever break up, just remember little old Amelia is out here on the plantation."

"I'll remember that, Amelia."

She disappeared through the entranceway, but before Brad could turn around, she leaned back to where he could see her through the opening. "I was just teasing, Mr. Yeary. Just having a little fun with you. You can't take me seriously." And she was gone, but Brad didn't know which was Amelia's true self. If he wasn't attached and committed he would have certainly found out.

# Eighteen

With what does a U.S. Senator and former governor of the state of Louisiana fill out all the shelves of a home library? Brad asked himself while he waited for Benjamin Ashford and the interview which was now a half hour late.

He first went to the window that faced toward Baton Rouge and looked out into the late afternoon sunshine over a canopy of barren oak trees that sloped down a slight hill. The grounds were immaculate even in the dead of winter. A dark young man a hundred yards or so away with a tractor and wagon collected broken branches that had fallen during the last wind storm. He picked them up by hand and then raked the smaller gatherings into piles that were placed into the half-full wagon. Beyond and to the right, a few head of cattle stood around a round bale of hay that resembled a brown thimble turned on its side from this distance.

Brad bent down and ran his hand along the hardwood floor near the window to feel the smooth texture of the ancient wood. At the base of the window, about midway to the floor, there appeared to be smoke smudges on the green plaster wall about even with the sides of the window if the lines were extended to the floor. While kneeling he reached back toward the middle of the room and let his hand glide beneath the edge of the fine Persian rug. The placement of the rug seemed odd. It was not centered but lay in a way that it came to within five feet of the window.

He noticed about a foot from the edge of the rug and toward the window a small "E" about two inches in length etched into the polished wood. He straightened back up and walked to the exact center of the fine fabric. Then he stepped to each edge and, going counterclockwise, saw the letters "N," "W," and "S" carved in small but clear detail in the floor at the center of each side of the rug about the same distance from the edge of the Persian as the "E" was toward the window.

Besides the five stacks of bookshelves that went from a short distance behind a massive wooden desk to the back wall, fine polished wood shelving lined the walls of the entire room except for an open area near the one window. The dark brown oak boards stretched to the twelve-foot ceiling and were filled with thousands of volumes.

He walked slowly beside the shelving. Ashford's collection included sets of biographies on all the Presidents of the United States, justices of the Supreme Court, and secretaries of state. One side of a stack that stretched thirty feet to the back wall contained only treatises, books, and diaries dealing with every war that the United States had been involved in from the Revolutionary to the Gulf War of 1991 and even to little skirmishes that Brad had forgotten about.

The largest section of that stack contained the history of the Civil War. Ashford had in his collection, Brad noticed as he pulled one fragile booklet from the shelf, handwritten notes and journals of soldiers who had actually fought in that war. There were at least fifty of these in one section. He lost track of time as he wandered around the room just glancing at the accumulation that he knew would be envied by many public and state libraries.

An eight-foot section from floor to ceiling at the front wall of the room was devoted to religion. Ashford had books and commentaries on all religions familiar to Brad and many that were not. Zen, Buddhism, Judaism, Catholicism, and many protestant Christian denominations along with the occult and mystic religions including voodoo, witchcraft, astrology, and numerology were all represented there. Commentaries on each book of the Bible took up another ten feet of shelf space. Just a little bit below his eye level was another long stretch of books dealing with Islam. Biographies of Mohammed were interspersed with histories of each Muslim country and several copies of the Koran. Brad pulled out one of the copies of the Muslim holy book and let the pages flip through under his thumb. He stopped at one page where he saw a handwritten note in the margin and began

to read. It was beside a two-page section headed "THE HYPO-
CRITES." There were two passages underlined.

       *"When the hypocrites come to you they say: 'We bear
witness that you are God's apostle.' God knows that you are indeed His
apostle; and God bears witness that the hypocrites are lying.*

       *"They use their faith as a disguise, and debar others
from the path of God. Evil is what they do.*

       *"They believed and then renounced their faith: their
hearts are sealed, so that they are devoid of understanding."*

And then a bit farther down:

       *"Believers, let neither your riches nor your children be-
guile you of God's remembrance. Those that forget Him shall forfeit all.*

       *"Give, then, of that which We have given you before
death befalls you and you say: 'Reprieve me, Lord, awhile, that I may
give in charity and be among the righteous.'"*

       Next to the last passage was a handwritten note that said, "I
must be charitable." But immediately to the left of the first passage,
in all capitals, was the printed denunciation: "DEATH TO THE HYPO-
CRITES!"

       Brad let the pages continue to fan in front of him. Other pas-
sages were highlighted or underlined at various places and little notes
made over and over in the margins.

       "Are you a reader, Mr. Yeary?"

       Brad had become so engrossed that he did not notice the pres-
ence behind him of Senator Ashford. The full, firm voice of the senator
so startled Brad that he dropped the Koran to the floor but quickly
picked it up and put it back in its place.

       He turned and faced the senator as Ashford extended his hand
and Brad put his cold hand out in return.

       "Yes, Senator Ashford, I read some. Mainly other newspapers
and magazines. Occasionally I'll read a novel for relaxation. But I
doubt if I had ten life times I could read all the books you have here,"
he said and swept his right arm toward the bulging shelves.

       "Me neither, Mr. Yeary. It's knowing where to find a passage
or section that's important. Most of these I've never read. Others, just
a chapter or two. Some of the most interesting, though, are the diaries
of those men who struggled through the War Between the States. Did
you see those back here?" he asked and began to walk down the aisle.

       "Yes, I noticed those, Senator."

       Ashford picked up one. "Yes, these are of value. Real men.
Many of them facing death for a cause they sensed would not survive.
They had wives and brothers and sisters and fathers and mothers back
home. Yet, they, for the most part, were willing to hang on, to stay in

camp, to fight, to give their lives in a losing effort. Why? Because they thought it was important. Now, that was true on both sides. That is one of the things I detest about our country today. Very few men and women have strong enough convictions about anything that they would give their lives for it. What about you, Mr. Yeary?"

Ashford sat behind his desk and Brad took a seat in front.

"What about me, sir?"

"Do you hold any belief or conviction strongly enough that you would die for it?"

Brad was quiet for a minute before answering.

"Well, I guess if the country went to war, I would be willing to." Brad thought a second and added, "If it was for the right reason."

Ashford managed a small laugh. "That's why we don't let men in their thirties and forties on the front lines. They're too philosophical. 'Should I pull this trigger? Is this battle for the right reason? Could we have negotiated this hill?' That's why we have to train our young men and women when they are eighteen to twenty-two to obey orders. They don't have the luxury of reflection on the good or evil of a policy.

"So, now that we've established that you wouldn't be dependable to give your life for the country in just *any* war, do you have any personal principles that you would give your life for rather than give up? Your religion?"

"I'm not very religious. Catholic, only by birth. Haven't been to mass or confession in a couple of years."

Ashford laced his fingers behind his head and looked at the ceiling. "Oh well, what about freedom of the press? What if you were locked up, not to be released, until you disclosed a source that you swore to protect?"

Brad jumped into that, having dreamed for the better part of twenty years of how brave he would be if it ever came to it. He would sit in jail, catch up on his reading, do push-ups, and wait till hell froze over before he would ever divulge a source. "I could handle that."

"Okay. What if they put you before a firing squad?"

He took longer to answer and he knew he would probably weaken then, but he wanted to affirm as much to himself as to the senator that he would stand as a stalwart for freedom of the press even though his blood was soaking into the ground.

"Yes, I would give my life for that."

Ashford leaned forward over the desk and looked Brad in the eye. "Good. Everyone should have one ideal or principle for which he would sacrifice his life. Not just generalities, but iron-clad, solid principles." He reached across and shook Brad's hand again.

"But Senator Ashford, we're not here to talk about me today. I've come to interview you."

"So you have. So you have. Get on with it then."

Brad reached inside his coat pocket and took out his mini-cassette recorder, placed it on the edge of the desk of the senator, and retrieved his note pad from his other pocket. He glanced at his watch as he noted the time and date on the opening sheet of his pad. In less than two weeks he had interviewed Vice President Harrot, President Teater, and now Senator and possibly Vice President-designate Benjamin Ashford.

This would be the most extended conversation he had ever had with Ashford even though he had been in the Senate as long as Brad had been a political reporter.

Ashford was an enigma. Of all the articles and columns that Brad had written over a period of ten years about all the politicians throughout Louisiana, he could not remember a comment from Ashford or his office about anything he had penned. On some occasions he had criticized votes and positions of the senator, and on others he had given him faint praise. Never, at any time, had anyone called to correct, condemn, or congratulate him for any comment. It was as though he was either totally ignored by Ashford, or else the senator had a tough skin that deflected criticism and withstood flattery equally well.

"Senator, you mentioned a weakness you see in people today of not having principles that they would die for. Is there any other great weakness either with America or its people here nearing the end of the Twentieth Century?" The question would give Ashford room to state some broad philosophy of government while it allowed Brad time to renew and hone in his mind the specific questions he wanted to ask about the Vice Presidency.

"Well, I'll approach that question from an individual standpoint first. There are many people who have no goal, no ambition, no driving force today like their parents and grandparents had.

"The first and second generations of immigrant families always prove to be the most hard-working, industrious people that you will find in the country. That is true regardless of ethnic background. It was true when the English came in the sixteen hundreds, and it's true now with those from the Asian countries.

"After a few generations, that zeal burns out in many people. They now seek to be entertained and amused rather than desiring to better themselves. And I'm not talking about bettering themselves from the financial standpoint, but bettering themselves through education—building up their souls and minds—or building better families.

"There's too much putting off and not enough gathering together. Many of our problems as a nation are just an extension of defects in character as individuals. Problems with alcohol and other drugs partly—and I need to emphasize 'partly'—stem from a desire to be entertained, to seek excitement, to pursue happiness in a very different way than was ever contemplated by Thomas Jefferson in the Declaration of Independence.

"Now, as to groups, we tend to have a growing problem that could be disastrous if it reached its natural end. That problem is more and more separation into groups or subclasses of Americans that tend to divide us rather than bring us together. There's a tendency to be what I term 'hyphenated Americans.' Ethnic, racial, and religious heritages are now becoming a wedge of division rather than what America has always been—which is a melting pot of diversity.

"Everyone should be Americans and leave off the prefixes and all the hyphenated ways in which we can be divided. If not, we could see the new century come in on heels of soldiers trying to keep warring, Balkanized factions of Americans apart. Do we want to become a Yugoslavia after the fall of the Russian Empire?" Ashford asked and shifted forward in his chair.

"Now, don't get me wrong. It's fine to have differing heritages and remember our roots and where we came from, but we don't need that to be a point of division. The only purposes of roots are to provide nourishment and support. The glory of a tree is not in its roots but in what its roots allow it to become."

Brad listened and took notes. Would what Ashford said come back to haunt him if he were chosen by the President to be the next second in command? He could imagine members of the House and Senate, who would be voting to confirm the next Vice President, trying to slice up Senator Ashford about not being sensitive to racial or ethnic issues.

But he gathered from the senator's first answer that he was speaking his mind and didn't really care who thought what. Perhaps that was why he had never heard a word from any of Ashford's staff on anything he had written—the senator marched to his own drum and could not care less what somebody said about him. Had he misjudged Ashford in labeling him as ambitious but without a quality record? The senator was a little deeper-minded than Brad expected. This answer and the large library were evidence of it.

For the next half hour, Brad plodded along through a series of questions on domestic policy and received well thought out and enunciated answers from Ashford. As a test of foreign policy, he went back to the line of questions he had asked to both then Vice President Harrot and, only the day before, to the President. "How should the United States respond to threats from Iraq, Saudi Arabia, and the other Mid-East oil producers when they say they might limit our supply of oil and raise prices?"

Ashford turned in his chair, put a finger to his lips, paused, and peered briefly toward the ceiling before answering.

"As a senator from an oil producing and refining state, I would have to say that we need to look inward. We should increase our own production and practice more conservation—not just fad programs that are forgotten in a year but real tough decisions that make us less dependent on foreign oil. Then we need to learn to negotiate and get along with our neighbors in the Mid-East—and I say 'neighbors' advisedly because the world is becoming smaller and smaller. They are our neighbors."

Brad took all of this down as he turned over in his mind a follow-up question to see how tough Ashford would be in suggesting the use of military force to insure a good oil supply. "What about sending soldiers there to make certain our oil will keep flowing?"

Senator Ashford leaned forward, his bald crown flushed a deeper shade of pink, and he brought his hands together to where his forefingers resembled a church steeple as he gestured with them, "That should not be necessary!"

For all his lengthy answers to other questions, the brevity of this response surprised Brad. Perhaps the senator and possible future Vice President did not want to step into a policy matter that rightfully belonged to the President who had said essentially the same thing in a little different phrasing. Brad turned finally to the questions that Jill and Ed Pinthater had sent him to ask.

"Senator Ashford, what about the Vice Presidency? Do you want it? And will you take it if it's offered?"

The senator relaxed, let a smile grace his lips, and leaned back in his chair with his hands behind his head. "I'm perfectly happy here. And I mean at Stratford Place. Being a senator is all right too. But I don't have to be a senator to be happy. I would just as soon stay in the Senate until the people of this state tell me they want somebody else.

"However, you know the President has called me in, along with many others, concerning the position of Vice President. And I'll tell you the same thing I told him last week. I don't want it. But if the President asks me to take it, I will serve my country and follow the call of the President."

Brad scribbled the response as his heart sank within him. The answer obviously meant that Ashford was available if the call came. Jill and Pinthater would have the answer they longed for, and he would have his heartache. While he contemplated his next question, there was a soft knocking on the library door. Amelia Tadford opened it just enough for her to slip in.

"What is it, Amelia? Mr. Yeary and I are into a good discussion concerning the fate of the country."

"I'm sorry to disturb you, Senator Ashford, but the White House is on the phone."

Brad looked first at Ashford and then at the lovely Amelia who made it a point not to make eye contact with the reporter.

"The White House? Since when did the White House grow lips, a tongue, and a larynx that allows it to talk on the phone?" the senator asked Amelia.

"I mean there's someone on the phone from the White House who says the President wants to speak to you," Amelia replied with a hint of irritation in her voice.

"Oh, okay. It's not the President? I wouldn't want to turn down the President. Just tell them I'm busy now with an important engagement, but I'll return the call shortly."

Brad was impressed. It was the first time in his life that anyone turned down a call from the White House in order to continue an uninterrupted interview with him. He could not recall anyone ever receiving a call from the White House in his presence. He shuffled in his chair and tried to come up with more questions for the senator since he had been so kind as to decline the call from Washington to finish the interview. Although he had asked the main questions he had come to Stratford Place to pose, he followed with three more rather benign queries.

When he concluded and stood to leave, Ashford surprised him by asking him to remain seated. "This may be some news that you might be interested in," the senator said. He picked up the phone from his desk and pushed the numbers to reach 1600 Pennsylvania Avenue.

"Yes, I'll hold," Ashford said and then, putting his hand over the phone transmitter, whispered to Brad, "I guess they're a little pissed that I put the President off, so they put me on hold. The President's busy."

In a minute the senator straightened in his chair. "Good afternoon, Mr. President . . . . What? . . . Yes, you know that was how I put it the other day. I don't seek it. But if you're asking, I will serve my country . . . . Yes, I will come up for a joint announcement." He looked at his desk calendar. "No, sir. I can't go on Friday. Monday would be fine. Sir, when are you going to announce this? I have Brad Yeary of the *Times-Gazette* here in my office now. Is it all right to tell him?" There was a pause as Ashford listened for nearly a minute. "Yes, sir, I will tell him. See you on Monday, Mr. President." He cradled the receiver back onto the pedestal of the phone and turned to Brad.

"The President says he has had nothing but praise since your story broke last night on television and this morning in the newspaper concerning his selection of a Vice President. He said the reaction quickly showed the support that I had for the job. He needs a half hour to call the other two mentioned candidates, and then you are free to 'speculate' that I will be the nominee. He will not announce it until tomorrow and will have no comment on your 'speculation' the remainder of today. I will join him for an official announcement on Monday at the White House."

Brad could not believe his good fortune. Perhaps he was on his way to a Pulitzer for being on top of the story of the Vice Presidency in 1998. From the death of Harrot to the appointment of Ashford, the gods or fates of inkwells and newsprint had taken him in timely fashion to places and people where the news was being made. He determined in his own mind that this story would be solely for the *Times-Gazette*. He would avoid Pinthater's addiction to Channel Five and write the story instead of broadcasting it. He could picture the banner headline in the morning edition:

ASHFORD TO BE NAMED V P PICK TODAY.

To avoid Pinthater's insistence on releasing the news through the broadcast medium as soon as possible, he would hurry back to the Baton Rouge bureau office and begin immediately on an in-depth story about the interview with Ashford and the phone call from President Stephen Teater. He would write and rewrite until after the Ten O'Clock news of Channel Five and then feed it directly by phone line through his word processor to the composition room of the paper just in time to blast all the other stories off the front page by the midnight deadline.

He said his goodbye to Senator Ashford and congratulated him on his appointment. Walking toward his car, Brad began to practice in his mind his acceptance speech for the Pulitzer that he saw gleaming in the not too distant future.

# Nineteen

From his chair at the headquarters of the *Times-Gazette* early the next morning, Ed Pinthater watched the sun rise and the traffic on nearby I-10 thicken with workers on their way into downtown New Orleans. He was filled with mixed emotions.

He smiled at the banner headline and the front page story. Brad had scooped them again. His was the only paper to have the story of Senator Benjamin Ashford being chosen by President Stephen Teater to be the nation's next Vice President. However, one of the media outlets that Brad had beat to the punch was his own Channel Five. Over the years, he had emphasized and even put it into memos and policy statements. All employees of the *Times-Gazette* would give their stories to his Channel Five if the deadlines were such as would permit the television station to be the first to broadcast the news. He reached into his desk for his bottle of Tums. He started with two.

He knew Brad disdained the broadcast medium. He had at times made it a point to override the intent of the publisher's policy by holding a story until it was too late to use on the late news broadcast so that it would appear on the front page instead. Brad was from the old school of journalism. He much preferred the ink and newsprint that allowed an in-depth report over the glitzy television with all of its smiling, hair-sprayed anchors. Had his chief political reporter resorted to one of those tactics again with this story?

Brad was supposed to have interviewed Ashford at three o'clock the previous day. That would have allowed plenty of time for the account to have been broken on the Six O'clock News and certainly by the late night broadcast. If anyone was going to hold a story, it would be the publisher who made the decision and not the reporter-columnist.

He had already tried to reach Yeary at his apartment in New

Orleans to no avail. Brad was probably with Jill Crenshaw in Baton Rouge, but Pinthater did not have her home number. He would deal with Brad later in the day. The reporter might be heading for a Pulitzer Prize, but Ed Pinthater was still the boss. He looked at the paper and then to his desk where there were three notes about calls from the major networks wanting to confirm the facts for their early morning news-talk shows. He smiled again.

COPIES OF THE *Times-Gazette* were also lying on the desks of Al Shanker and John Dobson at their investigation control center in the heart of New Orleans' business district on Poydras Street. Beneath the newspapers were copies of the seating chart for the Superdome and a computerized print-out showing to whom those in charge of the Sugar Bowl had sold or given each ticket in the stadium. In a locked and guarded file cabinet was the enhanced enlargement photo taken from the video tape of the man they believed shot Harrot, along with his friend who wore the Notre Dame jacket.

Since their discovery of the puff of smoke, Shanker, Dobson, and the other top investigators had followed the doings of the two suspects on all the video tapes that were available and had photos made from the tapes. Unfortunately, no video tape that they had access to ever showed the men for more than a few seconds at a time. They had them on tape for a total of thirty seconds over the three hours that they were in the Superdome.

But, they did possess a tape segment that showed the man in the Alabama sweater had shed his overcoat after half-time. Among ten torn and discarded coats that were found in garbage cans in a sweep for evidence after the game, they believed they had found the one worn by the shooter. They had already sent it to the lab for a thorough examination, along with copies of the photos for comparison to all mug shots in their files.

Dobson voiced the opinion that their tape of the actual shooting was more significant than the Zapruder film of the Kennedy assassination since it showed the assassin rather than just the victim.

When Dobson and Shanker arrived at seven-thirty, they sat across from each other and briefly looked at the newspapers. They drank coffee before turning to the job at hand—running down who had the tickets for the seats occupied by the assassins.

"This is interesting," Shanker said. He pointed to the story about Ashford. "That Brad Yeary is really on top of everything that's happening. I didn't think Ashford had a chance of being Teater's choice. Of course, he didn't ask me."

"Yeary was there at the Superdome when Harrot was shot, wasn't he?"

"Sure was. Had an interview with Harrot at halftime. I was

in the room. Seems to be a nice guy."

"Nobody's a nice guy until we find out who did this," Dobson said. He put down the paper and turned to his list of tickets. "Everybody who was on that west side of the stadium is a suspect until we eliminate them. We can't get tied completely into the idea the video shows the shooter for sure until we find the gun and the man who held it. That slight puff of smoke could just be a decoy to distract us from the real assassin."

Shanker looked at Dobson and then pointed to the seating chart. "But, John, you were sitting right here in Section 336. According to what you just said, you're a suspect. That section is right above where you saw the guy with the overcoat and Alabama sweater that you were so overjoyed about a few days ago." Shanker smiled and pushed the seating diagram over to Dobson.

Dobson pushed it aside and looked at the computer list of names and companies buying or receiving the tickets in the mid-field area. "The key word in what I said, Al, was *eliminate.* I hope I've been eliminated as a suspect. But very few others on that side of the field have been."

"That's true," Shanker said. He laid down his copy of the newspaper.

"By the way, Al, why was Harrot allowed to parade in front of seventy-five thousand people anyway? I thought your agency always tried to keep down the possible exposure of the ones you guarded. Putting a V P at mid-field with good elevated shooting angles doesn't make a lot of sense." He looked up as he continued to turn the pages of names and seat locations.

"I was against it. But it came down from the top. We had never had a serious attempt on a Vice President, so the chief let it go. It was against policy."

"Against policy?"

"Yeah, it never would've occurred with the President. But Steinheitz told the chief that it was a special request from the President."

"You're saying that the President's chief of staff asked the head of the Secret Service to by-pass your normal policy for this event?"

"Right. We hadn't had any threats against Harrot. Never in U.S. history had a Vice President been assassinated. The chief didn't raise a big fuss about it. Just assumed that everything would go smooth."

Dobson stared at the name of the one who originally had the ticket to the seat where they observed the person they believed to have shot Harrot. "Look at this, Al." Dobson circled the name and seat number assignments with a yellow highlighter pen. "Whose name is that?"

Shanker squinted. "It says J. Crenshaw."

"Hell, yes! That's State Senator Jill Crenshaw. She was given twelve seats in Section 264, and our shooter winds up in one of those prime seats."

Shanker rubbed his chin. "Jill Crenshaw. Who is she? A state senator you say?"

Dobson pushed a button on his top monitor to rewind the tape of Harrot falling to the ground.

"Al, my friend, remember the woman you pushed away from Harrot while he was lying on the ground at mid-field?"

"Yeah, I remember some woman in the official delegation kneeling over Harrot right before I got to him. Was that this Jill Crenshaw?"

Dobson rolled the tape that showed the shocked state senator bending down to comfort the fallen Vice President. "That's her right there. See, she's putting her hand on his chest and talking to him until you get there." He stopped the tape as it rolled to where Shanker, Crenshaw, and Harrot were all together for the frozen moment of time.

"So, there's a strange coincidence. She has the tickets to the seats originally that the shooter turns up in, and she's the first to get to Harrot?"

"Well, it's either strange or planned. No one else noticed that Harrot had fallen until a little later. She was the first. Governor Johnson was between her and Harrot, but she got to him first. It was like she was expecting it to happen, wouldn't you say?"

"No. I wouldn't say that yet. It may be that she was just more aware of what was going on around her while the men were staring into the crowd and smiling for the television audience."

"Maybe. But think about this. You're not a local so you probably don't know it's well documented that Jill Crenshaw and Brad Yeary are very close. They're romantically involved. It's no secret."

"The senator and the reporter are a couple?"

"Yeah, you could put it that way."

"So?"

"So, remember that everyone is a suspect until we eliminate them. Where was Brad Yeary when Harrot was shot?"

"I don't know," Shanker said, "but I bet you're going to tell me."

Dobson rolled another tape that showed a view from ground level from behind Harrot looking toward the west stands. He stopped it when it showed Brad Yeary and Liz Arzenhoff standing next to each other right before the shot was fired.

"Look at this," Dobson said. He pulled out an enlarged photograph from his desk drawer that had been taken from above and behind the shooter. A red dot had been placed on the location of the assassin, a blue dot on the figure of Harrot in the distance, and a yellow dot on a figure on the sideline.

"What is it?" Shanker asked.

"There's a straight line between the shooter and Harrot."

"Of course. A straight line can be drawn between any two points. I learned that in ninth-grade geometry."

"Yeah, but this straight line goes right over the head of Brad Yeary. He was below but in the plane of fire."

"So, what does that prove?"

"Nothing, really. It's either coincidence or else he's helping the shooter line up for the shot. He could be providing a reference point for the target."

"You must've been checking that theory out for some time, John. What makes you suspect Yeary?"

"What you said that first night. He had a bloody handkerchief. Where'd he get it? None of the tapes or photos show anyone putting a handkerchief to Harrot. Was it really Harrot's blood or just a prop he used to get through to you?"

Shanker bristled momentarily. He was certain the handkerchief contained the blood of Harrot just like Brad said, but he had no way to prove it. He didn't take the cloth from the reporter.

"Look, Al," Dobson continued, "I'm not saying it's your fault. But how could Yeary know that Harrot had been shot? Harrot's coat had not even been opened by the time you got to him? How big was the splotch of blood when you first looked?"

Shanker put his thumbs and middle fingers of both hands together making a rough circle. "About that size."

"And you didn't tell anyone that Harrot had been shot, did you?"

"No, just the chief of security and a captain on the police force. The paramedics knew it, but they were quarantined as soon as we got to the hospital. They couldn't have told anyone."

"So, seventy-two odd thousand in the Superdome and a national television audience believe that Harrot has only passed out. But Brad Yeary knows he's been shot. How? Unless he was in on the conspiracy."

Dobson sat silent for a minute while Shanker considered the prospect that Brad was one of the assassins, and he had entered into an agreement with the reporter to keep Yeary informed on the progress of the investigation. Shanker had not told Dobson or anyone else of that little deal.

"I don't like that word—*conspiracy*—and what it means. John, you're saying that it wasn't a lone, crazy gunner, but someone or ones with a plan who worked together?" Shanker closed his eyes and leaned his head back. He couldn't believe that Yeary was in on the killing, but as Dobson had just pointed out, there were some odd coincidences and unexplained knowledge on the part of the reporter.

"Unfortunately, we already know there was more than one person involved. That guy with the Notre Dame jacket standing next to the shooter had to know. They left together. They were talking in the little bit of tape that we have. There were some brains behind this." He paused while they both thought through the sequence of events that fateful evening.

"Al, the more I think about how accurate that gun was, the more I think it must have been laser-guided or something like that. To do that, a little tag of some kind had to be placed on the victim that would have reflected the laser beam that homed in on his torso. That raises two questions that I will let you ponder. Who saw Harrot and interviewed him during halftime? And who reached down to his suit coat exactly at the point of impact of the bullet when he fell?"

Al Shanker didn't answer either question aloud, but his eyes betrayed him.

"That's right." Dobson smiled and looked into the concerned eyes of Shanker.

"So you think that Yeary may have put a target on Harrot at half-time and Crenshaw took it off immediately following the shooting? That sounds crazy and outlandish to tell you the truth, John."

"I know it does, but we're dealing with a very sophisticated assassination. It didn't have to be very big, as small as a straight pin would have done it. It's just a possibility. We don't need to get locked in on this theory, but we need to check it out. Need to get that handkerchief."

Shanker nodded his head slowly. "What would be the motive? Why would Brad Yeary and Jill Crenshaw do this?"

Dobson picked up his copy of the *Times-Gazette* and laid it in front of Shanker. "Look at all the stories and publicity that Yeary has received since the assassination. His accounts have been on all the networks. He's had an interview with the President—which is very scary—and he's being mentioned as a possible Pulitzer Prize winner for his reporting."

"Yeah, but would anyone kill a Vice President to accomplish that?"

Dobson shrugged his shoulders. "Who knows? About ten years ago a woman reporter for one of the Washington papers faked a whole series of stories to win the Pulitzer. Those journalists have no ethics. And one like Brad Yeary might go off anytime and do something really crazy."

"But then you have Jill Crenshaw. What's her motive? It couldn't be that she liked this guy, Yeary, could it?"

Dobson pointed to a short side-bar story on the front of the paper written by another reporter for the *Times-Gazette* near Brad's account of Ashford's probably becoming the next Vice President. Shanker read it.

"Jill Crenshaw could be named to take Ashford's seat in the Senate when he's confirmed as Vice President?"

"Yep. That's it, Al."

"That's really too much," Shanker responded. He tossed the paper down on the floor. "She'd have had to know that Ashford would be appointed Vice President and that the Governor would appoint her as senator to believe that theory. That's impossible. No one could know that."

"Now wait a minute, Al. It's not as far-fetched as it sounds. Crenshaw is in tight with the governor. He helped her to be Speaker of the State Senate. He's sort of like a father figure to her. It's very likely that he would've appointed her to any vacancy that would've helped her political career. She knew that. So, all that was left was to know that Ashford was likely to fill the Vice Presidential vacancy if it came along. And once you consider Ashford, he does seem a logical choice for President Teater. He's from the South. He's not controversial. That's the first rule of selecting Vice Presidents: 'Choose someone who won't hurt the ticket.'"

Shanker continued to shake his head. "I just don't see it, John. I'm sorry, but I just don't see it."

"Well, it may not be. But I tell you what we need to do. We need to send a couple of agents over to the paper and at least ask for that bloody handkerchief. Just tell Yeary we'd like to have it examined. See if he'll give it to us. Ask him how he got a handkerchief with Harrot's blood on it. Then send another pair of agents up to Senator Crenshaw's office and see if they can account for the ones who received those tickets in Section 264. That'll give them a chance to explain the weird coincidences. Or it may start them to worrying if they're involved. And that's what we need. A break. Someone to get scared and start talking. What do you think about that?"

"Yeah, that's a good idea, but I think we're barking up the wrong tree in speculating Yeary and Crenshaw had anything to do with this." He picked the paper back up from the floor and looked at the by-line of Brad Yeary on the lead story. He shook his head.

"Oh, another thing, Al. I think that until we eliminate Yeary as a suspect, we need to let all the agencies know not to disclose any information to him or respond to any of his inquiries. What do you think?"

Shanker could feel his face flushing as he thought back to his pact with Yeary to give him background information on a non-attributive basis. Did his FBI friend know about that? Was he testing him to see what his reaction would be? "Sure. I guess you're right, John.

You're the boss on this. I'm just an observer. Yeary might suspect something, though, if you do that. He's a very bright guy."

"Maybe." Dobson nodded.

Dobson's telephone buzzed. "Yes. Okay, I'll hold." He put his hand over the phone and turned toward Shanker, "It's the lab at head-quarters. They have a report on the coat we sent up that we think came from the shooter." He turned back to the phone and listened.

"You're sure? Good. Send it to me on our secure fax as soon as you can." He hung up and turned back to Shanker. "Gunpowder residue on the sleeve of the coat, especially on the inside lining. They also found several hairs, some shed skin cells, and a bit of dried perspiration they can type with DNA testing. They'll run that through a comparison with every DNA screen in our files. Of course, there's not much chance of the shooter being in our files, but we might get lucky. Anyway, now we're sure we have our shooter on tape. If we can find him, he'll lead us to the others. I hope he didn't make it out of the country." Dobson smiled, and after a moment Shanker joined him. They shook hands, secure in the thought of a break in the case.

Another agent interrupted their small celebration. "Mr. Dobson, the sheriff of Plaquemines Parish wants to leave something with us, but he'll only leave it with the one in charge. Can you see him?"

"The sheriff of where? What's he got? Why can't he leave it with you?"

"He says it's urgent. He won't say what it is. Plaquemines Parish is south of here. It goes all the way to where the Mississippi empties into the Gulf. Should I send him away, or do you want to see him?"

Dobson shook his head. "Oh, hell. Tell him to wait just a minute. I'll see him as soon as I make a phone call or two."

Dobson found the sheriff patiently waiting in the main reception area near the elevator. He was holding a large manilla envelope. "Sir, I'm Sheriff Hickey, Plaquemines Parish, Pointe-a-la-Hache, the southern most parish in Louisiana." He extended his free right hand. He held the envelope and his hat beneath his left.

"John Dobson, Agent-in-charge, FBI. Good to meet you, Sheriff. What can I do for you?"

"Well, sir," the sheriff began and cast glances at all the other people in the room, "I have something in this envelope that you might be interested in."

"What is it?"

"A letter."

"A letter from whom? And to whom?"

"No, sir. Not a letter. A letter *A*."

"What the hell is a letter *A*?"

"Sir, if I could see you in private, I can explain."

Dobson led him into a small conference room just off the main reception area where there were a table and four chairs. They sat across from each other as the sheriff laid the envelope in the middle of the table and opened it. He pulled out a plastic-bag covered piece of cloth.

"Sir, an explosion of a boat was reported to us on the morning of January second. An old fisherman from Venice was on the Mississippi about six that morning. He said a high-powered sport boat came zooming down the river and not a quarter mile past him exploded into a thousand pieces. By the time he got there, he could only find this piece of cloth."

Dobson picked up the sealed plastic and turned it over. He looked closely at the large red A and the attached piece of clothing. "Did you identify the victims?"

"No, sir. We've yet to find one piece of the boat. Must've all been washed out to the Gulf. No bodies. No body parts. No I D of the boat. No one has reported a boat missing that would fit the description, and no one has reported any person missing who could have been on that boat."

"Why did you bring this to me then?" Dobson asked, and then it clicked. He had looked at so many Alabama fans in the hundreds of yards of tape that he had watched over and over during the past two weeks that he had gotten to the point he thought almost everyone wore a large A sewn to his sweater. The shooter? The shooter's sweater? he asked himself.

"I saw on our inquiry sheet that the FBI was looking for a person wearing an Alabama sweater in connection with the Vice President's assassination. I just saw it yesterday. So I thought I would turn this over to you for examination. I have no need for it unless we turn something else up. But I need you to sign for it so that I can give an accounting if anything ever comes up." The sheriff reached into his coat pocket and retrieved a small receipt paper which he handed to Dobson. Dobson signed.

"Sheriff, I want to send a team of our people down to look at the place where the boat exploded. We may be able to find something where you couldn't. We have more resources."

As soon as the sheriff left, Dobson told Shanker of the discovery and sent the package on its way to the lab. However, secretly he hoped that this was not the crimson A that he had been looking at for over a week now on the assassin. He needed a live murderer to arrest and make the country happy.

# Twenty

T he clean white Volvo stopped in the circular drive directly behind the limousine used by Governor Hugh Johnson for official business. Jill Crenshaw had been to the governor's mansion hundreds of times during her ten years in the state senate, and most of the time she enjoyed it. Her hand trembled slightly as she removed the key from the ignition. She was about to talk to "Papa Hugh" concerning the possible vacancy in the U.S. Senate.

The mansion was an imposing structure built in Greek Revival style in 1963 during the governorship of Jimmy Davis. Three stories plus a basement, the plantation-appearing house was surrounded on three sides by doric columns and a wide porch. Dark green shutters on brick painted white gave it the appearance of being smaller than it was. It served both as a residence for the governor and his family and a working office with staff when he wasn't at the Capitol a half mile away.

The pleasant surroundings of lake, swimming pool, and tennis courts belied the fact that this was a place of work and decision making. Most of the legislative deals during her career had been hammered out in the study of Governor Hugh Johnson, and arm twisting, however gentle, had been accomplished in the dining room and kitchen of the mansion.

Jill Crenshaw loved it. She secretly envied the residence. More than once as she had walked through the living area, she had

imagined how she would furnish and rearrange things when she became governor. *When she became governor.* She stepped to the front
door and was greeted by the guard. Now she was here to discuss being
a senator rather than the job she had planned for and dreamed about.
The guard checked his entry list just inside the foyer where he had a
little office from which he could monitor all the surveillance cameras
that constantly scanned the grounds.

She stood there on the Italian marble floor and looked straight
ahead toward the back of the house where the semi-circular staircase
swept upward to the main living quarters. There, standing like a
sentry near the stairway, was the stuffed grizzly bear that had been
left by a preceding governor who fancied himself to be "the great white
hunter." That would be the first thing she would remove. She could
not imagine how anyone could shoot such a lovely creature for sport.
It was a disgrace. She had repeatedly asked Governor Johnson why
he kept it.

"Hell, no one will take it. Ed knew that when he left," he had
told her. She would have at least given it a decent burial. The guard
cleared her on the list and picked up his can of beany-weenies to finish. He nodded for her to go in.

Governor Johnson, with rolled-up shirt sleeves, was down the
stairs and standing beside the big grizzly before Jill was halfway there.

"Let me look at you," the governor said. He spread his arms
and admired the woman he treated as a daughter. "My, my, Jill,
you're beautiful today. What color do you call that dress?" he asked as
he embraced her.

"Navy."

"Yeah, navy blue. I like that gold chain too. Brad buy that for
you?"

"No," she said and separated herself from his bit longer than
normal bear hug. "You don't hug everyone like that do you, Papa?"

"No, Jill, just the pretty ones like you," he said. He laid the
much chewed remains of his cigar in a tall standing ashtray near the
bear. "But you sure do look good."

"I didn't come here to be ogled." She smiled and gently patted
the briefcase she was carrying. "I came to talk to you about some
important business." She turned and walked toward the stairs and his
second floor study. "By the way, you should get rid of that bear. It's
disgusting."

Governor Johnson patted the bear on the head as he walked
by. "I know it. I asked Ed to take it back, but he says he doesn't have
room for it. By the way, just what does 'ogle' mean?"

She looked back over her shoulder. "Flirting. Lascivious looking."

"It's no fair to define one word with a bigger word. Is it okay for that Brad Yeary to ogle you?"

"I wish he would."

In his small study the governor invited Jill to take a seat in front of his desk. Off to the left, through an open door and down the hallway, a secretary and members of his staff were busy answering phones and taking messages between offices. He picked up the phone and pushed the button for his secretary. "I'm still unavailable for calls. Keep a list of the ones calling and the names of the ones they're recommending. And close my door. I'm with Jill Crenshaw and we may get a little rowdy." He winked at Jill who ignored him but smiled at the secretary who eased the door closed.

"See this paper, Jill? It's caused me a hundred calls already today." He held the front section of the *Times-Gazette* high in his left hand and thumped the story about Ashford with the back of his right index finger. "I'm putting everybody on hold. Good thing you made your appointment with me yesterday."

"I was just thinking ahead."

"Where is that feller of yours anyway? He's been raising a hell of a dust storm here lately."

Jill looked at her watch. "Right now he should be leaving my apartment to go back down to New Orleans. He's supposed to look up an old friend and source down there later today."

"Yeah? Is he going to have another bombshell of a story tomorrow?"

"Probably not. He likes to space them out. Gives people more time to absorb everything."

"Well, he could have one if you tell him what I'm going to tell you." He took another cigar from the top drawer of his desk, unwrapped the cellophane covering, bit off the end of the thick, greenish-brown tobacco rod, and clamped down on it with his right molars.

"What's that, Governor?"

He took a sheet of paper from his desk and slid it across to her. She looked at the single paragraph and his signature at the bottom. She read it slowly, then looked up at Hugh Johnson with eyes that were about to tear up, half from happiness and half from fear.

It was simply stated. The governor had typed it himself. It was obvious. There was one misspelled word and two typos. But it made its point. He had committed to appoint her to the vacant senate seat if Ashford was appointed and confirmed as Vice President. It bore the governor's signature in large John Hancock script.

"You didn't have to do this," Jill said. She looked back down and read it again as it fluttered slightly in her trembling hand. "I was coming to talk to you today about that, but you took all the fun out of it. I was going to be my most persuasive. I had my briefcase chocked full of good, sound reasons why you could do this. Now it's all a waste," she said and drew her briefcase up to the vacant chair beside her.

"Damn, Jill, I had to. Look at this list of calls." He pointed to a two-page typed list of names and phone numbers with notes beside each. "Ever since that story hit the streets, anyone who thought he or she had any influence at all has been calling, recommending, begging, threatening, whatever—to get their favorite appointed. I didn't want to have to go through that. I'm an old man. I'm about to retire after this term. I can do what I damn well please and, I may add, for once what I feel is best for the State of Louisiana. And that is to appoint you to the Senate. Besides, I didn't forget that I had put that bug in your ear a week or so ago anyway. So, this is my promise in writing."

"I'm flattered, Governor. But I don't need your promise in writing. Your word is good enough for me."

"Hell, I know that. It wasn't for you. It was for me. Now, I can tell everyone that I have made a written commitment. If it wasn't in writing, some of these 'statesmen' would tell me I could change my mind and nobody would ever know. I don't need that. You're the best for the job. You've worked hard. You're a good legislator—tough and honest. That's what Washington needs. Don't let me down. Don't let them change you." He took the cigar from his mouth and wiped a bit of moisture from the corner of his eye.

Jill breathed deeply. She sat there and tried to take it in. For so many years she had wanted to be governor. Now she had within her grasp a seat in the U.S. Senate and she was afraid to say yes.

"I understand the President is going to announce it officially later today to the rest of the media and have a joint announcement on Monday with Ashford at the White House. At least that's what your friend says in this story." He pushed the paper aside and leaned across the desk. "I'll need your final answer by the time of their meeting on Monday so I can get this out of the way as soon as it's official. I don't need this hanging over my head."

Now that it had finally arrived, Jill sat stunned. She didn't know whether to take the sure senate seat or wait and run for governor a year away when Papa stepped down and into retirement. "What do you think my chances would be of running for governor when you retire?"

Governor Johnson shook his head. "I don't know. You'd make a good one. But to run without a statewide base is very risky. There'll be all kinds of money getting behind candidates just as soon as they know that I'm not running again. A year is a lifetime in politics. Matter of fact, two days or two minutes often qualify as a lifetime. I know you've always wanted to be governor, but I don't see how you can give up this opportunity to be a U.S. Senator. Many governors would change places to be in Washington. You'll have a big staff, high visibility as the first woman senator from our state, and an ability to build a statewide base over the next two years. Take it. Then decide whether to run for governor or for election to the senate in the next election. That would be my advice."

"I'll have to talk to Brad. We're very close, you know. He could spend as much time in Washington as he does now in Baton Rouge if I were there. But I need his advice. He won't mention this in any of his stories. We have a pact. He doesn't write about me, and I don't ask him how to vote on issues."

The governor smiled. "I can see how the latter is very wise, but he could help you in his writing. And it's okay with me for him to break this story. He's hot right now."

"No. I'll tell him, but you'll never see a word about it in the paper from him. Another reporter is assigned to me. Brad says it's against his media ethics to be romantically involved with me and write about me. People would see it as improper promotion."

Governor Johnson leaned back in his chair and laughed. When he recovered he looked Jill in the eye, "That's a new one. Media Ethics. Isn't that what you intellectual people term an ox that's a moron?"

Jill grinned. "An *oxymoron*. A contradiction in terms like a 'holy war' or 'military intelligence.' But for Brad it's not. He's very serious about ethics. He preaches it to me all the time."

"Yeah, well we once had a House Ethics Committee that turned out pure bull legislative proposals that meant absolutely nothing. That's why I always giggle when I hear the term applied to a group who I know has very little."

Jill folded the paper that Governor Johnson had presented her and put it in her briefcase. She stood to leave. "Thank you, Governor, for your confidence, and especially for your friendship. I'll tell you my decision by this time on Monday. I need to talk with Brad."

Governor Hugh Johnson came around his desk and extended his hand. Jill almost took it but then said goodbye to her friend and mentor with a hug instead.

# Twenty–one

T wo miles separated the apartment of Brad Yeary and the home of Papa Legba. But in culture and affluence the two areas of inner New Orleans were divided by more like two centuries.

Brad's apartment squatted on the edge of the French Quarter at the corner of Burgundy and Esplanade. Bourbon was two blocks over but with the heart of its loud music and raunchy show area another eight blocks toward the central business district. He occupied the entire second floor of a remodeled, ornate home that was over a hundred and fifty years old. The deep red brick of the house assumed the same color as the name of the street. Black wrought-iron railing encased a balcony that swept around the front and side of the twenty by forty-five foot dimensions of the building.

Jill had helped him in placement of hanging and pedestal pots of flowers, vines, and shrubbery around the whole outside area adding verdancy and brightness to the otherwise dark hues. He thought it a bit much, and if the plants had depended on him for water and nourishment, they would have died a slow death. Black, functional shutters stood like sentries on both sides of each window and door to the balcony with each narrow, floor-to-ceiling window trimmed in nice off-white. The third floor of the structure was unoccupied, and the landlady allowed Brad ample storage space there. The only problem with

1001 Burgundy was that he had to contend with tourists for street-side parking.

Brad eased into his Ford and out onto the street. Burgundy crossed Esplanade while Bourbon ended there. Across Elysian Fields, a street whose name may have been appropriate when given but now was as ironic as any, Burgundy continued its sweep to the right as it remained parallel with the Mississippi a half mile to the east.

As in many of America's cities, the railroad tracks literally severed the haves from the have-nots. It was true in New Orleans. Burgundy changed from a street full of trendy, wrought-iron balconied homes stacked like dominoes on their sides to run-down, dilapidated, one and two-story houses. Plastic sheeting covered broken windows. These houses primary color was the grayish-white of paint peeling from wooden board siding that buckled and warped at many places.

Few tourists saw this side of town. They stayed in the French Quarter, the downtown business district, and the Garden District where Tulane and Loyola Universities sat like jewels among green and luscious trees and plants. Tourists viewed the Southern colonial homes with leaded-glass windows and crystal chandeliers from the St. Charles Trolley.

Outsiders who drove into this area had to know their business. It wasn't a place to wander after dark. The spirits of the dead weren't the problem; it was the walking zombies whose spirits had been taken.

Even Brad, who feared little after ten years on the police beat and an equal amount of time covering politics for the *Times-Gazette,* did not go aimlessly and without invitation down this end of Burgundy. Here junked cars sat like large, rusty mushrooms in small yards and the smell of expensive wine was replaced by that of cheap beer, open sewage, and rotting fruit.

He parked, as everyone else did, on the sidewalk. He checked the inside of his car to be sure nothing that appeared to be of value lay in sight. He didn't lock the door as he stepped out. It was no use. If they wanted in, they would get in. Might as well make it convenient.

A rusty, waist-high chain-link fence separated Papa Legba's small yard from the sidewalk. The squeaky metal gate had no lock. Unlike his neighbors on either side who had pit bulldogs tethered to metal stakes that allowed them free range of their entranceways, the doctor of voodoo had no dog, no alarm, no gun. He thought the spirits protected him. But better than that, all the young toughs in the neighborhood believed it too. No one bothered the old man. They were afraid of the spells that he could cast or the voodoo dolls they had heard about but not seen.

He let them believe it. It hurt nothing and gave him a special power and protection in the neighborhood. In reality, his only equipment was an old leather bag full of yellowed knuckle and small joint bones mainly of wild swine, a few candles that he burned more for the benefit of those in attendance than for himself, and a powerful mind and concentration. Many had passed out in his presence as he stared through them. They became hypnotized by his eyes and their lack of movement. Then there were the flickers of fire that could be seen burning in their depths.

Brad had met Papa his first year on the police beat when a vicious murder brought him to Papa's domain. A Creole woman who did business in the Quarter was killed. That was common enough. But the brutality that was displayed upon her body was not. She had been beheaded and her abdomen gutted. When her nude body was found lying on the hood of a car two blocks from Papa Legba's house, two candles cast an eerie light on her face while her nostrils served as candle holders. Her severed head lay staring skyward in the pit of her belly with her hands and arms positioned to appear as though they were holding it.

Papa Legba gave Brad the information that allowed him to write about the significance of the ritualistic carving and severing. Papa wanted no story attributed to him, but he thought the murder unnecessary and degrading to his religion. It was the work of a group of young gang members who thought they knew voodoo after reading a bit, but who Papa thought were using it for the wrong purposes. They did not honor their ancestors but rather debased them by their actions. He didn't need that kind of sordid competition and turned them in.

Over the years, Papa and Brad achieved a friendship of sorts. They saw each other rarely. But Brad would take special pains to visit the old man at odd times when he didn't need anything. They would sit during those infrequent occasions and talk about the old days and where they each had been.

Time would pass. Hours seemed like minutes. Brad would tell about being a son of a shoe salesman in the shrimping village of Lafitte. He would reminisce about how he liked to go on his friends' boats to the barrier islands in the Gulf and help raise up the nets full of brown or white shrimp. There they would stay on the boat for days at a time until the belly of the hull was full of a ton or more of the sea crustaceans that were so prized in the restaurants of New Orleans.

Papa would respond with stories of the days long ago when he was a barge hand and worked all the Mississippi between St. Louis and New Orleans. He had talked with every old person in his family and slowly learned about the whispered religion of Africa and the Caribbean—voodoo. He had learned over many years and at many ports that some were fakes and some had the real power. They gave him a token of it. It wasn't until Papa's right foot was severed between the hard steel of two barges scraping together that he went into the mystical, black religion of voodoo as a permanent priest. Among the animal knuckles and wild pig bones that he kept in the ancient leather bag were his own toe bones from his lost right foot. Only he knew them from the other yellowed, smooth joints.

This visit was at the invitation of Papa Legba. The talks with the President and Senator Ashford had intervened between the time Papa left the message and now, but Brad knew it would be worthwhile to make the trip. He wasn't sure what the voodoo doctor wanted, but whatever it was would not be a waste. Only four days had passed since he received the message, so Papa should not be too upset with him. He opened the rusty gate and stepped through.

He knew not to knock on the door but to go around to the rear of the house. There Papa held sanctuary on the floor of his small back porch where he shared space with an ancient washing machine. The yard was bare from use by those who would come, remove their shoes, and sit to listen to their spiritual leader speak to them from his pulpit of the barely raised wooden floor. He would sit in a colorful silk robe and a black turban wrapped around the crown of his head. The robe was the one luxury that the voodoo doctor allowed himself, as much to show the world that it was not a totally dark religion as for his own personal comfort.

Papa sat cross-legged with the robe flowing over his legs and foot. He disdained years before the prospect of having a prosthesis for his missing foot, and so delivered his lectures or instructions from a seated position with his back against a supporting post of the porch. His house was in no better repair than the others in the neighborhood. It was not for money that he gave audience but because this gift had passed into him from his ancestors and it was his destiny. To profit from it would be sinful.

It was late afternoon and he was staring out as though in a trance when Brad took off his shoes, came close, and sat in front of him. Brad waited to see if Papa acknowledged his presence by a nod, eye movement, or word. No one was to speak until he was recognized by Papa. For five minutes he sat there until Papa relaxed his eyes from whatever vision he was in and settled them on Brad.

"You have come. Late, but you have come."

"Yes, I got your message. But I've been busy."

"They tell me. Talk with the Big Man and the Senator."

Brad nodded. The old man was so trance-like and meditative, and he had the same effect on those who looked into his eyes. They were pale blue eyes that were probably now cataract impaired as far as sight but not as far as vision. They sat in a kingly head beneath a prominent brow bone that served as a canopy of sorts and shaded the deeply-set eyes. Short, crinkly white hair sat in tufts all around his head. His features were large. His ears and nose appeared especially

big as they adorned a lean face with the sunken jaws of a man of
eighty-five whose diet was not the best.

Brad was most amazed, though, at the size of Papa's hands.
His own were dwarfed by them. The large black hands with lighter
palms could have been those of a basketball player in modern times.
Fifteen years ago, Papa showed Brad how he could pick up and palm
a watermelon in each of his giant hands. They were especially impressive when they reached into the musky leather bag, cradled the knuckles and toe joints, and then rolled the bones onto the wood porch in
front of his admirers to discern from the position of the joints what
would be the course of events.

"I've been told that you have written much about the killing,"
Papa Legba said and leaned slightly toward Brad.

"Yes. Considerably."

"Do you know who killed him?"

"No. Do you?"

"I don't, but I believe Harrot does. And he wants to tell me,"
Papa said and rubbed his hands together as though to warm them.

Brad thought the assassination of Vice President Harrot would
have been out of the scope of Papa Legba and had not considered him
a source. But now, he paid more attention. Papa had his contacts
throughout all of the city, and maybe he had heard something.

"How do you think Harrot can tell you? And what makes you
think he wants to?"

"The night he was killed I was sitting here. Just looking at the
stars. All of a sudden I had a pain right here." He pointed to the middle of his chest below his breastbone. "It was a terrible burning that
hit and then spread like an explosion to all of my belly."

Brad leaned forward. "Point to where you first felt the pain
again, Papa." Papa placed a forefinger on the exact location where
Brad had witnessed the hole in Harrot as he lay on the gurney at
Bellevue Hospital. The precise point of the entry wound had not been
released. It had only been described as a chest wound.

"At first I thought it was just some bad shrimp," Papa said and
smiled. "But I have seen the face of Harrot in visions since that night.
It's him. But I can't get him to speak. I'm missing something. He will
tell me something if I can connect."

"What do you need?"

"Clothing, a shoe, a tie, some writing of Harrot's that I could
touch. Anything that could help me link up. He's a man like me. I
see me in him. I want to talk with him, but now his mouth is sealed."

They sat looking at each other for a time. Where could Brad
get any clothing of Harrot's? The FBI had body tissue stored away
some place, but they would not release any of that to a voodoo doctor.
Then it hit him.

"Blood! Blood! I have Harrot's blood on a handkerchief. How is dried blood?"

"Not as good as wet blood. But very good. Blood courses through every part of the body—heart, brain, tongue. You give me the blood-soaked rag, and I will talk to Harrot. Where is it?"

"Locked in the glove compartment of my car around front."

Papa Legba shook his head. "It's not safe to leave valuables in cars in this neighborhood." He reached behind him and withdrew a small bone that appeared to be a chicken leg bone from a box. "Go see if the handkerchief is still there. Bring it back if it is. Put this bone on the top of your car. It is a sign that your car is protected by the spirits that Papa Legba controls."

Brad took it softly into his hands not knowing whether he was holding a bone of one of Papa Legba's ancestors. "What kind of bone is this?" he asked as he got to his feet.

"Colonel Sanders. Chicken leg bone. It don't make no difference, though. The young punks in this neighborhood won't mess with it." Papa smiled while Brad put his shoes on.

Two young black men were sitting on the hood of his car when he reached the street and two more were on the front seat. "Pardon me, guys, Papa Legba told me to put this bone on the roof of my car and get something out of the glove compartment for him." The youths scrambled from the car and sprinted toward a distant house.

"This is good," Papa said. He closed his eyes and rubbed the blood-smeared cloth between his fingers. "This is good, Brad. I think I will connect. Of course, not in your presence. But later. Can you leave this with me? I will care for it."

Brad nodded. It was as safe with Papa Legba as if it had been insured by Lloyds of London.

"I'll reach you after I've talked with Harrot. It may take a while, but I'll let you know. It will be interesting to see how you write a story explaining that Harrot told you who shot him." Papa smiled again as Brad left.

Brad was thinking the same thing.

# Twenty-two

J ill drove straight from the Governor's Mansion to Brad's apartment to share the good news. She wanted his blessing on her becoming the next U.S. Senator from Louisiana. He wasn't there when she arrived. So, she let herself in, watered the many pots of plants on the balcony, and settled into the recliner for a nap.

Brad's elation at the day's events was not even sullied by the fact that tourists had once again taken all of the parking spots on the block. He had the top story in the nation, and he had a voodoo doctor who said he would be communicating with Harrot. What the heck? He had a few more questions to ask Harrot himself. A seance wouldn't be a bad idea. He would handle it like the politicians did. The communication would be on *deep background.*

The only disappointing development for him was Jill. If the governor appointed her to the Senate, Brad would have to make some decisions. He did not want to share her with the burden of Washington where her time would be eaten up with trivia. Her energy would be sapped by all the meetings and hearings. He was selfish. He knew it. He wanted her energy. He wanted to sit and talk with her, to walk along the bank of the Mississippi as the sun set gloriously across the other bank. He wanted to lie in her arms with the windows open and listen to katydids and the bellow of an alligator in the distance with the odor of magnolia blossoms drifting in from the plantations. He didn't want to share. That was a lesson he had not learned well in kindergarten.

Jill's sleep had been light and sporadic. She sat bolt upright when Brad opened the door. They embraced. "Where have you been?"

"With Papa Legba," he said and laid his jacket across a chair. "And where have you been."

"With Papa Hugh." She smiled. "Isn't it wonderful that we both have 'Papas' like Legba and Hugh?"

He nodded and sat down. "Yeah, I guess they serve the same purpose for us. Someone we can turn to for information and reassurance."

"Oh, much more than that. Papa Hugh has led me to become a mature leader in the political realm. And Papa Legba has helped you to become one of the top reporters in the country."

"One of the top?" Brad wrinkled his brow. "*The* top. I'm convinced. This story has led me to the top—at least for the first two weeks of the year."

Jill sat on the arm of his chair and put her arms around his shoulders. "I've got some great news and a hard decision to make."

She unfolded the sheet of paper that the governor had given her and handed it to Brad. There it was in black and white. The words that he feared. Jill had the word of the governor for the appointment. The deal was sealed.

Brad read it, folded it back up, and handed it to Jill without comment and, he hoped, without a change of expression that would betray his feelings. How could they maintain a relationship with her permanently in Washington? Yes, he could spend more time there—two or three days a week if he pushed it. But it wouldn't be the same.

Washington in the spring was glorious, with the cherry blossoms and all the flowers and plants that were guarded and cared for by public money, but the other times of the year were horrible. The stifling heat of summer was as bad as Louisiana but without the attractiveness of the Pelican State. It was then just a government town with busloads of school children and senior citizens walking around the monuments and into the White House with clothes more fit for the beach than to view the national shrines. Falls were all right, but winters could be unbearable.

But more than the seasons, he viewed the move to Washington as the beginning of the end for them. Jill would be exposed to parties every night where she would meet many wealthy and eligible men. Washington certainly had the culture and events that she would like and that he could bear occasionally. The Kennedy Center always had an inviting diversion. Then there were the lobbyists, all the staff that a senator would have, and the national media that would focus attention on the first female senator from Louisiana.

They couldn't survive short of . . . marriage. That would be the only way. They would be legally tied to each other as much as they were emotionally entwined now. Neither had mentioned the subject for the past year, and it would appear duplicitous for him to bring it up now. She would know. He looked up at her but didn't know what to say.

"What do you think?" she asked. She walked in front of him and stretched her arms toward the ceiling.

He sat there. He should tell her the truth, but he couldn't get it to leave his tongue. It was like peanut butter stuck to the roof of his mind. It was there and wouldn't go away until he swallowed it as truth or spat it out as though it were spoiled.

"What do you think, Jill?"

She sat down across from him on the arm of another chair so
that she still loomed above him. She wrinkled up her brow, half closed
her eyes, and pursed her lips. "Well, I always wanted to be governor.
And Hugh told me he's not going to run for reelection. But how can I
give up the opportunity to be a U.S. Senator?"

"Washington's an awful grind. They're vicious there. Everyone. Here, you know the assholes you have to look out for. Up there,
it's everyone. Proctology is the leading specialty around Washington
for a hundred miles."

"I can handle it. They won't grind me down. They'll polish me
like a diamond. I'll shine. I can feel it. I want it. But I want you to
want it for me too. I need that. Can you?"

"Can I want it for you?" How could he best phrase it so that
he could tell her his real mind without sounding like a jealous boy-
friend who was afraid to let her go forth into the horrible jungle?

"If we weren't so close, Jill, I could want it for you. But the
problem is, I can't want it for *us*. I think it will destroy us. We'll be
distracted. We won't have the same closeness we enjoy with you here."

"But, Brad," she stood now, "you're in Washington a lot. You
could be there more if I were there. You could justify it to Pinthater,
and if not, I'm sure you could write for a Washington paper or some
service where you could be stationed in Washington. We can work
through this. This is an opportunity of a lifetime for me. There're
ways that you can be there full time if you set your mind to it."

"Jill, the chief political writer for one newspaper can't just
change jobs like a cub reporter. There's only one of these jobs with
any large newspaper. I couldn't just walk into the Washington Post
and say 'I'd like to be your man. Throw the other lout out.'" He got
up from his chair and walked to the window. "Besides, I'm so immersed in this story of Harrot and Ashford that I'm going to have to
follow it through to its end. I can't walk away from the biggest story
of my life."

"And I can't walk away from the largest opportunity of my life."

Before he thought, he said it. "Well, maybe we should just go
our separate ways."

"Fine. I'm going back to Baton Rouge. Come and see me if you
change your mind." She grabbed her coat and walked loudly from his
apartment.

Brad slammed his fist against the wall without turning to see
her go. He opened the door to the balcony and walked out to where he
watched her getting into the white Volvo. He grabbed one of the hanging baskets of flowers and threw it down onto the hood of a parked car
of a tourist as Jill drove by. The exploding plastic container sent a
stream of dirt onto her windshield. She turned on the washer-wipers

and drove on.

"Dammit. Damn tourists. Damn politics." He walked back inside and fell into his recliner.

On the hour, each hour, from early that morning, Pinthater had left a message on Brad's answering machine to come to the office as soon as he arrived. He listened to his boss's voice. He rubbed his aching head. He didn't need this. Jill was enough to handle for one day.

But Pinthater's last message got his attention. He would send an armed guard to Baton Rouge and to Brad's apartment to bring him in if he didn't come to the paper immediately. He decided to go. He might as well face all the rage in one day.

His boss must still want to know why he didn't give the story to Channel Five first. But he was a journalist, not a damned made-up, prissy television reporter. Pinthater had caught him at the wrong time, and he would go on in and tell the old man off. He would stand up for his rights as a writer, not an oral purveyor of news. He had principles, and he would put his job on the line—if not his life—for freedom of the press—his freedom to write the stories and not to tell them over the airways. Pinthater wouldn't dare fire the journalist who was on the hottest story of the past decade.

AT EIGHT O'CLOCK THAT evening the publisher was still in the office where he had sat from early that morning reading Brad's front page story. It was good. No, not good, it was sensational, just as all his writing had been since Harrot's death. His anger had passed about Brad not giving the account to Channel Five first. But now there was something else—the visit he'd had from the pair of FBI agents.

They rattled off their requests so easily. "Mr. Pinthater, do you consider Brad Yeary's desk your property or his? Will you give us permission to search it? What do you know about a handkerchief supposedly soaked with the blood of Vice President Harrot? Is your reporter the type of person who could be disloyal to the United States? Is he violent? Do you know who he associates with? What did he think of Harrot? Has he ever been treated for emotional problems?" Those were bad enough, but the final inquiry really hit a nerve. "Mr. Pinthater, when is your Channel Five license up for renewal?"

He had refused to let them search Brad's desk. He had listened to the inquiries but had stood firm for his reporter. Brad was not disloyal or a conspirator as they had implied. He was not violent and had not been treated for any emotional problems to his knowledge.

He thought back to his first conversation with Brad after Harrot's fall on the field when Brad had told him the Vice President was dead. The words echoed forever in his mind: "He was shot in the chest. I have a blood-soaked hanky to prove it." But there had been no mention of the handkerchief since. Pinthater had read and reread all of the stories since the assassination. Brad had not once mentioned anywhere in the stories anything about his handkerchief or exactly how he knew Harrot had been shot in the chest before anyone else had that knowledge.

The FBI agents said they were only checking out every possible angle. Brad Yeary had information and knowledge that no one else had. They were curious. The Secret Service agents had mentioned a blood-soaked hanky to them, and they wanted it for evidence. They would examine it and see if it really contained Harrot's blood. How did Brad Yeary obtain it? Until they cleared up those details, they could not eliminate him as a potential subject of investigation. No, he wasn't a suspect, they emphasized. But until they had the handkerchief and these other questions were answered satisfactorily, they had to tell their agency and all other agencies not to release any information or cooperate with Brad Yeary in any inquiries concerning Harrot's assassination.

"Oh, by the way," they had said upon leaving, "best wishes on your application for renewal of your license for Channel Five."

Pinthater hated the dilemma he faced. He had been warned from the beginning that there could arise a conflict of interest when he had ownership positions in both the print and broadcast media. Here it was. He would ask Brad to turn over the bloody hanky to the FBI and cooperate with them in answering the questions they had. Then he could be eliminated as a suspect, go on with his job of reporting, and allow his boss to breathe easier about the renewal of his television license.

Brad walked through the busy newsroom where a score of reporters were meeting deadlines for the morning edition. He did not have a follow-up for his. He would allow it to soak in before hitting the public with some other big news. He had to talk with Shanker and get some inside dope on the investigation. That would be his next story. Shanker had mentioned some "interesting film" that concerned the assassination. He would do that tomorrow.

He walked to the rear of the room where Pinthater had one of his offices. He wasn't going to be pushed around. He'd tell his boss straight out. He was not a slick television broadcaster. If Pinthater didn't want him as a serious journalist, give him his walking papers and he'd look for another paper. Considering Jill's situation, he was a little tired of politics anyway.

Pinthater's door was open and his secretary had gone for the day. Brad walked in and sat down where he could look out the window toward the Mississippi. He couldn't see the river but did notice the lights from a few ships in the distant darkness.

Pinthater looked up and saw his reporter seated in front of him. "Where've you been, Brad? I've been trying to reach you all day."

"Out."

"Out? That's it?"

"I was busy. I was tired from writing that story. I had to get away from the phones. I slept in at Jill's and then drove down. I had to talk with another source."

"Another source? About the assassination? Or about the appointment of Ashford?"

Brad let the image of Papa Legba roll through his mind. He had never told his boss about the old voodoo doctor. There was no need to now. His sources were private. His methods might be unorthodox, but Pinthater shouldn't complain as long as they got results. "Both. Maybe," he finally replied. "Why did you need to see me so bad?"

The publisher shifted in his chair and turned it to where he was also looking out the window. He bit into the pencil he had been holding before he spoke. "First, I wanted to get your butt in here, and let you tell me why I didn't see your story on Channel Five last night?" He looked at Brad for a minute. His ace reporter just shook his head. "Then something else came up that I needed to talk with you about even worse."

Brad didn't even look at his boss. He continued to stare into the blackness of the night and think about Jill driving back to Baton Rouge alone. He heard part of the first statement of Pinthater, but the second didn't register.

"That story was too important to be messed up with television, Ed. It wasn't like New Year's night where I had to go with the television or lose the exclusiveness of it. I was the only one who had this story. I could do a better job with a little time to work on it and have it fully fleshed out for the morning edition."

Pinthater nodded his head. "I thought you'd say that." Brad's eyes still peered toward the outside blackness. Pinthater slammed his hand down on his desk to get Brad to look at him. "Have you talked to the FBI?"

Brad gave him a puzzled look. "The FBI? When?"

"Today? Anytime?"

"No. Was I supposed to?"

"They were here looking for you."

"Why?"

Pinthater stood and walked around his desk. When he got in front of Brad, he backed up and leaned against that side of the desk. "They're asking questions. Questions about your involvement in the assassination. Or at least about the information you had."

Brad stood, walked to the window, and then turned back toward his boss. "What are you talking about? What information I had?"

Pinthater walked to the door and closed it, blocking out part of the clatter and clicking of word processors and phones. "They never said it, Brad, but I get the feeling that they're looking at you as a suspect of some sort. Either as a plotter of the murder or one who knows who did it and is covering for them."

Brad fell back into his chair. "I can't believe that." He put his hands to his head and rubbed his temples with his thumbs. "What makes them think I had anything to do with it?" he asked and looked back up to his boss.

"Because you know more than anyone else. They don't think you could know that much without being in on it in some way."

"Bull shit. Just because I'm a good reporter they think I pulled the trigger?"

"No. They never said you pulled the trigger. Matter of fact, they never said you were a suspect. They wanted to search your desk."

"My desk?" He turned in his chair and looked across the room to where his cubbyhole of an office was. "Did they? Did you let them?"

"No. Of course not."

"What were they looking for?"

"I don't know. The only specific thing they mentioned was a bloody handkerchief. Do you have that in your desk?"

Brad propped his elbows on his knees and buried his face in his hands. "No."

"Do you know where it is?"

Brad thought before answering. There was no need to involve anybody else with what he knew and didn't know and what he had and didn't have. "I can't say."

"You can't say? Why not? All they want is to examine it. See if it's really Harrot's blood. If it is, they want to know how you got it. Can you tell them that? It'll get them off your back—and mine too."

He might have turned the bloody handkerchief in if the FBI had come to him and asked. But he didn't like their high-handed tactics. The very thought of them searching his desk sent him into a rage. They didn't understand the First Amendment. Now that he had bestowed the bloody cloth on Papa Legba, he wasn't about to retrieve it and give it to them. It was simple how the blood got on it. If they looked at all the tape they had, they probably would have seen it. There was no conspiracy. But he shouldn't have to explain all that to the FBI. They obviously had come to a dead end in their investigation if they were considering him as a suspect. It was too crazy to believe. He valued his sources and protected them. He would tell no one that Papa Legba had the bloody cloth. He certainly wouldn't tell them that Legba might bring the spirit of Harrot back in a seance.

"I won't tell them anything. I won't give them anything. Not now, anyway."

Pinthater plopped back down into his chair. He grabbed the pencil, broke it in half, and threw the pieces into the window. "Damn, Brad, you're making this rough on me. A little cooperation wouldn't hurt."

"They'll have a hundred more questions once you start talking to them. Then if you stop cooperating, they ask, 'Why aren't you answering any more? You got something to hide?' I'm not starting. They can do their investigation without me answering any questions. I'm supposed to be the one asking questions."

"Brad, you're a suspect."

"I thought you said I wasn't a suspect."

"Sure, I said that. But I can read where they were going with that line of questions. They're not going to give you shit until they clear you. Your sources with them are going to dry up. You've written your last story about the investigation as far as they're concerned. You're going to be useless to me on that story."

Brad thought of Al Shanker. "Hell, Ed, I don't need the FBI. I have my people at the top of the investigation."

"Who?"

"I can't tell you. I promised."

Pinthater shook his head. "Brad, where's Dan Boring? He's been working with you on this, hasn't he? He's a sharp young guy. He's written a lot of the side-bars on all of the incidental stories, hasn't he?"

"Dan? Sure, Dan's good. Inexperienced, but all right once he finds his way around. I've taught him all that he knows. He's coming along. But I haven't taught him all *I* know. I tell him where to go, who to talk to, what to write. He couldn't find the bathroom without a roadmap."

Pinthater bowed his head. "Well, I'm taking you off the story until the FBI clears you. I'm turning it over to Dan as of right now. You're off anything having to do with Harrot's assassination or the surrounding events including Ashford's appointment. You're not suspended or anything. You're back on the state political beat. I'm doing this for the good of the paper. Understand?"

Brad kicked a wastepaper can into the window, pushed a chair over, slammed the door against the wall, and left without speaking a word.

# Twenty–three

From Wednesday through Sunday, Brad did not leave his apartment. He saw no one. He spoke to no one. Jill was in Baton Rouge. Dan Boring had been handed the biggest story of the decade.

Brad's separation from Jill and from *his* story were a double death for him. But no one came to the wake. If death was a separation from life, then he had died twice in the same day. His life was his writing and Jill. Or Jill and his writing. Which came first?

He could have been mistaken for a thousand other lost souls who wandered the French Quarter in stubby beards and ragged clothes. Their odor preceded them like a proclamation of leprosy—"UNCLEAN, UNCLEAN." Their vacant stares loomed over things that once were or should have been. The only difference was that he didn't walk the streets of the Quarter, except in his mind. He sat on the balcony, propped his feet on the wrought-iron railing, and searched the recesses of his consciousness for an answer.

His eyes danced, unfocused, over the cars on the street and the pedestrians on the sidewalk. He had not taken his bathrobe off since that evening when he arrived back from his fateful talk with Pinthater. He picked up a dozen pints of Jack Daniels and two cases of Coke on the trip home. Those two friends had nursed him through the last four days.

Jill called at least three times a day and left her messages. "Brad, I know you're there. Please pick up." Pinthater did the same. Brad didn't answer. He was dead. He just hadn't been buried yet.

What could he tell Jill? He still didn't have an answer, and she wouldn't change her mind—unless he could convince her that his mental stability depended upon her staying in Louisiana.

Pinthater had helped him in that regard. He was off the national beat and back on the state. He couldn't go to Washington on official business and follow Jill. But Pinthater's answer was as bad or worse than the problem with Jill. Harrot's story was his life. Without the story, he was back to the humdrum of petty politics practiced on the provincial, proletarian level.

He listened to the phone answering machine for the repeated messages from Jill and Pinthater and heard a new voice. He recognized the slight twang of East Tennessean Al Shanker. The message was brief. "Tomorrow at 5 p.m. at the Cafe Du Mond on the Riverwalk."

Brad's ears perked up. Shanker had not forsaken him. He had told Pinthater as much. He still had his sources within the investigation.

He looked at his watch. What day was it? Then he remembered his interview with the Reverend Hutteth set for seven o'clock the next evening at the Hilton. This would be his chance to reenter the world of the living.

Hutteth would be a weird diversion from the everyday politics. Would he want the audience now if he knew Brad had been taken off the Harrot story? There was no need to tell the Reverend. Or Shanker. Just tell them things were slow. That was why he had not had any by-lines in the paper for the past few days. Had the FBI told Shanker about him being on their list to interview?

He would rise and eat. His supply of Jack and Coke was about exhausted. It had gone down smoothly the first day. Each day since his throat had degenerated into a feeling of coarser and coarser sandpaper. He needed food.

For the first time in four days he showered, shaved, and put on clean clothes. He would walk to Maspero's, one of his favorite eating places that had good food at reasonable prices. It was twelve blocks away on Decatur near the Jackson Brewery building, but it was safer to walk than to drive. His blood-alcohol level still had to be over the limit. He didn't need a DUI with all his other troubles.

"Where have you been, Brad?" Jill greeted him as he came out onto the street. "I've called three times a day for the last four days. Isn't your machine working? Or are you trying to ignore me?" she asked and slammed her car door.

Brad welcomed the surprising appearance of Jill. "How the

hell can you get a parking space right in front of my apartment when
I've never been able to?" He paused at her car. "Come on, Jill, lets go
eat. We'll walk and talk."

Jill glanced around her. "Walk through the Quarter?"

"Yeah, you're safe with me. It'll be just as fast as driving.
Wouldn't be able to find a parking space over there anyway."

Maspero's occupied the lower floor of an old brick building that
clung to Decatur just a block from the Mississippi. Brad and Jill had
eaten there often when they had taken afternoons to watch the artists
in Jackson Square. The atmosphere was rustic warehouse. A hundred
fifty could sit at bare wood tables while waitresses hustled amid the
clatter of plates and pans being banged around in the kitchen. Wood-
en arches gave a separation of sorts in the dining area and supported
unpainted rafters fifteen feet above the brick floor. Along one wall was
a bar with wine bottles neatly nestled horizontally into a wood grid
beside a long mirror reminiscent of an old west saloon. There were no
desserts on the menu, and Maspero's did not take credit cards.

Most of the food was deep-fried which Brad liked. He ordered
the seafood platter with fish, scallops, shrimp, and oysters while Jill
splurged with a baked fish sandwich. Iced tea replaced his Jack and
Coke.

Through the narrow windows they watched tourists headed for
the *Natchez* riverboat or on to more of the souvenir shops. The tourists looked in to see if the food there was any good. Brad always asked
for a window seat—not because he enjoyed viewing the tourists but
because window diners always received bountiful plates that were well
garnished to impress the ones looking in from outside.

Jill gazed out the window as she slowly stirred her iced tea.
"Jackson Square is filled with drunks and perverts."

"It's always been that way. It's just a different generation.
The great writers who came to the quarter—like Tennessee Williams—were considered the same way in their day. Williams lived
here when it was affordable—before they moved all the pig lots out.
The smell was worse then than now, if you can imagine that."

"Why do you keep living down here?"

"Well, I'm almost out of the Quarter." Brad said and looked
toward the kitchen.

"Yeah, but you could live somewhere real nice. Like over in
the Garden District. Pinthater pays you well enough to do that."

"I like it here. There are real characters on this side of town.
People who've lived life. They're not vanilla or generic people like you
find in the upscale neighborhoods. Over there they just count their
money and check their calendars for the next garden club meeting.
The whores and drunks and artists and singers and saxophone players
over here are the real people. I'd lose my edge if I moved out of here."

Jill looked at him over her iced tea. "I think you just said it. You like to live on the edge."

"No, I mean in my writing. My edge is my sharpness, my inspiration. That's what I'd lose if I moved into a sterile environment like the Garden District—or Washington." He looked at her for a reaction. Was this why she had come? To see if he would go to Washington with her? She had to see why he couldn't and why she should stay in Louisiana.

"Brad, you don't dislike Washington. You're up there a lot. You'll be up there tomorrow to cover the President's announcement of Ashford's appointment."

Brad looked away. His face flushed. He wouldn't be there. He assumed everyone knew—that it had been written in bold letters in the sky, "Brad Yeary is no longer on the biggest story of the year." At least until the FBI got through with its little games. Now he realized that everyone didn't know. He would have to go through the embarrassing process of telling anyone who asked that he had been canned—demoted to covering state and parish news as he had done years before.

"What's wrong, Brad? You look like you've been shot."

"I have. Or I wish I had. It would've put me out of my misery. You don't know?"

"Know what?"

Brad waited as the waitress placed their plates in front of them. Jill just looked blankly at him. The waitress moved toward the kitchen after refilling their iced tea.

"I've been demoted. Pinthater took me off the story. I won't be going to Washington. Not tomorrow, not anytime in the near future."

"Why?" Her eyes widened. She ignored her food.

"Because I killed Harrot," Brad said and flaked a piece of fish off with his fork.

"You killed Harrot? What are you talking about?"

"I'm on the FBI's list of suspects in the assassination. They don't really call me a suspect. I'm just someone they want to interview—and search my desk."

"Search your desk? What for?"

"For that handkerchief I wiped your hand off with when Harrot was shot."

Jill looked away and her eyes blinked. "I don't remember, Brad. That's all just a fuzzy haze to me now. I've tried to forget. You wiped my hand off?"

"Yeah, you passed out for a second. You had blood on your hand. I wiped it off and lied to you when you asked me if you'd had blood on your hand. I first thought I was hallucinating or something.

But I kept it and showed it to the Secret Service and told Pinthater about it. They're the only ones. Until Wednesday."

"Until Wednesday?"

"Yeah, I gave it to Papa Legba. He has this weird idea that he can communicate with Harrot, but he needed something that Harrot had been in touch with. So, what has a person been more in touch with than his blood? I gave him the handkerchief." He resumed eating, but Jill had not touched her food.

"But what does that have to do with the FBI?"

"They came to the paper. Wanted to search my desk for the handkerchief. They haven't figured how I could have a hanky with Harrot's blood. They want to question me. I'm surprised that you're not a suspect, Jill." He looked into her eyes. She turned her head and peered out the window.

"Did you talk to them and get them the hanky?" she finally asked.

"Hell, no. I wouldn't do that for anything now. They can kiss my ass. How dare them come into the paper and ask to search my desk."

"Is that why you're off the story?"

"Yeah, Pinthater's a marshmallow. They squeezed him and he caved in. Took me off the biggest story of my career until the FBI clears me, or until I get it straightened out with them."

"Wouldn't it be easy just to explain it to them and get back on the story? Surely, you couldn't be a suspect."

"I was there when he got shot. I knew he was shot. I had a bloody handkerchief. It adds up. I bet they're checking all the gun dealers to see if I have a gun. They'll probably come and talk to you."

Jill looked away again. "They have."

Brad quickly swallowed the oyster he had just forked into his mouth. "They what? They've talked to you?"

"Yes, not about you. They were at my office in the capitol on Thursday. They just said it was routine. They were tracking down where my tickets had gone."

"Your tickets? Your tickets for what?"

"My Sugar Bowl tickets. They always try to give high government officials tickets every year. I won't accept them, but I buy twelve to give away. Max takes care of it for me. I don't know where they go."

"Your secretary, Maxine?"

"Yes. Anyway, they wanted to know the names of everyone who got one this year. It turned out she had given a pair each to three different constituents and the other six to a lobbyist friend of hers. That seemed to satisfy them. They said they were checking all the tickets on the west side. I didn't know they were after you."

"That's strange. Your tickets and my hanky."

"Brad, you could just shoot straight with them and be back on the story tomorrow."

He shook his head. "No, it's a matter of principle. Freedom of the press. I don't have to tell them anything. I'm innocent until proven guilty."

Jill didn't move her head but her eyes darted back and forth. "You're just stubborn. And crazy, too. Tell them. And go on with your writing."

"No. I've just been sitting at home."

"Doing what?"

"Nothing. Just sipping Jack and Coke."

"You're not drinking, are you?"

"I was, but I've quit."

"When?"

He looked at his watch. "An hour ago. My source inside the investigation called and wants to meet me tomorrow. And I have that interview with Hutteth set up for tomorrow night."

"Well, that's good. At least you can occupy your time. You'll have something to go on when you get back on the story. Are you coming up to Baton Rouge on Tuesday?"

"What happens then?"

"Papa Hugh's going to make it official. I'm the next U.S. Senator from Louisiana. As soon as Ashford is confirmed. He'll announce it with me on the steps of the Capitol looking out over the statue of Huey Long. I want you to come. I want you to be with me. How about it?"

"You told him you'd take it?"

"Yes. He was under pressure. I had to make a decision."

Brad swallowed the last bite he would eat although his plate was still half full. He cast his eyes down.

"I'll come up. But I don't approve of it."

# Twenty-four

At one o'clock the next afternoon, Jill was on the balcony of Brad's apartment watering the dozens of potted and hanging plants. He came to the door and told her President Teater was about to make the announcement of Ashford's appointment. The TV showed the scene in Washington from the south lawn of the White House. Nearly five hundred dignitaries, friends, and family, along with practically every news organization, were crowded together in the brisk weather of the capital to hear the name of the newly nominated Vice President come from the President's lips.

The President came to the lectern, accompanied by Senator Benjamin Edward Ashford and followed closely by his chief-of-staff Rob Steinheitz and chief political operative George Garron. Brad and Jill sat together on the sofa facing the set. There would, in deed, be a Senate vacancy. Brad scanned the screen to see if Dan Boring was there. He didn't see him in the first few rows of the press. He smiled. Pinthater's new man on the story had been relegated to relative obscurity.

It took barely five minutes. The President made the required remarks expressing regret about the situation that forced his selection of a new Vice President but pointed out the fine qualities of Ashford. He hoped for an early confirmation by Congress so that the country could get on with its business, knowing that both high offices were filled. Ashford spoke for less than a minute. He accepted the President's offer and affirmed he would carry out whatever tasks the President assigned him with diligence and fidelity.

Brad pressed the remote button to turn the TV off. Viewing the scene had done nothing but put him back into depression. He should've been there. He could have been there except for the stupid FBI—and for Pinthater going along with them. He paced the room.

Jill watched him for a few seconds. "Brad, you know it was less than three weeks ago that we were watching Harrot on TV. He was coming into town for the game. So full of life. Things have really changed in a short time."

"Yeah. They've really changed for me. I went from the top of the world to the slime pits. I've lost my story. I may lose my job. You're going to the Senate. I'll be stuck here writing about councilmen and puny state legislators."

"You never called me *puny* before."

"I wasn't talking about you. Just the damn situation. I have no control over this."

"Yes, you do. Just tell the FBI what happened. It won't be so bad. They'll eliminate you as a suspect and you can go on about your business."

"No. I can't. It's freedom of the press. I don't have to explain my sources or how I know something," he repeated his reasoning, trying to convince himself.

"Bull. Your own boss doesn't think it's freedom of the press. He wanted you to cooperate. It's just you. You're bull-headed. You think you're always right. You have a martyr complex. You have a chance for a Pulitzer Prize and you're pissing it away. Excuse my language, but I've been around you too long."

"Pinthater doesn't care about freedom of the press. He's interested in the bottom line. 'Is it profitable?' That's the only question he asks. I'm standing on principle."

"You're not standing on anything. You're sinking in quicksand, and every time you kick you go farther down."

They both fell into silence.

She looked at her watch. "Brad, I have to go back to Baton Rouge. I have a late appointment at my office. Then I have to get ready for tomorrow's announcement. You will be there, won't you? It's very important to me. This will all work out. We have to work through it. Think about what I said. I love you." She stepped to him and they kissed. "Don't be drinking, okay?"

He nodded.

"Go see your source. I'm interested in your interview with the Reverend Hutteth. I wish I could be there. He scares me when he talks about all that Revelation stuff." She shuddered and pulled her coat tighter around her shoulders.

"I'll come up tomorrow. I may not be smiling, but I'll be there because you're happy about it."

He stepped to the balcony and watched Jill get into her car and start down the street below. She rolled down her window, blew him a kiss, and honked the horn.

He knew he didn't deserve a woman as good as Jill Crenshaw. Maybe, that was what God was doing. He was taking her away because she deserved better than Brad Yeary. He threw the last bottle of Jack Daniels into the trash can. Drinking wasn't the answer.

FOR A HALF MILE on the south side of Canal Street, Riverwalk perched near the Mississippi on three layers of stores, trendy shops, and food courts. It was convenient for tourists who still wanted to shop but avoid the drenching heat and humidity that was New Orleans from May to October. Turquoise and silver, paintings and prints, the latest fashions, sports equipment, and anything else that affluent Americans could imagine to purchase lined both sides of the rather narrow inside shopping mall. On the lowest of the three levels a branch of the Cafe Du Monde sold coffee and three beignets for two dollars.

By five o'clock, Brad had made his purchase and was sitting at a table in the corner overlooking a Navy destroyer that had docked nearby on the Mississippi. Secret Service Agent Al Shanker would be punctual. That was the nature of federal officers.

The area was sparsely populated at that time of day, and he had deliberately picked a location where they were unlikely to be overheard. He looked at his watch and then at the corner where an aisle allowed shoppers to go to other stores in the mall. He noticed Shanker surveying the area and nodded toward the agent. Shanker sat down with his order.

"Will anyone recognize you here, Brad?"

"No, I don't think so. What about you?"

"The only ones I know in New Orleans are you, John Dobson, and a couple of other FBI agents. Remember, I was just here to guard Harrot. I'm staying because of the investigation."

"Al, at the funeral you said you had some interesting film. What is it?"

Shanker finished a beignet, wiped the powdered sugar from his face, and looked toward the outside walkway and the ship beyond. "Yeah, it was interesting."

"What, Al? Is it film of the assassination? Does it show how they did it?"

"Listen, Brad. I'm under a little pressure right now. I told you I'd keep you informed. So, I'm going to tell you a few things, but I can't jeopardize the investigation."

"It won't, Al. And I won't. If I can't use it now, just tell me. I'll have it for background for a later story."

"Okay. What I was talking about the film was that we think we have the shooter on tape. We're not absolutely sure. It looks that way. But we have no ID. He was shot from the second level of the west stands. One bullet."

"And you think you have someone on tape showing him pulling a trigger on a gun?"

"No. We see no gun or trigger. Just a little whiff of smoke from beneath a sleeve of an overcoat."

Brad smiled. "That's not much."

"We have more, but I can't tell you right now."

"Anything unusual in the autopsy report?"

"Well, I can't tell you much. Just this. You remember seeing the entry wound in Harrot's chest?"

"Yeah, I saw it with you at Bellevue." Brad placed the forefinger of his right hand directly beneath his breast bone.

"That's the place, all right. But there was no exit wound. That's why there was no blood on the carpet at the Superdome."

"No exit wound? I don't get it. Did the bullet just stop inside Harrot, or did it disappear?"

"Neither. It exploded. Ten pieces pierced about every organ."

Brad was silent. He had not seen any evidence of that on Harrot's chest. Just the small entry wound was all. He thought. Then it hit him. Papa Legba had described the pain he felt on the night of Harrot's assassination. He had pointed to his chest to the exact place of the bullet hitting Harrot. Brad now remembered the words of the voodoo doctor saying that the pain "spread like an explosion to all of my belly." How did Papa Legba know? Was it true that he was connected with Harrot through the spirits? Or had someone connected with Legba actually fired the bullet that he knew would have exploded? Brad hoped it was the former and not the latter. If Legba was in on the assassination, Brad knew he was in deep trouble for turning over the bloody hanky to him. He felt his own blood draining from his face.

"What's the matter? You look pale."

Brad took a quick drink of coffee. "Nothing. I was just thinking about what you said about the bullet exploding. I haven't seen that in anything."

"And you won't. That's something that only we know. And the killer. And you. You can't use that until the murder's solved. Got it?"

"Sure. I understand. You have my word."

"Brad, I have a favor to ask."

"What?"

"You know that bloody handkerchief you showed Bob Clary on the night of the assassination?"

"Yeah."

"You need to turn it in to the FBI. Dobson has this crazy theory that you could be involved in the assassination."

"And you don't?"

"No. It's ridiculous. But you were standing directly in front of Harrot when he was shot. We have you on tape too. It's obvious that you didn't have a gun. But he thinks you may have been standing there to help someone else line up on the Vice President. And the bloody hanky is a mystery to him—and to me, quite frankly, since you never touched Harrot after he was shot."

"It's no secret, Al. Jill Crenshaw kneeled down to help Harrot. She got blood on her hand from his coat or shirt. She didn't notice. I didn't notice until I held her hand. When she saw it, she fainted. I wiped it off. That's how I knew he was shot. But I don't have the hanky anymore."

"Who does?"

Brad looked down. "I can't say. The one who has it is another source. A longtime source here in New Orleans. I wouldn't tell him your name, and I can't tell you his or hers."

"That's going to make it rough on me. Can't you see? I've got to be loyal to the head of the investigation—Dobson. He's given the word for no one to cooperate with you on any inquiry until we clear you."

Shanker looked toward the ships while Brad peered at what was left of his coffee.

"We just have to eliminate everyone, one by one, until we get down to the killer and any co-conspirators," Shanker said.

"Was the shot fired from one of the seats that Jill Crenshaw had tickets for?"

This time Shanker fell into silence. "What makes you ask that?"

"Because she told me the FBI were up talking to her about her tickets."

Shanker breathed deeply. "I can't say, Brad. Not yet. That's all I can tell you today about the investigation. None of it is to be used, yet."

"Okay."

"What's your next story going to be about?"

"I don't know. I'm officially off this story until Pinthater puts me back on. He feels the same way as you about the hanky. He wants me to give it to the FBI."

"I'm sorry to hear that. Maybe you can write a book about it."

"Not yet. You have to find the killer first. I have no concluding chapter."

Shanker smiled. "I hope we can find him or them. Then I can get back to my normal job. I was supposed to be visiting my parents in Tennessee, but I'm stuck down here."

"It's not that bad."

"Brad, think about what I asked you to do. I won't be able to talk with you anymore until that's straightened out. Understand?"

Brad stirred what was left of his coffee. "Yeah, I understand. I have no story. I have no girlfriend. I've lost my source inside the investigation."

# Twenty–five

S ilky blond hair softly lashed her back as the tanned young woman kept a rhythmic movement, sitting astride the Reverend William Hutteth. Pelvis to pelvis, they were both nude. She arched her neck and back bringing her breasts to where her erect nipples were pointing to the chandelier hanging above the bed. Hutteth was not moving, and with his dark glasses being his only apparel, she could not tell whether his eyes were open or closed. But he wasn't dead. She could feel that inside her.

She turned her head and looked out the window. The Presidential Suite of the Hilton took up the better part of the twenty-sixth floor. The drapes were open, and it was almost dark. No one could see in, but her act and the open drapes made her feel she was being watched. She liked it. She looked back at the preacher when she felt a slight quiver move through his thighs.

The music grew louder to her hearing, and she increased her tempo. It was as though someone had turned up the speed on the mechanical horse that she once rode outside the grocery store. "Another quarter, Mommy," she would say and continue to ride. Now it was three C-notes from the preacher for a half hour ride. He paid, not her.

She dug her knees into the sides of his lower torso and turned her pelvic action onto high until a shaking spasm like a shock of electricity ran through his body. His face contorted as he simultaneously reached up, grabbed her breasts, and squeezed.

"Stop, stop, stop," he gasped. She slowed her movement and stopped. She waited a second and gave two more thrusts. "No, no!" he screamed.

She smiled, relaxed her pelvic muscles, and relinquished her grip. "Is that enough, Reverend? Are we through having fun?"

"Yes, Sandy. I am drained. In more ways than one. Same time tomorrow, okay?"

She was already headed toward the bathroom. "Sure, Reverend. You got the money. I got the time. You're easy anyway. You're not as kinky as half the people who come to N'awlins."

Brad Yeary waited in the foyer reception area of the suite. The Hilton adjoined the Riverwalk and it took him only five minutes to walk over after his talk with Shanker. He didn't want to be here. He didn't want to be anywhere. He saw no use in it. An interview with a mad reverend who was spaced out on Revelation was the last thing he wanted to be doing now. But he had given his word. The promise had been given before the happenings of the last few days. Out of some inbred since of duty, he came.

He had no questions prepared. If the preacher wanted to talk, he would pretend to listen. He would set his tape recorder on the edge of another desk and let it do its work. He was too deflated to take any notes. Al Shanker had just driven another nail into the coffin of the felled journalist.

He thought back to his interview on Tuesday with Senator Ashford. He wished he could take back that silly promise that for principle he would die for freedom of the press. If he was going to die for something as noble as that, he had expected a spectacular execution rather than an anonymous wasting away—ignored, forgotten, and discarded. There was nothing heroic in that. God was punishing him for making such a blatant promise.

God was punishing him a lot lately. Maybe he needed a preacher. Perhaps he could confess to the Reverend Hutteth, and he could exorcise all those demons that had been afflicting him during the past week. Did Hutteth take confessions or just donations? If he could afford the Presidential Suite of the Hilton, he had donations enough. It was time for the Reverend to accept confessions. He waited. The Reverend Hutteth was in conference, he had been told by an assistant.

Brad reached into his pocket to see if he had brought along one of his many kaleidoscopes. He had forgotten. He leaned back with his head against the wall, closed his eyes, and imagined one. Through the years, he had mastered an ability to picture the glass prisms tumbling around into geometric figures with radiant hues of green, purple, blue, red, and yellow just as easily as Jill could close her eyes and imagine the perfect Thoroughbred horse.

"Hi there, good looking."

Brad opened his eyes just as the tall young woman walked past. She shook her head, letting her hair sway back and forth along the back of her red dress. She winked at Brad. "Are you one of the Reverend's boys?"

"No, I don't think so," Brad answered, shaking the cobwebs from his mind.

An attendant handed her coat to her. When she turned to fasten it, Brad glanced down her legs that were adorned with dark, patterned hose. "I like the way you look," she said before stepping through the doorway. Brad's gaze followed her until the door shut.

"The Reverend will see you now," the attendant announced and drew Brad's mind back to why he was there.

The Reverend William Hutteth was standing near the window looking out over the Mississippi in the study portion of the suite. He was dressed in white trousers and white shirt with no tie. He still wore the dark glasses.

He turned to Brad. "You must pardon the glasses, Mr. Yeary. I have an eye condition. It's sort of like my eyes are permanently dilated. I get too much light. Some people think I wear them for show. That's not the case. I can only take them off in near darkness."

They sat across from each other in comfortable leather, winged arm chairs with a coffee table between. The Reverend took a Dr. Pepper that the attendant opened. Brad took a Diet Coke.

Brad eyed the luxurious surroundings. He hadn't expected this from a man who preached from a tent, but he also knew Hutteth was at least a part owner of a cable television channel. He must be wealthy. He wondered about the young woman. He had gone to the bone in interviews with politicians. He saw no need to hold back with a preacher. If he made the Reverend angry, he'd be out of the interview quicker.

"Who was the young woman?"

"A whore."

Brad appreciated but was stunned by Hutteth's frankness. He went the next step. "Was she here to see you?"

"Certainly. Fucked my eyeballs out. That's why I wear these dark glasses." He smiled.

"You're rather open about that, aren't you? Aren't you afraid I'll use it?"

"Mr. Yeary, you're a professional. You have no reason to try to destroy me. I wouldn't just say that to anyone. But I know you have principles. We're not here to talk about my shortcomings and sins but about a larger subject."

"Well, that's right, Reverend, but I'm just curious. Don't you think it a bit unusual for a preacher of righteousness to be an adulterer."

"Fornicator, actually, Brad. I'm not married, except to my work. We're all sinners, right?"

Brad nodded.

"I just want to be honest with you so that you know that I'm shooting straight with you on everything else. My credibility depends upon whether you believe me. Understand? It doesn't depend upon me being sinless."

"I think I follow."

"Well, how about a quick sermon, before I get into what I really want to tell you? A man or woman is weak who doesn't know his or her weaknesses. Pretty women are my source of temptation. I don't crave money or power. I have both, but I didn't seek them. My vice is one. I'm fortunate in that regard. The devil cannot tempt me with anything else, so he tempts me with beautiful women. Sometimes I help him out a little by calling up the escort services like I did with Sandy. I'm working on my weakness, but I haven't overcome it. It may take a while.

"Others have different weaknesses. Alcohol, drugs, avarice, pride, a meanness deep within—whatever—Satan works on that. It's been true from the beginning with Eve—pride—the knowledge of good and evil."

"You mean with the apple?" Brad asked.

"Well, a fruit. It doesn't say what kind. Could of been a peach. Anyway, Satan continued that with the temptations of Christ—physical, pride, and power. It's the same today. People shudder when some little something comes out about a leader. What do they expect? We're all sinners. We just need to be sure that our leaders' weaknesses aren't in an area that would threaten the country. You agree?"

Brad nodded.

"Who cares that John Kennedy screwed everything that walked through the White House? Did it make him less a leader? No. No less and no more. If we each received a tattoo every time we sinned, our bodies would be like those guys in the circus—full of monstrous etchings—within a year.

"So now that you know my vice, you have no power over me because I readily admit it. I don't advertise it, but I don't worry about hiding it. That leads to other sins. One type of sin is enough for me. I don't smoke, drink, gamble, or do any of those other things."

"What about this suite, though? What do you pay for it? Isn't it extravagant for a preacher?"

"A laborer is worthy of his hire. My mission raises and spends enormous amounts of money. It's all freely given. There are no hoaxes, no time-shares, no miracles promised. Everything I spend is a matter of public record. This suite costs two thousand dollars a day."

"Yet, you preach from a tent?"

"I could rent an auditorium for a lot less than I pay to maintain my tents and carry all that equipment around. My people wouldn't come out to a fancy place. I play to an audience who feel more comfortable in the tent.

"And I can control the environment better there. Lights and sounds are all programmed. With a flick of my finger, all the lights can be doused and the sound muffled. With another snap of my fingers, lightning will flash and people will think the world is coming to an end. Thunder is the voice of God. The tent is my stage. It's the same in every city. I'm used to it and comfortable with it."

He finished the Dr. Pepper, stood, and walked to the window. "I can see the tent going up at the edge of town. I'll be there day after tomorrow telling everyone who wants to listen about the end of time."

Brad realized he had forgotten his recorder. He had none of the Reverend's confessions on tape. He took it out and set it on the coffee table.

"Do you tell the truth to the people, Reverend, or is it just a show?"

"Both, Brad. They want both. I could write it all out and sell it in a book. But people don't read anymore—unless—unless they know the author or want to get more of the story. I whet their appetites with the shows—the preaching—then they buy my books and videos. But my message is the truth. I believe it with all my heart."

"But your focus is Revelation. Isn't that what David Koresh and the Branch Davidians studied constantly before they were killed?"

Hutteth turned directly toward Brad, raised both arms the same as he did when preaching, and his face turned red, the veins popping out on his neck. "David was near the truth, but he was a fool. Just like Jim Jones. They retreated to a little compound. Their influence was limited. That's not my game. Interactive television and high tech shows around the country are where it's at. Once you retreat, your influence is reduced to just those around you. I have a cable television station, books, videos, and I tour eight months a year. My influence is on the ascent. You won't catch me in some jungle or in west Texas."

Brad was listening, but he didn't really care for those he thought might be charlatans of religion preaching all their world-wide application. He wanted it on a level that would relate to him. He decided to ask the preacher a personal question. "Reverend Hutteth, do you think God punishes people here on earth for what they do while they're here, or does he wait until they're dead?"

Hutteth paused briefly and took his glasses off. He looked directly into Brad's eyes and then slipped the darkness back onto his nose. A slight smile edged across his lips. "I don't have a confessional booth in the suite, Brad." He sat back down.

"Brad, there are some bad things we do that have natural

consequences which make it seem like God is punishing us. If you drink too much, you may have a wreck and get killed. Consequence follows action. If you murder someone, you may be put away for the rest of your life by the state. Again, consequence follows action. And if you—"

"What about the sin of pride, Reverend? What if I said I would be courageous? Would God test me or punish me? Or if I got to feeling that I was a pretty good journalist?"

The preacher smiled and twisted off the lid of another bottle of Dr. Pepper. "There is a tendency toward pride with anyone who is successful, Brad. I don't see that sin as having a defining natural consequence like in the others I've been talking about. It may in the long run lead to a downfall. God leaves a lot of things unpunished temporarily. And a lot of the bad things that happen to people have no connection with anything they've done. It's just life. Life is temporary. Eternity is permanent. Here it rains on the just and the unjust. Bad things happen to the good and the evil. So do good things. Has something bad happened to you that you believe is related to the sin of pride?"

Brad twisted in his chair and averted his eyes from the stare of Hutteth. "For the past six days, I've had nothing but bad luck and bad news. I boasted to someone that I would die for freedom of the press. Now, I've been taken off the biggest story of my life for reasons I can't tell you. I'm in danger of losing a lady I . . . "

"Love?"

"Yeah."

"Do you?"

"What?"

"Love her?"

"Yes."

"And she loves you?"

"Yes."

"You won't lose her. You'll find a way to make your love work. Otherwise it's not love—on both sides."

Brad wiped his eyes and wished he had dark glasses like the Reverend.

"Reverend, I've been taken off the Harrot story because I refuse to do something. I refuse to do it because of my principles. I believe in freedom of the press and the protection of sources."

"Is that the reason you've been taken off the story?"

"In a way. I won't give in to a request by the FBI and my editor."

Hutteth took off his glasses, rubbed his eyes, and stared directly into Brad's eyes. Brad could see the power, the dilated pupils, that made Hutteth appear ethereal. The preacher put his glasses back on before he spoke. "Brad, you have to examine your refusal. Look at it from the perspective of those requesting it. Is it a legitimate request? Would you actually be giving up a principle if you did what they're requesting? Or is it just a matter of pride with you? Are you so independent and full of self-pride that you don't want anyone telling you what to do?

"You know, if one person tells you that you're a jackass, it's just an opinion. But if several tell you that you are, you should start feeling for the long ears and see if you bray when you speak. Don't let pride masquerade as principle. Understand?"

Brad nodded his head. It was the best advice he had received in years. How was it that he was receiving it from a fornicating preacher who was hung up on the numbers in Revelation?

"And, I'm going to tell you enough that they'll have to put you back on the story of Harrot's death. It's revealed in the book."

Brad settled into his chair, sipping his Diet Coke. He prepared to listen to Hutteth.

"If there's one thing I'm an expert on, it's Revelation. I've committed all twenty-two chapters to memory and I have a passing knowledge of the rest of the Bible. The secret to the book is tied up in its numbers. Primarily four numbers: *Three*, which represents God or the power of God; *Seven*, which represents completeness or perfection; *Ten*, which represents announcements by God, like the Ten Commandments; and *Twelve*, which stands for the followers of God, as in the Twelve tribes of Israel and the twelve apostles. Do you have any fascination with numbers, Brad?"

Brad stirred to attention and thought. "Well, I pulled over to the shoulder of the road when my old Ford turned to one hundred thousand miles so I could watch the odometer pop up all those zeros."

Hutteth smiled. "Very good. Everyone—just about—has some fixation with numerals. Everything we do is determined by them. Numbers on clocks, numbers in our age, house and street numbers, phone numbers, social security numbers, credit card numbers—they all play roles in our lives everyday. So, it shouldn't come as a shock that God speaks to us in Revelation with numbers." Brad nodded as the preacher made his point.

"It's been over a thousand years—989 to 1001 A.D.—since we've had a twelve-year period bookended by numbers that read the same backward as forward. That is the period we are in now—1991 to 2002."

"Wait a minute, Reverend. Why is it significant that the numbers read the same backward as forward? I don't follow that."

"Good question. It denotes eternity. A mirror image. It never ends. You can go backward and forward and it's always the same. That is why the number of the beast—the servant of Satan—is 666.

It's the same backward and forward. He's there for eternity just like God is represented by 777—each seven representing one of the Trinity—God the Father, God the Son, and God the Holy Spirit. Seven, remember, represents completeness and perfection. The three sixes in the beast's number in Chapter Thirteen of Revelation represent the imperfection of Satan, the First Beast, and the Second Beast—all mentioned there."

"Well, I follow you, but I don't understand what that has to do with this year and Harrot's death. We're about two-third's through this twelve-year period."

"Exactly. And what did I say *twelve* represented?"

"God's followers. The twelve tribes and the twelve apostles."

"Correct. God's people. So far in this twelve-year period we've had peaceful overtones on many fronts—the fall of communism, peace accords signed between the Israelis and the PLO, South Africa has more peace between the races. You see, this is a time for God's people. But Satan hasn't given up. There is still turmoil and natural disasters. He's still alive and working. He'll make a great effort to wreak havoc before the end of this millennium and the beginning of the next. We're at that point."

"Well, Reverend, that's all well and good. But you told me this had something to do with Harrot's death. And you said this year, 1998, is the year of the beast. I was there in your tent and saw those numbers flash up on the screen. Then you pointed your finger at me and called me by name. By the way, how did you do that?"

Hutteth smiled. "That wasn't a revelation. I recognized you from the television. Plus my security people checked your license plate before they fixed your tire."

"I thought so," Brad said. "Tell me more about this being the year of the beast and how it's connected with the assassination. You know I won't be able to use this in any story. I'd be laughed out of the profession."

"Well, you can use it as background as you see future events unfold. I understand that you have at least one other source who's not strictly an everyday, factual person—one who delves into the mysterious—maybe even a little voodoo?"

Brad's mouth dried. Hutteth knew about Papa Legba? The preacher had more ways of finding out things than the FBI. Did he know about the bloody handkerchief? Brad didn't ask.

"Brad, if you'll take the word of a voodoo doctor, you need to listen to my theory of what's happening in the year 1998—the year that I've labeled *The Year of the Beast*."

"Okay, I'll listen, but I'm not saying I'm going to believe it."

"Very well. Just listen." The preacher stood and walked back and forth in front of the window. He used the blackness of the night as a backdrop and counted off points with his fingers. "The three sixes, beside representing the eternal imperfection of Satan and his beasts, also signify to us a time when evil things will be accomplished. You can go to the library and check this out, Brad, to be sure, but you'll find that I'm telling you the truth.

"Mohammed died in 632 A.D. But Islam reached its zenith for that century around the year 666 A.D. By that year the Muslims had taken practically all of north Africa and, more importantly, all of Palestine. Jerusalem, that was full of Jews and Christians, fell between 632 and 666, and by the year 666 the Islamic Mosque was built over the Temple Mound in Jerusalem. The Muslims treated the conquered Christians and Jews well at the beginning. But it's significant that this power reached its peak in that year.

"Now, the next appearance of 666 is when it's doubled to 1332. Follow me?"

"Yeah, I follow. My math is good up to that point but not much farther. What happened in 1332?"

"Good. At least you know what questions to ask. Another capital of Christianity fell to the Ottoman Turks, who were the predominant Muslims of that day. Constantinople fell to the followers of Islam around that time. There was fighting before and after. But its destiny was written. Isn't it odd that with the number of the beast and doubling of the number of the beast that two capitals of what had been the central religions of that day fell to Islam? And by that time, Islam had swept over all the Mediterranean area. It was at its height. The years around 1332 were another high water mark of Islam."

Brad watched from his chair. The preacher continued point after point with historical references that Brad was not certain about, but which he would check out—for whatever it meant. "Reverend Hutteth, I remember in the tent that you said 1998 is the third appearance of the number of the beast—666. That's because three times six hundred sixty-six is nineteen hundred ninety-eight, right?"

"Yes. But there's one thing more significant. It's the *third* appearance of the number of the beast. The third appearance is special—more powerful than the first and second. That goes back to the Bible and Revelation where three is representative of God—or God's power. So, this time the beast will take on or assume the power of God. The forces of good will react, but Satan will strike. Where? Where is the new capital of Christianity?"

"Well, I certainly don't think it's New Orleans, Reverend."

"No, it's not. It's the United States. The beast has stricken the second in command of the country. But that's only the start. He seeks to destroy our government."

"You think he's after the President?"

"It could be. Or someone else high up, or some high institution of our government that would create chaos or uncertainty. I don't have the full picture yet. I don't receive visions. I have to study these things. But you should be aware, so that when they begin to happen, you'll know why and can write intelligently about them."

"You think the Muslims are behind the assassination of Harrot?"

"Some fanatical element of Islam. Yes."

"You believe that Islam is the beast of Revelation?"

"Not Islam. The power of the fundamental fanatics of Islam. The beast will rise from within Islam. The book they follow, in theory and word, is not bad. Their application of it leaves out some of the mercy that Mohammed preached. Morally, it's a very good religion in what it says. But when they severed the head of the princess a few years ago for adultery, it showed a lack of mercy. Christ showed the woman taken in adultery mercy and forgiveness. The followers of Islam today don't show that. The law was the same—the judgment different.

"Mohammed in the Koran taught that Jesus was the son of Mary and was a great prophet. But he denied that he was the son of God. From Abraham came forth Isaac and Ishmael. Jesus came through Isaac. But Mohammed taught that Jesus was not Christ, the son of God."

"Who can I point the finger at and say they did it, Reverend?"

"I don't know. It's the work of the beast. He will reappear. The year is early. Be on the watch, Mr. Yeary."

Brad looked at his watch and retrieved his recorder. "I'd better be going, Reverend. I have a lot to think about."

"I enjoyed talking with you, Brad. I hope things work out for you. If you do what's right, I see you being put back on the story and renewing your relationship with your girlfriend."

"Thanks. I hope you're right."

"Brad, if you need more information about Revelation and its relationship to Harrot's death, stop by my house. It's only a short distance from where you'll be spending a lot of your time."

"Where do you live, Reverend?"

"Alexandria, Virginia. Suburb of Washington."

"I'm not in Washington as much as I used to be."

"Oh, but you will be. When your lady friend, Jill Crenshaw, is appointed to the Senate, I see you spending a great deal of time there."

# Twenty–six

At mid-morning, Tuesday, January 20, President Stephen Teater, along with Rob Steinheitz and George Garron, sat in the Oval Office reviewing drafts of the President's State of the Union speech to be delivered to Congress and the nation that evening.

"What do you think? Looks pretty good to me." The President laid his copy on the desk and leaned back in his chair awaiting his top advisors' comments.

"Rather inspiring to be so vague and ambiguous. Some nice phrases that the media should be able to pick up. Says we're doing well, but will do better with your leadership and the Congress' cooperation. I think we have a keeper here, Mr. President," Garron said and closed his copy.

Steinheitz was the picky one. It would be his ass if something slipped by that caused the President to have to answer questions or explain. "On page twenty, I don't know that we have to be so definite about revenue projections. That might come back to haunt us. I think our Friends Around the World theme on foreign policy is good. We might want to tone down the references to the Mid-East and oil dependence a little. That's on page twenty-nine at paragraphs three and four."

"Hell, Rob, we can't tone it down anymore without dropping any reference to it at all. It's as bland as it can be written." Garron gave a little laugh toward the Chief-of-Staff. "Besides, in a few months, all that will be changed anyway."

The President put a finger to his lips. "I think we may need to get a little fresh air. How about a walk?"

Outside and away from his paranoia with furniture that might contain listening devices, President Teater took his two long-time friends aside. "How long until Ashford's confirmed?"

"How fast do you want him to be?" Steinheitz asked.

"Well, I think we need to get that out of the way and get him settled into his job—his non-job—as soon as possible. Until that happens, he'll have to be seen with me and be around here to show that I'm entrusting him with all the important stuff. We don't need him overhearing our planning with the Arabs like Sam did."

Garron and Steinhietz nodded.

"Sam just didn't understand that sometimes you have to do things for the good of the country which could look questionable to strict legalists. Hell, this country didn't get to where it is today without some underhanded activity. The whole Mexican deal could have been avoided. But then we wouldn't have Texas, New Mexico, Arizona, and California. I've thought about giving California back as a goodwill gesture, but why should they take it—there's already more Mexicans there than U.S. citizens." The President laughed and his two advisors joined in. "Rob, you and George, do you think if word got out about these plans, that the people would think we're doing something illegal or wrong?"

"There's a good possibility. When you plan ahead to topple legitimate governments with simultaneous coups, there are a few of those bleeding-heart liberals who would raise a fuss. The newspapers would have a field day," Steinheitz said and looked at Garron for affirmation.

"I agree. But if it goes like we're planning, it's just that the U.S. is recognizing a citizen uprising in countries that we really haven't had much affinity for in the past anyway. They've threatened something that's very dear to us—enough oil and gas to race around all over the country. The people will support our decision to help these friendly forces—especially since they will announce that our supply of oil won't be diminished, and we'll receive it at lower prices," Garron, the vote counter and poll taker, said.

The President smiled. "Yes, re-election will come easy. Votes follow the price of gasoline." He looked at Steinheitz. "How are the plans coming?"

"Very well, they say. They're all veterans of Afghanistan. Most of them were trained by the CIA. They know explosives, armament, and how to plan a coup. They still need some time. I'll meet with them in March. We haven't decided where. They feel a little uneasiness dealing with me, a Jew. I've explained to them that I can put my religion aside for this project for the good of my country. But that kind of thing isn't within their thinking. They're still trying to dismiss from their minds that I might not be shooting straight with them. They want some proof in the form of military hardware. They're making up their wish list. That's one of the things we'll be talking about in March," the Chief-of-Staff said.

"They obviously know to keep this quiet, don't they?" the President asked.

"Yes, they more than we. We could only be impeached and thrown out of office. They could be summarily executed."

"We need to keep no memo's, recordings, or anything else in case something goes wrong. No trail of paperwork. Any arms need to be diverted from shipments already going to their areas. If shortfalls turn up with other governments, we just say 'we'll check it out.' We can check it out easily for several months like good government bureaucrats. Memo's, recordings, and paper is what's gotten others of our predecessors in trouble," Garron said.

"What about Harrot, George or Rob?" the President asked, turning first to the one then the other. "Are we sure he didn't write down anything he heard in that meeting?"

"He didn't hear much. There were no details discussed there. Just the overall operation. He knew the big picture, but he didn't have enough to substantiate anything," Steinheitz said and looked at the President.

"You think—and hope," the President responded. "He knew enough to tell me he was against it. He was thinking about stepping down. Boy, that would've been embarrassing. Even if he hadn't said anything, we would've had a hard time explaining the resignation of a Vice President. Fortunately, he was also enough of a team player that he was still considering his options when he went to New Orleans. Have you gone through his office files and his desk at his residence?"

"That was taken care of the day after his death. We sealed off his office here and, with the FBI, went through everything—under the pretense of national security. The residence here was done the same way. We found nothing that gave a hint he had documented anything about the meeting." Steinheitz tried to sound confident.

"What about his home in Montgomery? Did you go down there and look around? He spent a lot of time down there, you know."

Steinheitz looked at Garron, and then they both looked at the President and shook their heads.

"Don't you think we should do that? Just nose around. Take a couple of young guys from here who know something about surveillance and espionage. Tell his wife that they are FBI and you just need to check out to be sure there was nothing that Sam left there that could be considered of national importance. I'm sure she'll cooperate. Matter of fact, I'll call her and arrange it. I'll tell her that we hate to bother her, but that under the circumstances, if she doesn't mind, they need to look around. It's just routine. Okay?"

"Sounds like a good idea," Garron said.

"Now, Rob, what's the projected date for getting this operation with the Arabs underway?"

"The plans should be pretty well in place when I meet them in March. They've mentioned the Eighth of June as the target date. That's the anniversary of Mohammed's death, they tell me. He died June 8, 632 A.D."

Garron punched the date into his hand-held calculator and then some other numbers. "That's odd," he said, gazing at the numbers.

"What?" the President asked.

"That means that Mohammed will have been dead thirteen hundred and sixty-six years on June 8."

"What's odd about that?"

Garron wrote the figure down on a piece of paper and showed it to the President and Steinheitz. "See the numerals—one, three, six, six. You have two unlucky numbers put together. Thirteen and two-thirds of the number of the beast—sixty-six."

"I don't pay any attention to that numerology poppycock." The President waved away the paper.

"It's just odd," Garron repeated. He wadded the paper up and put it into his coat pocket.

"Yeah, it's odd okay. What's odd is we have a Jew, a Christian, Muslims, and a numerologist working together on a plot to overthrow several OPEC nations," Steinheitz said.

# Twenty–seven

**M**axine Hankins, Jill Crenshaw's secretary, ignored Brad Yeary who was sitting in the reception area of Jill's office in the basement of the State Capitol. He was too nosy. She busied herself with putting files away and straightening the folders.

Brad looked at her. They despised each other equally. He had nick-named her the Praying Mantis years before. He never used the term to her face but was tempted to now. Her angular, thin features, long neck, and the way she moved her limbs in a slow, deliberate fashion easily fit his name for her. She was a life-long state employee, and believed she knew more than any governor, legislator, or journalist. And she had always been quick to tell Brad as much, even after he and Jill Crenshaw became friends and lovers. Maxine, while loyal to Jill, did not let that spill over to Brad. She barely spoke to him.

"Maxine, I just want to know who you gave or sold the tickets to. You told the FBI. You can tell me."

She sat at her desk and brought her hands beneath her chin. With her hair in a tight bun, with very little makeup, and with just a thin line of eyebrows, she reminded Brad of a very strict Catholic nun he had as a teacher in the sixth grade. The boys had all made bets on who would be the first one to make her smile. They all lost. Maxine had the face of a mummy—well-wrapped and impossible to pry open.

"You ain't the FBI. You're just a jackass," she finally said. "I'm not telling you anything about tickets." She glanced at her watch. "You better get your little butt outside. The Governor will be making his announcement about Jill in just about two minutes. I'm going. Else you can sit here all by yourself." She rose and walked in her gangly gait through the doorway.

JILL CRENSHAW STOOD ON the eighteenth step from ground-level on the south side of the State Capitol. The twenty-seven story building towered behind her. She had one foot firmly planted on the state's name and the other on the date "1808" which were both engraved into the granite. Each of the steps from the bottom to the fiftieth bore, in order, the names and dates each state joined the Union. Louisiana was the eighteenth admitted, and from that height Jill had a very good view of the statue of Huey Long and the green maze of grass, trees, shrubbery, and sculptured hedge which formed the Zachary Taylor grounds on the south side of the Capitol.

She was ready for the announcement to be made by Governor Hugh Johnson who stood beside her. They were waiting for all the television cameras and microphones to be positioned. This was a first for the State of Louisiana. The Governor would announce that a woman would be appointed to the U.S. Senate to fill out the term of Senator Benjamin Ashford who had the day before been named as the President's choice for his new Vice President. Jill glanced around for Brad. He was late—if he was going to show at all. She saw Maxine Hankins walk to a place on the sidewalk in front of her.

Then, just before all the cameras and mikes were in position, she caught Brad out of the corner of her eye. He was away from the crowd, leaning against one of the low-limbed live oak trees where the gray Spanish moss almost, like a veil, obscured his face. He did not want to be a part of the festivities. At least he was there. Governor Johnson's press secretary began the introductions of dignitaries.

Governor Johnson lavished praise upon Jill. She barely recognized he was talking about her. He spoke of Ashford as the next Vice President, stating that the President had made a wise choice.

"There are many in Louisiana who would have honored the office and who are qualified to be appointed to the U.S. Senate. But no one is better qualified, better informed, more able, and more tenacious in representing the interests of all the people of Louisiana than State Senator Jill Crenshaw. And it is my pleasure to be able to take away the 'State' and replace that with 'U.S.' Subject to Senator Ashford being confirmed by the Congress as our next Vice President, I will appoint the Honorable Jill Crenshaw as Louisiana's next U.S. Senator," the governor said.

The sun shone on her face and a breeze barely moved her hair as Jill stepped over in front of the microphones. Resplendent with a glow of fulfillment on her face, she waited as the applause and the whine of film being advanced in still cameras continued unabated for what seemed to her an embarrassingly long time. On two note cards, she had made points for a short speech of gracious acceptance. This was not the time to be long-winded. This announcement by the Governor was just to relieve the pressure from him. Her real acceptance speech would come on the day of her swearing in—after Senator Ashford was confirmed as Vice President.

"I'm thankful for the confidence of Governor Johnson and of the people of Louisiana. I love this state and I love my country. For ten years I've done my best to serve my district and my state. I will be most happy and grateful if I have the opportunity to take my service to another level and try to help my state and my country. It is *our* state and *our* country. Strong leadership is demanded, and with your help and prayers, I know I will be up to the task that lies before me." After another minute of mentioning special people and points in her career, she was through. The applause this time was even longer. She looked over to the live oak tree where Brad had been. He was gone.

FBI AGENT JOHN DOBSON turned the television monitor off. He and Al Shanker had watched Governor Hugh Johnson's announcement from their headquarters on the third floor of the Annex Building on Poydras Street.

"She looks innocent enough," Shanker said. They both sat back down at desks that were piled with reports and files.

"They all do," Dobson mouthed from under tired eyes. "Al, it'll be twenty days tomorrow. Almost three weeks. And we haven't made an arrest. Matter of fact, we're not even close to making an arrest. That's what I had to tell the President's Chief-of-Staff just a while ago. The press is after us. We're being lampooned as inefficient. I've averaged less than four hours of sleep per night since this happened. I've about had it. Everybody looks like a suspect to me. You'd even be one if you weren't standing behind Harrot when he got shot."

"What was Steinheitz's reaction when you gave him the news?"

"I was surprised he didn't chew my ass out. He's known for being a tough SOB, you know. But he was actually calm about it. Didn't seem too upset. Just said to keep working on it. The 'Prez' appreciated our efforts. Said to keep him informed if we came up with anything," Dobson said. He began looking through the most recent reports from headquarters.

"Well, as long as the boss is satisfied, we don't really have pressure on us. We answer to the director and then the President. They both know it's going to be a tedious process," Shanker said and turned back to his copy of the *Times-Gazette* to look for a by-line of Brad

Yeary. There was nothing there.

Two young FBI agents entered the room, one carrying a sealed package beneath his arm.

"Agent Dobson, we have this back for you from the laboratory. You'll need to sign for it and make the notation in the chain-of-possession log." The other agent toted a larger box that was similarly sealed. Dobson signed for both and had them placed on the top of his desk. Their business finished, the two younger agents left.

"They're going to let us keep all the physical evidence in our vault here once it's tested," Dobson said. He turned to open the accompanying reports. He handed Shanker a copy of each.

It didn't take Dobson as long to get to the meat of the report on the large block "A" that had been found by the sheriff and turned over to him just a few days before. "Damn, Al. The DNA tests were positive. They found a splotch of blood and a few hairs on the cloth and compared them to the hair that was on the overcoat with the gunshot residue. Turned up a ninety-nine point nine, nine, seven per cent comparison."

"That sounds like the old Ivory Soap commercial. Is that good?"

"Hell, no, it's not good. Our killer is dead before we can arrest him and interview him. If this gets out, we're in it deep. They'll say that we'll never know the story. Of course, they may be right."

"Well, it wasn't a hundred percent. It could have been someone else, couldn't it?"

"Huh, uh. Too close. Not much room for error here, Al. The fact that both of these turn up within seventy miles of each other makes it even more likely that it's the same man. You add to that the fact that they both were wearing large Alabama block A's, and it almost clinches it. Plus, they were both involved in violent deaths—the one in the stadium of Harrot and the one in the boat of himself. No doubt to me that this is the same dude."

"That puts a crimp in our investigation, huh?"

"I'd say so."

"What's in the big box?"

"Those pieces of fiberglass that our divers found near where the boat blew up."

"What does the report say on them?"

Dobson opened the other envelope and scanned the report to the conclusion portion. "Not anything here we couldn't have guessed ourselves, Al. The fiberglass is a kind that is used in boat manufacturing. It was broken by an extreme blast, but there is no trace of explosive on any of the pieces which would normally be there with conventional blasting material. Therefore, it is the conclusion of the lab people that one of five different plastic explosives that leave no trace elements was used. A very sophisticated group."

"So, what happened? Did our killers get in a boat to escape, celebrate too much, forget that they had explosives on board, and blow themselves up?"

"If it was accidental, we may never know who did it. If it was deliberate, it may mean the conspiracy included more than just the two we saw on tape. The head honchos could have decided to get rid of the triggerman just to decrease the risk of being caught."

"John, what about the guy with the Notre Dame jacket? We don't even know he was on the boat. All we have is one piece of cloth. They haven't found anything else have they?"

"No, not a thing. The Mississippi at that point is carrying so much silt and the bottom is so soft that everything was washed out to the Gulf or sank before we were able to get men down there. I would speculate that the Alabama man was not alone on the boat. But I have no idea who was there with him. You're right that he and his partner may have split up. The guy in the Notre Dame jacket could have killed his partner."

"So, we don't have a gun. And now we don't have the person that pulled the trigger on the gun that we don't have." Shanker pulled the plastic-covered A from the package and looked at it. "All we have is an A."

"In this case, an A will not look good on our report card, Al."

"Our luck is bound to get better. We've used up all the bad. What about the tickets? Have the agents gotten back from talking with that lobbyist that Crenshaw's secretary said she gave them to?"

Dobson looked at his watch. "Not yet. But they're due anytime. I don't expect much on that either. The ticket business for the big events at the Superdome is a crazy mess. You've heard about laundering money by sending it through a maze of companies and individuals. Well, good tickets to a game or concert may change hands ten to twenty times before the event. They're all usually nameless, cash-ticket transactions. No one keeps names or addresses. It's the best black market going. No tax is paid on the mark-up of scalpers."

Dobson's phone line lit up. "Yes? ... Who? ... When? ... How much? ... Where is she? ... We get a name? ... Could be ... No, I want to talk with him myself. Just get me an address and Al Shanker and I'll drive down. The Secret Service has jurisdiction in that anyway. Great. Call as soon as you get the location." He hung up and a grin began to grow on his face when he turned toward Shanker.

"What is it, John? Did we finally get some good news?"

"Could be. A bank teller down in Venice called our local FBI office to report a strange transaction. A young kid—about eighteen—brought in a wad of hundred dollar bills to open a checking account. They had been wet and matted together a little even though he had tried to dry them—in an oven. Since it was ten thousand dollars, she had to make a transaction report to the treasury department.

"The kid said he had saved them up from his fishing business over the last two years and they had gotten wet because he had them buried in a can. But it could be that they were on that boat and got wet when it blew up. We need to talk with the boy and see if he did find them."

"I guess a kid finding ten thousand dollars in that part of the state isn't very likely, huh? If he made that much fishing, you and I need to go into that ourselves."

"Yeah, we both may if we don't get some answers on Harrot's assassination pretty soon."

The intercom interrupted their renewal. The sanitized voice told Dobson that the agents he had sent to interview the lobbyist with the tickets were back. "Send them in."

They came in and sat at the table with Dobson and Shanker. "Pardon us, chief," one of the younger agents said to Dobson, "is it all right to talk in front of him?" He nodded toward Shanker.

"Yeah, that's Al Shanker. He's with the Secret Service. He's with the team. You can tell him anything you can tell me."

They nodded.

"What did you find out about the tickets?"

"We haven't dictated it into our 302s yet, but we'll give it to you in rough form from our notes. The lobbyist admitted receiving the six tickets from Maxine Hankins of Senator Crenshaw's office. Seems that he does her favors sometimes and Ms. Hankins reciprocates when she can. He denied that Senator Crenshaw had any knowledge of the transaction. Says she is straight as an arrow in his opinion. He traded the tickets to a known scalper for twelve seats in a section of the Superdome where there was less demand. He had a party of twelve he needed to provide entertainment for that evening."

Dobson looked at Shanker and then back at the agents. "Tell me that's not all. Tell me we didn't lose the tickets when they were given to an unknown scalper. Boys do you have any good news for me?" he asked.

"Yes, sir. The lobbyist knew the scalper's phone number. He does business with him on a regular basis. We got the address for the phone number and went to visit him. He's a car salesman when he's not scalping. He was a little nervous that the FBI was interested in his scalping business." The agent smiled. "We told him that as long as he cooperated we would not use any information that he gave us against him and gave him some bull about immunity—like we would be interested in a small-time scalper anyway."

"Did he remember anything about the tickets?"

"Yes, sir. He remembered the six as being in a prime location—on the fifty-yard line, not very far up.  He said he remembered selling these in three sets."

"By any chance did he remember anything about the sales—like people's names or phone numbers or where they were from?"

"He said they were all sold in response to newspaper ads he answered like he usually does. He does remember that the reason he answered one ad was that it specifically asked for tickets in Section 264 or the section immediately behind it.  He thought if they knew where they wanted, they would be willing to pay a good price. They wanted three tickets, but he only had two left by that time. They took them—for five hundred dollars each, and he got them a single in another section in another level. He got no names. It was a cash transaction. He said it was a local number he called."

"Good, good," Dobson said, turning over in his mind the information. He looked back at the two agents. "Okay. Check the newspaper classified ads for the time we're talking about. Find that ad and then go to the newspaper. They're bound to keep some kind of records about placement of ads. They might have a name or checking account number. Check the number that was in the ad for a location, but don't go there yet. I want all of that done by this time tomorrow. Understand?  Report back tomorrow afternoon.  Agent Shanker and I are going on a field trip of our own south of town."

THE EVENING SUN HUNG low over the horizon by the time Dobson and Shanker arrived in Venice, Louisiana, at the end of Highway 23.  Dobson looked at his notes on the directions to the place where the youth lived who had the ten thousand dollars in wet hundred dollar bills. It was at the end of civilization in south Louisiana.

Game preserves, swamps, and state-owned marshlands lay between Venice and the Gulf. The Mississippi split up into four fingers in merging with the Gulf. Venice and the rest of the area was all part of the alluvial plain that had been deposited by the river over eons. They could now be driving on dirt that was originally in Missouri, Ohio, Illinois, or Tennessee. It stretched out like the palm of a man's hand laid flat with the fingers beckoning to the sea.

A shack—not much more than tar-paper over cyprus slabs—sat at the end of a dirt lane near the levee that kept the river contained and aimed at the Gulf. A cherry-red Suzuki dirt bike leaned against one wall. An orange extension cord ran from a nearby power pole and snaked its way inside the shack through a hole in a screen and window on the side facing the road.

"Hell, Al, this kid doesn't look very prosperous to me, judging by his house. What do you think? Two rooms and a path—to the river?"

They talked in whispers as they approached the little hut. Their car had been left another hundred yards down the road. "He has all he needs, John—a motorcycle, the river, and ten thousand dollars in the bank. He has electricity, and I believe I hear the sound of music—bad music—coming from in there."

They eased to the edge of one wall and listened for sounds from within. "You smell what I smell, Al?"

Shanker nodded. The aroma of marijuana drifted through the cracks in the wood slabs. They listened. There was a male and female voice. Shanker leaned down to Dobson's ear and whispered, "Like I said, the kid has everything he needs. He's realized the American dream."

Dobson retrieved his badge and ID from his breast pocket and stepped around the corner and to the open door with Shanker just a step behind. It was not until he blocked the sunshine that was filtering in through the haze of smoke that the two occupants in the room noticed him. They sat on the floor, leaning back against a legless sofa. A mattress lay on the floor at the juncture of two walls, bare except for a ragged quilt that was tossed to one corner. The extension cord was hooked to a black stereo. There was no light except for the sun.

The young man put a hand to his brow to shade the rays of the sun that backlighted Dobson's figure. "Who the hell are you? And what do you want?" He laid the smoking joint into a full ashtray and struggled to balance on his knees.

"FBI," Dobson said. "Billy Roach, I presume?" he asked and thought how appropriate the young man's name was.

The youth looked at Dobson's badge and ID. The tone of his voice changed. "FBI? What have I done?"

"Nothing of a criminal nature—that we're interested in," Dobson replied, casting his eyes to the ashtray where the smoking incense still rose from the cigarette.

The girl had not changed her position. She hunched forward on her knees, still puffing on what was left of her joint. Her eyes told Dobson that wasn't her first for the day. She hardly knew they were there. She weaved back and forth to the music while her long, greasy black hair fell from her shoulders toward her open blouse. Dobson looked down at the sight of her bare breasts swaying like dual pendulums within the white cloth. He knew there was no need trying to talk to her.

"Mr. Roach, can I see you outside for a minute?"

The young man stumbled, barefooted and shirtless, through the door. "Look, sir. That's just a little homegrown weed. I don't sell. My girlfriend just likes to sit around and smoke a little. Please don't bust me," he pleaded first to Dobson and then to Shanker.

It didn't take Dobson long to get to the point. They weren't interested in that law violation if the youth would cooperate. They wouldn't take away his ten thousand dollars. They wanted to know where he got the money. Did he find it? Where? He could keep his deposit and his marijuana. Dobson showed him that he had the wad of bills that the youth had taken to the bank twenty miles away. Billy Roach pointed to the levee, and they started walking toward it.

"Do you need to tell your girlfriend where you're going?" Shanker asked.

"Naw, I don't think she knows I'm gone yet," Billy answered. He looked back toward the jean-clad girl who was silhouetted in the smoke, still swaying to the music and puffing occasionally, her eyes closed in meditation.

From the top of the levee, he pointed to a clump of trees about a quarter of a mile down stream on the far side of the Mississippi. "It was there. Lodged in the base of a tree. I looked for more all up and down the river. But that's all there was."

"No more money?" Dobson asked.

"No."

"A piece of a boat? A container of any kind? A gas can? Anything?"

"No."

They walked back toward the shack. The music grew louder as they neared. Dobson kept up the questioning. He wanted more than just the money. He needed to tie it to the boat, to the man with the block A, to Harrot's assassination. The boy kept on shaking his head. He had not seen or heard anything on New Year's night. He and his girlfriend were up in New Orleans.

He did fish. Until he found the ten thousand dollars, he had scraped out a very meager living with the fishing and odd jobs. He was one of ten children. He left his home in Alabama when he was sixteen and hitchhiked to New Orleans. He had followed Highway 23 to the end and stayed. Now he had his eye on a used mobile home that he wanted to buy for him and his girlfriend. He invited them in. She had not moved.

"She's really a nice girl," he said, offering his guests the only two wooden chairs in the room.

Shanker and Dobson were ready to leave.

"You're sure there's nothing else you found around here about that time?" Dobson asked. He got to his feet.

Billy Roach continued to shake his head. Then he blinked. "Oh, I did find something over on this side of the river about a week later. Nothing of value. 'Tweren't nothing. I put it on the wall in my storage room," he said and pointed toward a door that hung from one hinge behind Dobson. "Go in there and look at it. It's hanging on a post."

Shanker and Dobson ducked their heads and were careful not to rub up against the unfinished door facing and snag their suits as they edged through the opening. The other room of the two-room shack was even darker than the main room. A small window at head height allowed just a trace of light into the dank, musky storage area. They looked all around the four small walls until their eyes fastened on a piece of material hanging from a nail driven into a support post. Shanker reached and took it off the nail. He held it up to his chest, spread it open, and turned toward Dobson.

Dobson's eyes grew wide as they feasted on a torn and ragged, green and gold Notre Dame jacket.

# Twenty–eight

B rad Yeary closed one eye and then the other. The last rays of sunshine were glancing off the dome of the Old Capitol Building just five blocks from where Jill Crenshaw had stood on the steps accepting the governor's public promise of appointment to the Senate.

Now used as a museum with archives of state relics, the Old Capitol drew mainly students and tourists to its ornate, marble-floored rotunda. Its restoration had been completed with the placement of the last stained-glass panel in the roof of the dome that sheltered the huge room. It was the Kaleidoscope Campaign and was one of the few charitable causes that Brad had freely supported. During the years of cleaning, refurbishing, and restoring, he walked over from his Baton Rouge office while Jill was going about her legislative duties and became an unofficial supervisor at the project. He would make suggestions on the placement of each colored glass panel and give his opinion as to which colors should be placed next to each other. The project superintendent humored him with an occasional nod.

Now, with its completion, Brad came to the edge of the great room, sat down against the cool stone wall, leaned his head back, and relaxed with the world's largest kaleidoscope. Already, he had been staring upward for three hours. If he would peer long enough, the images would begin to tumble in his blurred vision. And if he could encourage his eyes to water a bit, the reflections produced by the huge glass panels fifty feet above his head would become some of the prettiest and most relaxing mosaics that he had ever found.

This day he had no problem making his eyes tear. Three hours before, he heard the announcement that his love would be going off to Washington.

Only a very few lingerers were still in the Old Capitol when he heard the sharp, staccato steps of high heels against marble that he recognized from long association as belonging to Jill. He didn't move or shift his gaze from the dome.

"The big one that got away," she said and sat down near him on a wooden bench.

He nodded but didn't speak.

"I saw you at the announcement. At least at the beginning. But I couldn't locate you when it was over. I've been covered up with interviews and well-wishers. Have you been here all the time?" she asked and looked up toward the dome that was now growing dark.

"Yep. I've been right here. Walked over right after you said your last words—while the cameras were still rolling and the microphones were still on. I needed to relax."

"I knew I could find you here. It's a good place to relax—or run away to." She waited for his reaction.

"Yes," he said slowly, as though he had to force breath from his lungs to respond. "Run away? Maybe so," his voice was barely above a whisper. "I've considered it, you know. I'm just not sure where I could run to. There's not much left that hasn't been taken away."

Jill rubbed her hands together in her lap. She didn't want to say the wrong thing, but she was near her limit.

"Look, Brad, I've about had enough of you feeling sorry for yourself. You think the whole world revolves around you. Half of what's happened to you, you brought on yourself. You can straighten it out. There's still a world out there. You can get back on your old job, or you could work for another newspaper. This is a time when you should be celebrating with me, but I have to hold your hand because you've made a jackass out of yourself. I'm getting a little tired of it. Why should I have to come way over here and find you? You should have been the first in line to congratulate me." There. She had said it. It needed to be said. She sat back and waited for the explosion.

He turned to her, not exploding, but with the most innocent expression. "You're right, Jill, that I brought half of this on myself. The newspaper part I did. I grant you that. Your going to Washington, I didn't. I have no control over that. It never was within my grasp. You asked me my opinion about it. Then you didn't listen to me. I don't think you should go."

Jill flushed red. "Damn, Brad, just because I asked you your opinion didn't mean I was automatically going to follow it. It was an *opinion*. Understand? It wasn't like it came straight from God—written in stone. We talked about it, sure. That's what friends and lovers do. But it doesn't mean I'm always going to follow your opinions. I have a few of my own, you know.

"And it doesn't mean I love you any less because I didn't follow it. I'm a big girl. I can think for myself. I thought you knew that. I thought you liked that. That's what you said attracted you to me to start with. I could put sentences together in a thoughtful pattern that meant something. Now you don't like it because I thought something through and want to do what's best for me."

Brad looked down at the floor. "Is it best for *us*, though?"

"Yes, it is. It could be if you would work through it instead of sulking off because you thought I had to follow every word of your advice. We both can go to Washington. If worse comes to worse and you leave the newspaper, you could work as my press secretary. We're not related. It wouldn't be nepotism. Or you could work for a Washington paper. Even with you at the *Times-Gazette*, we both could be here and in Washington a lot. It can work if you want it to.

"Brad, you know I'm an expert on Thoroughbred race horses. I look at you and I know that you're a thoroughbred too. You have it deep within you to be great at what you do. Sometimes though, you're so mule-headed. And you know that a mule's father is a jackass. You act like one or the other. Even the mules that pull the tourist carriages down in the Quarter can be made up to look real pretty. But you still have the thoroughbred in you. You need to let her out."

"I'm at a loss, Jill. The year started off so exciting for me with the Harrot thing and all. I was on top of it doing some excellent work. Now, it's all fallen to hell. The same things that took me up are taking me down. Everything has happened so fast. The Harrot killing is responsible for me being canned. It's responsible for you going to the Senate. It's almost like Reverend Hutteth talking about it being the year of the beast. The same event has both lifted me up and thrown me down."

He turned to her and took her hand in his. "I don't know what I'm going to do. I don't want to work for another newspaper. I'm forty-four. I'm too old to start with another outfit. Working for you might really destroy our relationship. I've never been a mouthpiece for anyone. We might be in constant conflict. I need some time to think it through. A week. Ten days. Okay?" He rubbed his back against the wall and waited for her reply.

"Sure. You need to think it through. What are you going to do? Take off from work and hang out at your apartment with Jack and Coke? That won't solve anything. I'm going to need a couple of weeks to wrap up my state legislative office and get things directed to

Washington. I'm going to be busy. So, it won't hurt my feelings. But, please don't be drinking. It's not good for you—and us." She looked at him and rubbed her hand through his hair.

Brad stood up and took Jill's hand. "Let's go. All the light is gone from outside. The kaleidoscope has been turned off. I'll walk you to your office, and then we'll go eat."

They walked outside into the cool darkness and turned north toward the Capitol. "What are you going to be doing during the next week or ten days, Brad? I need to know where you'll be."

"I'm considering buying a shrimp boat down in Lafitte."

Jill turned to him. "You're what? A shrimp boat? Brad, you haven't been around a shrimp boat in a quarter century. What would you know about that business?"

"It's just you and nature. The sea, the boat, and the shrimp beds. You don't have to worry about pleasing an editor or the FBI. It's back to basics. The old reporter and the sea. It would make a good title for a book."

"Are you serious? Are you going out on a shrimp boat?"

"Yeah, I called up Barry Ledoux. We went to high school together. We're heading out day after tomorrow. I'm going down to Lafitte tomorrow and get set up. It will be just him and me and the boat. We'll be heading out to the barrier islands in the Gulf. We'll stay up to a week or until we take on a ton or so of shrimp. Remember his name. Barry Ledoux. I'll be back in ten days. I should have my mind made up by then."

"Brad, the only things those guys down in Lafitte care about are dogs, hunting, fishing, and racing. You would die a slow, mental death with that crowd."

"Now, don't go and judge everybody as stereotypical rednecks. You got onto me about doing the same thing with Harrot being from Alabama."

Jill nodded.

# Twenty-nine

Fresh dirt lapped around the roots of the old oak stump that squatted crab-like fifty yards from the white plank fence. The shorter Arab with the neat moustache, Nidal, hunched down low and peered through the fence toward the three-foot thick wooden behemoth. His partner, Ahmed, who stood over six feet tall, leaned over the fence, lowering his chin to the top plank. Nidal pointed a small antenna toward the stump and pressed a button at its base.

Leaving behind a cloud of dust, the stump rose like an illformed flying saucer to a height of fifty feet, appeared to hang there for a split second, and then plummeted back to the field of dormant Bluegrass. Nidal and Ahmed both jumped and clapped their hands together at the sight of the old tree trunk being lofted and settling back to earth.

"Powerful stuff," Ahmed said. He vaulted over the fence and ran toward the hole that was left by the explosion. Nidal looked back toward the green-roofed barns where two of their stallions stood looking toward the sound of the blast. He climbed over the five-plank fence and joined Ahmed at the crater where the trunk had moments before been rooted.

"The smell is one of power," Nidal echoed, his head deep into the six-foot cavern created by the blast. He took a package of chewing gum from his pocket, opened one piece, and handed another to Ahmed. "Remember, the plastic explosive was no bigger than this," he said, holding the stick of gum and then placing it in his mouth.

"Are we going to use the explosive next time?" Ahmed asked and walked to the nearby stump.

"It's backup. Mahmud and Siddig should be here soon with the new long rifle. We still want to use the gun if we can. Explosive is good but messy.  I like to be precise."

"Why are you a chemical engineer then?"

"Because my uncle thought I needed to be one in the petrol business.  I haven't used my training much here on the horse farm though, have I, Ahmed?  And neither have you used your degree in political science."

Ahmed smiled and looked away toward the barn where a black Jeep was stopping.  "I don't know.  We both may have used our expertise enough to make great changes.  I believe Mahmud and Siddig are at the barn."

"Remind me to get a tractor down here and fill that hole and pull the stump out to burn," Nidal said and walked beside his friend toward the white block building adjacent to one of the barns.

The two visitors took a long package wrapped in brown paper from the rear of the Jeep and laid it on the table in the barn.  They pulled down both garage-type doors at either end and waited for Ahmed and Nidal to make their way in from the field.  Mahmud, the older, taller, and fairer complected of the two, took a knife from his pocket and cut the string that bound the package.  He had sliced the paper open and peeled it back when his friends from the field entered.  They greeted with hugs.

Nidal looked at the package that still hid the contents.  "Do we have what we ordered?"

Mahmud leaned back over the table and loosened the last paper that encased a long, brown plastic rod.  He took it from the table and held it across both palms as he turned toward Nidal.  "It looks and feels as good as the last.  That young man in Memphis does an excellent job.  Look down the barrel and notice the rifling.  Hold it toward the light."  He handed it gently to Nidal who turned and placed an eye to the larger end.  He handed it back.

"Very nice.  How many shots is it good for?"

"From four to ten.  We need to test its accuracy one time before we use it.  But just once.  We can't be shooting it just for sport," Mahmud said.  He looked out the window toward a gathering of horses two hundred yards away.  "Nidal, do you have an old horse that needs to be put down?"

"No, not really.  But I guess we could spare one.  But what about the small thing there?"  He asked and pointed to a hand-sized, paper-wrapped package that still lay amidst the wrappings of the long rifle.

Mahmud picked it up.  He began to unwrap it.  "For close encounters of the serious kind."  He grinned and held up what appeared to be a medium-sized, silver-colored cigarette lighter.  He flipped the lid back and flicked his thumb against the edge.  A flame shot out six inches.  He adjusted it with a small wheel.  "Light, anyone?"

"What do we need with a flame-thrower cigarette lighter?" Nidal asked. He took the apparatus from Mahmud, extinguished the flame, and held it in his palm. He moved his hand up and down. "Very light. What's it made of?"

Mahmud took it back. "A plastic composite, just like the long rod." He rotated the top of the lighter a full half turn, snapped a hidden latch that released the plate covering the bottom, and pointed it toward Nidal's forehead.

Two barrel holes in the bottom aimed at Nidal while Mahmud gripped it in his hand. "A d . . . d . . . derringer. A two-barreled derringer!" Nidal exclaimed. "Is it loaded?"

Mahmud nodded. He turned away from Nidal, went to a nearby window, and slid it open. He aimed at a fence post ten feet away and squeezed. The report echoed loudly within the block building. The top of the post was lost in a haze of smoke, wood dust, and splinters. The other three joined Mahmud in gazing at the white post as the smoke cleared. There was now a neat hole at least an inch in diameter drilled straight through, as though by a high-speed blade.

"Pretty nice, huh?" Mahmud turned and restored the gun in a flick of his hand to what once again appeared to be a harmless cigarette lighter.

"For what distance is it accurate?" Nidal asked and examined the death instrument in his hand again. "So light."

"Ten feet is about the maximum," Mahmud explained. "Both barrels can be fired separately or simultaneously. I don't know if we can get anyone that close. But if the long rifle fails, this little man can do the trick up close. And the beauty of it is it doesn't show up on any kind of detector. It's not metal. I walked right through the airport machines with this on our flight from New York to Lexington. It didn't cause any kind of blip. I checked the long rod with the other baggage, but it wouldn't have shown up either."

Nidal walked to a cabinet and took out the cable and camera unit that once had been attached to the previous rod which had done its work in the Superdome. He attached the firing cable to the binoculars that served as the rifle's scope and aiming device. "Who wants to try it?" He asked and surveyed the eyes of his three friends.

Mahmud held up his hand. "Nidal, this will be yours. You must do the next one. We don't need to get anymore infidels involved. Their mouths are loose. For money they work for us. For money they betray us. The circle is drawn tightly around us four—and of course, the White Caliph."

Nidal nodded. "Yes, I suppose you're correct. The White Caliph says he'll meet with us soon. Maybe in a month. We'll exchange plans. He'll give us the go ahead." He took the long rod that had now been assembled with the cables, camera parts, and binoculars and walked toward the same window from which Mahmud had blasted the hole in the post. He looked toward the four horses that were grazing on the knoll fifty yards beyond where the tree trunk lay sprawled on the grass.

"Wait, Nidal!" Mahmud yelled.

"What?"

"My good friend. The rod is very accurate and very sophisticated."

"I know," Nidal acknowledged and looked back through the binoculars to one older, gray horse among the four.

"Yes, Nidal. But even it won't work without a bullet." Everyone laughed except Nidal. Mahmud took a cartridge from his coat pocket and walked to his friend. He unsnapped the chamber cover and placed the bullet in. He closed it and patted Nidal on the shoulder. "Now you are ready."

Nidal took his time. A half minute passed. They all stared silently toward the horses. Finally Nidal pushed the little button near the end of the barrel. There was a small puff of smoke and the sound like the hiss of a snake. In the distance, the gray horse's legs gave way at once as though they had been chopped by invisible axes. The horse dropped and rolled onto its side. There was no other movement. The other three horses sniffed and moved away, unaware of what caused their brother's sudden demise.

Nidal was not smiling when he turned back toward Mahmud. "It works well," he said and unloosed himself from the instrument. He looked at his watch. "It is time for prayer."

Nidal retrieved a small rolled-up rug from a cabinet and placed it on a line drawn on the floor. On a facing wall was a red circle. "Mecca," he said and pointed toward the circle. Each of the four kneeled on the rug and bowed toward the red circle until their heads touched the floor.

THE NEXT DAY BRAD made his way back to his roots—to Lafitte—thirty miles due south of New Orleans. No longer isolated, the shrimping village that spread along the Barataria Waterway was home not only to shrimping families but to the rich and upwardly mobile young families who wanted to escape New Orleans for the rustic life on the bayou. It seemed to Brad that the little community he grew up in changed drastically each year until he hardly recognized it.

Still, the smell was there. If anything, the aroma was the constant in a sea of change. It was hard to pretty up shrimpers. They smelled like shrimp and often had the personalities of shrimp—sullen and hardshelled. The village had lived on fish and shrimp for years. A flotilla of boats headed to the Gulf and the barrier islands daily during the seasons for brown and white shrimp. Some would come back in at night and some would spend days away until they filled the bowels of their boats with shrimp and fish covered with ice.  Docks, welding shops to repair the shrimp boats and the ocean going vessels, and the other businesses associated with the sea lined the waterway for miles north and south of Lafitte.

The Ledoux brothers were part of a core population that had been the heart and soul of Lafitte.  Generations back they had lived along the bayou and made a living from the water.  Now they had even expanded their business to give swamp tours to northern tourists who ventured south of New Orleans.  There were three of them:  Barry, who had been in the same high school class as Brad; Larry, two years younger; and Benny, who was in prison for murder.

Barry and Larry both had their own shrimp boats, but it was with Barry that Brad had made his arrangements.  He had packed enough clothes in his old Ford for a two-week stay.  He stopped at the side of the house that backed onto the waterway.  He saw Barry in the slanting sunlight of late evening preparing the boat for the next day's journey.  This was just what he needed—a getaway from the calamities of New Orleans and the world that were speeding by.

Barry Ledoux cared little for Brad's career.  He didn't even subscribe to the *Times-Gazette*.  Life to the Ledoux brothers was tightly contained within the sphere of a hundred mile arc between Lafitte and the Gulf.  Whatever happened outside of that was of little concern to them unless it intruded into their shrimping business.

Their father had tried to escape, only to come back after failing in the world to the north.  He learned to be a horse trainer and traveled the racing circuit up north to St. Louis, Louisville, and Arkansas, where he plied his craft until an errant hind hoof of a spirited mare crushed his chest and left him permanently gasping for breath.  The Ledoux family was chained to Lafitte.  It was their heritage and their anchor.

"What is it this time?" Barry Ledoux greeted Brad with a bear hug.  "Women, alcohol, or bosses?  Or two out of three?"

Brad looked at him knowing that Barry Ledoux with all of his non-education and lack of sophistication had struck at the heart of Brad's problems.  Life was simple.  It boiled down to women and bosses.  Throw in a little booze for good measure—either as a cause or effect of the other two.  "Just want to get away from the big city for a few days, Barry," Brad said.

"Sure, sure, buddy.  This is the place to do it.  We'll hit the water at four in the morning and be at the islands by the edge of dawn.  It'll make you forget all your problems."  For such a bear of a man, Barry Ledoux was light on his feet.  He practically dragged Brad toward the boat.  "You've got to see this rig.  I've got a new engine and swing-crane that just about takes all the work out of shrimping."  He laughed the laugh of one who was used to hard work. Not even modern machinery made the shrimper's life easy.

Barry persuaded Brad to leave most of the clothes he brought from New Orleans in the car. He wouldn't need them. On the boat for a week, they could get by with one or two changes. There were no night clubs, no civic centers, no theaters, and no women that would demand their attendance. The less on board, the less there was to keep up with.

With the necessities stowed, the shrimper invited the journalist into his house. The smell of the innards of the shrimp boat could be no worse than Ledoux's house. Clothes were scattered throughout, boxes lined the walls with contents spilling out, and food cans and cartons littered the kitchen. Barry scraped away a clearing on the kitchen table with his muscular arm where the two could eat. He retrieved a bowl from the oven, two paper plates from a package that lay on the counter, and two beers from a refrigerator that contained little else.

"The wife's gone," he said and snapped his can open.

"How long?" Brad asked.

"This one, six months."

"This one?"

"Yeah, she's my fourth. You married, Brad?" Barry helped himself to the hot contents of the bowl. "Take some, Brad, it's sorta Hamburger Helper baked with shrimp, rice, and beans. Pretty good once you get used to it."

Brad scooped him out a smaller helping. "I'm not married now. It's been fifteen years."

Barry shook his head. "That's a long time to do without."

Brad interrupted his tasting of the steaming concoction. "I didn't say I was going without. I'm just not married. I have a girlfriend."

"You must be having problems with your girlfriend. I haven't seen you except to say 'Howdy' and 'Bye' for more than an hour at a time over the past twenty-five years. Now you're coming down to spend a week with me?"

"I just have to straighten out a few things in my mind. This is the right place to do it. Just like when we were kids. You and me on your dad's boat."

"Yeah, I guess you're right. But if you look around here," he nodded to all the mess of his house, "you'll have to say that you must have some serious problems if you want to spend a week with me—a smelly old shrimper—instead of your girlfriend up in the city."

Brad nodded. His friend had hit at the heart of it again.

# Thirty

awn cut like a knife along the eastern horizon. Between the
dark Gulf waters and the gray cloud canopy that stretched
nearly to the water, the colors of morning poured in bloody
mary red and pumpkin juice orange.

The other boats that had sprinkled the waters of the black
night like small diamond lights had already disappeared to favored
shrimp beds around the barrier islands. Barry Ledoux's *Sweet Jasmine* rested at anchor.

For seven days the shrimper and the journalist had plied the
waters, letting nets down and taking nets up. Their catch was sufficient if not spectacular. Within the hull, fifteen hundred pounds of
brown shrimp, cooled on ice, awaited the final destination of restaurants around the country. One more day and the shrimpers would
plow back up through Barataria Bay to the waterway and on to
Lafitte.

The trip was routine for Barry Ledoux except for the company
of his guest. He usually worked the beds alone. The self-imposed solitary non-confinement was one of the reasons for his being on his fourth
marriage. It was the only way of life that he knew. He slept peacefully in the berth area that he had shared for the past week with Brad
Yeary.

The journalist was up early. He sipped coffee, held to the side
of the boat in a gentle sea, and awaited the sunrise a half hour away.
The colors equaled some of the better combinations that he had ever
achieved with his kaleidoscopes. Only his unresolved problems of love

and job kept him from complete enjoyment of the early morning soli-
tude and the spraying of deep hues. They were on his mind constantly—darting in and out like pilot fish and keeping him from his goal.

After the week with Barry Ledoux, Brad knew he was not cut
out to be a shrimper. His hands were raw from ropes and cables despite the gloves he wore. His back muscles ached from pulling and
lifting. His legs and head had barely become accustomed to the roll of
the sea. Yet, it was different—so different—from what he had been
doing for the last twenty-five years that he knew he would treasure
the week on the shrimp boat as a fond memory for the rest of his life.
But his life was not directed to the sea. He was a landlubber. He had
been gone too long. His dominion was with those who talked and
governed. He was the scribe who chronicled, cudgeled, and captured
the acts for all to read of those who made laws, policy, and decisions
that affected the state and republic.

How would he combine his love for his job and his state with
his love for Jill? He thought of all those he had spoken to and interviewed since the first of the year. Samuel Harrot wanted to talk with
him further but was gunned down before he could. Darla Puckett
wanted him back, but that relationship was over. Ed Pinthater loved
him when he was doing well for Pinthater's newspaper and television
station but turned his back on him at the first hint of controversy.
The Reverend Hutteth had told him everything between him and Jill
would work out if they both loved each other. Senator Ashford had
asked him the damning question of what principle he was willing to
die for. Papa Legba told him he could help with the mystery of
Harrot's death if he had something that belonged to the Vice President. Al Shanker promised him cooperation but was pressured into
reneging. Jill Crenshaw asked him to follow her to Washington, and
he had given her no assurance that he would.

For him, that was the biggest turnaround of all. He had, at
first, urged Jill to run for the Senate against Ashford, and she declined
saying she wanted to stay in Louisiana—the state she loved—with the
guy she loved. Then when it became possible that she could have
Ashford's seat without running for it, she was ready to go, and he had
begged her to stay. He was sorry he had ever given her any indication
that he thought she should run for the Senate. That was his mistake
to make her think that he was encouraging her to go to Washington.
He would regret that error for the rest of his life.

The thoughts and memories of the men and women who had
cast him into this net over the past five weeks surfaced and then dove
again just as did the school of dolphins in the distance. As dawn
brought more light to the surface of the Gulf, he could see the crea-
tures a hundred yards away playfully going about a morning workout
routine. They were old hat to Barry Ledoux who paid little attention

to them when Brad awakened him the first morning to enjoy the show. He had peeked out from his berth and turned back over. The enjoyment of dolphins was for newcomers to the sea.

They came closer and circled the boat. It was as near as they had been in the week that he had been shrimping. He counted them—six, seven, eight—circling, bobbing, and diving. They were a family. They came at the boat and dove beneath. Brad ran to the other side to see them reappear. They circled again. He ran back to the other side. It was better than a circus or a water show. The sleek gray bodies appearing and then disappearing beneath the boat. He lost count.

Barefooted, he ran to the far side again to watch them surface. The boat listed to that side in the mild rolling sea, and in his hurry, he couldn't catch himself. He hit the side like a gymnast turning a flip. His torso went over the rail. His legs and feet followed. The sensation was peculiar—sliding down the side of the slick boat toward the gray water. He was in a dream and would be yanked back to consciousness.

When he struck the cold water and went under, he knew it was for real. His heart raced. Fear and panic seized him by the gut. He opened his eyes but couldn't see. Water gurgled in his ears and burned his nose. Sense of up and down was lost in darkness. He held his breath and hoped he would surface. The seconds in the black water stretched into years in his mind.

His thoughts raced back and forth. He didn't want to die without telling Jill how much he loved her. He didn't want to drown beneath Barry Ledoux's boat. He spewed out a few bubbles and followed them upward with strong strokes. He bobbed to the surface less than ten feet from the boat.

He swam to the side of the craft, reached out to grasp it, but his fingernails scraped through the slime on the wood. He couldn't hold on. He looked around for his dolphin friends. They had deserted him—a hundred yards away by now—scared by the sudden splash of the dead weight that dropped from the *Sweet Jasmine*. He wasn't dressed to swim. The water-logged shirt and pants were dragging him down. Iron chains around his body couldn't have been heavier. He stripped off his pants and shirt. Then he wondered if that was a good idea. The cold water began chilling him to the bone.

He barely treaded water and maintained contact with the boat. His eyes searched for any place to grab onto. There was none. He yelled for Barry. His voice sounded pitifully faint against the water and slick wood of the boat. Shivers racked his body. His teeth rattled. He swam as forcefully as he could, trying to make a circuit of the boat. There had to be an anchor line someplace that he could hold onto and maybe use to climb back into the boat. If only he could find it.

The cable lay off the stern on the far side. It was a short distance but an exhausting one that took him fifteen minutes to navigate. He shouted for his sleeping friend until he became hoarse from the salt water that splashed into his mouth. He bobbed like a fisherman's float alongside the boat. He was not fit to climb the metal anchor cable when he was dry, warm, and strong, let alone when he was wet, cold, and weak. His attempts brought his waist almost out of the water, then he would plunge back down and under. His eyes burned. He blinked to a blurry vision. His nose bled from the irritation of the water and the pounding of his heart.

He was so chilled that his mind began to play tricks on him. He saw visions. He looked up and Papa Legba, Samuel Harrot, and the Reverend Hutteth were looking over the rail toward him. Jill was there beside them. She pointed toward him, laughed, and then walked away with the Reverend. Then they were all gone.

Little by little, the cold took away the use of his limbs. First it was his fingers that lost their grip on the cable; then his legs cramped. He reached down to massage them and went under. He swallowed water. He surfaced, coughing and sputtering. He wrapped his arm around the cable and rested it in the crook of his elbow. He was becoming sleepy. Hypothermia. But he couldn't resist its inviting comfort. He banged his head against the boat, more to keep himself awake than to stir Barry. He thought he might give himself a concussion, but he continued anyway. If he was going to drown, he would beat himself unconscious before he plunged to the bottom. It would wake him momentarily. Then he would nearly doze off again.

The voice of an angel could have sounded no sweeter to Brad's ears than that of Barry Ledoux. He looked over the wall of the boat, saw his friend blue-skinned in the water, and yelled, "What the hell? Is that you, Brad?" He quickly threw a round life-ring attached to a rope to within three feet of his cold friend. Brad's arms wouldn't reach for it though his mind told them to. His head sank into the water. Barry pulled the ring back up and dropped it over Brad's head.

"Put your arms through and hold on, Brad. I'll pull you in."

Brad wanted to, but he couldn't move. He was chilled, barely able to keep his mouth and nose above water. Barry threw a net over the side, stripped naked, and jumped in with a splash that rolled over his friend's head. He came up within five feet of him. In seconds he secured the ring around Brad, took him to where the net lapped the water, and rolled him into it. He tied it so thate Brad was barely lying in the water and climbed back up the remaining nylon and over the side of the boat looking like a walrus going ashore. He rotated the crane's arm that was already hooked to the net to over the side. Barry landed his catch that looked like a large fish in the midst of the brown nylon mesh, blue skin poking out through every opening.

Barry couldn't tell if Brad was breathing. He rolled him onto his side and watched water dribble out his mouth. He rushed below and returned with blankets. He wrapped two around Brad and huddled in the other himself.

"Speak to me, boy," he said and pounded Brad on the back. "Please say something, Brad. Tell me you're breathing. I don't want to kiss you." He turned Brad onto his back and looked at his blue lips. "Oh, shit, don't die on me." Barry Ledoux shivered and cried at the same time. He held the back of his hand near Brad's mouth and felt for breath. Brad coughed, and Barry turned him onto his side again.

"That's good, Brad. Cough it all up. You'll feel better." He rubbed Brad with the blankets. Brad's arm flinched, and he moved his hand ever so slightly. An hour later, Barry and Brad sipped coffee around the small table in the galley. They still wore their blankets.

"I was scared, Barry. I thought I was a goner. I thought I was going to drown, and you would never know what happened to me." Brad's hoarse voice was barely above a whisper.

"You weren't half as scared as me. I first looked over the side for you and just saw your pants and shirt. I thought a shark ate you plumb out of your clothes."

"That was dumb. A shark would've eaten my clothes too."

"Naw, Brad, sharks around here have better taste in clothes than what you wear."

For the first time that morning, they both laughed.

"Then I rushed over to the other side. And, man, I didn't recognize you at first as being a human. Your color was all wrong. Then I thought you were already dead and just lodged onto the anchor cable some way. You scared me to death. When I got you on board, I was afraid I was going to have to do that mouth-to-mouth breathing with you. You were the most unappetizing looking thing that I'd ever seen." Barry spit on the floor.

"Thanks, Barry. I was really stupid to fall over."

"Now, I've told you all week not to be out there alone without a life preserver. The Gulf can look real calm, and then here comes a great swell that'll about knock you over. What were you doing out that time of morning?"

"I was watching for the sunrise. A school of dolphins were playing around the boat. I was running from one side to the other to watch them. When I fell over, I thought the dolphins would save me. They just went the other way."

"This ain't no movie. Those dolphins don't give a shit about you." He looked out the galley window toward the horizon. "And did you say you were running? You were running barefoot on a boat? I tell you. You're bound to have your own way, aren't you? You're stubborn as a jackass. Matter of fact, it sounds like you're braying from all that saltwater you swallowed."

Brad sat silently, looking into the black coffee that reflected his face. He thought back to what Reverend Hutteth had told him: "If one person tells you that you're a jackass, it's just an opinion. But if several tell you that you are, you should start feeling for the long ears and see if you bray when you speak." He named them to himself. Maxine Hankins, Jill, and, now, Barry Ledoux had all told him that he was a jackass. They had used that exact word, although to illustrate different aspects of his character. Barry was right; his scratchy, hoarse voice echoed the throaty bellow of a braying donkey.

He gazed deeper into the smooth surface of the coffee to see if his ears had grown to match his voice. He didn't notice any difference. He set the cup down and reached with both hands to the cold, still-numb appendages on the sides of his head. It was odd. They gave no sensation. His hands could tell they were there, but they felt like dead flaps of skin. At least they had not grown to the size of those of a jackass. Perhaps it was only a matter of time.

He was beginning to have more faith in the Reverend Hutteth. He couldn't dispute his number theory, nor the Reverend's knowledge of his and Jill's relationship. He knew about her being receptive to the idea of going to Washington. He had warned him about the possibility of pride masquerading as principle. He made the analogy of being called a jackass. It was clear to Brad that the Reverend was right more than he was wrong.

Then he thought back to the other thing he had said about his and Jill's relationship: "You'll find a way to make your love work. Otherwise it's not love—on both sides." Of all the terrible experience of almost drowning, Brad remembered most the thought and the vision. He did not want to die without telling Jill how much he loved her. Then he had hallucinated about her pointing at him, laughing, and walking away with the Reverend Hutteth—the fornicating teller of truth.

"Dammit, Barry! Let's weigh anchor. I'm going home," he said as forcefully as he could for a man who was still hoarse, cold, and weak.

# Thirty-one

**A**l Shanker came to headquarters early. He wound and rewound the videotape machine. A few employees were beginning to filter in. He had to find it when Dobson wasn't there. He needed the scene that would verify what Brad Yeary had told him about the bloody handkerchief—that he had wiped the blood from the hand of Jill Crenshaw. He couldn't just tell Dobson that. Then he would know that he had been talking with Brad—a possible suspect in the assassination.

If he could find it, then he could show it to Dobson, send an agent or two to interview Crenshaw, and be done with the suspicion that hung over both her and Brad. Of all the tape and film they had, it had to be there.

An hour later he found it. Shot from the east side of the field at ground level, a camera had focused on Harrot with Yeary and Crenshaw in the background. He pushed a button to enhance the area that showed the two lovers. She slumped into his arms and momentarily went to the turf. A handkerchief appeared from his pocket, and he wiped both her hand and his. Yeary returned it to his pocket and Crenshaw was up and about in a matter of seconds.

Shanker pushed a few more buttons to copy that segment with an enlarged close-up onto a different machine. He had his proof. He pressed a phone button and found a couple of agents already in the building. He told them to interview Crenshaw about her fainting. "Ask her specifically if she knew she had blood on her hand."

"Got some more reports back, Al." Dobson sat down across the table. He laid two sealed envelopes and two bulky packages in the center. "Let's just take pot luck," he said and picked up the envelope on top. He opened it and handed Shanker a copy. "This is on the jacket." He patted the bigger box, scanned the report to the conclusion, and laid it down. "Well this helps a little. Blood stains and hair. The blood doesn't match anything we have. Neither does most of the hair. But a few hairs are similar to what was found on the A cloth."

Shanker read the same report. "Where does that put us? The same guy wearing both jackets?"

Dobson shook his head. "No. It connects them. Hair from the Alabama guy on the Notre Dame guy's jacket. Pretty much says they're the same two we saw in the Superdome tapes. If you hang out with someone, there's probably going to be some of your hair or something on the other guy's clothes. Right now, there's probably a hair or two of mine that've found their way to your jacket. Hair falls out all the time. If you spend a few hours with someone, you're going to have a hair or two. Just be careful that they don't show up long and blond when you go home to your wife. Women have microscopic vision. We hire a lot of them for our lab work." He laughed and laid the papers down.

"So, our team of assassins was blown up on the boat? Where does that leave us?"

"Up shit bayou without a paddle." Dobson tore open the other envelope and again gave a copy to Shanker.

"Uh, oh, this one's mine to explain." Shanker flipped to the second page. "That wad of hundreds that Billy Roach found was sent to the Treasury lab for analysis. Couldn't identify the bank that distributed them—because they're counterfeit."

Dobson looked up. "Counterfeit? Boy, they looked good. Where're they from?"

"Syria. They're part of a billion dollar batch that started circulating in '93, '94, and '95. We hadn't seen many lately. Thought the bills were all gone and they were out of business. They were made by a terrorist group that was seeking to undermine the U.S. currency system. Very good counterfeits. Even our sophisticated sorting machines couldn't detect the difference. Same paper, same fiber content, same iron oxide, even had the horizontal bar imbedded in them that you had to hold up to the light to read which said '100USA100USA' all across."

"So, that skinny Billy Roach got his hot little hands on ten thousand in bogus money. I guess the Treasury Department will take the bite on this, Al. You wouldn't want to take money away from that kid, would you? Aren't you the one that kept mumbling that he'd found the American Dream?"

"Yeah, let him keep it. We have bigger problems."

"You thinking what I'm thinking?"

"Probably not. Tell me what you're thinking?"

"We're going to have to go international on this. Maybe the CIA. Counterfeit currency from Syria. Oh, I hate to get the CIA involved. I wanted to keep this just in the FBI."

"The FBI and . . ."

"Oh, and you, of course, Al. Hell, I'm beginning to think of you as FBI."

"Please don't."

"What I'm going to have to do is have a conference with the Director. He may want to go to the President or his right-hand man—Steinheitz. We can't sit on it. They can make the final decision of whether to involve the CIA or not. I'm covering my ass on this one."

Shanker pushed a button on his video machine. "John, before you run off, I want you to look at this. Here, scoot around so you can see it."

He played the tape for Dobson. And again.

"That's the mysterious handkerchief?" Dobson asked.

"Yeah, it answers the questions we were asking. Crenshaw got blood on her hand when she touched Harrot. Yeary wiped it off. That's how he knew Harrot was shot. It's Harrot's blood on there."

"So?"

"So, I think we should cut Yeary and Crenshaw some slack. I don't like possibly ruining someone's career when they haven't done anything."

Dobson replayed the tape for himself. "Well, Al, Yeary still hasn't given us the handkerchief. I'd like to see it."

"You know how those reporters are. They think everything is privileged and protected. But we don't need the handkerchief if we know how the blood got on it."

Dobson turned the tape off. "You may be right. I talked to Governor Johnson myself. I told him about Crenshaw having the tickets and being connected with Yeary who had the bloody handkerchief. I knew he was thinking about appointing her to the Senate. I just wanted him to think about it."

"What did he say?"

"Well, obviously, he didn't take me too seriously. He announced her appointment the next day. He said he didn't really care much for the FBI, he was retiring, and he would do what he damn well pleased. He said he knew Jill Crenshaw like a daughter, and she would not be involved in any criminal activity. He said he hated to vouch for a reporter, but if Jill Crenshaw liked Brad Yeary, it pretty well cinched it that he was one of the good guys."

"John, after I found this on tape, I asked a couple of agents to go out and ask Senator Crenshaw if she remembered having blood on her hand. They're out there now. I hope you don't mind."

Dobson shook his head. "No, Al. You're part of the team. I'm glad you're taking some initiative." He leaned back and closed his eyes.

"How can we handle it?" They sat there in silence, Shanker staring at Dobson wondering if he'd gone to sleep. Finally, Dobson sat back up.

"Okay. I'll go along with your hunch and the governor's. If the agents come back with verification from Crenshaw that she had blood on her hand, we'll loosen up on Yeary. I'm going to Washington with the news on the money. You can get word to Yeary and his publisher that we don't need the handkerchief at this time. That he isn't a suspect. However, I'm telling you that I'm going to keep a close eye on him and, if I have my way, he won't get within fifty yards of the President until we break something on this. How's that?"

"Fine. I'll get word to them."

A knock interrupted their planning. Another agent-messenger from the lab handed an envelope to Dobson and had him sign a receipt.

"What else did we send off?" Shanker asked.

Dobson slowly opened the sealed paper. "I don't know. They have so much from the Superdome sweep that we get stuff everyday. Most of it's useless."

Again, a duplicate was provided that he handed to Shanker.

"It's the bullet. Or the stuff that was in the bullet." Dobson paused as he skipped to the summary and conclusion. His eyes widened.

"Is this supposed to mean something, John?"

"Yeah, they've identified the poison that was in the hollow of the bullet."

"I see the name for it. But what is it?"

"On the next page, Al." Dobson turned Shanker's copy to the second page. "It was a very concentrated equine anesthetic. It's used to put down—to destroy—horses."

# Thirty-two

P lease place your hand on the Bible."

Jill Crenshaw stood in the well of the Senate ready to repeat the oath of office. The day before, February sixteenth, Benjamin Edward Ashford was confirmed as the new Vice President. He presided on this occasion, but allowed the first female U.S. Senator from Louisiana to be sworn in by one of the two female justices of the Supreme Court. Beside her stood her father and Brad Yeary.

In less than five minutes the ceremony was completed. She made a short acceptance to her colleagues from the floor. Then, hand in hand with Brad, she strode through the congratulatory throng toward the steps of the Capitol where she would speak longer to the press and to the people back in Louisiana.

Channel Five from New Orleans provided live coverage. Dan Boring of the *Times-Gazette* wrote the story for the paper. Brad had the day off.

"I want to thank Governor Johnson for his confidence in me. I pledge to all the people of Louisiana that I will be the best U.S. Senator I can be. I appreciate the support of my family and friends. A lot of work lies ahead of me, and I'm ready to get at it." She spoke for ten minutes and answered questions for fifteen more.

Brad tried to stay in the background. This was Jill's day. He had had many of his own. This one they would celebrate on her time. He would be by her side as much as possible. They would make this work. He was determined.

"Let's go to my new office," Jill said to Brad and her father.

"You and Brad go ahead," her father said, "I'm regretfully going to have to get back to Louisiana. Important business. I'm proud of you." They hugged. The Senator shed a tear. "Do the state a good job. Brad, you keep her straight, okay?" With a wave, he left them.

Brad and Jill walked to her new offices. The staff was busy unpacking boxes and moving furniture when they tiptoed through the maze. With the lowest seniority, she received the least attractive suite of rooms. Time in office still stood for something in the U.S. Senate. She pointed out to Brad the equipment and where everyone would be working.

"I think it's just great, Brad."

"Not bad. At least you're not in the basement like you were in

Baton Rouge."

"And I get to choose the carpet and drapes that I want. They're going to change that next week. I'm so excited."

"Now, don't go and spend too much of the taxpayers' money."

"I'm in the Russell Long Building, Brad. They named a building after another Louisianan. I stood on the steps of our Capitol just a few weeks ago when Hugh announced that he was going to appoint me. I looked out toward the Huey Long statue. Now I'm here in a building they named after his brother."

Brad looked around. He was glad for her. "Mr. Long of Louisiana. I guess they name a lot of the buildings up here after famous people. The Washington Monument, the Jefferson Memorial, the Watergate Building."

"Oh, Brad, there was no Mr. Watergate."

"What about Nixon?"

"I hardly think Nixon would have wanted to be known as Mr. Watergate."

Brad moved a couple of boxes from a couch and sat down. He motioned Jill to join him.

"Nixon will always be known by that term—Watergate. Don't you think so, Jill?"

"Well, yeah, that's true. But he did a lot more than that. Even I, your diehard Democrat, will have to admit that he did some great things in foreign policy. Opening up with the Chinese and all. He accomplished a lot."

"Very true. I was just testing you. But you have to remember that in politics, as in many other aspects of life, you'll be remembered for what you did last—not necessarily what you did best. A first day senator needs to know that. As Vice President Ashford asked me, 'Do you have a principle that you're willing to die for?'"

"He asked you that?"

"Yeah."

"And what did you say?"

Brad looked at the floor and then back at Jill. "Something I soon regretted. That I would give my life for freedom of the press."

Jill nodded. "That's noble. That's very good. I'm proud of you. How did you come to say that?"

"It's my life. Freedom of the press and writing is what my life is about. If it didn't exist, my life would be meaningless. So, it really wasn't anything noble to say. It was just a fact."

"Yes, Brad, but freedom of the press would exist without you."

"And so it should." He got up and walked to the window that had less than a spectacular view.

"Did you ask Ashford what he was willing to die for?"

"No."

"You should have. What kind of journalist are you anyway?"

He turned back from the window and thought for a minute. "I don't know. Did you know it was Watergate that really got me into journalism?"

"No. How did that happen?"

"I was nineteen when Nixon was reelected in 1972. I was in LSU, but I wasn't really sure I wanted a career in journalism, although I was taking courses there and had it as my major.

"But when this Watergate thing really took off in '73 and into '74, I read everything I could get on it. I cut my teeth on the *Washington Post* and the articles of Bernstein and Woodward. That was investigative reporting at its best. From that time on, I was determined to be a journalist. And if it ever came to it, I would be prepared to follow in their footsteps. Their writing brought down a Presidency."

"Well, their writing and the Senate committee that investigated the mess. I was in the seventh grade and our civics and history teacher let us watch the hearings of the committee for two hours every day. I remember Sam Ervin—the old country lawyer—asking questions and John Dean answering. That's what got me interested in government. I'd just sit there mesmerized. And when his own party's senators—like Howard Baker—started asking those hard questions about 'what Nixon knew and when he knew it,' it sealed the case for me. I was forever hooked on politics. I saw that honorable people from both parties working together could do what was best for the country."

"Pretty astute for a seventh grader."

"Well, I was an eighth grader by then. And I didn't use those big words."

"So, we both got our drive from the same event. Me from the newspaper stories. You from the committee. It's sort of like we're twins. Not identical but . . . what's the word?"

"Fraternal."

"Yeah, we're fraternal twins. That probably prevents us from getting married."

"Not in Louisiana." Jill winked. "It's strange that we'd talked about so much before but hadn't talked about what spurred either of us on to be what we are."

"I guess it could sound kind of corny if one of us had brought it up out of the blue. But here and now, it has some significance. You're in the Senate that you watched on television years ago and I'm writing about the investigation of the murder of a Vice President. It's not exactly Watergate, but nothing else is either. You know something else interesting about Nixon?"

"I know a lot, but I don't know what you're referring to."

"He resigned on my birthday. I became a man on the day he resigned—August 9, 1974, was my twenty-first birthday."

"Interesting." Jill counted on her fingers. "That means you're going to be forty-five this August, right? What am I doing running around with an old man?" She leaned over and kissed him on the cheek. "Let's go to the apartment so I can change clothes and then go out to eat."

"Yeah. Maybe at the apartment I can demonstrate what you're doing running around with an old man." Brad kissed her on the lips. "Isn't your apartment within a block or so of the Watergate?"

"Yes, I'm afraid so."

"You live in the historic part of town. They have a special tour for all the infamous places. The Watergate, the Tidal Basin where the guy from Arkansas chased Fanny Fox, and the restaurants where all the co-conspirators from the Nixon administration went to eat. How about me taking you to one of those places for dinner? Who knows, we might run into the spirits of Haldeman, Erlichman, John Mitchell, or even Nixon himself."

ROB STEINHEITZ AND GEORGE Garron sat together at a table in a dark corner of the elite restaurant. By prior arrangement, the owner always knew when they needed privacy and hid them away from the boisterous crowd out front and from the prying eyes of reporters who also made this a favorite gathering place. Within two thousand square feet of floor space, on an average evening, could be found those who had power, those who coveted power, and those who told about power.

The President's men would sit in the more public area when they wanted to be seen or wanted to corner a reporter and plant a story. But when they didn't want the glaring light of public scrutiny, they stole in through a private entrance to this little corner where they could enjoy the good food, have a hushed conversation, and then leave through the public area and slap a few backs on the way out.

"I've arranged to meet with our Muslim friends next month in Lexington. The President feels it's about time to take Ashford out in public, and I'm going with him to the basketball tournament there in Lexington at Rupp Arena," Steinheitz said.

"Well, that's good. We have a few fences to mend in Kentucky. That should be a good gesture."

"Yeah, and the President wants us to show the country that we're not afraid of assassins. He's going to let the Vice President sit right out in public."

"Teater's going to let Ashford show that we're not afraid of assassinations? That's a safe way for him to do it, right?" Garron laughed at the thought. He looked at Steinheitz. "Well, I guess he will be safe, won't he? You're going to be with him?"

"Yes. And what makes it real safe is that you're not going to be there."

"Why do you say that?"

Steinheitz glanced around to see who might have wandered into their space. "Harrot. New Orleans." He whispered the three words even though no one was within fifty feet of them.

"I wasn't in New Orleans with Harrot."

"Yes, and that was a very good cover, too, I might add."

Garron leaned back in his chair and opened his eyes wide. He swept his hand back over his mostly bald head and then leaned forward.

"Wait a minute, Rob. Don't put Harrot's death on me. It wasn't from my side of the White House that it was done. Hell, yes, I'm the chief political operative. But that wasn't in my job description. That came from your side. Didn't it?"

Steinheitz stared at Garron. Then he looked around. He grimaced and leaned over near Garron. "George, I didn't have anything to do with Harrot's death. I'm not just saying that to save my ass. It didn't come from me. I thought you did it."

"Rob, ever since the President talked to us outside that day about how good a job we did, I thought it was all your doing. I didn't want to say anything in front of the President. The less I knew the better."

"I thought you ordered it through some domestic operation. I was the same way when the President said that. I was stunned. He acted like we both were in on it, and that he would protect us. I knew I didn't do it, but I thought you did." Steinheitz sat in silence. He and Garron exchanged long stares. "Shit. If we didn't do it, who did do it? And why?"

"Do you think the President could have done it himself? Ordered it through the military, CIA, or something?"

Steinheitz bowed his head. "Why would he say that to us if he had it done? No, Teater's not a detail man. Everything that's done goes through one of us. He always uses us for a sounding board even when he's going to tell a cabinet member to do something. I don't think he has the guts for it."

"Well, maybe, maybe not. He didn't want Harrot around. He could have been accepting that award in New Orleans, but he arranged for Harrot to go, didn't he?"

"That, George, was part of my doing. The Secret Service wasn't going to let us put the President out in front of seventy thousand people. Especially where they would be elevated and the President at the center of the field. That's to invite some crazy to take a shot. I said to send the Vice President. The Service squawked about that. But I persuaded them it would be okay. No Vice President had ever come under attack. I did my bad ass routine and they caved in.

I put Harrot in New Orleans but I didn't kill him."

"I didn't even know he was going. When I heard he'd been shot, it was news to me that he was even there."

"No one knew until that morning except for Harrot and a few others who were making the arrangements."

"When did Harrot know?"

"Two weeks ahead of time."

"Damn. We'd better start paying closer attention to the investigation then. What do you know about that?" Garron asked and pushed his plate away. He had suddenly lost his appetite.

"Oh, the chief guy down in New Orleans—I think his name is Dobson—with the FBI was up here a couple of weeks ago. I met with him and the director. They don't have a clue, really. He tells me they have the assassins on tape. Believes they were blown up in a boat as they escaped. They have some of those scientific DNA tests they did to connect up a few shreds of evidence. Hell, I was sitting there real pleased that you had done such a wonderful job."

"Was he up for anything in particular or just a routine report?"

"That's what I forgot. He came up to ask whether we should get the CIA involved. He said he had found some counterfeit hundreds that were manufactured in Syria. He thought they were connected to the killing some way that never was clear to me. I told him and the director to just keep it in the Bureau. Told them the President had great confidence in the FBI and there was no need to involve the CIA. Just a bunch of bull at the time. I really thought that old George had financed it with some money through our Muslim friends in Syria and I didn't want them to be nosing around too much. That was my first act to protect you." Steinheitz smiled at his longtime friend.

Garron was silent for a minute. He then leaned closer to Steinheitz and whispered, "That could mean that the President arranged it himself. He knows a couple of our Arab contacts. He could've just dropped a hint and then they did it on their own. If they saw Harrot as a threat to them being successful in a coup, they could have popped him. Did the President know Harrot's schedule for going to New Orleans?"

"Sure. He knew. I told him myself."

"Let's go, Rob. I've got to go home and think this over. We don't need to lose control of this operation. If people are out there doing things on their own, we may have problems down the road. We need to find out definitely who was responsible for Harrot's murder. Can you push that Dobson to give you all the dope they have? We don't need them to solve it. We just need to know how close they're getting. From what we know, maybe we can put the pieces together before they do."

"Yeah, I'll push for a weekly briefing. I may have to go down to New Orleans to get it. But I could use a little time on Bourbon Street." They pushed the chairs back and made their way into the busy part of the restaurant.

BRAD NUDGED JILL'S ELBOW with his finger. "Look coming toward us—the President's chief aides—Steinheitz and Garron. Aren't you glad I brought you to this restaurant?"

"Thrilled. Should I say hello to them?"

The two men were walking a line that would take them right by the table of the new senator from Louisiana. They stopped at three tables in between to chat with two reporters and a couple of cabinet members. Brad was determined to make the introductions. Jill tried to hold him down.

"Mr. Steinheitz, Mr. Garron," Brad almost shouted to get the men's attention as they walked near. "I'd like you to meet Jill Crenshaw—sworn in today as Louisiana's junior senator."

Steinheitz and Garron appeared puzzled at first but then extended hands toward Jill and Brad. "Good to meet you, Senator Crenshaw. Sorry we couldn't make it to your swearing in. We'll be calling on you soon, no doubt," Garron said and turned toward Brad. "I know I should know you too."

"Brad Yeary. I'm with the New Orleans *Times-Gazette*."

"Oh, yes. You were up here about a month ago for an interview with the President. You're doing a great job. You both were there the night that Vice President Harrot was shot, weren't you? What a shame. A great loss to the country."

"Yes. Very shocking," Jill said.

"Well, Mr. Yeary, I'll let you get back to your interview with the new senator," Garron said to Brad and then turned toward Jill, "I know he'll write a great story about you, Senator. I look forward to working with you."

"The same goes for me," Steinheitz added and shook hands with Brad and Jill before leaving.

Brad and Jill watched the two most powerful men in the world, next to the President, walk out onto the street before they turned toward each other and laughed.

"They thought you were interviewing me. I guess word hasn't made it to Washington yet."

"I was upset that they recognized you and not me."

"This is exciting. My first day and I get to meet the top men."

"From what I hear, they are. If you want anything from the White House, you have to go through one of them."

"How long can you stay? Does Pinthater want you back right away?"

"Have to go back tomorrow for a few days. I've got to come up with something to write on the Harrot investigation."

"So, what did Pinthater say when he told you that you were back on the story?"

"As little as possible. Said that Agent Shanker from the investigation had stopped by to see me while I was down in Lafitte. Told Pinthater they decided the bloody hanky wasn't all that important. They'd still like to see it, but it wasn't that big a deal."

"And Pinthater told you to go back on the story?"

"Yeah. Said they'd had a lot of people calling asking where I was and why they hadn't seen anything on the investigation lately. Made me feel good to know there were some people out there calling in asking about me."

"Well, I've been meaning to tell you. I had all my staff call in anonymously and ask where you were. So, don't go thinking too highly of your readership." Jill grinned.

"I thought so. They always teach us to write for a readership assuming a sixth grade level of education. That must be where your staff fits in."

Darkness was complete when they finished dinner and walked back out onto the sidewalk. The mid-February chill had Jill pulling her coat tightly to her and walking arm in arm with Brad.

"Is it safe to walk here?"

Brad looked in front and behind. "As long as you're observant and not alone, it's probably as safe as any large city. Probably as safe as New Orleans. You want to walk a ways?"

"Yeah, I can't come down yet. I'm still way up here." She held her hand above her head. "I'm so glad you're adjusting better to having me up here. I was about to back out when you went down to Lafitte. I didn't know whether it was worth it. But I knew deep down, this was what I wanted to do. I just wanted you to be with me and be supportive. I love you."

"Me, too."

"Me, too, what? You love me, or you love you?"

"Both."

"Say it then."

"I love you."

"That's better. Now tell me about your shrimping trip. Anything exciting happen?"

Brad paused in his walk. Then he started up again. "Naw. Just two old smelly seamen out on the Gulf in a wooden boat for a week. I knew after a week with Barry Ledoux that I didn't want to spend the rest of my life doing that. It's a great job if you're born into it. But it has to be in your blood. Very hard work. Harder and harder to make a living from it. I admire those like Barry who can."

He pointed toward the Washington monument in the distance.

"I just decided to come back, and if I had to work for another newspaper or be on your staff, I would. Ink's in my blood. I'm bound to write."

"You could still be on my staff if you wanted. We could really give this town a run for its money. The best journalist and the best senator on the same team."

They eventually made their way to the Jefferson Memorial and sat near the base of the steps on the cold marble. A full moon was rising through the skeletal branches of barren oak trees. There was no breeze. Their breath hung in sparkling crystals in the frigid air. Only a few tourists braved the cold night and lingered at the monument reading and observing the stone figure of one of the country's founders.

"My parish is named for him," Brad said.

"Yeah, he's the one who said if he had to choose between government without newspapers or newspapers without government he'd choose the newspapers. Isn't that right?"

"Very close. Of course, that was before he was attacked so viciously by some newspaper owners."

"Do you ascribe to that? That newspapers are more important than government?"

"Fortunately, we don't have to make that choice. When they're both doing their jobs, we don't need to." Brad turned to Jill. "Have you ever been kissed at the Jefferson Memorial?"

"No."

"Me neither. Let's see what it's like."


IN NEW ORLEANS, AL Shanker was looking through a thick file containing all the information many agents had compiled on the search for the purchaser of the tickets to the seats where the assassins sat. John Dobson walked in and sat down across the table.

"You're late, John. Did you find a hot lead?"

"No. I've been to the doctor. They're going to have to scope me. Think I may have an ulcer. I tell you, Al, it's this damn investigation." He slammed his fist down on the table. "A month and a half and we don't have shit. Even the rumors are beginning to run out. We're at a dead end. Congress is appointing at least three committees that are going to look into the assassination and probably into our investigation. Why couldn't Harrot have been shot in some other city?"

Shanker got up from the table and walked to a file cabinet. He ignored his friend. He didn't need to be reminded that his failure may have allowed Harrot to be shot in any city.

"I'm sorry. I didn't mean to imply that you would've let him get shot in another city. I know you did your best. Like we're doing our best here. It's just that we're under a lot of pressure to put the finger on someone."

"John, I was going through that ticket file again. That holds the key. If we find out who bought the tickets, it'll give us someone to talk to."

"How do we know that the guy who ran the ad even kept the tickets? He or they may have resold them and on and on."

"Well, the newspaper said it was a cash transaction. The ad gave a telephone number of a pay booth in the bus station just two blocks from the Superdome. We have two maintenance employees at the bus station who remember seeing a guy hanging around that telephone for two days during the time we're looking at."

"Yeah. But no name. No address."

"But they both agreed to describe him under hypnosis. We might at least get a composite drawing."

"I hope they both come up with a similar picture."

"Yeah, we sent them to independent specialists. If it turns out similar, at least we have a picture we can circulate."

"But if it turns out to look like one of the guys we have on the tape then we're back to square one."

"Well, it's worth a try. Anything new on the money?"

"No, our people and yours say those Syrian hundreds haven't circulated here in a couple of years."

"Remember, the newspaper said the ad was paid for with a hundred dollar bill."

"Yeah, I wished they'd kept it. It would be easy enough to match up," Dobson said and rubbed his stomach. The pain was apparent on his face. "When I met with the Director and the President's man, we decided to keep the investigation inside the FBI with help from Treasury where necessary. Steinheitz didn't act very concerned that we hadn't put the finger on anyone yet. Said the President had confidence in us."

"Yeah, but wait until Congress and the press start screaming. Then you can bet that Steinheitz will be on our asses."

They both pored over the papers in the file for another five minutes.

"John, do you think the money and the plastic explosive give the assassination a foreign flavor?"

"They do. But our lab experts say the horse anesthetic is made in this country."

"Well, that solves it then. The assassin is a Syrian veterinarian with a green card who dabbles in explosives. How's that for a profile?"

# Thirty-three

T he blue screen flickered with the dreaded message: FILE NOT FOUND. Brad Yeary slammed his coffee cup down, sloshing the few papers on his desk at the same time. For fifteen years he had failed at understanding how computers worked. He could barely process his stories through the intricate mechanisms without losing a line or page.

Now he had lost an entire file. He pressed the button that was supposed to display the file directory. The list scrolled upward in neat alphabetical order. What had he named it? It would come to him if he stared at the screen long enough. It didn't. He finally gave up and turned to read a Washington paper. He wanted to see how the capital's press played the swearing in of Jill the day before.

On page A-10 he finally found a two-paragraph story. "Damn, they don't give much coverage to the first woman senator from Louisiana," he said and threw the paper into a heap in the floor beside his desk. He could tell this wasn't going to be a good day. His mind was on Washington and Jill. Pinthater wanted another story on the Harrot investigation, and Brad was running out of new story-lines. By looking through some of his old files that he had stored in his trusty computer, he thought an idea might flash its fresh face.

"Danny, Danny, come over here, my friend," he shouted at the university intern who was a computer wonk. Danny edged into Brad's territory a little hesitantly. Just the month before, Brad had caught him playing a game on his computer and had given him a good tongue lashing. "Danny don't be afraid. I need your help. I've lost a damn file on here, and I can't find it. Can you help me? Please."

Danny set down the bundle of papers he was carrying, squinted at the screen through thick glasses that sat on a hawkish nose, and waved Brad out of his seat.

"Mr. Yeary, do you know if you deleted the file?"

"No. I could have. My elbow scraped across several of the keys. That control button sometimes sticks and makes me not know what the hell I'm doing."

"I see. Well, just give me the name of the file."

"I forgot. It has information in it about Harrot's assassination. Names and phone numbers. Some notes I made but never used. Just a lot of otherwise useless information."

"I see," Danny said. He stared at the screen and his fingers flashed across the keyboard more deftly than any piano player's. "Wait a minute. I have something back in my area that I need. It's my tool for finding lost files." Danny sprinted to the back of the building and was gone less than a minute when he returned holding a disk. He pressed it into the slot on the computer.

"Will that do the job?"

"I hope so, Mr. Yeary. I've done wonders with it before. How long has your file been missing?"

"I was working on it just a few minutes before."

"Good." The keyboard rattled out with the cadence of a train going clickety-clack down the rails at seventy miles per hour. "There's nothing on here you mind me seeing, is there, Mr. Yeary? No pornography? No government secrets?"

"No," Brad said and thought back to all the years he had used the computer. He wasn't sure what was buried deep in its innards.

"This will draw up every file you've ever had on it."

"Even if I've deleted it?"

Danny smiled. "Sure. That's what a lot of people don't know. Delete only makes that disk space available for use. It doesn't erase the file until something else is put on top of it. Most deleted files can be brought back unless you're near the capacity of your disk and have written over it." He rattled on with the keys, occasionally stopping to look closer. Then a list of file names began scrolling up the screen. Danny slowed it to a crawl, moved out of the chair, and motioned Brad to sit back down. "Tell me if any of those file names rings a bell."

Brad watched intently as name after name rolled by. He saw some that he knew he had deleted intentionally, never wanting the contents to see the light of day. It was like judgment day with God playing back every deed he had ever done. Then he saw the one that he thought was the Harrot file and pointed to the screen. "Try that one."

Danny looked and smiled. "Yeah, that one was deleted." He sat back down, struck a few more keys until the screen filled with the file that Brad thought he had lost.

"Great, Danny. That's it. That's what I was looking for. And you did all that with that little disk there?" Brad asked, pointing to the flat square of plastic that Danny retrieved from the machine.

"That and this," Danny answered, pointing to his head.

"You're a marvel, Danny. I'm really sorry about jumping on you that day. I was in a bad mood. You can play with my computer anytime you like. Okay?"

"Glad to help, Mr. Yeary. If you ever need any advice about computers, feel free to call me." He picked up the bundle of papers and trudged back through the row of desks toward the back of the room. Brad resumed the perusal of files hoping to be inspired to write the story that Pinthater wanted.

After another fruitless hour where he just sat and stared at all the notes he had made on the Harrot investigation, he decided to get out of the office. He looked at his watch. It was still early morning. There would be plenty of time to write a column before the midnight deadline.

Out on the street and in his car, he drove down Burgundy toward his apartment but didn't stop. Across Esplanade, he found himself aimed toward Papa Legba's as though by some strange power. He wondered if his friend was putting out a voodoo call for him. For the most of the month since he had given the bloody hanky to him, Brad had felt as though someone was sticking needles in a doll that must have carried a close resemblance to him. Bad luck had tracked him like a bloodhound. Legba would throw him out of his yard if he mentioned voodoo dolls. Papa had told him more than once that they were highly overrated. Voodoo was more positive than negative.

But just like in the other aspects of life, the negative, dark, and different drew the most attention. The White Magic of voodoo shouldn't be confused with the Black Magic of witchcraft gone bad. There were good spirits and bad. Papa Legba urged the use of the good but let some people believe that he was also in league with the bad demonic powers. He would have either respect or fear.

The red stump of his right ankle stuck out from beneath his robe as Papa Legba sat in his familiar place on the back porch of his small house.

Brad took his shoes off and found a seat on a thick slice of a cyprus stump five feet from the porch. He waited for his friend to open his eyes from meditation.

Legba raised his head, opened his eyes, and saw the reporter seated in front of him. "My young Mr. Yeary. What honor brings you to my humble share-cropper's hovel?"

"Thank you for the compliment. But I'm reminded daily that I'm not young. How're you doing, Papa?"

"Fine, just fine. I could use a stick or two of wood for my stove or even a lump or so of coal. The house is cold. The power has been turned off. I eat scraps from restaurants that friends bring by. But I'm doing fine because my soul is free, not burdened with the cares of this world, but able to meditate and receive some discernment of the mysteries of the universe. Some, but not all. There are many great secrets still to be revealed."

"You'll have wood, coal, and food this afternoon, Papa. I'll see to it."

"I don't want much. I might get too comfortable and not know the joy of fasting and meditation. You ever fast?"

"At Lent, I used to give up something."

"Whiskey or sex?" Papa asked and laughed.

"If I gave up one, I gave up both," Brad answered, smiling at his friend, "because until recently I had to drink to have sex with some of the women I ended up with. But that's all behind me. I've been true to my lover for the past five years."

"Yes. Much safer that way."

"Papa, I came to ask you. Have you had any luck in contacting Samuel Harrot? Did the hanky with his blood help any?"

Legba shook his head and pulled his robe tighter around him as a late February breeze whipped around the corner of the house. "Harrot has been one hard spirit to contact. I tried every morning, evening, and night with no success. Until last night."

Brad leaned closer. "Last night? You talked with him last night?"

"I didn't say talked. I made contact. He's a reluctant spirit. He finally appeared, but he was ill at ease. He was agitated."

"What did he say? Did he say anything?"

"Yes. He said, 'Why do you bother me? I'm at rest. What do you want?' " Legba paused. He picked up the leather pouch of dried bone joints that lay beside him. His big hand entered the bag as carefully as if it contained rattlesnakes. Part of the treasure of yellow bone pieces was withdrawn. He kneaded them in both hands as Brad looked on.

"Did you ask him about who killed him?"

"Yes." Legba rolled the bones out onto the bare wood floor in front of him. They scattered to a stop in a random arrangement. He stared at them for a minute and committed their position to memory. He picked up two. "He was upset that I asked. He said it was not his to point the finger at the causer of his death. That was the word he used—*causer*. He said vengeance belonged to God. He was at peace."

"Didn't he say anymore?"

"I apologized for disturbing him. Before he left, he looked back, and said, 'Look at the White House.'"

Brad sat in silence. Legba continued to pick up the bones one at a time. "Look, Brad." He held up one small piece of bone, yellowed with age. "That's my big toe." He put it back in the bag.

"You know, even though I lost my foot years ago between those barges, I have the sensation sometimes that it's still there. I start to walk sometimes before I remember that I don't have a right foot. 'Phantom nerve sensation' is what the doctor told me. I think it may be the same way for the recently departed. I'm talking about the ones who have been severed from this life. They may have a 'phantom sensation' that they are still here. They don't want to be, so they regret being called back. Those who are gone longer—a hundred years or more—I can call back easier. They know they don't have to come back to this sorry world." He placed all the bone fragments back into the pouch.

"What were the bones for that you threw out this time, Papa?"

"To see if I should tell you what Harrot told me." He looked at Brad with eyes shaded by his prominent brow.

"And?"

"They said you could handle it." He pulled the string tight on the bag.

"Look at the White House." Brad repeated the message from Harrot.

"Brad, in a hundred years or so, Harrot will open up more when we call him back. But now he wants to be at peace. He doesn't want to be reminded of this place."

"In a hundred years, Papa, neither you nor I will be here to call him back. It won't matter then."

Legba smiled. "Does it now?"

THE DRIVE UP I-10 to Baton Rouge and then to Lafayette sped along interrupted only by Brad's phone calls to the grocery store and coal and wood supplier for Papa. Brad's mind was speeding faster than the Ford. He would compare the backgrounds and lives of Harrot and Ashford for his next story. What were the similarities and differences? It would give him an excuse to go to Stratford Place and visit Amelia Tadford. Perhaps she could enlighten him as to anything in Ashford's history that was unique or at least unusual.

By noon he was pressing the door bell.

"Mr. Yeary. It's good to see you. Come in. I'm afraid your visit is a waste. The Senator . . . I mean the Vice President isn't here." Amelia showed Brad to the parlor to a chair in front of the fireplace where logs smoldered awaiting a poke to ignite them. "May I get you something to drink? Or a sandwich?"

"No, I'm fine. Thank you."

She walked in front of him, took an iron from a rack near the fireplace, bent slightly, and prodded the logs to life. Flames licked up the sides. Small, blue and orange, but it was a start. "We have central heat. We just keep the fireplace going for the atmosphere. The Senator likes it. Even when he's gone, I keep it going."

"It's like a love story. It just needs the right punch now and then to keep it going."

Amelia smiled. "I guess so. It can go either way. It can smolder out. Or you can give it a little chuck and it's on fire again. Of course, then shortly you need more fuel. It'll smolder longer than it'll burn."

"True. You could've been a philosopher, Amelia."

She sat down in a chair facing Brad but a comfortable distance from him and the fireplace. "Well, maybe so. I read a lot of the Senator's books." She nodded to the library.

"I came to see you, Amelia, not the Vice President."

"I'm flattered, Mr. Yeary, but—"

"Brad. You can call me Brad."

"Well, Brad, I know I flirted with you last time, but I don't know if I'm ready for you to drive all the way up here just to see me. Didn't you say you had a lady friend?"

"Yes, I do. And if I didn't have Jill, I'd be up here to see you for a different reason. I find you attractive and intelligent. But I came today to ask you about the Vice President."

"Oh. That's good. That's real good. Because I didn't know how I was going to tell a white man that I was attracted to him too, but I didn't feel we should get involved." She put her hands together on her lap. "It's better that we two stick to official business." She smiled.

"How long have you lived on the plantation?"

"All my forty-two years. My parents and their parents before them. Back six generations counting me."

Brad scribbled on his notepad. "Such loyalty. Do you find it easy to work for Senator Ashford?"

"Yes. I don't consider it work. It's more like I'm family. I'm just taking care of the house. B. J. takes care of the farm."

For an hour, Brad delved into the memory of Amelia Tadford for stories about Benjamin Ashford from his youth and through adulthood. What he liked to eat, what he liked to wear, what he liked to do when he wasn't in Washington and what he talked about when no one else was around. He had heard most of it before, but he was panning for nuggets that could be used to lay beside the portrait of Samuel Harrot to contrast the two men.

"They had no children. His wife passed on. She was a lovely lady. But the Senator did so want an heir to pass this plantation on to." Amelia shook her head and wiped a tear from her eye.

"Are any of his school teachers alive that I could talk to about his youth before you knew him or were even born?"

Amelia thought. She shook her head from side to side. "I guess all those folks done passed on by now, or they'd have to be pretty old." Then her eyes lit up. "Oh, I know there's one old lady just a few miles down the main road here. She's in that fine nursing home you'll go right by on your way back to the interstate. Mattie Lewis. She was his sixth or seventh grade teacher. I've heard him talk about her. I think he still even goes by and sees her when he gets a chance. Miss Lewis could tell you a lot about the Senator."

Brad jotted down the name and location. He would stop there on the way out. He had just a few more questions for Amelia. "What about religion, Amelia? Does the Senator go to church often?"

Her lips tightened, her eyelids blinked, and she kneaded the small handkerchief she had in her hands. "No, I don't know much about him going to church. His family were all Catholic, but the Senator didn't much ever follow that. I don't ever recall seeing him even leave the house on Sunday to go anywhere to church. I would always go to my Baptist church about seven miles over yonder," she pointed toward Lafayette, "but I don't recall much about him ever going. He's religious in the sense of being good and all. And he reads and has all those books on religion up in the library, but he don't go to church much, if any."

"By the way, Amelia, could I see the library again? It's very interesting. So many books."

She glanced up the stairway toward the closed doors. "I reckon so. The Senator loans books out to anyone who asks. He's particular about getting them back. But I've often heard him say that the library is open to anyone who wants to study. He's had some college kids come by to read part of his Civil War journals."

The air was cool in the dimly lit large open room. The one lone window allowed very little sunlight. Amelia turned on the desk lamp and the lights over the stacks and shelves of volumes stretching the length of the room. The desk of Ashford was clear except for two books that lay side by side.

Brad stepped to the window while Amelia stayed near the door. "It's a little spooky up here to me, Brad. It's so dark without the lights on. But that's the way the Senator likes it."

Brad walked around the Persian rug. "Amelia, do you know why the letters for the four directions of north, south, east, and west are carved into the floor?"

"No, except Mr. Ashford has a surveying hobby. He has those instruments that you stand up to give the exact degrees and everything from north. He probably had that done for a reference point of some kind. He uses this library a lot for studying and meditation."

Brad wandered around the stacks for a few minutes taking an occasional book down to read the title. He ended back up in front at Ashford's desk. He looked at the two volumes on top. There was a large hardback that was intricately inlaid with gold lettering. It contained the Constitution Of the United States, the Amendments, and the Declaration of Independence. Beside it lay a paperback copy of the Koran. He picked it up, thumbed through, and placed it back. He walked back toward Amelia who still waited near the door.

"You know it's funny, Brad."

"What's that, Amelia?"

"Us being right here talking about Mr. Ashford, and you having written about him and Vice President Harrot who got shot."

"I don't follow."

"Well, the night the Vice President was shot, Mr. Ashford was up here in the library. I didn't know whether to disturb him with the news. But finally I come tiptoeing up the steps and knock real lightly. He doesn't answer. So's I open the door a little and come on in. It's all dark except for a couple of oil lamps over by that window. Mr. Ashford's sitting on that rug, just wearing a robe, and facing toward the window and lamps. I thought he was asleep or dead. I guess he was praying or in meditation."

Brad walked back to the rug. "This was where he was when he learned about his Vice President being killed?"

"Yes. I told him. I said, 'Mr. Ashford, they've just announced that the Vice President was shot dead at the Superdome about two hours ago.'"

"How'd he take it?"

"He paid it no mind. Just sat there. Said something like 'that's enough,' then he just continued to meditate. I went back downstairs."

Brad didn't open his notepad. He would be able to remember that. "That's all? No shock, no tears, no phone calls, nothing?"

"That's it. I was all upset. But he just said ball games are stupid and dangerous and went about his meditation."

They walked back down to the parlor and talked for another half hour. He got up to leave. He had enough for a background story with what was already in his files. Amelia would give it a human touch. It was obvious to him that she considered herself more like family than like a servant. Now, with Ashford living primarily at the Vice President's residence in Washington, she had the run of the place. With her son's help, they had kept the plantation in remarkable shape. He didn't know how he could use the library episode. He would have to sort that out as he went.

"Are you going to move up to Washington, Amelia?"

She was in the doorway. She gave a faint smile and tilted her neck a little to her right. "No. I don't think I'd like it up there. Too busy a place. I like this." She swept an arm around showing him all the fields and gardens. "He's told me I could come up there and work in the home they have for him. But I don't think so. Besides, I'm waiting for you to give up on that woman friend and come calling on Amelia." She waved him away as though she was teasing.

"Thanks, Amelia. I'll remember that. This area looks a lot

better to me too than D.C. does. Mattie Lewis, you say?"

"Yes, you can't miss her."

SHADY ACRES, A NEW nursing and residential home that occupied the area where a former plantation house had stood, sat amid aging oak trees with Spanish moss veils that almost touched the ground. The sparkling new brick of the buildings and the walkways gave away that it was only recently constructed, but the builders had done an extraordinary job in retaining the trees and natural surroundings of a plantation.

Despite all they had done, the owners could not mask the smell of a habitation for those who were so old that they often lost control of bodily functions. Bleach, soap, and air fresheners only went so far. He was hit with it as soon as he entered the lobby. He supposed those who worked and lived there became accustomed to the odor, but for him it always conjured up death and dying. There was something in a body that didn't like a nursing home.

He passed the recreation room and looked in. The only indication of activity there was the sound of the television used to entertain or sedate the residents. He wondered how many knew what they were watching. Some sat in wheel chairs, their heads slumped over in sleep, as they silently drooled onto the floor. One alert old man waved and called out a name. Brad didn't know him but waved back. He remembered why he was always depressed after a visit to one of these places. They were necessary. People were living longer, if not totally useful, lives. Children couldn't take care of parents in the shape of some of these. Others had outlived their children.

"Do you have a Mattie Lewis here?" he asked the receptionist.

"She's in 108B," she answered without looking up. "But you'll probably find her in the sun room. First hallway on your right, halfway down, and to your left." She looked up. "Are you another one of her students? There're a lot who stop by."

"No. Just a friend of one." He had no problem considering himself a friend of Ashford. He found his way there. It was brighter. More colors. And the residents, at least some of them, were up and walking about. Airy and light, the room had a different smell. There were rows of flowers resting on tables near where the glass panels of the sloping roof met the south wall. A worker and some of the aged women were tending the plants. It was like a greenhouse. He looked around. This would be the room he would occupy if he was ever put away.

Another attendant directed him to a lady seated alone in a chair at the end of a table of flowers. Her hands were still occupied with a marigold that she looked at as though inspecting it.

He scooted up a chair. "Are you Mattie Lewis?"

She looked around and cupped a hand to an ear. "I'm sorry. I don't hear very well." She looked at him for a bit longer. "Are you one of my students? Charles . . . Charles . . . I can't call your last name."

Brad leaned closer and spoke slowly and louder. "No, Miss Lewis. I'm Brad Yeary. I'm a reporter."

She nodded that she understood, smiled, and put the flower in her lap. "Lawsy, son, I don't reckon I've done anything that needs reporting. Did Oscar send you?"

"No. Who's Oscar?"

"He's my fellow. But sometimes he gets jealous and sends people to check on me to be sure I'm not running around on him. Like there'd be someone here I'd be interested in." She looked around the room. "He lives on the outside. He's a young fellow—eighty-eight. I'm ninety-two."

Her eyes told the story. Her body was wearing out, but her mind was still there. Her sense of humor had carried her well through the years she'd traveled. Her left hand had a tremor, and her pallid loose skin said she was her age. But he could see the fire in her eyes that told him she hadn't given up. He decided to let her tell him about Benjamin Edward Ashford instead of asking her questions.

"Do you remember Senator Ashford being one of your students? Tell me about him."

"Bennie Ashford? Shucks, there was one boy. You want me to tell you about Bennie?" She smiled and her eyes turned toward the window.

"Yes. Just anything you remember." He didn't get his pad out. He would just listen and see if there was anything he could use. He would let her rattle on without thinking that he had to write down every word she was saying. Maybe she would relax and open up.

She closed her eyes and leaned back in her chair. When she opened them, she was ready. "Bennie was one of my better boys. Probably top ten out of the thousands I had over forty years as a teacher. Very spunky youngster. I knew he was going to amount to something. Of course, he came from a good family. The Ashfords have been prominent around here since way back."

She rambled on for a good fifteen minutes telling Brad all that she remembered. She was his primary teacher in the sixth and seventh grade. She also taught him high school English.

"Bennie could do anything. Every year we'd read some stories, and then toward the end we'd let the kids dress up like their favorite characters. One year he dressed up like Caesar when we were studying Shakespeare's *Julius Caesar* in high school English. Earlier though, in grammar school, his favorite thing was to dress up in a robe and turban when we were reading stories from the *Thousand and One*

*Nights.* He was Ali Baba."

She leaned back in her chair and laughed as though she had been transported back in time to when Bennie Ashford stood before her in turban and robe. "He was so convinced he was really Ali Baba that he wore that get up for a whole week. I finally had to talk to his mother. Turns out he'd made the robe and turban himself. Quite handy with a needle and thread."

"He was one of your more creative students then?"

She squinted toward Brad and put her hand to her ear again. "I can't hear you. You have to speak up. The Lord's not letting much come through my ears to my brain. Reckon he thinks I've got enough stored up here already. I'm ninety-two, you know."

Brad mouthed it and spoke louder. "He was a good student?"

"Oh, yeah. Tops. He didn't stand for anyone doing something wrong. Straight as an arrow and expected everyone else to be the same way. One day he said, 'Miss Lewis,' that's what he called me. He said, 'Miss Lewis, why do Christians go to war when Jesus said to love your enemies?' I said, 'Child, don't ask me. Ask your preacher or priest.' It just came out of nowhere. We'd been talking about World War II."

She looked at Brad and then at the large clock on the wall. "I've got to go take a nap. I'd like to talk with you longer. Tell Bennie hello for me. I have to nap more than I used to. Did I tell you I was ninety-two?"

THE TRIP WAS BENEFICIAL. Brad laid out a story in his mind while I-10 sped beneath his car on the drive back to New Orleans. He would do a short profile of Ashford relating his early childhood. He would tell about his love of books and how he enjoyed literature from an early age. He would probably leave out the fact that he sewed his own robe and turban. There was no need to embarrass a sitting Vice President.

From what Amelia had said, Ashford still liked playing Ali Baba. Brad would also omit, for the time being, Ashford's very cool reaction to Harrot's death that Amelia had related.

He wished there was some way he could use the two books on his desk as symbolic of Ashford's life or philosophy. If it had been the Bible and the Constitution, it would have been easy. What's more American than the Constitution, the Declaration of Independence, and the Bible? However, the Koran would not go over as well. Besides, it was probably coincidence that both books were there side by side. He had seen many books in Ashford's library on other religions, including Christianity.

By the time he arrived at the New Orleans office of the *Times-Gazette*, Brad had already composed in his head the lead and at least

the following ten paragraphs for the feature. He would wait to contrast Harrot's life for the next column. Ashford was the present story.
His confirmation was less than a week old.

Danny, the computer whiz-kid, came running to his desk as
soon as Brad sat down. "Mr. Yeary, there's . . . " He started, almost
spitting each word and out of breath.

"Danny, you can call me Brad. We're friends. Okay? Now,
what's the matter? Just slow down and tell me."

"Brad, there's a policeman waiting for you with a package.
He's been here for six hours." Danny pointed to a uniformed officer
having a cup of coffee at a table near the reception area.

Brad ducked his head. "A subpoena. Damn, I bet it's a subpoena for that hanky." He sank down even lower with his head on his
desk.

"He wouldn't tell us," Danny said and pushed his glasses back
up his nose. "What do you want me to do?"

"What the hell. Just send him back here. It's inevitable.
Might as well get it over with." He straightened back up.

"You sure?"

"Yeah."

Danny went to the front and accompanied the policeman back
to Brad's desk. Brad tried to look as nonchalant as possible.

"Are you Brad Yeary?"

"Yes. Do you have some papers for me?"

"Yes, but I have to see some identification first. I have my orders. How'd you know I had papers for you?"

"Just a lucky guess," Brad said and began fumbling for his wallet. "Will this do?" He took out his driver's license and a picture Visa
card.

The officer looked closely at both and then at Brad. "Not a
very good likeness." He handed Brad a letter-size brown envelope that
was sealed. The officer waited.

"Am I supposed to say 'Thank you' or something?"

"Well, it wouldn't hurt. I came all the way from Alabama."

"Alabama?" Brad looked at the return address on the envelope.
The name jumped out at him. "This is from Lenora Harrot?"

"Yes. She wanted me to hand deliver it to you personally. I'm
a policeman in Montgomery. I need you to sign a receipt for it."

Brad took a pen from his pocket. His hand was shaking. He
barely was able to sign. "Thank you, officer. I'm sorry. I thought it
might be a subpoena." They both smiled.

# Thirty-four

I t lay there beside his keyboard. The long brown envelope from Lenora Harrot appeared harmless enough. It could be a harbinger of good things to come. Or, it could be a cobra waiting to strike.

Brad tried to ignore it. He typed away on the word processor. From time to time, he would catch himself casting a sideways glance at it. It was eleven, and he just had an hour to the midnight deadline. The Ashford feature would appear in the morning edition. He'd have time to concern himself with the Harrot part after he finished. If he ever opened the envelope, he would be consumed with its contents, whatever they might be, for the remainder of the evening. He would not be able to get his mind back onto Ashford's story.

He wrote and rewrote, honing the article to his level of excellence. He rearranged paragraphs, checked his pronouns for antecedents, switched a participial phrase from the beginning of a sentence to the end, and deleted an unkind opinion or two.

For the third time, he reread the complete story. The copy editor might catch something, but he had proofed it enough that he could argue he meant to say it that way. A political columnist should have some artistic license. He pulled up on his screen the three photographs to go with it—a current head and shoulders of Ashford, one of Ashford's plantation home, and the one he borrowed from a Washington paper of the Vice President's residence in Washington.

He had mentioned the library and its vast collection of Civil War journals, diaries, and maps. He quoted Miss Lewis saying she knew young Bennie Ashford "was going to amount to something." He left out the part about his propensity to dress as Ali Baba or Julius Caesar. The Constitution was mentioned but not the Koran. It was enough for the public.

He pressed the save and transmit keys and then turned off his word processor. Everyone except for a few interns and the police beat reporters had already gone home. He walked to the window and looked out through the darkness toward the Mississippi where he could see the lights of docked ships. In the distance, the bright strobe light that sat atop the Hilton flashed on and off. Who was occupying the Presidential Suite tonight? Hutteth was gone.

But not forgotten. He and his Year of the Beast would not let go of Brad's subconscious. The mental picture of Ashford in his robe on the Persian rug on the night of Harrot's assassination would not let go of him either. Why did Harrot's spirit say to "look at the White House" when it was called back to Papa Legba's back yard? And how could a colleague of Vice President Harrot take so calmly the news of his violent death? He needed to see Shanker.

"Brad, aren't you going to open it?"

The voice had sneaked up behind him and startled him momentarily. He turned and faced the gangly Danny staring back at him through his dark-rimmed glasses.

"Open what?"

"The envelope the policeman brought."

Brad looked toward his desk. It still lay there on the corner. He had forgotten. It was an old problem. When he finished what he thought was a good story, he got on such a high that he often overlooked appointments.

"Yeah, I guess I better. Mrs. Harrot went to a lot of trouble sending it down to me from Montgomery. The policeman and all." He walked back to his chair with Danny following behind.

"Danny, I appreciate you, but I'd rather read this alone." He didn't want to be hard on the computer whiz who had found his lost Harrot files, but he didn't want someone reading over his shoulder either.

"That's all right. I just thought with the policeman bringing it, it might be something important. Will you at least tell me that after you read it?"

"Sure, Danny, I'll let you know." The youth retreated toward the area where he waited for anyone else who might call with a problem with word-processing equipment.

Brad carefully sliced open the envelope. A handwritten note from Lenora Harrot was paper-clipped to five pages of typed, double-spaced print. Brad admired momentarily the beautiful large script of the late Vice President's wife. It reflected the Southern gentility of her cultured heritage.

*"Dear Mr. Yeary,*

*"I so much appreciated the way you wrote concerning the untimely passing of my dear Sam. Your stories reflected a feeling of loss, concern, and sympathy that many of the other journalists did not. They sometimes tended to sensationalize.*

*"When I found these pages of Sam's notes in a drawer of our bedroom dresser, I decided that you would be the right person to give them to. I don't really know what they mean. I stopped reading after seeing that they dealt with a rather ominous warning or concern about things happening in our government.*

*"Anyway, please use this as you see best. If I can be of any help, please feel free to call me at my home in Montgomery.*

*"Lenora Harrot*

*"P.S. I had Mr. Bradshaw deliver these personally because of the nature of the material."*

His hands began to sweat and his heart beat faster. He looked around the room to see if anyone was near him. He paper-clipped Lenora Harrot's note back to the five pages, folded them, and placed them back into the envelope. He didn't know if he wanted to read the late Vice President's reflections. At least not at the office. If there was an "ominous warning" in these sheets, perhaps, he should turn them over to the CIA or FBI unread.

The bloody hanky had caused him enough bad luck. If he was now the possessor of otherwise unseen words of Harrot, the tide of black happenings might just be beginning. At least he would not begin this at midnight. He would take the envelope home, leave it unread for the night, and decide in the brightness of the sunlight of morning what to do. He passed Danny on his way out. "I'm taking it home to read in the morning, Danny. I'll see you then."

AS THE SUN BEGAN its morning arc from behind the brown, slow-flowing Mississippi, Brad sat on his balcony on Burgundy Street with coffee cupped between his hands. It was only by gripping the cup with both hands that he could stop the trembling. The vapor drifted upward in the cool morning air. Wrapped in a bathrobe, he shivered in the coolness of air and spirit. His decision to wait until morning had been of little benefit. He had tossed instead of sleeping.

The few fitful minutes he had slept were filled with visions. He had dreamed of Papa Legba and of Samuel Harrot. His mind flashed back to when he thought he was drowning beneath the boat of Barry Ledoux and had seen Jill and the Reverend Hutteth standing hand in hand behind the rail.

He had asked Papa Legba to bring Harrot back to speak to him words that might help with the mystery of his death. He had been rewarded with words from Harrot brought to him from Montgomery. It was like a prayer being answered in a very different form from what the petitioner had expected.

The brown envelope lay beside him on a little metal stand. As soon as he thought Jill would be up, he would call her and, for the first time in his life, ask her advice. Mrs. Harrot apparently didn't see the sheets as the last will and testament of her deceased husband. Brad didn't want them to be his either.

He could wait no longer. His fingers punched in the buttons of Jill's number from the phone on the balcony. It was nearly seven. She should be awake enough to discuss it.

"Jill. It's me. How's everything in Washington? . . . Yes, I know it's early. I'm having a cup of coffee on the balcony. Getting ready to water all these plants you got me." He looked around at the dying jungle of brown and yellow leaves. "Hey, I need to ask you something."

"What is it, Brad? I'm in a hurry. I've got to get to an early committee meeting. I'm trying to hit the ground running. My office is still not unpacked. I barely can find my way around."

"Lenora Harrot sent me some papers—about five pages of her husband's typed notes of some kind. She thinks they have what she calls an 'ominous' ring to them. What should I do?"

"You're asking me? What do they say? Why does she think they sound ominous?"

"I haven't read them yet. I'm a little afraid I might be stumbling into something over my head. I got into enough of a problem with that hanky. Should I read them or just turn them over to the FBI?"

"Brad, you're the journalist. You even have a year of law school. If Mrs. Harrot thought you were the one who should see them, I'd say you should honor her wish and read them. If it's something then that you believe the FBI should know, you can worry about it then. Read them and call me back tonight. I gotta run. Okay? I love you."

"Thanks. I'll talk to you tonight. I love you too." He hung the phone up. She was right. Just the month before he had told Ashford he was willing to die for freedom of the press. But, now that something was given to him, he was scared to death even to read it.

He finished his second cup of coffee, turned, and picked up the brown envelope. He took Mrs. Harrot's note off and scanned the neatly typed pages of Samuel Harrot.

His hands began to shake again. He didn't know if it was the coffee, the cold air, the contents of the papers, or a combination. He walked inside and stood in front of a portable heater that he turned up to high. He now read the five pages more closely.

It was like a diary. There were three entries—October 15, November 15, and December 15. He could see why Mrs. Harrot had stopped with the first page. He didn't recognize some of the names, but he did recognize one obvious title and the setting of the first entry. Harrot referred to "Mr. P" which he concluded was a reference to the President.

"Met with Mr. P, Ross, Gigi, and visitors. The discussion turned to our problems with oil supply from Mid-East. P is irritated. Says the f . . . ing OPEC leaders are about to strangle us. He has plans though. He has already put in motion 'unconventional' means of dealing with problem. Do I agree? Well, it depends, I said, on exactly what the unc. means are. He gave me more details than I needed to know. My face must have turned white. He backed up. Said it was just an idea to kick around. What did I really think?

"I confessed I could not support such 'unc. means.' He laughed and said to forget it. They all appeared concerned that I knew and would not support. I told Mr. P that I did not want to cause a problem. If he wants, I would resign."

He continued with private musings that the Vice Presidency was not what he thought it would be. He wanted out. He didn't want to cause the President a problem, but he decided to talk with him about resigning.

The November 15 entry related the results of the conversation with "Mr. P." The President encouraged him to stay on. He told Harrot to forget the October fourteenth meeting. The President said he was upset but thought things would work out now. It would be a black eye on the administration if the Vice President resigned. It would open up a Pandora's Box.

In his December 15 entry, Harrot had just found out he would be going to New Orleans for the Sugar Bowl. He said that he would take a few days off after the first of the year to make a final decision. He wanted to go home to Montgomery and spend some time with Ellah. He would visit Aunt Bea while he was in New Orleans or in Montgomery.

The last entry began, "I have determined that I would not be a candidate to be included in an updated version of *Profiles of Courage*. I must do something, but I am lacking in courage. I think too much about Alabama and home. I should be thinking more about what's good for the country. Decision time must be soon. I should consult with my friends and family. I must—" And it ended there.

Brad looked for another page in the envelope. There must be more. Mrs. Harrot would have known that if she had read the whole five pages. The December 15 entry was incomplete. He wanted to read on, but he was left holding five pages that raised more questions than they answered.

He examined the pages. He ran the tips of his fingers over the edges of each one. He could feel it. The pages had the remains of perforations. The paper was from a printer with continuously fed sheets that had been torn off and separated. There could be other pages missing. At least the remainder of the sentence, perhaps a paragraph, or page, or even a whole diary. Some senators were known to have kept diaries of their careers. Why not a Vice President?

He looked at his watch. It was still early. He would walk to Jackson Square and have breakfast at La Madeleine's. Then he would take his precious discovery to Danny. Danny could guide him to the other pages.

It might take a trip to Montgomery. Samuel Harrot must have had a home computer or word processor that these last thoughts were stored in. If Mrs. Harrot allowed, he would have words directly from

the late Vice President's mouth to use in some future story after he
put all the pieces together.

He mulled over the contents of the five pages while having
French coffee and a sweet Saint Tropez roll. Who were these other
people Harrot referred to? Ross and Gigi with "Mr. P." and Ellah in
Montgomery or Aunt Bea? He hoped that Ellah was not some hidden
mistress of the late Vice President. Lenora Harrot had been through
enough tragedy. But the Ross and Gigi who met with Harrot and the
President were of more concern. Who were the visitors? Were they
the operatives who would carry out the "unconventional" means of
dealing with the OPEC nations? Once again he had more questions
than answers.

He looked at his watch. What time would Danny be at the paper? He didn't even know the young man's last name. He had used
him without ever inquiring. Someone at the paper would know.

"Danny Spurling," the lady in employment said. "We can't give
out his home phone number without his permission."

Even the bureaucracy at his own newspaper was hindering
Brad. He paced back and forth. Pinthater wasn't in. There was no
one there to tell the lady that it was all right to give him the number.

"Then don't give me his number. Just call him and tell him to
call Brad Yeary at the paper as soon as possible." He looked across
the counter. She reluctantly agreed. He headed to his desk.

His phone was ringing by the time he got there. "Danny?
Yeah, I need you in here quick. I think I have a job for your expertise.
Tell whoever you need to that you might be late getting home today.
We may be going to Montgomery, Alabama, to let you help on my
Harrot story, okay?"

Brad hung up knowing that Danny was busily getting ready to
head to the office.

Danny turned the paper over and over in his large, slender
fingers and peered at the pages through his thick glasses. "Hm."

"That's all you can say?" Brad asked.

"No. I just want to be sure. This looks like medium weight
micro-perf paper that was fed though a push-type continuous-feed
printer. It's a cheap nine-pin dot matrix print. Probably an old Epson.
I would hazard a guess that it was generated by an older WordPerfect
program on a three-eighty-six DX home computer. The pages aren't
numbered. But as you guessed, there should be something to follow
this last phrase. There would probably be some preceding pages too."

Brad shook his head. "You can tell all that by looking at a few
pages?"

"That's my business. Besides, I may be wrong on the type of
computer. But it's definitely WordPerfect word processing. I can tell
that by the word and line spacing."

"Danny, get that little disk you used on my computer. I've got to call Mrs. Harrot. If she says that the Vice President had a computer there at his home in Montgomery, I'll ask her for permission to take a look at it."

"I'll take my whole tackle box, " Danny said and started walking to his hideaway.

As soon as 9 a.m. arrived, Brad dialed the number that was embossed on the note paper from Lenora Harrot. A maid answered and took his name. In a minute, Mrs. Harrot was on the line.

"Mrs. Harrot? I wanted to call and thank you for your note and papers from the Vice President. They're very interesting."

"Well, yes, I guess they are to you. It started out a little scary to me. That's why I sent them on over. I didn't even look at the other pages."

"I was wondering, Mrs. Harrot—"

"Please call me Lenora. 'Mrs. Harrot' sounds so old."

"Thank you, Lenora. I was wondering. Did you find any other pages with these?"

"No. That was all. Just neatly folded in an envelope in our dresser. I don't know why Sam put them there. His other files and things are in his study where he used to go and peck and tap on that little computer of his."

Brad straightened up in his chair. She had said the magic word. Computer. He and Danny were in business if she would let them look at it.

"Mrs. Harrot—I mean Lenora—do you know anything about Sam's computer?"

"No. I can barely use a typewriter. But he liked to fool around with those new gadgets. He'd always go off in there and write letters and things. It was off-limits to me."

"Would it be possible for me to take a look at the computer, Lenora? I think there were some other notes that maybe should have been with these that you sent me."

There was silence on the line for a few seconds. "I don't see why not. You're welcome to come look if you like. When would you want to?"

"Now. Today. I can be there in five or six hours if I drive fast. Is that all right?"

"Sure. I'm going to be here all day. Don't drive so fast that you'd have a wreck. You know where our house is?"

"Yes, I drove by it when I was there for the . . . the funeral."

"Yes." Brad could hear her sniff. "Just come on over then. I'll be happy to show you his whole study."

Danny packed his tackle box of computer disks and programs. Brad left a message for Pinthater that he and Danny were off to see

Mrs. Harrot and not to expect either one back until late that night.

The 1993 Ford Crown Vic sped along I-10 to Mobile and then I-65 to Montgomery. Five hours and one speeding ticket later, they were pulling into the long driveway of the Harrots off Highway 331 south of Montgomery.

Lenora Harrot was a gracious host. She insisted on Brad and Danny sitting down with her for a cup of tea and a bit of conversation in the early afternoon.

"Sam was so concerned about the country. But for the last couple of months before his death, he seemed preoccupied with something. He wouldn't talk about it. You know how men keep things to themselves." She looked up at her two male guests and smiled. "Well, maybe you don't know, but it seems that way. We women talk about everything to our friends and family, but the menfolk just seem to bottle it all up. At least the men that I have known in my family. I'm sure you two young men are different."

Brad and Danny looked at each other, then at Lenora Harrot, and nodded.

"Did he talk very much about his job to you, Lenora?"

"No. Just 'everything is fine' type of talk. He didn't carry his work home with him. He'd talk your ear off about Alabama football, his boat, or bird hunting. Just superficial stuff, if you know what I mean. I understand that the younger generation of men is more sensitive, will talk to their wives or girlfriends more. Do you find that to be true?"

Again, Brad and Danny nodded their heads simultaneously.

"Are you both married?"

Brad shook his head. "No, I'm going pretty steadily with a lady, but I'm not married." He glanced over at Danny whose eyelids were blinking rather rapidly. "What about you, Danny?"

"No. I'm so busy with school. I don't have much time for socializing."

"Well, you better make time. Life shouldn't be all work or study. When you get nearer the end, you'll see that the things that mean most are family and friends. That Sam was Vice President means very little with him gone. Nobody remembers Vice Presidents except their families."

After a half hour of chit-chat, Lenora Harrot showed Brad and Danny through the spacious house to the second-story study of her late husband. She unlocked the door and turned on the overhead light. The three stepped into the cool room. Maple hardwood was partly covered with a large area rug that bore the seal of the state of Alabama. State and federal flags flanked a large mahogany desk to their right with large double windows overlooking the front lawn situated behind the desk. The flag of the Vice President was stretched on the wall opposite the desk. Immediately in front of them and on an outside wall of the house was a fireplace and mantel.

Samuel Harrot's computer and printer sat conveniently beside his desk on stands of their own that matched the desk. One file cabinet stood behind the desk and another beside the windows. Built-in book shelves lined the wall from the door toward the front windows. Framed family pictures sat on the mantel.

Brad looked around before going farther. Everything appeared so neat. There were no papers on the desk, computer stand, or the file cabinets. Samuel Harrot was certainly a more organized man and tidier than Brad.

"This is a very nice study, Lenora. The Vice President sure had a comfortable place to work. And it's so clean and organized too."

She walked to the middle of the rug and turned slowly to view the entire room. "Yes, this was the way Sam liked it. It wasn't nearly so neat after he worked here a while. Books would be scattered, papers thrown everywhere, news magazines on the floor, file drawers opened, just a real mess. I started to leave it that way. But the President's men cleaned it up for me when they were down here a few weeks ago." She smiled and walked to her husband's desk. "It does look nice, doesn't it?"

Brad felt the familiar palpitations of his heart. He leaned against the door facing. "The President's men? Who came here?"

"Oh, Rob Steinheitz and a couple of young men. Some type of agents I believe they said. FBI or CIA, I really don't know. We had tea right down there where you and I talked just a few minutes ago. Mr. Steinheitz was so nice. He told me how everyone in the administration was going to miss Sam. Said they needed to look through his study to see if there were any matters related to national security that Sam might have left lying around. The President had called to arrange it."

"National security? Did they take anything?"

"Just a box of papers or documents. Mr. Steinheitz said they needed to go back to Washington—that they dealt with sensitive matters. Who was I to know? I just said, 'Sure, take what you need.'"

"Was that before or after you found those papers you sent me?"

"Before. I didn't find those until just a couple of days ago. If I had had those then, I might have been more careful about what they took. They were in here a couple of hours. I heard file drawers opening and closing, boxes sliding along the floor."

Brad looked around at the sanitized room. Yes, they left it neat. Probably too neat for what he was trying to find. "Do you mind if we look in the file and desk drawers? I'm trying to find the other pages that went with what you sent me."

"Go right ahead. I'll be down in the parlor if you'd like another cup of tea."

She left them alone in the study. Brad locked the door behind her. He was becoming paranoid about people looking over his shoulders.

"Danny, you go to work on the computer. I'll check the files and desk to see what I can find."

"Wait a minute, Brad. Look at this." He pointed to the printer and grinned.

"Yeah. What is it?"

"Epson nine-pin dot-matrix," he said and then pointed to the computer. "Three eighty-six DX. I got 'em both on the first guess."

Brad turned to the file drawers and began a systematic search from front to back and top to bottom of all the files remaining. The drawers were less than a third filled.

"Uh, oh, Brad. We got trouble," Danny said as soon as he flipped the switch to turn the computer on.

"What is it?"

"There's nothing. Absolutely nothing. No document files. No word processing program. Nothing shows up."

"Can you fix it? Can you find it like you did my lost file? That's why I brought you—to find the files I need." Brad looked over Danny's shoulder to the blank screen of the monitor.

"Yours was just one lost document file. That was a piece of cake. All the files and even the word processing program have been deleted on this. It'll take me longer. But if they were as sloppy as most are in just deleting the files, I'll eventually be able to find them."

He opened his tackle box and took out a number of small computer disks. "I have all kinds of search programs on here. Some of them may even be illegal. I've never checked or asked. Give me an hour or two and I should have everything restored to where it was before those government boys started messing with it."

"You got it. You find what I need and you'll get a bonus."

"Just mention me in one of your stories."

Within a half hour, Brad had done all the searching he could do. The files in the cabinets and the papers in the desk all had to do with things other than the last three months of Harrot's life. He was only looking for notes, documents, letters, or anything from October fourteenth and forward to the end of December. The space was replete with emptiness as to anything having happened during that time.

"How are you doing, Danny?"

Danny's fingers once again were playing the music of train wheels against track sections as they sped across the keyboard. "I've got the word processing system back up. WordPerfect like I thought," he said without looking up from the screen. "I'm beginning to restore the document files."

"How do you know what he named them?"

"I don't. Most people are lazy. They name them something with one of their names in it, a birth date, a Social Security number, or something. I have all that on Harrot from his death certificate."

"His death certificate? How'd you get that?"

"Brad, you're not the only one who knows how to investigate something. I knew you were working on Harrot. I wanted to be of help. I have my own file. Probably have some things you don't."

Brad shook his head. "Look for anything from October on through December. I'm going back downstairs and talk with Mrs. Harrot. She might know who some of these characters are that her husband referred to in the pages that I have."

"You want me to print it out or just copy it for printing later?"

"Copy it to a disk we can use and print it out if it's not too long. I don't want Mrs. Harrot to think we're taking something we shouldn't."

"I can copy all his document files that are on the hard disk on ten of my floppies. If he was like most lazy computer users, he probably put everything on the hard disk unless it was completely full."

Brad's eyes began to glaze over from all the computer talk. "Whatever, Danny. Just see what you can come up with. Here's a copy of the five pages. Don't lose them."

Mrs. Harrot was still sitting in the parlor reading a book of poetry when Brad came down and joined her. He was hesitant about bringing up the names mentioned in her husband's entries. He was afraid Gigi, Ellah, and even Aunt Bea might either be females that Lenora was unfamiliar with or would renew any suspicions she might have had of her husband's wanderings.

"Did Sam like to come home to Alabama, Lenora?"

"Oh, dear, yes. That was one of the things he didn't like about being Vice President. We didn't get down here as often as when he was in the Senate. He was thinking about not being on the ticket next time because of that. He would say, 'Ellah, I miss my bird hunting and walking the farm.'"

Brad's ears perked up. "Sam called you Ellah? I didn't know that was your middle name."

She closed the poetry book. "Oh, it's not. My name is Lenora Ann Harrot. He's called me Ellah since way back during LBJ's administration when he first was elected to the state legislature. Those are my initials—L. A. H. If you turn that into a word, it comes out Ellah." She smiled. "He enjoyed doing that with everyone's name."

"Why's that?"

"It was Johnson. He was making fun of LBJ. Remember how Lyndon always made up names for his wife and daughters that had LBJ in them? Lady Bird Johnson, Lucy Bird, and Linda Bird. Everything was LBJ. Sam was just spoofing the President of the other party by taking people's initials and turning them into words or names."

Brad took the five pages from his coat pocket that Lenora had sent to him. "How much of this did you read, Lenora?"

"Only part of the first page."

"Well, maybe you can help me with some of these names. I don't recognize them."

She leaned forward. "I'll try. How many are there?"

"Four, I believe. Now I know who Ellah is. That's you."

"Did he say something about me?"

"Yes, he wanted to come home to Montgomery and spend some time with you."

She reached for a box of tissues and dabbed at her eyes. "That was sweet. Just like Sam."

"I'm sorry, Mrs. Harrot, . . . Lenora, I didn't mean to upset you."

"Oh, that's all right. I'll miss Sam from now on. Go ahead."

"What about Ross, do you know who he is?"

"Ross is R. S. Rob Steinheitz. Of course when he was down here a few weeks ago, I didn't call him Ross, I called him Mr. Steinheitz."

Brad made a note beside the name. He looked at the next one and prayed that it was an innocent one. "What about Gigi? Who's she?"

She laughed into her tissue. "Oh, Sam would be proud of that. Gigi is not a she. It's a he. G. G. George Garron, the President's right hand man, besides Steinheitz."

Brad was relieved that it wasn't Harrot's mistress. His hands began to sweat with that entry. The circle of power was present at the fateful meeting. He pressed on. "I suppose that your husband did refer to the President as 'the P' or Mr. P? He didn't have a pet initial-type name for him?"

"That's right. He couldn't. He was afraid he'd slip up and use it in his presence. You know the President doesn't have a middle name. Just Stephen Teater. Those two initials didn't lend themselves to anything that Sam could use in public. He tried 'Stubborn' or 'Stupid' with the ST sound, but it was less than satisfactory. He even tried . . . oh my, I don't know whether I should say this in mixed company. Please excuse me, but he used 'Six Teats' for a while. Then he went back to just Mr. P. He didn't want to diminish the dignity of the Presidency."

"I see. There's just one more that I don't know then, Lenora. Who is Aunt Bea?"

She laughed again. "Did he mention Aunt Bea? That's so ironic. Aunt Bea was his best political friend and colleague. Benjamin

Edward Ashford. B. E. A. Our new Vice President. They would visit very often. He came to our farm, and we visited his plantation house. Have you ever been there to Stratford Place? It's very lovely."

"Yes, I've been there."

"Did you get to meet Amelia Tadford? She's so very bright. The Senator was lucky that she worked for him."

"Yes, I've met her too." Brad busied himself with making notes. He felt a warm wave move up his neck and across his face. He hoped the blush wasn't noticeable.

"There was always a little gossip about the Senator and Amelia, especially since his wife died. But I didn't believe a word of it for a second."

"Gossip? That they might be . . ." Brad tried to think of a delicate way to put it, "that they might be involved."

Lenora nodded her head. "Isn't it terrible for people to say something like that?" She paused and wiped her eyes with the tissue. "I know Sam would be happy and proud that his beloved Aunt Bea, Senator Ashford, succeeded him as Vice President. He always said that Senator Ashford was so much smarter, so much braver, and so much more the patriot than he was. I didn't believe it. Sam, in my estimation, was just as intelligent and brave. He loved his country and Alabama."

"I'm sure he did." Brad had all the names figured out in the pages, and he wished Danny would complete his work in the study so that they could head back to New Orleans and make some sense out of the last written words of Samuel Harrot. He glanced toward the stairs. There was no sign of him coming down.

"Would you like to walk over the grounds a little, Brad, while you wait for your friend to finish?"

"Yes, that would be fine."

For the next hour, he and Lenora Harrot walked through the orchards and gardens that her husband loved to come home to. Brad could see why. It was beautiful and relaxing. He silently wished that Samuel Harrot had made it back from New Orleans to retire to his estate here in Montgomery. He stood on a little arched bridge with a small stream gurgling beneath and looked back at the house. The light in the study suddenly went off. Danny was through.

As Brad and Lenora approached the front entrance, Danny opened the door. He held his tackle box of magic computer openers in one hand and a couple of sheets of paper in the other.

"Are we finished, Danny?"

Danny nodded. "Yep, I checked as much as I could and got a little bit." He waved the paper toward Brad and moved his eyes toward the plastic box.

"Well, I do hope you can make some sense of Sam's notes. It

seems so scary to me. Is there anything else you young men need?"

"No, Lenora. You've been a great help." Brad reached out and took her hand. "Have they given you any indication that they've found or are getting nearer finding the one who killed Sam?"

"No. I know less than probably anyone. I learn more from the television and newspaper than I do from anyone on the official investigation team. They've called a couple of times, but no one has come to see me except for the President's men."

As soon as they were out of the driveway, Brad looked over to Danny. "How'd you do?"

Danny patted the box that was now sitting securely on the front floorboard. "I got all the document files that were on the computer copied. The one with the diary-like entries he only began last January when he was sworn in as Vice President. It seems as though he was starting a journal where he would enter his thoughts on the Vice Presidency into the file about once a month."

Brad glanced over to him as he aimed the Ford onto Highway 331 and back toward Interstate 65. "Anything interesting there?"

"Not that I noticed. Just routine stuff and his reminiscences. I just scanned those. They're here on the disks."

"What are those two pages?"

"That's from that last December fifteenth entry. They follow the pages that you had. I didn't want to print out the whole file and have Mrs. Harrot think I was taking something I shouldn't be."

Brad pulled over in front of a fruit stand that was closed for the winter and slid the car to a stop in the loose gravel. "Give me those pages."

He reread the whole entry for December, beginning with the pages he already had to refresh his memory. "I must" was where his last page ended. The next page that Danny was able to coax from Harrot's computer completed that sentence. ". . . call Aunt Bea before I go to the Sugar Bowl. He'll know what to do." Harrot continued with self examination similar to what his wife had just told Brad. He believed "Aunt Bea" to be more knowledgeable and patriotic.

For the next several paragraphs there was little of immediate interest. The final page contained only three lines at the top of the page. They were the last words that Vice President Samuel Harrot had committed to paper during his life. There were just three short sentences.

"I still feel down and depressed even though I have talked with the PREACHER.

"I must look at the White House.

"Told **BEAST** was about to move on plan, and I don't know what to do."

# Thirty–five

The rental car chugged listlessly along Duke Street, the main thoroughfare of Alexandria, Virginia, while the driver's eyes searched the side street signs for the place he was to turn. Duke Street severed the instep of the geographical boot formed by the Potomac River at the back and the toe created by the intersection of I-95 and I-395 in the Washington suburb.

They could be numbered on the fingers of one hand—places that bore the names of Chevy Chase, Maryland, Arlington, Virginia, and even over to Oxon Hill, Maryland—where there existed the appearance of real civilization. This was the plush, near hinterland of the Capital City where the wealthy lobbyists and the members of Congress who they lobbied fled from the crime-riven streets of downtown. The government areas were fortresses guarded by all the modern sophisticated electronic surveillance equipment possible but still in need of moats.

In those places where lawns of stately homes abutted swimming pools and tennis courts, the residents could still jog or mow their yards in summer without being concerned about a drive-by shooting—usually. It was on one of these streets, regally named Gloucester, that the Reverend William Hutteth had his mansion-house. Brad Yeary's eyes strained for the name of the adjoining street that would lead him to salvation at the hands of the Reverend.

He glimpsed the street number and wheeled into the entrance. He was met by a guard who walked from a small brick guard shack that matched the color of the house. Yes, the Reverend was expecting him he told the uniformed attendant and showed him his driver's license and picture Visa card.

Straight from Lenora Harrot's house, he had gone to New Orleans and did his story on Samuel Harrot that would be published in
the next day's *Times-Gazette*. It was good, but it wasn't his best. His
mind had been preoccupied with the things that he could not yet write
about. His thoughts reeled from the last three lines of Harrot's computerized diary. Four words kept flashing before his eyes as though
he had been hit across the forehead with a billy club or as though one
of his kaleidoscopes had exploded in his eyes while he was looking.
*Preacher, White House,* and *Beast.* Those hot coals had not left his
mind for the past two days.

As soon as he had landed in Washington, he called Hutteth and
then Jill. Hutteth would talk to him again. He didn't tell him the
questions he had—just that he needed to talk more about the Beast.
Jill had told him he was crazy. Hutteth was crazy too, for that matter.
But he insisted. It was essential. He felt he was closing in on a picture of why Harrot had been shot. But as soon as he thought he had
captured the vision, it tumbled away and a new one appeared. He was
haunted by kaleidoscope images.

Harrot's words had sent him now to the mystical preacher who
knew the secrets of Revelation.

Hutteth was watching a monitor showing one of his taped programs when Brad was ushered into what was termed the sun room although it was overcast and dreary on this Saturday afternoon as it
often was in Washington from November through March.

He bounced up from his chair and greeted his guest. "Good to
see you again, Brad," Hutteth said and momentarily took off his glasses. After two seconds of eyes meeting eyes, he placed them back on
and waved Brad to a light and airy cushioned deck chair which
matched all the other furnishings in the room. Hutteth pressed a
button on his control box and the video shut off. "Reviewing my latest
tape on Revelation. Did you buy a set?"

Brad shook his head. "No."

"You should have. As interested as you are in the Beast. You
should buy a set and listen and watch. Seven tapes. Three hours
each. You'd be an expert by the end."

"Yeah, an expert or a candidate for a mental hospital." Brad
smiled, hoping that his host would see his comment as a joke.

"That's good. But I haven't received any reports back of anyone watching the tapes having to be transported to a facility for the
mentally infirm."

"Maybe they were already there. Have you checked the addresses of where they're being mailed to?"

Hutteth laughed. "You're good. You have a way with words.
No wonder your writing is so compelling."

"I'm here about the Beast, Reverend. I need to clear up a point or two."

"So, you've come to accept my theory?"

"Let's don't go that far. It's intriguing. And it keeps turning up at points to where I need to clear up what your theory is exactly." Brad paused long enough to take his pad from a coat pocket. "You said the Beast will rise from Islam. Right?"

"Yes, your accuracy is amazing. Not Islam—but arise from Islam."

"And you said the Beast killed Harrot?"

"Your accuracy fails you slightly. It was the *work* of the Beast. The Beast was behind it, if not actually pulling the trigger."

"You believe his death arose then from a fanatical movement within Islam?"

"Well, let me say this. Muslims are a lot more moral generally than your run-of-the-mill Christian. That's good. I disagree with their belief that Jesus is not the Son of God. The Bible says he is, and the Koran says he's not. They don't agree. The Bible said any future prophet would not say anything contradictory to the Bible. That's my difference with the Muslim religion."

"Okay, I know all that. I need more specifics. Do you see anything in Harrot's death having to do with the White House?"

Hutteth leaned forward with the mention of the White House. "What makes you say that? Has someone indicated that the White House itself is involved?"

"I'm sorry, Reverend. I'm the one asking the questions. I can't disclose that now. I'm just checking all possibilities."

"Well, that's strange." Hutteth rested his chin in his hand and leaned more toward Brad. "The White House could be involved. If the Beast was in the White House already, it would be easy enough for such a cancer to destroy our government or part of it." He spoke more to himself than to Brad.

Brad turned to the other question he wanted to ask Hutteth. "Did you ever personally meet Vice President Harrot?"

Hutteth took his glasses off and looked straight at Brad. "Why? Did he mention me somewhere?"

"Reverend, I'm sorry. I can't say right now. I'm just asking."

Hutteth put the dark glasses back on, leaned back, and clasped his hands together. "Yes. I first met him when I was lobbying a Senate committee concerning my television channel a few years back. He developed an interest in some of my theories. He's sat right where you're sitting on at least three occasions over the past five years. He would ask me dozens of questions about Revelation.

"Then when I took my tent ministry to Montgomery, he was there. He tried to disguise himself. But he was there. He was a very kind and nice gentleman. He always wanted to learn. He said he had

a friend who knew so much about all religions that he felt very igno-
rant. He was trying to catch up."

Brad was getting more than he expected. "Did he call you any
special name?"

"Like what?"

"I don't know. You tell me."

Hutteth smiled. "He just called me *Preacher*. He had this
thing against calling men *Reverend*, so he always just called me
*Preacher*."

"Did you talk to him in November or December before he was
killed?"

He reached over to a stand next to his chair and picked up a
black appointment book. "I guess since he's dead, it wouldn't be di-
vulging any confidence. This one goes back to the last month of last
year." He flipped back a few pages and ran his finger down a page.
"I spoke to him on December the eighth," he said and closed the book.

"What did you talk about?"

"Oh, some general questions about Revelation. He wanted to
know if I thought there would be a literal battle of Armageddon. Or
if that was just figurative."

"What did you tell him?"

"Literal. To occur before the year Two Thousand and Two."

"Was that all he asked?"

"No. He wanted to know where it would begin and who would
be involved. I told him that Armageddon was an actual place in Palestine. That it would begin somewhere in the Mid-East and spread. It
would involve the powers of the Beast arrayed against the forces of
good."

"What did he say to that?"

"Not much. He seemed nervous. I do remember him asking
whether it could be stopped."

"And?"

"I told him, 'No. And woe to him who helps to start it.'"

"Anything else?"

"He mentioned that he was worried about the Mid-East situation. He hoped we were not near a flash-point of a war or something.
He said he had a friend he was going to talk to about it too."

"Did he say who this friend was?"

"Not by name. It was the same one he had talked about before
who he felt knew so much about religions and everything else."

Brad looked at his notes from Harrot's last diary entry. "Reverend, did you by any chance tell Harrot that the Beast was ready to
move on its plan?"

Hutteth wrinkled his forehead and brought a forefinger to his
mouth. "The Beast was ready to move on its plan?"

"Yeah, something like that."

"No. I wouldn't have said anything like that. I don't know what the Beast's plan is. I'm on the other side. I may have told him that I believed that 1998 would be the year of the Beast. But I wouldn't have said anything about a *plan* since I don't know if there is one."

"Thanks. If you remember anything else, give me a call. Sorry, I can't stay any longer."

BRAD DROVE STRAIGHT TO a downtown library. He had meant to check out the dates of the Muslim conquests that Hutteth had described to him before. He hadn't. But now it was more urgent. A good library would do. He didn't believe he needed the Library of Congress—yet.

In a musky corner of the library where he hoped he would be undisturbed, Brad laid out the first five books that he could find on Muslim history and two on the chronology of world events. Hutteth was right that Mohammed died in 632 A.D. June eighth he found to be the accepted date. The Muslim Arabs were invading and conquering North Africa in 664 and had pretty well completed it by 666. Asimou's *Chronology of the World* said that Jerusalem was taken in 638 along with Damascus, but it didn't state the exact year that the Mosque was built in Jerusalem where the Jewish Temple had stood.

He looked to the 1300s to see what was happening with the Muslim movement at that time and how accurate Hutteth was. The dates varied in the several books from the late 1200s to the mid 1300s as to when the Ottoman Turks were finally successful in their conquering efforts. The fall of Constantinople and change from Christian to Muslim occurred during the time frame that Hutteth was talking about although the exact year never appeared in any of the books to be 1332. It wasn't perfect, but Washington was famous for the phrase, "It was close enough for government work."

Brad took his pad and started writing his own numbers. He added six hundred sixty-six onto the date of Mohammed's death and got the year 1298 A. D. He checked the chronology book again. There was just more about the crusades ending and the Ottoman Turks securing themselves in the conquered lands.

He added the doubling—1332—to the Prophet's date of death and came up with 1964. The only thing he could remember happening around that year was that President Kennedy was assassinated less than six weeks before the year began and LBJ defeated Goldwater in the 1964 election. Goldwater might have seen LBJ as a form of the Beast—but that was more a question of political opinion than religion. He put his pad away, returned the books, and headed for the car and Jill's.

MOST OF THE AGENTS were off, but Al Shanker and John Dobson came in Saturday afternoon for a special purpose. The drawings were to be delivered. Under hypnotic induced recall, the two employees of the New Orleans Union Station had described the person they had seen taking calls at the pay phone booth that was used for the ticket transaction. They were interviewed separately. They had on two different occasions given their best verbal description to different reconstruction artists. They were examined with different teams of hypnotist and artist to insure there would be no unintentional influence of the resulting depiction.

Dobson and Shanker had before them four separate, large brown envelopes. The outside was marked with the name of the witness, artist, and hypnotist.

"I hope these aren't the same person that we had on video who was on the boat," Dobson said and began to unclasp the first. He and Shanker sat side by side to view their last best hope of putting a face to anyone who could be connected with the assassination.

Dobson pulled the first colored-pencil drawing from its cover. He and Shanker stared for a full minute at the head and shoulders depiction of a neat man probably in his early thirties. His ears lay flat against the sides of his head. Expressive eyes sat anchored beneath dark eyebrows on a handsome oval-shaped face. Even and dental poster caliber, sparkling white teeth glistened beneath a well-trimmed moustache. A larger than average nose and olive or tanned complexion led Dobson to say it first. "Arab."

"Semitic, at least," Shanker said. "White shirt and tie. Could be a bank vice-president."

"Let's see how close the others are. Remember we have four different artists doing these. Two for each of the two witnesses." Dobson laid the first drawing back on its envelope and opened the next.

It was amazingly similar. The white shirt and tie, eyes, ears, moustache, and nose were as close as two artists looking at the same person could draw. Only the hair was slightly different. Fuller in one than the other but still neatly trimmed. He looked at the envelope. "This is great."

They opened the other two and then laid all four side by side. The two witnesses through four different hypnotists and four artists had described the same person so closely that the drawings differed in only minute detail.

Shanker read the two page description that went with each. "Short," he said after reading all four narratives. "The man is described as short. No taller than five-foot-three or four. They both say that twice. Neat, handsome, short, well-dressed, and with an olive complexion."

"Good. That's not either one of the guys we saw on the tape. We have something now. Al, look in that drawer and hand me the drawing that was made from the scalper's description of the one he actually handed the tickets to."

Shanker went to the file cabinet and retrieved another large envelope. He took out that drawing and laid it below the line of four that they had just been examining. He read the description that went along with it.

"Definitely not the same man. We have a pair who were involved in the tickets who are not on our tape."

Dobson looked at the lone drawing. "Yep. That guy is tall. What's it say? Six-feet-two. He has a beard and moustache. Ears that stick out like a car with its doors open. Slender face with thicker lips. Wearing a sweater over a dark T-shirt. These are not the same guy. They were just working together.

"Al, we need to make a computer composite of these four and get our scalper under hypnosis with another artist. Then make a composite of that one and this one," he said and pointed to the drawing of the tall, lanky young man. "I think we have a couple of Arabs."

"That really changes the complexion of this whole thing, John. Where do we start?"

"I'm going to go back to Washington. The director and the President need to know this. These drawings and the Syrian counterfeit money is enough to point to a foreign involvement. It's a political problem as much as a criminal one. They'll have to call the shots on this."

BRAD LAY WITH HIS head in Jill's lap while she stroked his hair.

"Brad, what you need to do is go back down and talk with your guy in the investigation. Tell him what you have. To tell you the truth, it doesn't sound like much. It's certainly not anywhere near proof beyond a reasonable doubt."

Brad kept his eyes closed. He felt safe and secure with Jill. He wasn't sure about the safety and security of the country.

"Jill, it's plain as day to me. The President had his own Vice President killed because he knew too much."

"You think you have enough that Pinthater would let you write that kind of story?"

"Get serious. Two sources for everything? This wouldn't get by the first two sentences to Pinthater. I only feel safe in telling you."

"Well, tell me. And I'll shoot it down from a lawyer's perspective."

"Okay. My sources are Harrot's diary from his computer and—"

"In his handwriting? Did he sign it? Or did anyone else have access to it?"

Brad sat up. "Wait. Don't cross-examine me yet. Listen to it all, and see what it sounds like to you." He laid his head back down in her lap and closed his eyes.

"Okay, go ahead. I'm sorry for interrupting." Her fingers played with his hair.

"Harrot's diary said the President was planning 'unconventional means' of dealing with the OPEC leaders. Harrot didn't like it and told the President. He was thinking about resigning. His last entry said he must look at the White House. He had talked with the *Preacher*. He was told that the Beast was ready to move on its plan."

"The Beast? Is that why you went to see Reverend Hutteth before you came here?"

"Yes. It turns out that Hutteth and Harrot had talked about the same thing. Revelation and Armageddon. Anyway, when Papa Legba called back Harrot's spirit, the spirit also said, 'Look at the White House.' Word for word what was in the diary entry."

"Has Papa Legba been to Montgomery?"

"No. Of course not." Brad opened his eyes. "Now listen. Senator Ashford was not at all alarmed or surprised when he was told by his maid that Harrot had been shot. Why? Because he is in on this with the President. I believe the President needed Ashford as Vice President and needed Harrot out. Ashford is a closet Muslim."

"A what? A closet Muslim? What's that?"

"He's a Muslim, but no one knows it. What's the Muslim holy day?"

Jill thought for a few seconds. "Friday, I think."

"Right. The Sugar Bowl started on Thursday night, but by the time it was announced that Harrot was dead it was after midnight. It was Friday. His maid finds Ashford in his library sitting on a Persian rug in meditation or prayer. He's facing toward Baton Rouge but really toward Mecca. No one prays to Baton Rouge."

"Why does the President need Ashford?"

"If he takes unconventional steps toward the Muslim OPEC countries, he can always smooth it over by saying, 'Hey, wait, this is not a religious or ethnic thing. My Vice President is Muslim.' "

"But if Ashford is a *closet Muslim*, then no one knows he's one. How's that help?"

"The President knows. He'll take him out of the closet when it's time."

"Go on."

"I have several reasons for believing he's a Muslim. He had a copy of the Koran on his desk and his ninety-two-year-old teacher said he liked to dress up like Ali Baba."

"So? J. Edgar Hoover liked to dress up like women. That didn't mean he was one. All you have there is a senile old woman and a copy of the Koran that you can probably find in any library."

"But, the Reverend Hutteth keeps on saying that the Beast will arise from a fanatical element of the Muslims."

"You don't believe that Beast stuff do you, Brad?"

"Well, I checked out the dates of the years he referred to. They pretty well match up. But on Ashford, I've checked his calendar while he was Senator and now as Vice President. No official appointments on any Friday. There's no record of him being of any other religious faith. He must be a Muslim."

"This is a free country, Brad. There's still a First Amendment the last time I looked. He has religious freedom."

"Yeah, but that wouldn't go over too well politically, would it?"

"Probably not."

"And I checked the President's appointment schedule for that October fourteenth meeting date. It shows that Harrot visited the White House. There were a few other names along with Garron and Steinheitz. Then there were just lists of groups. It was a big photo op day."

"So, that's all you've got? Let me list them. You have a diary entry that may or may not be authentic. You have a spirit that was called back by a voodoo priest. You have the stories of Ashford's maid and ninety-two-year-old school teacher. You have a charismatic evangelist who's preaching *Apocalypse Now*. Does that about sum up your evidence?"

"Yeah, pretty close."

"And from all of that you have deduced that the President of the United States is a murderer and the Vice President is a closet Muslim. And they're getting ready to start Armageddon?"

"Right."

"Brad, if I were you, I don't think I'd tell another soul. Let it rest with me. You tell this to someone else—they won't take you to that nursing home where Ashford's teacher is—they'll put a straight jacket on you and take you directly to the loony farm."

"Maybe you're right." Brad sat up, reached for his jacket, and pulled a copy of the Koran from his pocket.

"Uh, oh, Brad. Looks like you're a closet Muslim. You have a copy of the Koran," Jill mimicked in a sing-song tone.

"I just have it for research purposes. This was one of the sections that was marked in Ashford's copy in the library." He opened it and handed it to Jill.

"The Hypocrites?"

"Yeah. Read it."

She was silent for a minute. "Looks like a little dissention there."

"In Ashford's margin, someone had written 'Death to the Hypocrites.' "

"What does that mean?"

"I don't know." He took it back from her. "There's a passage here that you might like, Jill. It's from the section titled *Women*. Let me read it to you. 'Men have authority over women because God has made the one superior to the other, and because they spend their wealth to maintain them. Good women are obedient. They guard their unseen parts because God has guarded them. As for those from whom you fear disobedience, admonish them and send them to beds apart and beat them.' " He looked at her for a minute trying not to smile. "What do you think about that?"

Jill remained outwardly composed and calm. "Does it say 'beat them'?"

"Yes, but just the ones we're afraid might be disobedient." Brad could not hold back the grin that was taking over his face.

"Well, I thought beating women was the Christian way to do things. All the battered women workshops I've been to have women saying their men beat them because they thought the Bible told them to. It's good to know that violence toward women transcends religious dogma."

"What do the Jewish men do? Turn them into pillars of salt or send them off into the wilderness?"

"No, Brad. You're thinking about Lot's wife and Abraham's Hagar who was his mistress, concubine, or handmaid—take your choice. Lot and Abraham weren't Jews."

"Oh, well, you have to remember that I'm a Catholic. I just heard the stories. I didn't read about it." He laid down his copy of the Koran and lay back down in Jill's lap.

"Brad, you know what I've been thinking?"

"No, what?"

"I'm thirty-six. I've got the job I want, but I'm missing something."

"What's that?"

"I want to have a baby."

Brad's eyes popped open. "A baby?"

"Yeah, you know, one of those little things that look almost human. They cry, and eat, and wet, and cry, and crawl. You've seen them on television, haven't you, Brad?"

"Yes. Whose baby do you want to have?"

"Mine. And yours. I want us to get married."

# Thirty-six

A baby?"

"No, I said *baby-faced.*" Dobson gave Steinheitz a hard stare.

He had just laid out before the President's representative and the Director of the FBI the drawings of the two men he and Shanker had worried over the previous Saturday in New Orleans. This Monday meeting at FBI headquarters in Washington was necessary to see what would be the next step.

"I see what you mean, now." Steinheitz held the drawing of the nice looking man up closer to his eyes. "He does look very innocent. You would never take him for a murderer."

"No, just the boy next door. Isn't that what all the serial killers' neighbors always say. 'Well he was just so nice and quiet. Never had a bit of trouble out of him.' Then they dig up about thirty bodies from his basement or start taking body parts from the freezer. Then they remember 'an odd smell' having come from his place or the sound of saws in the middle of the night. Yeah, this kid's nice looking all right. He could smile while he carved out your liver," the Director said.

"Well, we figure him and his buddy may be Arab terrorists. They look like they could be. And we have the Syrian counterfeit money, remember?" Dobson asked.

"You don't have much though, do you, John?" the Director asked. "No names, no motive, just hypnotic induced recall for reconstruction artists."

"Those terrorists never have needed a motive. They feel there's ongoing reason for their actions. They just wait for a good time to get plenty of attention."

"This would be a touchy political problem right now, Agent Dobson, if we start pointing the finger at Arab terrorists without having more proof. We're having tough enough times with the OPEC people without starting a rumor that someone with foreign connections killed our Vice President. Hasn't some of that Syrian money been circulated in the United States before?" Steinheitz asked. He and the Director looked at Dobson.

"That's true. In 1993 on through part of 1996. But we thought we'd gotten rid of all of it."

"But the point I'm making is that this money could've been in the United States for the past five years. It could have gotten into other people's hands and then passed on to the assassins. It even may have been used to make it appear that Arab terrorists were involved. Don't you agree?"

Dobson nodded his head. "Yes, that's one possibility."

"And there was just a small amount of counterfeit money recovered, right? What did you say? Ten thousand?"

"Yeah."

"And there was more than a billion of that in circulation just a couple of years ago."

"Yes. But we do have these two fellows."

"You're right on that count. I think you should pursue their identification. But as quietly as you can. Understand? Until we know more. We don't want to have an international incident based on what we have here. Find out who they are, but keep it quiet as far as spreading around that Arabs may have killed Harrot. Okay?" Steinheitz looked at the Director, then to Dobson.

"That sounds like the rational and professional thing to do," the Director said. "John, you're doing great work. We still feel this can be handled within the Bureau. Isn't that right, Rob?" He looked at the President's man. Steinheitz nodded.

The Director looked back to Dobson. "John, I know this is exhausting. But keep it up. This is a break," he said, pointing to the drawings, "but we need names. And then we'll check these guys out."

"Oh, Agent Dobson, I was wondering if I could get a copy of those drawings, perhaps in a little smaller size?" Steinheitz again looked first toward the Director and then at Dobson.

"Why?" Dobson asked.

"Well, if you're correct, I'd at least like for the Secret Service men who guard the President to be acquainted with their faces. I don't want them turning up in a receiving line for the President and gun him down."

Dobson looked at the Director. "Is that all right?"

"Sure. Rob speaks for the President."

"Okay, I'll have our lab send you a couple of eight by tens. Be careful who you show them to. We don't want these to get in the wrong hands."

"Certainly not, Agent Dobson. Keep me informed on the investigation. It's been close to two months now. These Congressional committees want to start their own investigation, but we're trying to hold them off. We . . ., and I can speak for the President on this, are getting a bit anxious to see an arrest or at least a name of someone who we know is responsible. You understand?"

Dobson nodded. "Yes, sir. We're working on it."

THE NEXT DAY, BEFORE Dobson returned to New Orleans, Shanker and Brad met again at the Cafe Du Monde in the Riverwalk. Brad hoped their first meeting in over a month would be more productive than the last one. He was back on the story now, but he needed more hard information. It would also give him a chance to feel out Shanker on the things he had learned from Harrot's diary, his trip to Ashford's plantation, and the more exotic information he had garnered from Hutteth and Legba.

The crowds were still relatively scarce. In a short time though it would be Mardi Gras, and from then until the end of the year, throngs would flock continuously to Party City. Brad relished the quiet times of the year in New Orleans when he could walk the streets and see the sights for his own renewal without the press of unknown flesh against his.

Small chit-chat occupied their first five minutes while they finished off the beignets and refilled their coffee cups. Tugs plowed the Mississippi, visible through the glass wall in the slanting sun of late afternoon, seeking tankers and large freighters to take to berths.

"How's the investigation going, Al?"

"Slow, but we're making some progress. How's life in Washington since your lady's been appointed to the Senate?"

Brad shook his head. "I don't like it as well as here. Baton Rouge, New Orleans, and Lafitte are where I'd rather be. I'm trying to adjust. I don't know if I'm going to make it."

"I know what you mean. I've been stuck here for the past two months. I need to be in Tennessee. I need to see my folks. It's near time to prepare the tobacco beds. I have a 'hankering' to go up there, as we say where I'm from. Home may be where the heart is, but there's something coded or embedded within me that makes me want to go back to the soil of my home. It's like the Monarch butterflies, the migrating birds, or the salmon. It's in us to get back to our roots, and when we're gone too long, it works on our souls."

"That's a fine way to put it, Al. I never had thought of it that way. But I feel the same. I wonder whether it's a stronger urge in men or women?"

Shanker shook his head. "I'm afraid I don't know much about women. I've never been married—except to my job. But I know it's a deep need down in me. I called headquarters today and told them I want to get back out on assignment. I'm tired of being tied down here. We're moving very slowly. They told me to give it another month. Then I'd have a few weeks off and be put back on the roster for duty assignment."

"You're not going to stay with the investigation?"

"What investigation? We're running into stone walls. We have very little, Brad. But don't worry, I'll still be involved. Just not on a day to day basis like I am now. I'll keep you informed as I can."

Brad looked toward the river and took another swallow of coffee. "Anything new?"

"A little. We have some leads—at least faces—of a couple of guys who were involved in the ticket transaction."

"Any luck on the film of the one pulling the trigger? Have you got an ID on him or them yet?"

"No." Shanker cast his eyes downward. "Brad, give me your word that you won't use this yet." He looked back up.

"Okay. What?"

"The actual shooters were killed the next morning in a boat explosion."

"Where?"

"South of New Orleans on the Mississippi. Near a little place called Venice."

Brad nodded his head. "Yeah, I know the place." He fell silent for a minute. Then he looked Shanker in the eye. "Then you think that they were knocked off by somebody who was behind the assassination? A conspiracy?"

"I can't say. You have to keep what I tell you quiet for the time being."

"Al, do you have pictures of these other folks involved in the ticket transaction? You said you have *faces*."

"No, not pictures. Drawings. Composite drawings produced from descriptions given by witnesses who were put under hypnosis."

"Can I have a copy?"

"No, absolutely not!"

"Okay, I'm going to tell you something. I won't be able to say how I know, but I just want you to acknowledge if it fits in."

Shanker wrinkled his brow. "Well, go ahead. I don't know if I can acknowledge anything. I'll see."

"First, from what you saw of the shooters or of the fellows who were involved in the ticket transaction, would there be anything that would lead you to believe that Arabs or Muslims were involved?" Brad was staring straight at Shanker when he made the statement. He watched for the slightest reaction. Shanker's eyes didn't blink, but Brad saw a faint quiver at the corner of his mouth.

"What makes you say that?"

"I told you I can't say what leads me to say that. Do you think Arabs are involved?"

"I can't say."

Brad took the last drink of coffee, looked at the boats on the river, then back across the table to Shanker. What he was going to say next he had to word just right. He didn't want Shanker to think he was some nut case, someone who was creating outlandish conspiracy theories.

"Al, have you ever considered whether someone higher up had Harrot killed?" This time he saw the reaction. Shanker set his cup down with such force that Brad wondered why it didn't break.

"Higher up? There's no one higher up except for the President or God. I gather you're not referring to the Deity."

Brad nodded his head.

"No, we haven't considered the President as a suspect. Why should we?"

Brad decided to throw in the entire boat load. If he was going to sink, he might as well go down with the weight of all the chains of his theory. "Did you know that Ashford is a Muslim?"

"No, I didn't know it, and I don't know it. Is Ashford in on this too?"

"Not on the murder. Just that he was necessary to replace Harrot as Vice President."

"So, if I follow, the President had Harrot killed, and Ashford knows that he did—either before or after the fact?"

Brad nodded. That was as far as he was going to get involved. He had divulged more than he needed to. He hoped it served its purpose. Give Shanker something to think about and see where he went with it.

"Brad, I need a break from this investigation. And I think you need a little rest yourself. Take a few days off. You might want to go out on a boat or something and relax. Those are some crazy theories you have."

Shanker looked at his watch. "I've got to go. Dobson will be back in about an hour. He's been meeting with the President's man—Steinheitz. He was unaware that the President was the murderer." Shanker laughed for the first time since he had sat down. He left Brad there alone. Then, as he reached the corner of the restaurant, he turned, looked back over his shoulder at Brad, shook his head, and smiled again.

MARCH WOULD BE UPON them in less than a week and breeding season would be in full swing. Nidal and his tall friend and cousin, Ahmed, scanned the schedule for the first week of March.

"Looks like the stallions are going to have a great coming out party this season. Twenty mares next week and even more the following. We already have twenty requests for *Jacob's Ladder*. They like his bloodlines," Nidal said. He turned from the desk in his swivel chair and watched the lanky Ahmed scan the list of horses. "And the fact that he won over five million in his racing days."

Ahmed was in charge of the actual operation of the stud farm. He enjoyed the day to day oversight. He would feed, comb, and exercise the horses himself if need be. He liked to ride but his appearance on a horse resembled a large animated rag doll trying to hold on for dear life. Nidal had teased him that as tall as he was he should be able to wrap his legs all the way around the belly of the horse.

Nidal was the businessman. As small as most jockeys, he had never been on a horse in his life. He preferred to wear the silk-blend suits and mingle with the elite of horse breeders at the sumptuous parties thrown by the blue-bloods of Bluegrass country. After ten years of ownership of one of the top breeding farms in Kentucky, he was almost considered part of the establishment. Almost—but not quite. Money would buy many things, but it did not purchase the five-generation Kentucky pedigree or heritage that was necessary to break some of the social barriers.

Even at the barn, Nidal dressed nattily in starched white shirt and tie. Many of the older socialite women almost adopted him as one of their own sons. His clean looks, bright teeth, and ready smile mesmerized them at their first meeting. He was a salesman. He had sold the services of his and Ahmed's farm very well. His father and uncle, Ahmed's father, had provided the early financing, reaching into the millions of dollars. Now they were clear of debt and making a profit. Neither he nor Ahmed had been home to Saudi Arabia for the past five years. He wasn't looking forward to explaining to a distant relative what had happened to Ali. Their cousin had died as a warrior in the battle to determine who was going to govern their homeland.

They had won that battle, but the war was not over.

Ahmed finished his perusal of the breeding schedule and turned his attention to the Lexington *Herald-Leader*. He was the sports minded one of the two. He had season tickets to watch the Kentucky Wildcats play basketball just twelve miles down the road at Rupp Arena. He was looking at the probable tourney schedule when a side story caught his attention. He read it and then handed it to Nidal.

"Look, Nidal. This is one game you may want to go to. I have seats side by side."

Nidal looked at the three-paragraph story and smiled. "That's great. He's coming to Lexington. We don't have to go to Washington. The only thing that could be better is if he would request a tour of a horse farm while he was here and it would turn out to be ours."

Ahmed took the paper back. His smile almost met his ears. "Vice President Ashford is coming to Kentucky for two days of the conference tournament." He walked over to the wall calendar and circled the dates with a large black marking pen. "Two weeks from Saturday he'll be here for the semi-finals."

Nidal was just as pleased but more under control. His emotions were the same as his religion—in submission to his spirit. He walked to the safe, turned the rotor of the combination, and swung the door open. He took out a small box, opened it, and laid in his hand the cigarette lighter that his friends from New York had brought down the month before. He lifted it up and down in the palm of his hand, still amazed at its lightness.

He walked to the window and looked at the fence post that Mahmud had shot with the derringer. The neatly drilled-looking hole was a testament to the force and accuracy of the small instrument.

"Do you think we can get close enough?" Nidal asked before putting the lighter back into its box.

"Yes. He's bound to be going to a party, a reception, or something. We can get close enough. And if not there, why not at Rupp Arena?"

Nidal shrugged his shoulders. He would have to think about it. They had two weeks until another Vice President would be in town.

IN WASHINGTON THE NEXT morning, Vice President Ashford sat in the kitchen at his residence reading the Washington *Post* that his staff had already marked with the stories they thought would be of interest to him.

On the last page of the front section was a two-paragraph story saying that he would be going to Kentucky to help patch up some political problems for the President. The story didn't mention that he would be the honored guest at an athletic event. He despised sports, but for the good of the country, he would feign high enthusiasm while he was there.

Farms and animals did interest him though. So, he wrote a short note with pencil and paper to his chief-of-staff. "See what horse farms are available in Kentucky for touring while I'm there. Get me the name of two or three that have fine examples of breeding stock, and I'll choose one I would like to visit while in Lexington."

When he finished breakfast, he walked upstairs to what he was slowly turning into his new library. He had taken none of the volumes from Stratford Place, but instead had already purchased close to fifty thousand dollars worth of used books he had found on several trips to stores in the Washington vicinity. He liked the near anonymity of being Vice President where he could walk into a book store with a

Secret Service agent or two without creating much of a stir. The President couldn't do that. He wasn't certain if he wanted to be President anymore.

The room was nowhere near as large as the one at his plantation house, and most of the boxes still lay on the floor unpacked. It did have more windows than his library at home. On a small stand near one of the windows sat a large geography book containing the exact longitude and latitude designations for all cities of any significant size. In front of the window and near the stand, he had set up his compass on a tripod.

He knew the longitude and latitude of Mecca by heart. He looked again at the listing for Washington. He did some brief calculations on a pad, taking into account the location of the residence of the Vice President from downtown Washington, and then walked to the tripod and compass. He took a knife from his pocket, kneeled down to the hardwood floor, and made a small indention. Then he went to the wall, and with a red felt-tip pen, made a dot on the wall that was barely visible. He went back to the tripod one more time and gazed at the alignment of the compass. It was exact.

He scooted the tripod away, kneeled with his knees right at the small nick in the hardwood, and bowed his head to the floor toward the mark on the wall for his morning prayers.

# Thirty–seven

**E**arlier than normal for a Saturday morning, Brad walked out onto his balcony holding a steaming cup of coffee and clothed only in his bathrobe. The vernal equinox and the official first day of spring were just a week away. He could smell it.

The odor wasn't like Lafitte where families turned over a layer of topsoil and worked it up for gardens. There the aroma of damp, dark, warm soil filled the nostrils with the sense of planting time and the hope of harvest. On Burgundy Street at the edge of the Quarter, the smell was more one of rancid decay, the rotting of vegetables, fish heads, and shrimp thrown into the alley garbage cans awaiting the big green dumpster trucks.

Occasionally, though, there were whiffs of lilac and rose from the parks at the river's edge, or even from Jackson Square that made their way through the mugging stench as though they had been carried on angels' wings. He breathed deeply and savored the rare delight.

Along the L-shaped balcony, the plants, vines, and flowers that Jill had so lovingly planted, placed, and nurtured were making their own revival from the deadness of winter. If the plants had survived his benign neglect, he felt encouragement for Jill and him. Perhaps even the country would make it into the next millennium.

Jill would be at the airport at noon. He would enjoy a leisurely cup or two of his home-brewed French coffee and then make his trip to the corner of Royal and Toulouse to the little jewelry shop. A week before, he and Jill had spent all of Saturday afternoon looking at engagement and wedding rings. She wanted him to pick them out. He knew he had no taste in that kind of thing and wanted her to at least suggest what she liked. She had tried on more than a dozen and said she would be satisfied with any of them. She hinted especially toward three different sets, each in a different price range.

Brad opened his checkbook and glanced at his balance. He then retrieved his last Visa statement to see what his credit limit was. Jill and this marriage were worth an investment. He had not responded with a definite "yes" when she suggested marriage and babies at her apartment two weeks before. He was old-fashioned enough that he wanted to be the one to propose. Tonight in Baton Rouge on the river bank with the moon at their backs he would do just that. Spring had always encouraged him to move forward. He could feel it in the air. He would ask her to be his wife, or at least formally respond and accept the invitation to be her husband.

His mind was so enmeshed in the thoughts of a fresh start with Jill that he had sat on the balcony looking down Burgundy for a half hour before he noticed the large brown envelope that was alone on the wrought-iron stand next to his chair. He didn't remember placing it there. Jill had been in Washington for a week. No one else, to his knowledge, had been at his apartment.

He set his coffee down beside it and picked the envelope up. Turning it over, he saw a handwritten note on the opposite side. "To Brad—From Al." He opened it and withdrew the contents. Paper-clipped to two eight-by-ten color drawings was Shanker's note: "Dobson gave a set of these to Steinheitz, so I guess I can give you a set. Do Not Use Yet! For Your Information Only! (See how safe you are in your apartment!)"

Brad held first one and then the other up and in front of his eyes. He knew when he studied them that they were the two that Shanker had talked about. The more he looked at them the more he knew they could be Arabs. The breeze seemed cooler now when he thought back to Hutteth's warnings. He carefully placed them back in the envelope and then took them to his desk inside. He looked back out toward the balcony. Shanker was a slick one. When and how could the agent have delivered the envelope to the table? It was scary what the government could do.

At the jewelry shop, Brad became rattled again looking at all the sparkling rings. He hoped he had not forgotten the set he was seeking—or worse yet, that it had been sold. The more he peered through the glass cases, the less sure he was about his selection. Then he spied what he believed to be the set—a large diamond perched upon antique, filigree yellow gold. Yes, Jill would have that. It would adorn her finger until "death do them part." The shop owner was happy to put the set in a nice box. He should have been. The amount drained Brad's checkbook and approached his credit card limit.

He didn't mind the price. He smiled broadly as he put the box in his jacket pocket. This would be the happiest day of his life until they married, and then their wedding day would be.

VICE PRESIDENT ASHFORD ARRIVED in Lexington at noon. Accompanying him on Air Force Two were three staff members, his Secret Service contingent, Rob Steinheitz, and Steinheitz's staff. Tip-off for the first semi-final game of the tournament pitting Kentucky against LSU was set for 2 p.m. Arkansas against Tennessee would follow.

After greeting local and state dignitaries, he and his party were whisked to the Hyatt Regency Hotel that adjoined Rupp Arena where the tournament was being held. He would have a half hour to freshen up before a reception in the hotel at one o'clock and the game an hour later. The trip was purely political although some semblance of official business would be conducted in order to quiet the opposition party's urging reimbursement of the expense of the trip from the President's party's coffers.

Nidal and Ahmed arrived at the arena an hour ahead of the first game. It wasn't that unusual. Thousands of Kentucky fans did the same thing. Kentucky's basketball fans were similar to Alabama's football followers. Both would travel to the far reaches of the world to view their teams' successes. When the Kentucky team began preseason practice at one second past midnight on the first allowable day, Rupp Arena filled with twenty-three thousand or so fans who just came to view their team go through wind sprints and perhaps scrimmage each other.

The team from LSU similarly drew a large following and an equal number who despised them. Their coach brought out the best and worst in his and the opponents' fans. He had played by the rules of the recruiting system and up to the edge. Each year there were at least one or two players on his team whose names could not be easily pronounced. It wasn't that they were Cajun. He recruited from Europe and Africa the behemoths who could reach up on tiptoes and touch the orange metal rim ten feet above the floor.

Making their way to the first-level seats twenty rows behind the scorer's table, Nidal and Ahmed, along with the hundreds of others entering, were closely scrutinized by ushers and an extra contingent of police and security guards.

Since the Vice President would once again be in an open area, the Secret Service moved to minimize the potential for another assassination. Metal detectors were set up at the entrance to each aisle. Fans who came in and went back out for a Coke or popcorn would have to pass through the detector each time. It had slowed the entrance of fans, but it had been announced the previous day. Even players, coaches, and referees were scanned by hand held detectors before they were allowed to enter the arena floor. Many of the media grumbled for having to go through the gauntlet of security mechanisms. The referees raised the biggest stink because the Service insist-

ed that they use plastic whistles instead of metal. Neither the reporters nor the officials garnered any sympathy from the fans. It was one
time they were treated equally.

Nidal winced when he passed through the detector the first
time with the cigarette-lighter-derringer in his back pocket. There was
not a squeak, so he made a game of going in and out of his seat and
through the device for the next half hour. He bought candy, a program, popcorn, and finally a Coke before he sat down to enjoy the
game.

The three rows immediately behind the scorer's table were
roped off for the Vice President's party. The Secret Service had the
names of each seat assignment within a ten row radius. Fans having
those seats were checked for identification before being allowed to sit.

Nidal and Ahmed had seats on the aisle. Ashford and his
entourage would have to enter either down their aisle or the next one
over. They had prayed for theirs to be the one. They hoped the Vice
President would pause and shake hands with well wishers on his way
down the aisle, as was customary with American politicians. That
would be their chance.

Nidal took the cigarette lighter out of his back pocket, put a
small cigar between his lips, and began to light it. He was immediately set upon by two ushers.

"We're sorry, sir. Smoking is not permitted in the arena.
There's a designated area outside."

Nidal smiled. "I'm sorry. I should have known. Smoking is
not permitted anywhere in America any longer." He flipped the lighter
closed and put the cigar back into his pocket.

One minute before tip-off, there was a stir. People turned
around to look at the entry of the Vice President into the aisle where
Nidal and Ahmed sat. Allah had blessed them. Ashford was flanked
by six Secret Service men. He waved to a few nearby fans as he was
briskly escorted down the walkway. He was still fifteen rows behind
the two horsemen when Nidal stood up and palmed the derringer in
his right hand.

Ashford smiled and appeared to enjoy being in Rupp Arena as
he was ushered down the steps with guards on each side, in front, and
behind. He made eye contact with as many of the fans seated nearby
as possible, considering the speed at which he was descending. A few
reached out to shake hands, but the guards would not allow him to
respond. Their job was to get him to his seat as quickly and safely as
possible.

Nidal waved his left hand and kept his right down to his leg.
"Mr. Vice President!" he shouted. Ashford looked directly at him when
he got to his level. Ashford nodded but did not reach out a hand. The
Secret Service man nearest the left side of the Vice President shielded

Ashford from contact, and he passed safely by the row where Nidal and Ahmed stood.

Ahmed looked at his shorter friend. "Maybe he'll come back up. Or else tomorrow at the farm."

BRAD LAY ON THE couch while Jill finished showering and changing after her flight in from Washington. He had zipped the ring box safely inside a pocket of his jogging jacket that was draped across a chair near the door.

A few times a year he watched LSU basketball on television or he would drive up and take Jill to a game on campus. They were both alumni. It didn't hurt to yell for the Tigers. They had an exciting team—the best since the Shaq Attack left.

"What are you watching?" Jill asked. She came through the doorway to the kitchen and bathroom wearing Brad's terry robe and towel-drying her hair. No make-up, no fancy clothes, just wet hair and squeaky-clean skin.

Brad looked over his shoulder. "LSU and Kentucky. Kentucky's up by five. They're just ten minutes into the first half. Come around and sit down." He watched her combing through her hair, carrying a portable dryer under an arm. His blood began to flow a little faster. "You have on anything underneath my robe?"

She laid the hair dryer down on the end of the sofa, sat down, and continued the stroking of her hair. "No," she said without taking her eyes off the television.

"Then I want my robe back." Brad reached toward her waist and began tugging on the cloth tie belt.

"Stop, Brad. I don't have anything on. I'm wet and it's cold in here."

"I was hoping you were wet," he said and continued his playful tugging. She stood and headed back toward the kitchen door. He jumped in front of her and put his arms inside the robe where he had managed to loosen the belt and brought her body to his. Her skin was cool to his touch at first, but he felt it begin to warm. Slowly she gave in, rested her head on his shoulder, dropped her comb, and wrapped her arms around him.

He ran his lips along her neck from just beneath her ear to her shoulder and began to give her little nibbles as he traversed the area in the slow rhythm of an impassioned pendulum. He brought both hands up her flanks and along her sides until his fingers were just beneath her arms and his palms lay flat against the sides of her breasts. He let his lips move to hers and kissed them, parting them slightly with his tongue. She tiptoed and pressed her pelvis to him.

"That three-pointer ties the game at twenty-seven!" the announcer shouted, and Brad swung Jill around so that he could see the screen over her left shoulder.

She pushed him away and tied her robe back. "I wouldn't want you to miss any of the ball game," she said, picked up her comb and dryer, and walked back toward the bathroom.

Brad sat back down. He wanted to save the best for the evening anyway after he gave her the ring. He watched his school's players run up and down the hardwood court as they tried to stay up with Kentucky.

By the second half, Jill relented and rejoined him on the sofa. She had her hair fixed and make-up on, but still lounged in a sleek purple and gold satin jogging suit. "I thought if I dressed like a cheerleader, I might could keep your attention," she said and ran her fingernails along his thigh to his knee.

"Well, Jill, it's our school. You went there too. You should cheer for them."

"We probably should've gone to the game and made an appearance. I'll need all the positive publicity I can get when I have to run for election."

"I don't know. They showed Vice President Ashford there a few minutes ago. I'd feel kind of nervous with another Vice President in a large crowd at a sporting event. He might get shot. You and I may be the harbingers of bad events."

"I don't think our being there would affect it anyway. We just happened to be there when Harrot was shot."

"Just kidding."

"Brad, let's walk down to the LSU horse stables when the game's over. It's less than a mile, it's a pretty spring day, and I love the smell of horse barns."

Brad winked at her. "You have strange tastes for a U.S. Senator. But okay, we'll go see the horses. We'll come back and go to dinner. Then I want us to go out to the riverbank with a bottle of wine and your portable CD player and listen to some funky music."

She turned and ran her fingers through his hair. "Brad, you sound like you just walked in from the seventies."

He nodded. "Yeah, I'm your funky reporter."

"Will I have all your attention?"

"Yes, my lady."

ROB STEINHEITZ LOOKED UP at the television screen in his suite at the Hyatt Regency. With five minutes left in the game, Kentucky had pulled out to a seven point lead. He was more interested in the play that Ashford was receiving as the goodwill ambassador for the President. The national network had already shown him in three close-ups. Ashford even appeared to be enjoying the game.

Steinheitz had ensconced himself in the comfortable rooms

three floors beneath where the Vice President would be staying. Except for the perfunctory greetings of dignitaries at the airport, he had left the official business to the Vice President and had come straight to the hotel. Since one o'clock there had been a steady stream of power-brokers and politicians who had made their way to his floor for private meetings. He had his list of the ones who had scheduled appointments. They came from Kentucky, Tennessee, Ohio, and Indiana. They knew where the real power rested. He could see them and listen to their concerns without a Secret Service check. The Vice President was guarded but he wasn't.

He looked at his watch. He had left two hours in his appointment list unfilled. He told his clerk to take a break and go to the ballgame. He handed him two tickets for mid-court seats. He wouldn't need him the rest of the day. He was going to take a nap.

Ten minutes later the phone rang. "Yes, where are you? Sixth floor? I'll be right down. You're right next to the stairway like I asked, aren't you? Have the door open. I don't want anyone to see me."

He eased out of his room, down the stairway, through the door to the sixth floor, and looked for the open door to the room where he was to meet with his Arab plotters. He carried a large envelope and a note pad.

There were three of them that greeted him. A fourth stood guard at the door with some type of automatic weapon that Steinheitz didn't recognize. Why was he called upon to do this dirty business rather than Garron? To be the lone Jew in a room with four Arab terrorists was not his idea of a comfortable and friendly afternoon. For some reason though, these men had taken a liking to him once they had overcome their initial hesitancy in dealing with an American Jew. For many, in some of their homelands, Steinheitz would be the embodiment of evil. They shook hands in the Western tradition and hugged in the Eastern.

"President Teater sends greetings to all of you," Steinheitz said and looked at each of them and then back toward the one at the door.

One of the Arabs motioned to him to have a seat. "We cannot be too careful. We are at a critical point. The time is nearing. We have checked the room for bugs. We hope that few know we are here. How're our supplies coming?"

"Here's the list you gave me," Steinheitz said and retrieved a paper from the envelope. "We've shipped most of it already to the port that you mentioned. Will arrive next week. It's up to you to secure the shipment. More will come in April. How's your support coming at home?"

"I speak for all of us," said the first one who had been doing the talking already. "Things are in preparation. June Eighth will be the day of execution. We believe we have a great following. They just need a little leadership and show of strength. The weapons we asked for, and that we hope you have sent, will go a long way toward that."

"They'll be there. What about detection? Is there any indication that anyone knows something's brewing, that something's being planned? What about in the official family?"

The spokesman shook his head. "No. They always have rumors of coup attempts. There's been questioning on a periodic basis, but nothing's suspected as far as we know."

"Abdul, let me ask you a few things. Suppose the coups and rebellions start and there's resistance. Do you have enough people, enough troops committed, to carry it to the end?"

"Yes. In Iraq, Kuwait, Saudi Arabia, Nigeria, and even in Iran we are strong and will be successful. You'll have oil. We'll be in control. You will support us. After the initial attacks on the leaders, we'll ask for official recognition and help from you to keep order. Things must move swiftly and forcefully. That's why we need to see the President again face to face."

"Well, we'll talk about that later. It's a little touchy to get you back into the White House again. Unfortunately, our meeting in October did not go over well with the Vice President who was there." Steinheitz looked at the three who nodded their heads in agreement. "If I may touch on a delicate matter for a moment, Abdul, do you have information as to who killed Vice President Harrot?"

Abdul, sleek with close-cropped hair and dressed in the best western attire, blinked and then smiled at his companions as a bit of nervous laughter engulfed them. "Best guess we had was CIA. They trained us for Afghanistan. Looks like a CIA operation to us. What do you say? You had him killed? Right? He knew too much?"

Steinheitz shook his head. "No. I didn't. Garron didn't. We thought maybe some of your people volunteered to the President to do it. Maybe to show your good intentions? You can tell me. It won't go any farther. I'm just sort of curious why someone else would kill him if it wasn't one of us or you."

"No, it wasn't us," Abdul said and received nods of the heads from his companions. "We would have if anybody had asked us, but we didn't. Who does that leave?"

"I don't know. The investigation hasn't turned up much. They did find a little Syrian counterfeit money."

Abdul and his companions smiled again. "Yes, that was very good fake currency. We've seen some of that. It started in 1992 or 1993. We all saw some of it. Very professional. Do they have anything else?"

Steinheitz took the two drawings from the envelope. He handed them to Abdul who studied each and handed them on to his companions. "These two guys were implicated in buying the tickets for the seats from where Harrot was shot. Do you recognize them?" After another minute, they each shook their heads.

"What else does the investigation have?"

"That's all I know of. They're supposed to tell me everything, but I don't know if they have?"

"Do you want us to find out what all they know? We can do that. Where're they headquartered? New Orleans, right?"

"Yes. Well, if you could do it without being caught, that would be fine. They may be hiding something from me. I don't want any Watergate burglary though. It can't lead back to the White House."

"We have professionals working for us. Not Cubans. We'll check it out. Report to you when we meet the President."

"Yes. Well, I'll check his travel schedule for the next couple of months and see where we can arrange a meeting. Away from Washington. At a reception or big gathering where you could get in. Trust me, the shipments are on the way. You have my word."

"I trust your word, Rob. But for all of my people whose lives I'm putting on the line, I have to have the handshake of the President and look him in the eye."

"Abdul, you've heard the term *Armageddon*? The Christian prophecy about a great war of good against evil?"

"Yes, I've been to the place."

"Is there any chance that if this goes bad, we could have a big war?"

Abdul looked around the room at his companions and smiled. "Remember how Saddam Hussein said when the U.S. was preparing to push him out of Kuwait that it would be the Mother of All Wars? Well, if something goes wrong, this will be the Mother of All Wars. Your Armageddon. But we're not going to let anything go wrong, are we, my Jewish friend?"

THE LITTLE EXCURSION TO the LSU Equine Pavilion, as the horse barns were officially known, had been interesting to Brad. Jill spoke with one of the professors and compared notes on the background and pedigree of the horses that had been mentioned early on for the Kentucky Derby. She curried a bay mare and was allowed to ride. The people at the barn were honored to have a U.S Senator visit them.

Dinner at one of the swankier restaurants had gone well. But Brad felt Jill was anticipating something that didn't occur there. Had she known him long enough to be able to read him and know that he had a ring for her?

Now they were back to one of his favorite places in Baton Rouge. From her apartment, they had walked the elevated crossing to the park that hugged both sides of the levee. The languid Mississippi flowed toward New Orleans on the far side. Walkers and joggers chugged along the path that capped the spine of the levee.

They sat on the cool grass. The fragrance of spring was still in the air. The moon had just begun its ascent in the eastern sky behind them, like a huge translucent pearl being pulled along a backdrop of black velvet by a chain of tiny stars. No one seemed to notice that Louisiana's newest senator and the state's best known reporter were there near the crest of the levee staring deep into each other's eyes. The others in the park had agendas of their own.

They sat facing each other side by side. Jill could see the necklace of orange and white lights off to the north of town that decorated the oil refineries and metal towers and walkways. Brad looked to the southwest where Lafayette sat below the horizon more than fifty miles away. A slight orange glow showed him where Lafayette's street lights reached up toward the sky. Ashford's Stratford Place and Amelia Tadford were over there still wrapped in a mystery he had failed to unravel.

He turned his thoughts back to why he was here, drew Jill closer to him, and encircled her with his arms. He looked down at her face where she had now closed her eyes. The soft moonlight bathed her face in an angelic and childlike glow. He was sure he wanted to spend the rest of his life with her.

"Jill."

She opened her eyes and stared up at Brad's but didn't say a word.

"You want to have a baby?"

"You romantic devil you."

"No, I mean . . . I want to do it the old-fashioned way." For someone who dealt with words everyday on paper, he was having the most difficult time of his life trying to put his feelings into verbal expression.

She wrinkled her forehead. "Brad, I want to do it the old-fashioned way too. If I didn't, I could've already visited a sperm bank and made a withdrawal or tried that in-vitro fertilization. But I always said to myself, 'Do it the old-fashioned way.'"

"No, Jill. I mean let's get married first. Will you marry me? Or may I still accept your proposal?"

Her eyes moistened. "Yes. And yes."

He fumbled for the ring box and finally found it in an inside pocket. The diamond and gold sparkled in the pale moonlight as he slipped the ring on her finger. They leaned together and kissed.

THE SECRET SERVICE HAD already checked the backgrounds of the employees and owners of Darby Run days before Vice

President Ashford's visit to Lexington. Of the three farms that his staff had recommended to him, he chose the one that was only twelve miles from the Hyatt Regency Hotel where he would be staying. The farm was reputed to have some of the best Thoroughbred stallions in the country.

Most of the farm hands were local boys who had a few public drunkenness and DUI charges but nothing so serious as to raise a question with the Service. The owners, Nidal and Ahmed, had been in Lexington for over ten years. They were two of the many rich Arabs who had invested in multiple horse farms in the area in the 1980s. Most of them had departed the Bluegrass after losing most of their investments, but Nidal and Ahmed had toughed it out and stayed.

They were both from Saudi Arabia. Their families were upstanding lower echelon government functionaries who, like many from that country, bathed in the vast riches of oil. There was no criminal record for either Nidal or Ahmed, and the locals gave them a glowing report. The Service decided Darby Run was a safe place for the Vice President to visit.

Benjamin Ashford dressed casually for his Sunday morning visit to the farm. He and the Secret Service officers who accompanied him would be the only outsiders. He had invited Rob Steinheitz to join them, but Steinheitz declined and stayed at the hotel. He cared as little for horses as he did for Vice Presidents.

The limousine wheeled into the long, tree-lined lane, stopped to allow two of the Secret Service agents to stand guard at the gate, and then proceeded between the white-planked fences toward the green-roofed barns in the distance. A few warm days had brought the green to the grass and a horse or two turned their heads and looked fleetingly at the sleek black car. Nidal and Ahmed stood beside the barn awaiting their honored guest. Nidal was resplendent in his dark suit, sparkling white shirt, and sunglasses aimed toward the early morning sun. Ahmed wore jeans, a sweater over a blue denim shirt, and cowboy boots that made his six-foot-three-inch frame appear even taller. Nidal still carried the cigarette lighter in an inside coat pocket.

A preceding car load of Secret Service agents had already fanned out around the barns and stood as sentries. Only Nidal was better dressed than they.

The Vice President extended his hand. "Good to meet you. I hear you have a wonderful farm. I want to see some of your stallions. You have *Jacob's Ladder* here. Is that right?"

Nidal extended his hand. "Yes, Mr. Vice President. We are honored to have you. This is my cousin, Ahmed."

For an hour Ashford, Nidal, Ahmed, and two Secret Service agents walked through the barns, the lanes between fences where the stallions were enjoying the early morning air, and to the horse cemetery where monuments had been erected to great stallions of the past. Ashford asked a myriad of questions about horse breeding and the training of race horses.

"At least two of the horses that will run in the Kentucky Derby in May were conceived right here on our farm. You should come back for the Derby, Mr. Vice President," Nidal said as they neared the breeding barn.

"Maybe I can. When is it?"

"The first Saturday in May at Churchill Downs in Louisville."

"I'd like to see your charts on the breeding history and the results of the offspring of these stallions. I mean, if it's not confidential. I breed beef cattle, and it's interesting to me to see the history back through several generations."

Nidal looked at Ahmed. "Certainly. We have all that in the office area in this barn we're coming to. We'd be happy for you to come in, have a cup of tea, and let me explain the history to you."

They got to the office door just inside the barn. "Is this the only door to the office?" Ashford asked.

"Yes."

Ashford turned to his Secret Service guardians. "Why don't you two stay here and guard the door? We'll go inside and talk for a while."

The agents were hesitant, but agreed if they could do another sweep of the room before leaving the Vice President alone with the two Arabs.

No one was more pleased that Ashford asked to be alone with them than Nidal. He closed the door, showed Ashford to a chair in front of the desk, and opened the large book that detailed the history of each stallion on the farm. Ahmed pointed out a few lines to Ashford who hunched over the desk to look at the diagrams of mares, stallions, and offspring. Nidal reached into his inside coat pocket, removed the cigarette lighter, and flipped the bottom out of the way revealing the two-barrelled derringer. He stepped up behind Ashford and extended his arm.

# Thirty—eight

**A**hmed touched Ashford on the shoulder. "We have a gift for the White Caliph." He nodded toward Nidal. Ashford turned in the chair and saw the derringer lying flat in the extended hand of Nidal. Ashford glanced toward the door.

"That's the little gun you told me about? Some type of plastic that's not picked up by metal detectors?"

Nidal smiled. "Yes. I've been swept with detectors three times this morning. Not a single blip."

"Is it loaded?" Ashford asked.

"Yes. The bullets are the same way. No detection." Nidal gave Ashford a brief run through of how to use the small weapon, closed it, and handed it to his guest. "It's for you to use in case we can't get close enough or fail."

"Very ingenious. It would have to be a last resort. For me to use this would ruin our plans for the future. We could've had Teater killed without killing Harrot, but getting rid of Teater is only part of it. If I have to use this," he said and looked at the weapon, "our plan will have only been half successful. I don't believe they will let a Vice President who killed the President succeed to his office. It's sort of like killing your parents for the insurance money."

"It's only as a last resort, Mr. Vice President," Nidal whispered. "We hope to be able to use the long rifle again if we can get the President in the open. Do you know his schedule for the next month?"

Ashford smiled and looked toward the door where the Secret Service agents stood just outside. "I'm only the Vice President. I'm like the wife who's been cheated on. I'm usually the last to know. But I'll let you know as soon as I do. What's our deadline?"

Ahmed remained silent. Nidal continued in a low voice, "We don't know. Our friends in New York have been back to the homelands. Everything's calm. The leaders don't believe there's a threat. They've been told. They've interrogated dozens, but all's quiet. They don't believe the U.S. would get rid of them with simultaneous coups. We don't have names of suspects. We only have the word of a dead Vice President. This is March. Three months are over. We know it's going to be this year. We have to move soon or our past efforts will be in vain. Your friend Harrot would've given his life for nothing along with my friend Ali."

Ashford put his deadly gift into his pocket. "If it becomes necessary, I'll do it myself.  Cut the snake's head off, and the body will die.  They know they have to be supported by the President to be successful.  They would have no deal with the Speaker of the House who's next in line after me.  Oh, but we need *you* to do it.  Then I could be President.  Your homelands would remain safe with their present rulers or with those you choose."

"Yes.  That's best.  We'll do our part.  I'm willing to die for my country if it comes to that.  Aren't you, Ahmed?"  Nidal turned to his tall cousin who acknowledged with a nod.

Ashford shook his head.  "Sam was a patriot.  He was a friend.  But he was a coward.  He couldn't do what he had to do.  I miss him.  He was like a brother to me.  I hurt for Lenora."


MARRIAGE PLANS WERE BUZZING through his mind on Monday morning when Brad returned to his office.  That was all Jill could talk about the remainder of Saturday and Sunday after he had slipped the ring onto her finger.  He looked at the three names he had scribbled on the paper.  She wanted him to prepare a list of people he wanted to invite to the June wedding, and she would have hers within the week.

This was moving a little faster than he had anticipated.  June was just three months away.  He would be married.  Then she wanted a child.  He would be a father at forty-five if all went well.  His child would be in the first year of college when he turned sixty-four.  He had trouble imagining it.  The same way he had trouble making out a guest list for the invitations.

He had put his sister and brother down and Papa Legba.  Three.  How had he managed to know so few people well enough to invite them to his wedding?  He would have put down Amelia Tadford's name, but Jill probably would have asked why.  Hutteth was out.  Brad had asked Jill if Hutteth could do the wedding and received a resounding "NO!"  She didn't think it would go well with the setting of the St. Louis Cathedral in New Orleans.

He glanced up and saw his new friend, Danny Spurling, coming down the aisle with a sheath of papers.  He penciled in his name.  Danny stopped at his desk.

"Danny, would you like to come to my wedding?  I don't expect a gift.  I'd just like to have you there."

"Sure, when is it?"  Danny wiped a lock of his long, stringy hair out of his eyes.

"June."

"June what?"

"I don't know.  I just told Jill to be sure it wasn't June Eighth."

"What's June Eighth?"

"It's a long story, Danny.  It's Mohammed's date of death."

"Oh. Yeah, you're right, it must be a long story."

"Thanks, Danny, I'll put you down for an invitation."

Danny laid the stack of typed pages on Brad's desk. "I thought you'd like to see what a good printed copy of Harrot's diary looked like, Brad."

"That's what this is?" Brad picked up the first few pages. "I've read it three times during the last month. You didn't uncover anything new did you?"

"No. It's just that you were reading from the copy from his cheap dot-matrix printer. I wanted to show you how neat it looked coming from my laser printer. It's still about fifty pages from January through December."

Brad admired the nice dark print that was crisp and clear. "This does look a lot better. I'll scan it again to see if I come up with anything new. Thank you."

For the next half hour, Brad reread the entries of Samuel Harrot. It was pretty boring up until the October entry. A Vice President's biography just would not be a best seller, he once again concluded. He looked closer at the October, November, and December entries to see if another reading would bring out anything missed before. There was nothing until he got to the last page. He waved for Danny to come back to his office.

"What is it?"

"Danny, this last page wasn't like this before." He took his copy of the printing and handed it to Danny. "See that."

"What?"

"There's a comma there that wasn't there before." He pointed to the last sentence on the last page.

"No. It was there. The old dot matrix and the worn ribbon just made it very faint. The laser brings it out nice and neat. Your eyes are probably a little weak from all your reading and age. You're over forty, aren't you? I don't mean that you're really *ancient* or anything, but you might want to check on getting glasses or contacts."

Brad frowned at his young friend. "You still want to be on my wedding invitation list, Danny?"

"Yes."

"Don't call me old."

"Okay."

"Thanks." Brad sat back down and examined the two pages side by side. He still couldn't see the comma in the first copy. It put a whole new light on the meaning of the last entry that Harrot had made. He looked at the sentence now as it was printed from Danny's laser.

"Told **BEA,ST** was about to move on plan, and I do not know what to do."

# Thirty-nine

The Delta 747 began its descent into Atlanta with Brad Yeary fidgeting at a window seat. The whole South had welcomed spring. The grass was bright green and the trees were beginning to leaf out. Even from twenty-seven thousand feet, he could see the mystery of the season roll northward.

For three and a half weeks, he had tried for another meeting with Shanker. No contact. Shanker was in Washington, then in New Orleans, and now at his parents' home in East Tennessee. He had finally called Brad and invited him up. "Twenty miles from the Knoxville airport," he had told him. All the flights from New Orleans went through Atlanta or Nashville to get to Knoxville. Brad had taken the first available one. An hour in Atlanta—just long enough to change planes—and he would be a short hop to Knoxville and the gateway to the Smoky Mountains. He had been there only once during his college years to an LSU-Tennessee football game. He didn't remember much. It had been a long drive home.

He looked at his watch. Jill would be leaving now from Washington headed the opposite direction to New Orleans. Congress was taking its traditional long break for Easter. He would visit with Shanker this evening and fly back on Good Friday. It was the best time of the year for New Orleans, and Jill had plans for them. They would stay at his apartment on Burgundy and finish their wedding preparations. The DAY was now set for Saturday, June Twentieth.

Samuel Harrot had written his own death warrant. That was Brad's conclusion from all the information he had. When Harrot followed up on his diary entry by telling "BEA" that President Teater was about to move on his plan, he confided in the wrong person. Brad was sure that Ashford had run straight to the President with the news that Harrot was talking. In less than two weeks he was dead. Harrot did not even have the opportunity to confront his friend who was in on the conspiracy or to utter an indictment similar to the words that Shakespeare put in Julius Caesar's mouth,—*Et tu Brute?*

Brad had it all neatly typed out—double-spaced on five sheets of paper. He had summarized all he knew. The notes included his conversations with Reverend Hutteth, Papa Legba, Amelia Tadford, and Harrot's diary entries. Omitted were the conversations with Mattie Lewis. He had wrestled with his duties as a reporter against those as a citizen for all of the three and a half weeks he had sought Shanker.

He could just sit back and wait for any further events to unfold, report on them, and be perfectly all right ethically.  He didn't have any direct evidence that a crime was going to be committed—just a feeling and conclusion that something was terribly wrong.  Or he could, as he was going to do, disclose to an agent of the government all that he knew and hope it would fall into the honest hands of someone who would do something with it.  Shanker, if anyone, fit that description.  Then if nothing came of his efforts, he could rest comfortably knowing he had done all he could to find Harrot's killer and prevent whatever "unconventional" means the President was proposing to use against the nations of OPEC.

The rental car company at the Knoxville airport gave him a map of Tennessee and Knoxville.  He laid it beside the directions he received from Shanker and aimed the Ford toward the foothills of the mountains and the small village of Townsend.

Shanker had described the route perfectly.  Brad expected no less from a Secret Service agent who had spent his entire life traveling with Presidents and Vice Presidents.  He rolled down the window and breathed in the aroma of lilac and locust blossoms.  Small farms that clung to cleared ridges dotted the sides of the highway, interspersed with businesses, campgrounds, and other tourist attractions.  He turned onto a side road and finally back right again onto a long gravel drive that ended at a farmhouse.

He needed no introduction.  The solitary figure sitting on the porch in a rocking chair, smoking a pipe, with a straw hat shading his face was clearly Al Shanker's father.  Brad could have picked him out of a line-up any place.  He didn't get up or acknowledge Brad's presence.  He just kept rocking and peering in the visitor's direction, occasionally putting the pipe to his lips.

"Hi, I'm Br—"

"Brad Yeary.  New Orleans *Times-Gazette* reporter.  Here to see Al," the old man said and kept rocking.

"Yes.  Good to meet you, Mr. Shanker."

Shanker's father nodded.  "Pull you up a chair and sit a while.  Al's out beside the barn tending to the 'baccer bed.  You know he guards the President, don't you?"

"Yeah, he's very good at it," Brad said and looked toward the barn.

"Yep, he's going back on assignment next week.  'Tweren't his fault the Vice President got shot.  He's going straight back to the White House.  The President needs him."

"Yes, your son does a wonderful job, Mr. Shanker.  I believe I'll just go on out toward the barn and talk with him.  Good to meet you."

"Same here.  Call me Clyde instead of that Mister stuff.  He's over there," he said and pointed the pipe toward the barn behind and to the left of the house.

Al Shanker was on his hands and knees in the middle of a small tobacco plant bed when Brad rounded the barn.  A huge collie lay in the warm sun near Shanker but came awake with staccato barks when he saw Brad.

"Hush, Henry, that's just a reporter.  He's not dangerous." Shanker brushed the dirt from his hands and stepped to meet Brad.

Brad shook his hand.  He looked around at the few head of Hereford cattle across the way and toward the ridge where maples, oaks, and poplars were just coming to full leaf.  He knew why Shanker wanted to come back to the hills of East Tennessee.  "This is wonderful, Al.  Are you going to retire here when you finish with the Service?"

Shanker turned and took in the spring beauty himself.  "Yeah, I guess so.  When I'm through with the Service or when they're through with me—whichever comes first.  It's nice here.  Quiet. There's a stream down the way that you can still wade in and drink from without worrying about the crud.  I always try to come back in time to help them put out their tobacco allotment.  They get a little cash from it in December."

"Still growing tobacco?  Still subsidized too?"

Shanker smiled.  "Yeah, a little.  It's harder and harder to make anything from it.  Sort of like shrimping down where you're from.  My dad said if they ever legalize marijuana, he wants to sign up for his allotment to grow that too.  I think it's already the largest cash crop in the state."

"At least in tobacco farming you can't fall off the boat like you can in shrimping."

Shanker nodded.  "You said you wanted to talk to me.  You were going to bring me something.  You know there's not much headway being made in the investigation.  I'm going back on assignment next week."

"Yeah, your dad told me.  He's real proud of you."

"He took the shooting hard.  Probably harder than I did.  He's proud now that I'm going back to the White House for two weeks with the President and then I'll be rotated to two weeks with the Vice President."

"What about the investigation?  Are you stepping away from that?"

"I'll still be on the team.  There's just not much happening now. I needed to get back to my job.  I've got to see if I can do it.  If something comes up with Dobson in New Orleans that I need to be involved in, he'll let me know and I'll go back."

Brad took the rolled up papers from his coat pocket and handed them to Shanker. "I want you to read these, Al. I have to tell someone. You may think I'm a nut, but I've got to give it to you."

Shanker took them and motioned toward the barn. "Let's sit over there while I look at what you brought." They both walked to the side of the barn and sat on a bale of hay wedged against the door.

Brad studied Shanker while the agent read. At home, Shanker could have passed for any farmer. His hair lapped over his forehead where he had been bending over tending to the young tobacco plants. Attired in overalls and a blue denim shirt with sleeves rolled up to his elbows, Shanker looked just as at home in the barn lot as he did in blue suit and tie guarding the highest officers of the land. His ruddy face and huge hands spoke for all the hours he had spent outdoors and for his strength. He still looked as though he could break bodies like match sticks.

Shanker shook his head and turned toward Brad. "The only things I see here that are of interest, Brad, are what you describe as diary entries of Harrot. I don't think we have those. Where did you get them?"

"At his home in Montgomery. Steinheitz and some men had been there before me, but we were able to restore them on his home computer. Didn't you say one time that the White House wasn't pressuring the investigation? That they thought you were doing all right?"

"Right. At first that was true."

"Well, doesn't that go along with the theory that the President or someone there was involved. They don't care whether you ever catch the killer."

"It's not true now. Steinheitz calls every day. He wants to know every move. He wanted the drawings of the ticket people. He wanted the enhanced photos we made from the video of the shooter. In the last month, there's probably not a day gone by that he hasn't been on our asses."

"Maybe he thinks you're getting close to something that points to him, and he wants to know."

Shanker stood and squinted toward the sun. "It's almost four. I'm going to have to think about this. We should check into that computer. If Harrot thought that the President was doing something illegal, then that does provide a motive. I'll see to it that Dobson gets your memo as soon as I figure how I can get it to him without his knowing that we've been talking so much."

"Al, in the Secret Service, do you take an oath?"

Shanker wrinkled his brow and stared at Brad. "An oath? Sure, we take an oath when we're sworn in."

"What does it say?"

"We swear to protect and defend the Constitution of the United States from all enemies, foreign and domestic."

"Is the essence of your job to protect and guard the President and Vice President as persons or to guard and defend the Constitution?"

Shanker looked down at the ground, folded the papers Brad had given him, and put them into the front pocket of his bib-overalls. He didn't say anything but motioned to Brad to walk with him.

For the next two hours, he and Brad walked the farm with the big collie, Henry. They talked about tobacco, corn, beef cattle, shrimping, football, and basketball. Neither said another word about the investigation. Finally, as their circuit brought them back to the barn, they talked about music.

"Brad, this is just your second trip to East Tennessee. We need to go to the Music Barn, get some good food, and introduce you to some music that's different from the Blues of New Orleans."

The Music Barn sat just off the highway between Townsend and Maryville. Its name derived from the fact that it was a remodeled farm building. The cow and horse manure had been scraped out and the floor bricked. Old gray wooden beams still predominated, and the hay loft had been transformed into the control and lighting center for music and theatrical productions on an elevated stage at one end. It was a restaurant too. On this Thursday, nearly two hundred sat at tables with red and white checkerboard cloths or around a bar on the opposite side from the stage and ate barbecue. Laughter and the clanging of pans and plates greeted them. It reminded Brad of some of the Cajun out-of-the-way places.

He was hungry and greedily attacked the slab of ribs when they were set before him. It was simple. Pork ribs, slaw, baked beans, and a choice of tea, coffee, soft drinks, or beer. There was no hard liquor. It was more a family place than a pickup parlor for singles. The waitress tied a paper bib around the neck of each person ordering the house specialty of ribs. It was needed. Barbecue sauce laced with pork grease soaked his fingers and ran in brown rivulets down to his wrists before Brad finished half his plate. He requested more napkins and bread. They served the same purpose.

The locals knew Shanker. He had been away most of his life, but he never lost contact. Several times before and after their meals arrived, old and young came by to greet the Secret Service agent and cast a curious glance at his companion. Brad learned, not from Shanker but from the snatches of conversation that he heard between his friend and the greeters, that Shanker was held in high esteem. He was the first from Friendsville High School to go to the Secret Service or FBI, for which some mistakenly thought he worked. He was a high school football star and then also at the University of Tennessee. His family was five generations deep in Blount County. No one said a word about him losing a Vice President to a sniper's bullet.

"Now for the entertainment," Shanker announced when the lights began to dim. He scooted his chair around to face the stage more directly.

The five-member Smoky Mountain Travelers—three old men, one young man and a young woman—walked out onto the stage in matching blue jeans and navy shirts. All but the girl wore a western style hat. The men carried their stringed instruments—banjo, mandolin, guitar, and bass. The lady played a fiddle. It had been a while since Brad had heard only stringed instruments in harmony. Jazz City leaned more toward the brass.

As they started, he closed his eyes and was lifted to the bayous. He was taken back to his youth when he and one or two of the Ledoux brothers would take a small boat on summer nights and paddle out into the dark waters, unafraid and innocently unaware of the dangers of alligators and snakes. There they would fish, fight mosquitos, and weave tall tales into the early morning hours until they slipped off to sleep with the stringed instrument accompaniment of cicadas and crickets. He could feel that freedom as the Travelers played on through several Bluegrass favorites.

He and Shanker were alike in that they appreciated the small towns of their births. It was obvious though that Shanker could fill out a wedding invitation list a lot quicker than Brad.

"You want to come to my wedding, Al?"

"What? It's hard to hear with the music." Shanker cupped a hand to his ear and leaned closer.

"I said, do you want to come to my wedding?"

Shanker looked at Brad with raised eyebrows. "Congratulations, Brad. Jill Crenshaw?"

Brad smiled. "Yes."

"When is it?"

"June Twentieth in New Orleans. The St. Louis Cathedral there off Jackson Square. You're the only Tennessean I know. It would be nice if you could. For me and to represent General Jackson."

Shanker nodded. "I'll try to work it into my schedule." He scribbled a note and handed it to the waitress.

The Travelers took a fifteen-minute break between sets. Brad ordered some iced tea and watched again as another five to ten lined up to shake the hand of the man who guarded Presidents and Vice Presidents.

Shanker was finally able to turn back to Brad. "You like it?"

"Sure, they're great. Those old men have been playing for a long time, haven't they?"

"Yeah, the three of them have been up and down these valleys for the past fifty years. How does this kind of music compare to the jazz of Louisiana?"

"We have a similar strain in Cajun music. There's a lot of the stringed instruments."

"I bet you're a brass person, though, aren't you, Brad? The cornet, trumpet, bass horn?"

"Well, my favorite is a sax. I love a sax solo. The sax combines the richness of the brass with the delicacy of the wind instruments. It has a reed like a clarinet, you know."

Shanker nodded and looked toward the stage. "Yeah, it's like us. There's a place for the sax and the fiddle. Politicians, reporters, guardians. They all play a part. Which one is most important or best depends on what you want to listen to at the time."

Brad didn't say a word. His friend was working through something he didn't need to ask about. The Travelers were back for their next set.

Near the end of the last half hour of the show, just after the five instruments had combined in a rendition of *Amazing Grace* that brought the audience to its feet in applause, the young lady with the fiddle stepped to the microphone.

She tiptoed up. "We are pleased to announce that Al Shanker has with him a friend who is engaged to be married on the Twentieth of June."

"Not to Al, is he?" Someone from the back shouted. Laughter rolled over the crowd.

The young lady continued, "No. Brad Yeary is to be married in New Orleans." She looked down at the note Shanker had passed to the waitress to give to the band. "He's a Cajun lost in Big Orange Country. Mr. Yeary, would you like to request a number?"

Brad looked at Shanker, shook his head, but then stood and hoped that the blush on his face wasn't noticeable. "Thank you. You all did a great job. See, I can talk like an East Tennessean already. Do you think you could do a solo on your fiddle of 'When the Saints Go Marching In'?"

There were a few chuckles from the crowd. The young woman pondered the request and then lowered the mike to the level of the fiddle and put the bow to the strings. She started a stringed instrument version of the song he had heard so many times from the tubes of saxophones in New Orleans, and Brad led the applause. The beauty of the mountain instrument lifted him and carried his spirit back to New Orleans before his body.

ON THE MORNING OF Sunday, April 12, five hours before the sunrise Easter service, the streets of New Orleans were practically deserted. Wet from a late night shower, they were silent to the tread of three men crossing Poydras and darting to the side entrance of the Annex Building. Hooded and each carrying a bundle, they pressed their bodies against the side of the building, out of sight of the street. There they caught their breath and steeled their nerves for the entrance.

One of the three lifted the covering from the load he was carrying and looked at a black kitten with white paws inside a small wire cage. "Be quiet little cat. We have big plans for you." One of his companions ran a flat, broad blade down the slit between the door and its facing. He struck the door bolt, maneuvered the blade with his hand, and then pulled it open. He motioned for his friends to follow.

Inside, they unrolled a paper with a diagram of the wiring for the building and looked at it one last time with a small flashlight. They were on the first floor of the fire escape stairway that went the entire height of the building. Their interest was only in the third floor. Stepping quietly through another doorway, they walked into the lobby and around a corner to a service door. In a minute it too opened to the efforts of the man with the flat blade. Inside, he left his friends and squeezed his small body along a passageway that contained wiring conduit.

In fifteen minutes he was back, stringing out thin wires behind him. He reached for the contents of a bag held by one of the other two. He took out five small monitors, each of which could be held in the palm of his hand, along with a smaller digital clock. He attached a wire to each of the small screens and tuned them in. They came aglow with each showing a portion of the third floor investigative headquarters.

"This is what the guard sees from the control room. They have a surveillance camera on the third-story door from the stairway. The other four are all areas inside." He studied the small images further with his companions looking over his shoulder. "As I thought, they do have a time readout on the screen." He then hooked a wire from his own digital clock across all five of the other tiny silvery strands that linked the monitors. He set the clock to the exact same time as was being shown on the screens.

"Bilal, take the cat up near the third floor. See the camera angle?" he asked and pointed to the monitor showing the third floor stairway and door. "You stay out of sight. Send the cat to the door. I'll see her on here when you do, and that's when I'll splice in and freeze their video. Go now."

Bilal took the black cat from her cage, put her under his arm, and slithered back into the lobby and into the emergency stairway. Up almost to the third floor door, he stopped and tossed a nugget size piece of fish toward the base of the door another six steps up. He gave the cat a shove in that direction. She sat silently at the base of the door eating the morsel until called back by Bilal a minute later. He put her under his arm and walked back down to where his friends waited in the service area.

"Look at the monitor now," his friend said to Bilal. Bilal stared at the screen which showed the cat as though she was still there. "That's what they will see from the control room if they look. All their monitors are on freeze frame, but the clock makes them appear to be continuing to work. Time for the real work. Let's go."

The cat was left at the base of the stairs. The three made no noise as they slipped toward the third floor.

Only two deputy U.S. Marshals guarded the headquarters on the holiday weekend. The FBI agents and staff hadn't been there since Thursday. They would also have Monday off. The next shift change would be at eight o'clock in the morning for the two who were picked for the lonely duty in the early hours of Easter 1998. One sat just inside the stairway door. The elevators were sealed in the lobby and at the third floor. The stairway door could only be opened from the inside. The other deputy marshall sat in the surveillance control room and looked from time to time at the five overhead monitors that scanned different areas of the floor. It had grown so routine. There had been no incidents since the third floor was commandeered for headquarters for the assassination investigation the first week of January.

The deputy heard the faint scratch at the door and the soft mewing of a cat. The solid metal door prevented his looking at the source of the sound. He ignored it. Then it was there again. Claws against the metal door and the sound of a cat wanting in amused him. It was a diversion for an otherwise dull morning. He wanted to open the door and let the cat in, but orders were to open the door to no one without knowing who was there. He walked around the corner to the control room.

"Ralph, I hear a cat in the stairway. She's clawing on the door." He smiled and pointed to the overhead monitor. "Look, there she is. She's awfully still now. Just sitting there. I believe I'll let her in."

"Okay, Wendell. How'd she get in? I'll keep an eye on the monitor. Don't go anyplace else. Run her off or let her in. I don't care."

Wendell walked back toward his chair and the door. He slowly pushed the bar that opened the door, not wanting to scare the cat. He couldn't see her when he edged the door open. He kept one hand on the door and stepped through.

He felt only the cold looped metal cable around his neck for a split second before it bit deep into his flesh and crushed his windpipe. He didn't have time to gasp or raise his arms. His weapon was never unbuckled. His body slumped to the stairs next to Bilal's feet. The metal garrote was removed. His neck was circled by deep red and blue remnants of burst blood vessels.

Inside the control room, Deputy U.S. Marshall Ralph Witherspoon was still watching a motionless cat on his screen. He shouted for his co-worker. "Wendell, I thought you were going to get that cat. What's taking you so long? Wendell? Wendell?" He looked back at the monitor. Still there was just the cat. The clock said two-thirty-three. He walked out of the control room and toward Wendell's chair. He looked around the room and then headed toward the door.

He touched the door and barely opened it. The loop of cable flew over his head from behind and cut into his neck. The door swung open, and there facing him was the partner of his killer. In three seconds he passed out. In ten he was dead. The cat was safe at the bottom of the stairs.

They laid the two bodies side by side on the third floor landing of the stairway and propped the door open. Bilal stood guard listening for any entries from below or above. They expected none for five hours. The other two set about with the contents of the bags they carried entering computers, file cabinets, desk drawers, and anything else they could observe that would help them know what information the investigation had gathered.

For two hours, they rifled through everything available. Locked file cabinets opened to the masterful touch of the one with the blade. Computers spewed forth their hidden contents to the other who copied on a hundred disks thousands of pages of information for later review. The only room they could not enter was the one that Shanker and Dobson called home. Their inner sanctum remained inviolate. Only they had keys to the four locks that secured the solid metal door. The intruders tried the air vents but abandoned their effort when they ran into solid steel bars they were not equipped to cut. Dobson's and Shanker's notes and conclusions lay undisturbed, but the information they were based on was taken from the outside files and computers.

They were still busily copying and opening at fifteen till five when the phone in the control center rang. All three froze and listened to see if a machine would answer it. It rang ten times and quit.

"Time to go," the leader shouted to Bilal who was still standing by the door. "We have much. Someone may check since the phone went unanswered. Let's get out." They gathered up their tools, closed the computers down, and looked around one last time. It was as neat as when they entered. Only if the meters on the copy machines were checked, would anyone know that information had been lifted.

They closed the door to the third floor, stepped over the bodies of the two deputy marshals, and proceeded downstairs to disconnect and pick up their little monitors and digital clock.

The task completed, they headed back to the side door and picked up the cat and her cage before slipping out onto the damp alley.

# Forty

On Monday, a week and a day after the marshals were killed, Shanker and Dobson sat in the inner office reading the reports on the murders.

"Eleven hundred pages were copied right here in our headquarters. There's no telling what else they looked at or got their hands on," Dobson said and rubbed his stomach. "Al, this has gotten out of hand. Not only don't we have much on Harrot's killing, but now we have two federal officers murdered right here at headquarters. I'll be off of this assignment within a month. There's too much pressure. Congress. The press. The White House. They'll replace us. Hell, they'll probably transfer me to Alaska. 'Career enhancement,' they'll call it."

"I guess I got out just in time," Shanker said. "I'm on the President's detail the rest of this week. Then, I'll be with the Vice President for two weeks. I just wanted to come down and give you my condolences and see what's turned up."

Dobson tapped the ten sheets of reports with his forefinger. "That's it. Not much, is it?"

Shanker shook his head.

"They lured them out and killed them. No forced entry. Two seasoned marshals killed without drawing their weapons."

"And the security cameras didn't catch anything but a cat?"

"Yep. A first class job. They spliced into the monitor wires, froze the picture for over two hours, and then reconnected a little before five. We have the cat for two and a half hours and then the marshals' bodies."

"Did they get in here?" Shanker asked.

"Who knows? They were so clean that we couldn't tell they had been in at all except for the copy count on the machines. Everything was real neat. They probably have everything we have."

"That's not much, is it?"

"No. They're probably sitting somewhere laughing at how little we developed on the Harrot assassination in over three months. The only thing that would be important would be the photos of the shooters and the ticket people. And the hundred or so suspect profiles we had developed."

They sat silent for a few minutes. "John, if they have that information, why don't we release the drawings, or at least leak them, to some newspaper or television station to publish or broadcast?"

Dobson closed his eyes and thought. "You mean put them out there because they already know we have them?"

"Well, we don't have any names to go with them. If they're published, somebody may recognize one or more and call us."

"It's risky, Al, because it could also cause them to run. But I see your point. We're not getting anywhere with just the investigative network seeing them. It's worth a try, but we need to get them to someone where we can disclaim any knowledge of it if things go wrong. If they're leaked locally, we could always say they may be copies that the burglars made. How's that?"

"Great. The drawings and the enhanced photos of the shooter and his companion?"

"Might as well. We think the shooter and his friend are dead. But who knows, they might have jumped off the boat and met someone on the bank. They may have left their clothing there just to make us think they were dead. Go for the whole thing."

"How about Brad Yeary?" Shanker asked. "What if I get the pictures to him? You have him on your possible suspects list anyway. If something goes wrong, you could say that he must've gotten them from the burglars."

"Good. That's real good."

"John, you know that crazy reporter looked me up in Washington and gave me a five-page memo on how he thinks the President is in on this."

"He what?"

"Yeah, here it is. I told him I'd get it to you. You might want to read it and check out the part about Harrot's computer." Shanker handed the papers to Dobson.

ON FRIDAY, APRIL 24, Shanker met Brad at a restaurant in downtown Washington. They both thought they were as anonymous there as on the Riverwalk in New Orleans. At a window table, Brad looked at the photos of the shooters for the first time while Shanker sipped coffee. The first rays of dawn's sunlight glistened a deep orange on the burnished walnut trim of the window.

"So this is what you were telling me about? This guy is the shooter and this one was with him?" Brad asked, pointing first at one and then the other.

"That's them. We believe they're dead. But we don't know for sure. You can use them. And the drawings of the ticket people that I gave to you before."

"Why? Why now, Al?"

"It's the murders of the U.S. Marshals. Somebody was trying to find out what we have. They think we're getting close, but we have very little. If we don't break something soon, it's going to be taken out of our hands. It's a last resort. We give them to you. If we get an ID on any of them, it's great. If we don't, we can blame the publication on a leak or on the burglary and deny any involvement."

"You're using me."

Shanker shifted in his chair, looked away, and then looked back at Brad. "Yes. We're using you. But we're also giving you a big scoop. No one else will have these. Everybody uses everybody else. You're getting something in return. Also, you may be helping your country to find the assassin of Harrot and the killers of the marshals."

Brad drank from his coffee, put the pictures back into the brown envelope, and looked back at Shanker. "What about attribution? You don't want me to say that I got these from the investigation, do you?"

Shanker shook his head.

"You don't want to be a source. It's just like these floated onto my desk from nowhere."

"Yes. We'll have to deny any help with it—in case anything goes wrong."

"What if a Congressional committee calls me before it and asks where I got these?"

"We hope that you would be true to your source and not reveal it."

Brad shook his head. "So you think I'm being treated fairly for being used?"

Shanker raised his eyebrows and slowly nodded his head.

"Will you visit me if they put me in jail because I don't answer their questions?"

"Probably not."

"I'll think about it, Al. I can't even tell Pinthater? You know he's going to want to know."

"He trusts you enough on this story now that if you tell him it's from a confidential source, he'll believe you."

"Maybe." Brad looked out the window at the thousands of bureaucrats on their way to offices all across downtown Washington. Each of them depended on the government continuing to run smoothly. "It would be a big story all right. Jill and I are going back to New Orleans tonight. I'll think about it. If I'm going to do it, I'll run the story by a week from tomorrow. Sound okay?"

"Sure, our time is running out, but I don't want to rush you. You have to write a good story to go with the pictures and get your defenses ready to head off any questions. Our line will be that we didn't release anything for publication." They nodded their heads in agreement.

ROB STEINHEITZ WAS PASSING through the Atlanta airport after a trip to New Orleans to meet with John Dobson for an update on the investigation. Dobson told him nothing that he didn't already know. He walked to the pay phone booth and dialed the New York number. It was answered on the first ring.

"Abdul, is that you? This is Rob."

"Yes. What's the news?"

"I've just got a minute. The face to face you need with the President. Next Saturday in Louisville, Kentucky. He'll be there for the Kentucky Derby. He knows he needs to see you in person. We will have your name, Ramzi's, and Abdo's on a guest list for a reception after the Derby. Stay at the Hyatt Regency there. The Secret Service has your names for a background check. You are clean, aren't you?"

"Yes. We'll see him after the Derby?"

"Right. It won't be released until the middle of the week that he's going. How's everything else? The plans?"

"All is ready for the Eighth of June. We received the shipment. We're anxious."

"Good. Keep it cool. See you on Saturday. I may call you before in Louisville."

VICE PRESIDENT ASHFORD WANDERED through the aisles of the bookstore in downtown Washington. He was still filling his library. His two Secret Service agents were accustomed to it by now. He would dress as inconspicuously as possible. With his jacket collar pulled up, and a baseball cap for headgear, no one recognized him. The guards had more problem remaining focused on their task than keeping anyone away from him.

He had already filled two boxes with old volumes when he stepped to a pay phone. The agents remained a discreet distance away. He dialed the number and put a handful of quarters in the slot when asked to do so by the operator.

"Nidal? The President will be at the Derby next Saturday. It's our opportunity. Will that give you and Ahmed enough time to plan?"

In the sterile looking office at Darby Run, Nidal looked at the calendar that hung over the desk. Ahmed stood next to him. "We will be there anyway. Two of the horses in the race were sired right here at the farm. The owners of both have seats for us. We have plenty of time. We'll have Mahmud and Siddig come down from New York. When should we take him?"

"That's up to you. I don't know the seating arrangements yet. There'll probably be a reception or two that he'll appear at. It's a political trip. I'll be there too. They thought I did such a good job at the tournament that they want me to go again."

"We'll start the plans now. Tell us as much as you know when you find out. And . . . Mr. Vice President, we need your assurance of pardons when this is over and you are President."

"Don't get caught. But if you do, you know I'll do everything I can. I've got to go. I'm at a bookstore. It's hard to slip the Secret Service. Do your job."

"Yes, Sir."

GEORGE GARRON AND PRESIDENT Teater walked alone along the path through the south lawn of the White House. "Rob's on his way back from New Orleans, Mr. President. He flew commercial this time. The press doesn't follow his movements as closely when he goes that way."

"What's he doing? Checking on the investigation again?"

"Yes. He's also arranging the meeting that Abdul and Ramzi wanted with you. We're going to do it at the post-Derby reception next Saturday. Everything's in place. They just have to have a handshake and a nod of the head from you to set it in motion. The Eighth of June."

"Yes, that'll be good. This trip to Kentucky should be the last one we'll need there before the election. They're back in line aren't they? For my re-election?"

Garron nodded his head and smiled. "You know, Sir, you did a great job in choosing Vice President Ashford. The Kentucky pols were impressed with him last month when he was there. He smoothed a lot of ruffled feathers. We're going to take him again to the Derby."

"Good. He's certainly doing a lot better job than Harrot would've done. I hate it that you boys had to kill Harrot, but it's all worked out for the best."

Garron and the President walked another few steps in silence. They had been friends and worked side by side for over thirty years. Garron decided it was time to be frank with him.

"Mr. President, Rob and I have discussed the Vice President's assassination. While we both agree that it wasn't a great loss, neither of us had anything to do with the arranging of it. Somebody else out there killed Harrot."

The President stopped and turned toward Garron. "You mean you didn't do it?"

"No. Neither of us. We're in the dark about it. Matter of fact, we thought maybe you had it done on your own. A hint to our Arab friends or something. But they also say no."

"If you didn't do it, and I know I didn't give the word, who did it?"

"That's why Rob is going to New Orleans and talking with the head of the investigation so much. We'd like to know."

"Al Shanker of the Service was with Harrot when he was shot. He's been on my detail for the last week or so. I like Al, but if he can't keep the Vice President from being shot, I don't want him guarding me. Check to see when he rotates off. I don't want him on my detail on any trips. He's all right around the White House. Shanker's getting old."

"We all are."

BRAD WAS LYING ON Jill's couch at her Washington apartment squinting into one of his many kaleidoscopes when she burst through the door.

"Brad, Brad, I was hoping you'd be here," she said and set her briefcase down. She took one look at him and her enthusiasm ebbed. "What's got you staring into your escapist glass images again? You up tight about the wedding? You don't want to marry me?"

Brad sat up and laid the metal tube next to him. "No. It's nothing like that. I'll tell you about it in a minute, but what were you so excited about?"

She walked in front of him. "Brad, remember where we met? Where we really met?"

Was this a test? He thought back. "I had met you before. But where we *really* met was the night before the Kentucky Derby five years ago."

She sat down beside him and hugged him. "You do remember. Well, guess what?"

"What?"

"We're going back there next week. I've been invited to go along with the President. He found out I knew Thoroughbred racing stock and asked me to go along. Of course, it also helps to make it a 'non-political' affair for him. I'm the only senator not of his party in on the trip."

"Jill, that's great. I'm happy for you."

"For us, Brad. For us. The Kentucky senators are hosting a reception for you and me on the night before the Derby. They know we're getting married, and I let it slip that we met at the Derby. So, we're to be honored at a party. There'll be all kinds of big people there. The President is going to stop by, and Vice President Ashford. I'm so excited."

"Great," Brad said with little enthusiasm.

"Brad, get excited. You can rent a tux, can't you? It'll be fun."

"I'll try. I've got a big week ahead of me at the paper. Are you going to fly on Air Force One with the President?"

"Yes. Isn't that great? I've been a senator for about two months, and I'm going to fly with the President." She got up, went to the kitchen, and brought them both a soft drink. "Now, tell me what was on your mind when I came in."

He took the Diet Coke and drank a long, slow swallow. "I've got the pictures."

"What pictures?"

He patted the envelope lying on the coffee table. "I've got the pictures of the guy who shot Harrot."

Jill set down her drink and scrunched up her shoulders. "How? Where? Who? I don't understand."

"Jill, you have all the right questions to be a reporter. The shooter is right here," he pointed to the envelope, "and I have at my apartment the ones of the people who wound up buying your tickets. Shanker gave them to me. He says it's time to run them. I don't know."

"Can I see them?"

"No. You want to be able to deny ever seeing them—ever being involved."

Jill thought and took a sip of her drink. "If you don't use them, will they give them to someone else to use?"

"Probably."

"Why are you holding back? Why shouldn't you use them?"

"I'm being used. Don't you see? The feds want to use me to flush the killers or conspirators out of hiding."

"What's wrong with that?"

"I don't know. It's just that I should be writing about the events, not creating them."

"Yeah, but if you don't, then somebody else will run with the story. They won't worry about being *used*. They'll be happy to. What did you tell Shanker?"

"I'd decide this coming week. If I was going to use them, I'd do it by next Saturday."

"Brad, our reception is Friday. Do it by Friday. I need you in Louisville at the Hyatt Regency by eight o'clock. I'll fly down from Washington with the President. I'll meet you there."

# Forty-one

May Day. On Friday, May 1, at 4 p.m., Brad read for one last
time the story that would accompany the four drawings in
Saturday's editions of the *Times-Gazette*. He had a car and
driver standing by to take him to the airport for his flight to
Louisville. He would barely make the evening reception, but he would
be there.

Years before, in his youth, May Day had been simpler. The
Maypole and the games of spring were so much more relaxing than a
deadline to meet for the paper. It was the holiday that most Americans had forgotten. Back when the Soviet Union was in full blossom,
they always had the parades and displays of military hardware. It
was the day for the workers. In America, it was Law Day. In his only
year of law school, he was drafted to speak to a high school civics class
about the Constitution and Declaration of Independence on May Day.

More and more his life had funneled down to mayday rather
than May Day. Distress had elbowed celebration out of its way.

It was good though. He would have to give himself that. This
story would put him back into the spotlight. It took up the majority
of the front page with four columns and a bleed-over to the next page.
There were two side-bars on the front page. All sat below his by-lines.
He had seen the layout of the front page, changed it, and then approved it. It wasn't often that he had that authority. Pinthater was
already off to Louisville since the President and Vice President would
be there. He left Brad in charge of this story.

"Do it how the hell you think best, Brad. This is your baby."
Those had been his words when he left the office at ten. Yes, this
would be his baby. He hoped it wasn't soon left an orphan.

One thing he had pushed Pinthater into doing. Danny Spurling was receiving a battlefield promotion. Brad dialed Danny's number.

"Danny, get your ass back to my office. Now!" He slammed the phone down.

"What'd I do, Brad? Did I screw up something?" Danny sputtered when he entered the office.

Brad played it for effect. He stood and glared over the nervous youth. "I'm just going to tell you this once, Danny. So, listen good."

"Yes, sir."

"You've lost your job." Brad waited for it to sink in. Danny began shaking his head. "You've lost your job because you've been promoted to my assistant. Congratulations." Brad extended his hand. Danny stood, but instead of taking Brad's hand, lunged toward him and wrapped him in a bear hug.

"Assistant? Wow! What do I do?"

"First off, Danny, I'm leaving. When this Harrot story hits the streets in the morning, all hell's going to break loose. You're my nerve center, my damage control, my headquarters. Don't tell anyone where I am, but take every message. You can bet your ass that every Sunday talk show and the networks are going to be after this. You've got to get me the word on what's happening without steering anyone to me. Got it?"

Danny nodded. "I think so. This is going to be big?"

"Yes." Brad looked at his watch. "I'm leaving. If I were you, I'd go home now and get some sleep and be back here at four o'clock in the morning. There's no telling how long you're going to have to man the phone without sleep. I'm depending on you."

AL SHANKER MET WITH the other three Secret Service agents who were stationed outside the door of Vice President Ashford's suite at the Hyatt Regency Hotel in Louisville. He looked at his watch and then at the log of their rotating schedule. "At six I'm taking off. I'm going back to my room and get ready to go to the reception for Senator Crenshaw. I'll be back on with the Veep tomorrow from noon until after the Derby, right?"

"Yeah. He'll get there first. The President will come in last. You have the seating chart already, don't you, Al?" The agent looked at Shanker who nodded. "Al, you're not working the reception, are you?"

"No. Not unless you need me. I'm just going because I met the guy the Senator is engaged to. He's that reporter from New Orleans who's been writing so much about the Harrot assassination."

"Oh, yeah."

"Does the VP have many left on his appointment list for tonight?"

The other agent looked at the paper naming those approved for entry to the suite. "No, he's going to the reception about nine. He just has about five or six left."

Shanker ran his finger down the names. Four Kentucky office-holders and two names that sounded foreign to him. "Who are these two guys?"

"Horse friends of Ashford's that he met in Lexington back in March. He left tickets for them for all the receptions. They're coming over to chat with him for a while. He's big on animal breeding."

"Oh, well. They've been checked out, haven't they?"

"Sure. They were checked before his visit back in March."

"I'll see you at noon tomorrow." Shanker took his briefcase and went to the elevator. His room was on the fifth floor. An hour's nap would do him good. Then he would dress, eat dinner, and go to the reception. He needed to know if Yeary was going to run the pictures or if he and Dobson were going to have to find someone else.

A HALF HOUR LATER, Nidal watched as Ahmed punched the elevator button for the eleventh floor where they would visit with their friend and Vice President of the United States. This time Ahmed dressed in a suit and tie. His cowboy boots made him tower even more over Nidal.

It was a brief check-in ritual. Their names were on the list. They had ID. An agent patted them down and ran a looped, hand-held detector around their bodies. Cleared, they were permitted passage to the suite where they were met by Ashford's chief-of-staff.

Ashford stepped up. "Good to have you men visit. I need some expert advice on the Derby. I might want to bet a dollar or two. Come on in." He pointed his visitors toward another room—a bedroom that had been converted to a study for Ashford's visit. All three entered and Ashford closed the door behind them.

"It's going to be a great race, Mr. Vice President, and a great day," Nidal said and took a seat facing Ashford. Ahmed pulled his chair near as they made a little circle where their knees almost touched.

"Are we ready?" Ashford asked.

"Yes, Sir. Ahmed and I, along with Mahmud and Siddig. Where will be the best place?"

"We have three places. The President will be at a reception for Senator Crenshaw tonight at eight downstairs. Tomorrow at the Der-by. Or after the Derby at a reception and party. Do you have the long rifle?"

"Yes, back at our hotel. We also have another little pistol," Nidal said and took a duplicate cigarette lighter derringer from his pocket. "If tonight, I have to use this. Tomorrow, the long rifle. To-morrow night, again the derringer."

"The sooner the better."

"Yes, Mr. Vice President. But we're bound to get caught if we use the derringer. I have to be within ten feet. Accuracy is no good for more than that. I would be swarmed by Secret Service before I could make my escape."

Ashford reached over and took Nidal's hand. "Yes, my son. But remember, I'll be President. Then we can work on getting you released if you stay quiet."

Nidal shook his head. "Very risky. I'd rather have an opportu-nity to get away in a crowd—like at the Derby—so there'd be no need for pardons. We melt away to Saudi. You don't authorize extradition." Nidal glanced at Ahmed who nodded agreement. "Do you have the route the President will be taking in the car and walking to his seat? Maybe a seating chart also?"

"Just the seating chart. I'm going in separately. They don't even disclose his route to me. This is the way we'll be seated in the box for dignitaries. It's enclosed, I understand." Ashford handed Nidal a paper with the diagram of the seats. "The President will be here," he pointed to a seat circled in red. "I'll be a row in front of him. Sena-tor Crenshaw will be to my left. Kentucky's governor and senators will be in the same row with the President, but his sidekicks, Garron and Steinheitz will be on either side of him."

Nidal passed the paper to Ahmed. "This is good. We'll be seat-ed in the open in front of the VIP box about fifteen rows from the front. That's plenty good for the rifle."

"What about shooting through the glass? Will that stop the bullet or deflect it?"

"No. Not the kind of bullet we'll use this time."

Ashford got up and walked to the window. The sun was sink-ing low on the western horizon. He looked at the Ohio River a half mile away. "I have to know when you're going to do it, Nidal. If you don't do the job, I have to finish it." He took his derringer from his pocket. "Like I say, the sooner the better. Tonight if you can. Sacri-fices have to be made. You're a soldier. We're doing this for your homeland and for Allah. Those planning the overthrow in your own country are hypocrites. If we knew who they were, we would not have had to kill Harrot and now Teater. I regret Harrot, but Teater is a different story. He's planning murder himself."

Nidal looked at Ahmed. "Yes, Allah will provide a home for his valiant warriors who die serving him. I know that. Ahmed knows that. Siddig and Mahmud are willing to be sacrificed also. But there is no need if we can do it and also escape."

Ashford sat back down and scooted closer to Nidal. "Let's do it at the reception tonight if there's an opportunity. If not, tomorrow at the Derby. Agreed?" He looked first to Nidal and then to Ahmed. Ahmed remained silent.

Nidal relented. "Okay, tonight at Senator Crenshaw's reception. If not there, at the Derby. Mr. Vice President, if it goes to the Derby and we haven't done the deed by the time of the running, then this is what I plan."

He stood up. "In the homestretch when everyone is standing and shouting for their horses, I will then raise my cane and dispatch the snake. You need to remain seated to give me a clear target. Understand? Don't get up."

Ashford looked at the chart one more time. "Yes, I have it. Tonight. But if not tonight, then at the Derby tomorrow."

They all stood. "Have you prayed?" Ashford asked.

"Yes, but one more time wouldn't hurt," Nidal said and looked around. "Which direction is Mecca?"

"This way," Ashford led them toward his bedroom. "We must remember. We are doing this as agents of Allah. It's up to us. The great evil they are planning will go unchecked unless we kill the snake. Let our resolve be steadfast." They all kneeled toward a red circle on the far wall of the bedroom.

TWO FLOORS BELOW, GEORGE Garron and Rob Steinheitz slipped down the stairway unnoticed and through an open door to the room of Abdul, Ramzi, and Abdo. Another Arab with a Mini-mac 10 stood guard at the door.

"Is the room clean, Abdul?" Steinheitz asked.

"Perfectly. No bugs. Swept by our people each day. We've been here for two days. What's the plan?"

"The victory party after the Derby. We have tickets for you. You'll go through a receiving line and shake hands with the President. You'll get your handshake and look eyeball to eyeball. I'll be by his side. He'll say to each of you, 'Let's do it soon.'"

"Good. Tomorrow night? Why not sooner? Isn't there a reception tonight and a speech tomorrow?"

"The mayor and governor made up the guest list for the speech tomorrow at noon. We couldn't get you into that. He's just meeting privately with fundraisers and politicians tonight. There's a list. The press will see it, and we don't need questions as to why he's seeing three Arabs. The victory party's a different matter. A lot of Arabs are still involved with horse racing. Farm owners and such. You'll fit right in."

"What about the reception tonight for Senator Crenshaw? I heard the President was going to be there."

"Wrong. He won't be going. Crenshaw's fiance is a reporter.

The head of the Harrot assassination team has him on a list not to be
in the President's presence. I don't know why exactly. They must've
had him on their suspect list to start."

Abdul pointed to a storage box sitting on a small table. "Abdo,
bring me the list."

Steinheitz looked toward the box. "Is that what you got in
New Orleans?"

"Yes."

"Why were the marshals killed?"

Abdul shrugged. "We had to get in. Americans are such soft-
ies. They gave their lives for a cat."

"A what?"

"Never mind, my friend. The less you know the better. But
the investigation did have a list of a hundred or so suspects. They did
profiles. That reporter you mentioned was on there, but they have him
ranked at the lowest end of the scale. What's his name?" Abdul ran
his finger down the pages of suspects.

"Brad Yeary."

"Yes, here he is. Native of Louisiana. Flunked out of law
school. Police reporter and then political. Same paper for twenty
years. Possessed a bloody handkerchief after Harrot was shot. Finally
decided it came from wiping blood from his girlfriend—now U.S. Senator Jill Crenshaw."

"Anybody else we know who's on the list?" Steinheitz asked.

"No. They have nothing. Practically all the suspects have been
eliminated. They have the drawings you showed me of the people who
purchased the tickets. They mention photos of the shooter. But we
didn't get them. They must have been in the one room we couldn't
penetrate. They're believed to be dead."

Steinheitz shook his head. "You got that whole box of documents, and there's no real suspect and no motive?"

"Right."

"What do you think?"

Abdul again shrugged his shoulders and looked at his three
Arab companions. "Don't know. It was fortuitous for us. Perhaps
Allah sent an angel."

Garron gazed at Steinheitz and then turned to Abdul. "After
you get your handshake, what do you do then?"

"We have a little over a month until June Eighth. We will
leave immediately and go to our countries. For the month, we will
make final plans. A week before, you will receive word as to the exact
hour. All depends on your support. The coups have to be followed up
by recognition, and force if necessary, from you. Remember, we're
doing this for Allah and our countries. Our leaders have declined into
decadence. Pardon me, but they have become similar to the great

Satan of the West."

"But the oil will be secure? We have your word on that, don't we, Abdul?" Garron asked.

"Yes, you'll have your oil, and we'll deliver our countries back to Allah." Abdul looked at his watch. "Would you two want to join with us in prayer?" He smiled.

Garron looked at his watch and then at Steinheitz. "No. We have to get back to the President. We have a deal."

THE LIGHTS WERE LOW, the music soft, and the dress formal. No more than a half dozen times a year could Brad take this. He stood next to Jill who was the star of the party. The Kentucky senators had done a resplendent job in arranging the reception. Brad had met more horse owners and trainers in the past two hours than he had ever encountered in his lifetime—or wanted to.

Jill turned to him. "Brad, the President isn't going to get here. They say it's because you're still on some kind of list from the investigation."

Brad looked around the room. "Jill, I can leave if you'd rather have the President here."

"No. But that means you won't be able to sit with me tomorrow at the Derby. If they won't bring the President here, I'm sure they won't let you in the VIP box with us."

"It's just as well. They told me there would be just one pool reporter in there. It's a private party. They don't want a bunch of snoopy journalists."

A large woman of some maturity with a bluish tint to her hair stepped up with her husband next to the honored couple. "Senator Crenshaw. I wanted to offer my congratulations to you and your fiance and wish you the very best."

"Thank you," Jill said and took her hand. "This is Brad Yeary."

Brad shook the lady's hand and then her husband's. The lady turned back to Jill. "I hear that you're an expert on Thoroughbred pedigrees." She took out a card and handed it to Jill. "What do you think of the bloodlines of this one? I've already put twenty-five thousand on him."

Jill looked at the name. "Good lines, but not for the Derby. He needs a longer race. Sorry, but he'll finish no better than fourth. If you want to save your money, you should try one of these three. I've put a thousand on them in this order, but they could finish just the opposite. Two of them have *Jacob's Ladder* as their sire."

Brad raised his eyebrows. The couple walked away after the lady wrote down the three horses that Jill recommended. "Jill, what are you becoming, a horse handicapper?"

"Relax. We're just having fun. Let's go dance. Look, there's

Vice President Ashford," Jill said and nodded across the room. "They let him come in, but not the President. That's odd, isn't it?"

Brad looked toward the Vice President. "Naw, they don't care if they lose another Vice President as long as the President survives."

Before they reached the dance floor, Al Shanker stepped up to Brad and shook his hand. "Any word on the pictures?"

"It's done, Al. The morning edition. I'm nervous about it. I'm glad I left New Orleans where I won't have to answer questions."

"It'll be okay, Brad. Everything will be fine. Introduce me to your lovely fiance."

AT ELEVEN O'CLOCK, AFTER all the money men and women and politicians had left, Garron and Steinheitz sat alone with President Teater. The eighteenth floor Presidential suite provided an excellent view of the city at night.

"I like getting away from Washington. It's exhausting, but I always feel refreshed. Today was especially good. Financing is good for this area. Everybody is falling into line. There's only one problem on the horizon—oil and gas prices—and we're going to take care of that, aren't we, boys?"

Steinheitz had his feet up on a table, his shoes off, and was leaning back in the overstuffed chair. He rubbed his eyes. "Everything's go, Sir."

Garron stood and walked to where Teater was looking out the window. He spoke low. "Sir, at the post-Derby party, Abdul, Ramzi, and Abdo will be in the receiving line to meet you. When they get to you, you'll say to each, 'Let's do it soon.' Those are the words they need to know that you're still backing the operation."

"Let's do it soon? Those words? How soon will they be doing it?"

Steinheitz sat up. "June Eighth is still the date, Sir. On our trip to Israel for the Fiftieth Anniversary of its statehood, we may have a little side conversation with one or two then. That's just two weeks from now."

Teater smiled. "Good. With that resolved, we'll be in office another term."

"Yes," Steinheitz said. "If everything goes according to plan. I've never liked dealing with Arabs."

"Don't worry, Rob," the President said. "They know what they're doing. If we didn't do this, those other Arabs in power now could strangle the United States with their oil prices or withhold it altogether. We're doing this for the good of the country. God and country. You agree?"

Garron and Steinheitz looked at each other, then at their boss. "Yes, Sir. It's necessary. And it's to save our country," Garron said.

The President turned to Steinheitz. "Rob, I know that you especially don't like to deal with Arabs, but we have to."

"Yes, Mr. President, it's my heritage, and I'm not sure we can trust them."

The President smiled. "Rob, we have to trust them. As LBJ told me one time, 'When you're dealing with skunks, it's better to have them inside your tent pissing out, than outside pissing in.' "

Garron laughed. "He was eloquent. As always."

# Forty–two

T he cirrus clouds hovered over the eastern horizon like a golden washboard. Sunrise was still a half hour away. The colors changed from gray to orange to pink while Brad sat next to the window and stared toward Washington, six hundred or so miles away. The constantly changing aurora challenged his kaleidoscope images in beauty.

Sleep had come in fits when it came at all. His and Jill's rooms adjoined. He had spent the night in hers. He awoke at two, then two-thirty, three, three-thirty, and finally four arrived. Sneaking off to the phone in his room, he had dialed his desk at the *Times-Gazette*. Danny Spurling was there, as he was supposed to be. Interest in the front page story started to perk as soon as it hit the street. Ten calls already, according to Danny. Then every half hour, Brad was back to his phone for an update.

Danny faxed a copy of the front page and inside conclusions of the story to the Hyatt Regency's message center for Brad. In a jogging suit and houseshoes, he retrieved it and a pot of coffee from the lobby. He needed both. He always had to see it in black and white before he really believed it had been published. The fax copy was not as crisp and clear as a real newspaper. It didn't feel the same to his hands. And it certainly didn't smell the same. But he had it. The story was making its way across the country.

By five-thirty, a hundred inquiries. Now he sat with his feet propped on the window sill, bare toes clinging to the cool metal. A half empty pot of coffee sat beside him while he listened to the unending bleeps of the phone behind him. It didn't take them long to find him despite Danny's valiant efforts to fend them off. The story would speak for itself. He was determined not to give in to the questioners until after the weekend.

Pictures. That's why it was so big. For four months, there had been stories, speculation, and theories. But no pictures. The public wanted to see. Americans craved to be shown. They didn't want to read. They didn't want to think. Show it to them and they would believe. Now they had their photos, and they would be the biggest story of the day, the week, and the month.

He thought back thirty-five years to Dallas in November of 1963. Four pictures told the story of those three awful days. Zapruder's frames of the fatal shot. Jackie reaching for the Secret Service agent. Ruby sticking a pistol into Oswald's gut. And little John John saluting his fallen father. The sum of history is spoken not in words but is splashed into the brain on waves of the patina of old images.

He knew where Shanker was. Dobson was also unavailable. He would have a monopoly on the story behind the pictures of the shooters and ticket buyers until Monday. After twenty years as a journalist, he had learned about timing. A Saturday morning bombshell of a story presses the competition to respond. Weekends are low-staffed. The people who are needed for a quote are usually unavailable. Then, to react with a story on the front page of the five-pound Sunday edition is to lose it. Sunday papers are put back to be read at leisure. Coupons are clipped before the front page is read. If television picked up the story, all the talking heads could do would be to quote Brad Yeary and say, "According to a copyrighted story in Saturday's editions of the *Times-Gazette* . . . ."

He would call out, but he wasn't taking any.

Jill slept like the proverbial baby, unaware of the hub-bub the story was creating in pre-dawn America. She tossed only with the sweet memories of the reception of the evening before and the hopes of the Derby. Brad was restless, but she didn't care.

THE KENTUCKY DERBY WOULD be the sixth race of the day. A jewel in the Triple Crown, it sat at the head of the stretch with the Preakness and Belmont Stakes following at two-week intervals. Those three races would determine the consummate three-year-old Thoroughbred for 1998.

While President Teater spoke at a downtown luncheon and Vice President Ashford remained at the hotel, Brad and Jill left early for Churchill Downs. It was a request with which he gratefully complied. Anything would have been preferable to staying near the constantly beeping phone. CNN picked up the story by eleven. Brad watched the short clip where they showed the front page of the *Times-Gazette* and zoomed in on the pictures. His by-line was flashed across the country. As he imagined, the network could not say anything more than he had already written.

By noon, the sun was bright on the Kentucky Bluegrass. The high clouds had moved to the east. Thousands were already packing the infield of the race track. The sun beat down in burning rays on the winter-white skin of all the northerners who had come south for the race. Young men shed their shirts and hundreds of young women stripped to halter tops and mini-shorts. Coolers were opened with their displays of stocks of beer. Portable tape and CD players dueled with deafening steely music. By race time, the infielders would have no recall about which horses were in the race—let alone who won—until they checked their two-dollar tickets afterward. The Derby was the modern May Day celebration—only a day late.

Jill had managed passes for them to walk through the stable and paddock areas. Horseflesh abounded. Stallions snorted and flicked their tails at real or imagined flies. Ladies in billowy hats and fashion plate sun-dresses and men in white linen suits and matching hats paraded around this area where only the elite were permitted. It was class separation at its pinnacle. Jill held to Brad's arm as they walked among the largest assembly they'd been a part of since the prior New Year's Eve in New Orleans.

Brad liked horses—the sinewy, muscle-powered machines covered by tight, glistening brown and black coats—but not nearly as much as Jill did. She would point and tell him a horse's name, owner, jockey, dam, and sire. He was glad she was having fun, but his main desire—as it had been on New Year's Eve—was to make it through the day near the one he loved. From two until the Derby ended, they would be separated. She would have to go to the VIP booth early and stay until the President left. He would be in the press section in front but below the enclosed dignitaries.

FEAR TWISTED LIKE FISTS in the guts of Nidal and Ahmed when the screen filled with their likenesses on the CNN report. They stared in fascination at the noon report in their hotel rooms two miles from the race track.

"Those drawings are better than some of the pictures we've had made, Ahmed. How did they do that?"

"We could shave. My beard and your moustache. Then we wouldn't be recognized."

"Yes, and perhaps we could cut off your ears and I could grow a few inches. They have us described perfectly. We can't shave anyway. Our passport pictures have us the way we look now. Our flights are confirmed. Louisville to Atlanta to London to Saudi."

"You still think we can get by airport security?"

"They have no names, Ahmed. Just the drawings. We'll be out of the country before they can put names to us. The White Caliph will be President, and we'll be safe. We'll do our job and Siddig and Mahmud will get us to the airport. We'd better get on our way to the track now."

Nidal took the white cane from the clothes drawer. The cigarette lighter disguised derringer already lay on the top of the dresser. He retrieved the special binoculars from a drawer of the room's desk, connected the fiber optic cable between the port in them and the cane, and then stretched his arm and cane toward Ahmed while holding the binoculars to his eyes.

"Yes, perfect. You're in the crosshairs of elimination, cousin."

Ahmed stepped to the side.

"Don't worry. It's not loaded."

Nidal put the cane back down to his side. He tapped it against the floor and measured it against his leg. "Ahmed, this is way too long for me. I'm short. We didn't take that into account when we placed the order. I would look out of place with it. You must do the deed." He handed the cane and binoculars to his cousin. "Look through the glasses and point the cane at what you want to shoot."

Ahmed took a few steps backward and tried his hand at using the weapon. After a few minutes, he smiled. "I see. It looks easy enough. Just get the target in the crosshairs and pull the trigger, right?"

"Well, actually, it's not 'pull the trigger' but 'press the button.' It's simpler this time. The cane crook just rotates down and then the trigger button appears." Nidal took hold of the cane and turned the handle exposing a small button. "One shot, Ahmed. We have only one chance. Be sure you have the President in your sight before pressing the button. Anywhere in his body and he'll die."

"I can do it," Ahmed said and continued looking at different objects in the room through the glasses and pointing the cane toward them.

"We need to wrap your foot and ankle with some tape as though you have a need for the cane, Ahmed. There'll be tight security today. One shot and we're gone."

Nidal took a roll of wide white tape, had Ahmed sit on the couch, and began to wind it around his bare foot and ankle. "Good," he said and stood back up. "Just enough to show anyone who needs to see that you have a slightly sprained ankle. Let's head to the races."

FOR THE THIRD TIME within twenty-four hours, dogs, trained to sniff out explosives, walked around the inside and outside walls of the VIP booth at Churchill Downs and then on to the perimeter of the nearby area. Six Secret Service agents were stationed in and around the booth from the time the track opened for business. Two of them were now inside and the other four outside. The official delegation began arriving at a few minutes before two.

Jill Crenshaw left Brad near the track and made her way up the steps to join the others who waited to enter the room they would share with the President and Vice President.

AL SHANKER STOOD ON the outside of Vice President Ashford's suite at the Hyatt Regency and talked to two other agents. They went over their schedule, the emergency routes to hospitals, and their coordination plans with the local police for travel to and from the track. Shanker looked at his watch.

"It's two-thirty now, guys. We need to be walking out of here at fifteen till. We're supposed to arrive between three and three fifteen. He'll meet the elected officials at the VIP room and have about an hour before the race. The President will arrive around four. Is everything all right?"

They nodded agreement. Shanker knocked on Ashford's door and was greeted by his chief-of-staff. "We need to leave within ten minutes. Is the Vice President ready?"

"Yes, I believe he is. He's watching a newscast right now. We'll be at the door here in just a few minutes." He closed the door and walked to Ashford's study.

CNN was rerunning the story and pictures. Ashford sat solemnly in his chair staring at the screen. He shook his head.

"Sir, the Secret Service are ready for the ride to the track. Do you need to take anything?"

Ashford patted his pocket where the derringer lay deep inside, looked at his aide, and shook his head. "No. We'll be returning to the suite afterwards. I don't know of anything I'll need." He got up, buttoned his jacket, and walked to the door to meet Shanker.

JILL CRENSHAW AND ANOTHER twenty elected officials and dignitaries watched the fifth race of the day from the booth before either the Vice President or President arrived. It was a group that abounded with laughter, loud talk, and shouts as the horses thundered across the finish line directly in front of them. For nearly an hour, they had been enjoying the company of each other along with refreshments that lined one wall in abundant proportions. A bartender stood in a rear corner behind a large assortment of liquors, wines, and soft drinks—all at no expense to the guests. It was a frivolity heightened by the knowledge that each had been chosen to be in the presence of the two highest office holders in the world. They would partake of the Kentucky Derby with the President and Vice President.

"Senator Crenshaw, I'm so happy that we were able to have the reception for you and your fiance last evening. It was a wonderful affair. How romantic to have met here at the Derby and then come back for a pre-marriage party," the wife of one of Kentucky's senators said. "And I understand you are quite an authority on Thoroughbreds. How have you done on the winners today?"

Jill shook her head. "Not as well as I had hoped. I got the winner in two races but finished out of the money in two others. This fifth race I came out even. My choice finished third."

"Who do you like for the Derby?"

Jill showed her the card that named three horses. "I picked them in that order. I don't bet much though. It's just recreational to me. I have to put a little money where my mouth is or else nobody would take my expertise seriously."

"I say. Well, you're doing much better than me. I haven't chosen a winner all day."

"It's not too late," Jill said and showed her the card again.

A hush came over the group as the Secret Service escorted the Vice President into the room. He came in from the rear entrance and stepped down into the main reception area. Tiered seating took up the middle portion of the room where they would sit to watch the race. He methodically made his way around the room in a counterclockwise circuit of shaking each person's hand and smiling a greeting. He declined an offer of refreshments.

He finally made his way to Jill. He grasped her hand firmly. "Such beauty. I've never seen such a lovely person in the Senate before. It's an honor to have you here, Senator."

"Thank you, Mr. Vice President. Call me Jill, please."

Ashford nodded. "Jill. A lovely name to go with a highly regarded lady." Then he leaned closer to her ear while the other voices increased to a raucous din again. "Your fiance had another bombshell of a story in the paper this morning."

Jill smiled. "So I understand. I haven't seen it yet."

"Oh, yes. The television is giving it huge play. CNN has it on every half hour. Quite a scoop for him to get those pictures. How did he manage that? Do you know?"

Jill shook her head and swallowed the drink of wine she had been tasting. "No. He's amazing. Never tells me a thing. Would you care for some wine, Mr. Vice President?"

"No. I don't drink anything with alcohol," Ashford said and turned to his Secret Service guard. "Mr. Shanker, have you met Jill Crenshaw? She's my replacement as U.S. Senator."

"I met her last evening. At the reception," Shanker said and continued to look around the room and outside as he was trained to do.

"Have you met her fiance? Brad Yeary. He's quite a reporter."

"Yes, I saw him last night also. Very nice gentleman. I also met him shortly after the incident in New Orleans."

"I see," Ashford said.

BRAD MADE HIS WAY to the press section situated in the open in front of the VIP box. His seat assignment had him to the left of the box and about ten rows in front. He turned to his right and could barely make out a few figures wandering around inside. He couldn't distinguish one from the other. Jill was in there somewhere, but he could see no sign of her. Most members of the press were waiting on a walkway for a glimpse of the President and the opportunity to shout a question or two at him. Brad was thankful that members of the national media knew him only by name and reputation and not by appearance.

Between races the area had emptied and was beginning to refill with those who owned, trained, and raced Thoroughbreds. He noticed an odd looking duo of young men descending the walkway. They had already passed him when he saw the tall one was limping slightly and walking with the aid of a cane. His companion kept his head down and pointed to their seats five rows in front and to the right of Brad. Their seats were positioned directly on the finish line. Brad shook his head. How much money was represented by the two hundred seats in that section?

Precisely at 4 p.m., the band struck up "Hail to the Chief," and most of the spectators in the stands turned their heads in hope of getting a glimpse of the President. The announcement that he would be there added to the excitement of those who came to see the fine horses and enjoy the glorious spring event. Brad turned and looked toward the walkway behind the VIP booth. He could see a flurry of activity but could not make out any individual. He turned back toward the track and saw that practically everybody else was peering toward the walkway also. The man with the cane was looking through a pair of binoculars and pointing his cane in the direction of the movement. His shorter companion also pointed in that direction.

PRESIDENT TEATER, ALONG WITH a Secret Service contingent, Garron, Steinheitz, and another ten dignitaries who had been to the luncheon, entered the side door of the reviewing booth to the standing ovation of the ones already there. Jill Crenshaw was nearest the door when the entourage entered.

The President waved for quiet and everyone stopped talking. Only the tinkling of ice in glasses could be heard. "Don't mind me. Go on with your party. I came to see a good horse race. You know I've been in some of my own in my lifetime," he said and was answered with an outburst of laughter. "I'll get around to seeing all of you. Remember the party after the race. All of you are invited. See George here if you haven't received your written invitation," the President said and pointed to Garron.

He turned to Jill. "Senator Crenshaw, I see you made it through the reception last evening. I'm sorry I couldn't make it. Secret Service rules," he said and pointed toward two of his guardians. "They're very careful about where I go in crowds. This is the largest group I've been allowed to mingle with in a long time. Apparently all of you are harmless," he said and looked around the room.

"Thank you again, Mr. President, for allowing me to fly down on Air Force One. I've had a great time."

The President saw Ashford, excused himself from Jill, and moved toward the Vice President. He grasped Ashford's hand, "I'm glad the Secret Service thought it was safe enough to put us both in the same room. It's rare you know. But you got such a friendly reception in Kentucky in March, they didn't feel there was any danger."

"Thank you, Mr. President. I was only doing my job."

"And a great one you've done. You stepped into a difficult situation and have performed marvelously."

NIDAL LEANED OVER AND spoke softly toward Ahmed. "Couldn't you get him in your view?"

"No. I think I saw him, but there were too many surrounding him. Not a chance."

Nidal took a paper from his pocket and unfolded it. "Let's review the seating chart again." Ahmed leaned over and looked at the small diagram and the red circle around the seat where the President would sit. "Unhook the cable from the binoculars and just see if you can make out the seat from our vantage point. Third row, third seat."

Ahmed kept the cane to his side, stood, and turned toward the booth. He focused the binoculars while he held them to his eyes. The glass of the booth made it a bit difficult to see in. Finally he nodded his head. "Yes, third row and third seat. It's directly behind this row. It's on the finish line too. I should be all right."

Nidal turned his head toward the booth. A line of uniformed police stood in the row below the window. "Don't worry about the police, Ahmed. If they see anything, it'll just be a gawky young man pointing a cane. I guarantee you they will be focused on the horses in the stretch just like everyone else. You could piss in the aisle and no one would notice."

Heads turned, fingers pointed at favorites, and eyes checked betting tickets in the stands and infield as race time drew nearer. In

the paddock area the twelve horses that would run for the roses were
being saddled and made ready for their jockeys to mount. Television
reporters were still interviewing owners and trainers. Each was giving
an analysis of the race and stating a preference as to the favorite.

On the horse and rider shaped weathervane, a painter was
removing the colors of the last winner of the Derby in preparation for
painting the new winner's as soon as the race concluded. In the victory circle, the blanket of red roses lay across a wooden stand awaiting
the sweating winner. Some of the infielders forsook their revelry and
surged toward the retaining fence in order to have a fleeting view of
some part of the race.

Brad surveyed the crowd and wished he was with Jill in the
booth. At least for the next few minutes, his story would not be the
center of the nation's attention—the Derby would be. He leaned back
and closed his eyes. Another newsman, sitting next to him, elbowed
him. "Don't go to sleep and miss the most exciting two minutes in
sports," he said and looked at Brad's ID badge. "Yeary? Yeary? Are
you the one from New Orleans? With the great story and pictures?
Hey, I'm just a sports reporter, but that was a great job. Congratulations."

Brad shook his hand and hoped that no one else heard. Anonymity was his sought-after companion.

AT TEN MINUTES BEFORE post time, the band began its me-
lodic playing of "My Old Kentucky Home" accompanied by the voices
of thousands in the stands and infield and a few in the VIP booth who
were native Kentuckians. Jill Crenshaw joined in. She had learned
it many years before—the melancholy tune that brought joy to the na-
tives. The post parade with the Thoroughbred entries, their jockeys,
and lead horses began with the first notes of the tune. As soon as the
band concluded, the thirty guests in the VIP booth began to take their
seats with only the ten Secret Service agents remaining standing.

They began to take their places from the back of the six rows
of raised seats. Everyone behind the President's third row remained
standing—not sure of what the protocol was in a booth at the Kentucky Derby. The President's row filled with Kentucky's two U.S.
Senators to his extreme left, Steinheitz to his immediate left, and
Garron on his right. The last seat to his right was for a Secret Service
agent, but he remained standing as did all the others.

Vice President Ashford took his place on the second row immediately in front of the President with Jill Crenshaw to his left and his
chief-of-staff to his right. None of the first row of seats was occupied.

Jill squinted toward the track and looked at the card that had
her three picks listed. She located them and smiled as they walked by.
In good-natured tones, voices from behind the President asked which

one he had bet on.

"Oh, I've got a favorite or two, but I forgot to ask Senator Crenshaw. I understand she's the expert," the President said and gave Jill a nudge on the shoulder. She looked around and smiled.

The horses and outriders made their way to the loading gate. Television monitors along the front top of the booth gave the guests close-up views of the three-year-olds being placed in the starting gate. The crowd drew quiet as the last horse walked in. There would be only a slight pause before they were released to run.

With a loud clang of metal against metal and a simultaneous bell, the gates opened and twelve Thoroughbreds shot out and bore to their left, attempting to gain the inside rail position. A shout went up from some in the booth.

Jill Crenshaw's eyes followed the burst of spirited horseflesh while the Vice President's were fastened on a row of seats in the stands sixty feet away. He reached his right hand into his coat pocket and with his thumb flipped the bottom of the lighter away.

"Mine's ahead!" the President shouted.

"That's a bad sign, Sir," someone said from behind him. "He needs to be ahead at the end of the race." A little laughter echoed through the booth.

The horses disappeared around the first turn and a shout went up from the infield fans on that side who now got a glimpse of the race. Eyes in the booth focused on the monitors for a better view of the far side of the track.

AHMED TURNED THE CANE'S handle and felt for the button. He reached down and released the cover plate from the end of the barrel. Nidal turned briefly for a look at the booth. He could see they were all seated except for the Secret Service. He leaned over to Ahmed. "Are you ready?" Ahmed nodded affirmatively but continued to look toward the track.

Five rows back and to the left, Brad was engulfed in the excitement of the moment. He had lost sight of the horse he placed twenty dollars on. It probably wouldn't matter anyway since it was not one that Jill had recommended.

THE RACE ANNOUNCER CALLED out the order they were running at the half-way point. Jill's three were among the top six. The President's horse had dropped from first to third. Brad's was tenth but gaining. Al Shanker and the other agents looked toward the track themselves. They had also made their bets.

In another minute, the horses appeared at the head of the stretch. They were a quarter mile from the finish. Jill's horses were out of order but now all were among the top five. The booth vibrated as those in the stands around began to stand and stomp their feet in hope of spurring on their horses. All eyes looked left. Those in the booth began to stand. Jill bounced up and down in her seat as her picks pulled to the front, now in the order that would make her a trifecta winner.

Ashford looked straight ahead. "Don't stand!" he said. "You'll block the President's view." He clamped his hands around Jill's arm on his left and his chief-of-staff's on his right.

Sixty feet in front, Ahmed stood, stepped into the aisle, turned, and aimed his cane toward the window. Quickly, he aligned the crosshairs in the binoculars on the figure in the third row who was now standing.

The ears. When Brad saw the man pointing the cane toward the booth, it flashed through his mind. Those were the ears of the tall man that he had seen so often the past month when he stared at the drawings Shanker had given him.

"You!" he shouted. No one heard. The stands vibrated more and more as the horses neared with thundering hoofs, less than a hundred yards from the finish.

Jill couldn't take it. She had to stand. Her horses were going to win. She shouted and escaped Ashford's grasp. She was halfway up, cheering the horses' approach to the finish line when the plate glass window in front exploded.

All those in the booth threw their hands up reflexively while the thousands of pieces of glass settled in sparkling chips to the floor. All except for Rob Steinheitz, who toppled over onto Jill's back. His forehead had exploded at the same time as the window. Blood and sticky gray matter sprayed all those near him like a geyser as his heart pumped its last beats.

Ashford turned as Teater wobbled and stared at Steinheitz. The President wiped at the side of his face that was covered with Steinheitz's blood. The Secret Service agents reacted first toward the window for a split second and then, almost as though their heads were turned by the same invisible string, toward the President and Vice President. They both had blood on them.

"Everybody fall down!" one of the agents yelled and moved toward the window.

Steinheitz's limp body slid off Jill toward a Kentucky senator. All of the agents had drawn their weapons. Shanker was nearest the window when it shattered. He held his gun but there was no one near the opening except for the police. Most of them still watched the horses, oblivious to the fact that the window behind them no longer existed. He turned toward his charge—the Vice President he was sworn to guard.

Agents rushed toward the President to shield him with their

bodies. Ashford turned. The President was not hit. He drew the derringer. Teater turned toward the back of the room. Ashford raised his
hand and pointed toward the President's back. Jill slapped at the
barreled lighter when she saw it aimed at the President.

It fired before Ashford squeezed. The President gasped as the
shot ripped through him.

Shanker hesitated for a split second and then fired his weapon
into the Vice President's back before the derringer's second barrel
could be emptied.

In his fall to the floor, Ashford pulled Jill with him. They lay
face to face. His eyes opened. Blood oozed from his mouth.

He looked straight at her. "Death to the hypocrites," he whispered his final words.

Nine guns pointed at Shanker's head. Each of the other Secret
Service agents now bore down on him. "Drop it, Shanker! You gone
fuckin' crazy? Drop it and on the floor!"

# Forty-three

The hospital room was quiet. Jill lay in the bed with Brad at her side. Her eyes stared weakly at the ceiling. Her lips were tightly drawn over her teeth. She had recovered nicely from Harrot's assassination in her presence in January. But this was different. She had lain face to face with another dying Vice President just after Steinheitz's lifeless body had fallen across her shoulders.

"I don't like politics, Brad."

"Everything's going to be all right," he said and squeezed her hand.

The day before when the cane fired and smoke belched from its end, Brad had turned to see the glass explode in the booth where Jill sat. It didn't matter to him at that moment that the President and Vice President were also in there. His thoughts had been only on her. Instead of running down the shooter, he had sped up the steps toward the booth. Again, he had been intercepted by a line of police and not allowed to enter.

Nidal and Ahmed made their escape. Siddig and Mahmud drove them to the airport where they boarded a flight for Atlanta and eventually Saudi Arabia. Ironically, a half hour before post time, a Lexington socialite who had been watching CNN called the Washington headquarters of the FBI and Secret Service to report that she knew the names of two of the men who appeared in the drawings on television. By post time, police had gone to Darby Run in Lexington to check on Nidal and Ahmed. There they discovered the two had been in Louisville for three days.

Knowledge of what had occurred crept slowly through the Derby crowd. All eyes had been focused on the finish. Once the ambulances began arriving everyone knew something was terribly wrong. The President was taken out first, badly wounded and unconscious. Then two bodies were removed with sheets pulled tightly around their faces or in one case what was left of his face. A neatly dressed man in suit and tie, manacled and with his head down, was then led to a waiting police cruiser. Jill had been carried out on a paramedic cart also with her eyes closed.

On another floor of St. Andrews Hospital in Louisville, President Steven Teater lay between life and death. His prognosis was not good. A bullet had ripped through his right lung. There was internal bleeding. Hours of surgery had, for the moment, stabilized his condition.

Brad cared little for any of that. He just wanted Jill to survive. And not only to survive, but to be Jill again. He wanted her laughter and beauty. He had not asked her about what happened. But in the hours when she was awake, she had volunteered the information to him.

Her psychiatrist and the other attending physicians indicated that it could be therapeutic for her to talk about it with someone she loved. She didn't need to keep her feelings bottled up, they told him. So he listened and nodded when she spoke but left his questioning nature outside her room.

Steinheitz must have been hit by the shot through the window, she told him. Blood and brains gushed from him and splattered her and everyone nearby. He had toppled over onto her back, spilling what remained in his skull. She had seen Ashford turn toward the President with a small, twin-barreled gun in the palm of his hand. Her push at his arm had only changed the course of the bullet slightly. It struck the President.

The next moment she heard another loud blast and Ashford slumped to the floor, taking her with him. He still grasped the little gun when he spoke his last words to her. She recounted it at least three times to Brad. He sat, listened, held her hand, and said over and over, "It's going to be all right. I'm here with you."

Brad knew when he saw the television news accounts that Shanker was the one led from the area in handcuffs and into custody. From what Jill told him, he began to put together what had occurred in the VIP room the day before. Apparently no one saw Ashford shoot the President except for Ashford's chief guardian—Shanker—who was trained to keep his charge in sight at all times. And Jill. All other eyes were on the President. They arrested Shanker, thinking he was part of an assassination plot.  In the confusion, they didn't know whether he shot Ashford or Teater or perhaps both.  No one had interviewed Jill yet.

He learned that Shanker had been released within an hour from the time that he was taken into custody.  He was flown out of Louisville in a government plane to an undisclosed location.  With all the politicians who were in the room at the time, the remarkable thing was that no one was giving any public interviews.  The FBI and Secret Service had requested it.  Two or three people in the stands said they saw a young man point a cane toward the window just before it exploded.  But no one could give a good description, and he had disappeared into the crowd during the ensuing pandemonium.

The basement of the hospital was a flurry of activity.  Half the floor had been commandeered as press rooms for the myriad of reporters who were already there and for those who swarmed to the Kentucky city within hours.  It was an international story that had, at four-forty the previous day, ended all the talk about Brad's front page scoop in the *Times-Gazette*.

"Brad, go write your story.  You have to.  I'll be all right."

"Jill, there's plenty of people writing stories, but I'm the only one here with you.  It can wait."

A nurse came into her room with her next medication.  Jill took the pills and swallowed.  "Brad, these are going to make me sleep for at least four hours.  When I wake up, I want you here beside me.  But I want you to be able to tell me that you've written the story.  Got it?"

He nodded.  "I'll be here."

"And you will have written the story."  She raised a hand and pointed an index finger toward him.

Pinthater was in the little area he had managed to claim for the *Times-Gazette* in the basement of St. Andrews.  All around the phones were ringing, keyboards singing, and people shouting at one another.  All of the Sunday stories had speculated on how many bullets had been fired and from where.  This generation of reporters and editors had grown up on the abundant conspiracy theories of the Kennedy assassination and were framing their reports in a manner that would leave them open to go in many directions.  Pinthater had written the front page piece for his newspaper.  He sat admiring the only writing he'd done in ten years.

"Get up, Ed.  I've got to get this done and get back up to Jill," Brad said and swept all the loose papers off the desk with his arm.  He took out his pad and started jotting down notes while Pinthater vacated the chair.

"You got something good?"

"You bet your sweet ass.  This'll be bigger than anything to date.  Is this line secure where no one can intercept it?" Brad asked, pointing to the phone and computer terminal line.

"Hell if I know."

"Okay, I'm not transmitting on it then. I'll put it on disk. Get you a plane chartered to New Orleans and you'll have it in time for the deadline." He looked at his watch. It had been a mere twenty-four hours since the shots were fired.

He phoned Danny Spurling at his desk in New Orleans. Danny had been at the paper for thirty-six hours straight, and he sounded like it. "Danny, I need four photos ready for the front page of the morning edition. Listen carefully. Head and shoulders of Ashford and Teater. Got it?"

"Yes, sir."

"Okay, look at Saturday's edition and get me the bottom left. Understand?"

There was a pause while Danny shuffled through the papers to Saturday's. "Ears?" He asked.

"Right, ears." Brad smiled. Danny was catching on. "Now get me a file photo of the Secret Service agent who is on the Harrot investigation. That's all. Those four across the top of the page. Pinthater's bringing the copy for the story back on a plane. Tell the make-up people to clear the whole front page." Brad looked at Pinthater who nodded agreement. "That's the word from the boss."

Brad looked back at Pinthater. "Get your ass out of here, Ed. I've got work to do. Get the plane arranged." Pinthater stood and walked out the door.

Brad slipped the disk into the computer and began the clickety-clack on the keyboard. He had two eye-witness accounts. His and Jill's. A heartbeat of panic struck him. What would happen once the story came out that he saw the first shot fired? He could identify the one who shot Steinheitz, and Jill's account put the finger on Ashford as the one who wounded the President. With what he had heard from Jill, and knowing Shanker first hand for the past four months, it fit that the Secret Service agent had killed the one he was there to guard—for a higher good. Shanker shot Ashford protecting the President of the United States.

He shook his head. He had been so wrong to believe that Ashford and Teater were co-conspirators in the death of Harrot. Silently, he gave thanks that he had not written anything about that notion. He was still as puzzled as ever as to the why of it all. Was the big-eared youth aiming for Steinheitz, the President, or Ashford? Why was Harrot killed? Why did Ashford shoot the President? He shook his head again. He would deal with those questions in followups if he could ever get the answers.

MONDAY AFTERNOON JILL AND Brad sat in her Baton

Rouge apartment admiring the story that took up the entire front page of the *Times-Gazette*. Shanker was the hero, according to Brad's version. He had saved the President by shooting the Vice President. He told it all. The bullets. The shooters. The fallen. Three—there had been three of each.

The FBI and Secret Service were not confirming nor denying his version. He knew they couldn't dispute much. He was the eyewitness to one and Jill to the other. Shanker's shot was the only speculation, but it was a safe guess, taking everything else into account. The FBI would be in Baton Rouge to interview him and Jill before nightfall. He didn't mind putting the finger on the tall Arab who had now been identified.

The doctors, when they released Jill early Monday, told her to take it easy. Talk about it as much or little as she liked. She should be her own guide. Seek further counseling or therapy at home, they told her.

President Teater's condition was unchanged. The Speaker of the House had been named as acting President under the provisions of the Twenty-fifth Amendment and the Presidential Succession law. There was no Vice President. If the President died, the new President could name one. The Speaker would serve until Teater was well enough to resume office.

Ashford's body had been returned to Stratford Place for the funeral the next day and burial on the grounds. Brad's story would decrease the amount of mourning for the Vice President and the number in attendance at the service. Jill told him that he should go. Brad didn't know if he could face Amelia Tadford after writing the terrible facts about her boss and long-time overseer of the plantation.

Shanker was missing. Brad tried the Washington office and the New Orleans office of the Harrot investigation. Nothing. No comment. Very short. His Tennessee phone was unlisted, but Brad was sure Shanker would have sought refuge there.

He asked Jill if it would be all right for him to make a quick trip to Tennessee to see Shanker and to Washington to see Garron. He would go after the Ashford funeral. He had done a fine story with the Who, What, Where, and When, but he needed the Why for a conclusion. Harrot's diary was part of it. He began a story based on that, but it would never get past Pinthater's "second source" requirement unless he could get Shanker or Garron to back it up.

THE GATES TO STRATFORD Place were closed and locked the next day when Brad drove up. Four uniformed guards stood in front. He told them who he was. They still refused entry. "The service will be private," they told him.

He went to the gate and looked over. The house was barely

visible at the end of the long narrow drive. He made out several cars. Big limousines—shiny and black. The walkie-talkies of the guards crackled with occasional talk. Other cars drove up and were turned away. No press allowed. At least fifty camera crews were rolling and snapping from this vantage point. They had telephoto lenses. Brad didn't.

"Dammit, at least call in there and ask if I can come in."

"Not a chance," one of the guards said and pointed at the Monday edition of the *Times-Gazette*. "You call him a Muslim and a would-be murderer, and you expect to be a guest at the funeral?"

"Is Amelia Tadford in there?" Brad gestured toward the house.

"Yeah, she's in there, and she's the one who gave the order for no press."

Brad folded his arms across his chest. "Just call her. Tell her Brad Yeary's here. If she says 'No' then I'll go quietly back to Baton Rouge."

The guards looked at one another. Finally, one pushed a button on his phone. "There's a Brad Yeary here. Says Ms. Tadford's expecting him at the funeral. He's a stubborn asshole. Won't take 'No' for an answer. Want's to be sure. What? Yeah, I'll hold." The phone was silent for a long period while the officer rocked back and forth on the balls of his feet. Then a voice came back through. "Who? Yes. Okay, then." He handed the phone to Brad.

Amelia Tadford invited him in. "Thanks," Brad said and handed the phone back to the officer who was scratching his head.

Brad parked behind a Saudi Arabian embassy limousine that was immediately behind a similar one from Kuwait's.

In the parlor, fewer than thirty people, many of them with olive complexions and dressed in expensive suits, talked in hushed whispers. Amelia Tadford stood before the closed casket of Benjamin Edward Ashford, hands clasped to her bosom, and stared at a framed photo of him that stood on a small table near the head. When she turned to face Brad, she held a single rose in her delicate hands. He could barely see the sad eyes beneath the black lace veil that she wore. She was dressed for mourning in a floor-length dress and hat that held her veil. All black.

She pointed to an adjoining room. Brad followed.

"Would you care for some lemonade or tea, Brad?"

"No, thanks, Amelia." They sat down in chairs on each side of a window that looked out toward the orchard. "I'm sorry it turned out this way. I just wrote what I knew. I certainly didn't mean any harm to you."

She took a tissue from the little table that stood in front of the window between them. "I know. The whole thing was unfortunate."

"I just wanted to come by and pay my respects."

She looked at him. "No, Brad. You wanted to come by so that you could write a follow-up story on who attended his funeral and what was said."

Brad smiled and blushed. "You got me. Is he going to be buried here?"

"Yes." She pointed out the window. "The family cemetery. Six generations of Ashfords. Out on the far side of the barn are six generations of Tadfords."

"He was the last, though. The Ashford line comes to an end. Right? He had no brothers? He and his wife were childless?"

"Yes. And no."

"No? What do you mean?" Brad leaned nearer Amelia.

"The Ashford name is gone. The Ashford blood lives on. My son is his."

Brad sat silent while Amelia rose, went to a desk, and returned with a document she handed to him. "His will. B.J. and I inherit Stratford Place. B.J. is at this moment upstairs in *his* library." She nodded upward.

Brad opened and read the Last Will of Benjamin Ashford. The plantation passed from the overseer to the overseen. From master to servant. From father to son.

While he was busy reading, Amelia retrieved another envelope and handed it to Brad. "He said to give this to you if anything happened to him."

Brad laid the will aside and took out ten neatly typed pages from the envelope that she had just passed to him. He flipped through all the pages and saw that the last page had been signed and notarized. Each page bore the unmistakable signature of Ashford at the bottom. He went back to the first page and began to read.

"The fact that you are reading this means that I was at least partly unsuccessful in what I attempted."

Brad read on in silence while Amelia looked out the window. It was all there. A signed and notarized confession of a murderer. He had Harrot killed. Harrot would not turn on Teater. Ashford didn't pull the trigger on Harrot, but he took responsibility. He named the President, Steinheitz, and Garron as being plotters with unknown Arabs to overthrow certain Mid-East countries. He referred to and quoted extensively from the Koran. "The Hypocrites" was repeated word by word.

His plan was to kill Teater, end the conspiracy, and as a logical consequence, also assume the power of the Presidency. He would protect the countries that would have been under attack from Teater. If Teater wasn't killed, Ashford asked for Brad to use this to bring him down. Ashford believed that the present governments in the Mid-East were sufficient, although not perfect. His Muslim faith prevented him

from advocating a military overthrow of them. He despised the plotters. "They are the enemy. Guard yourself from them," he again quoted from the Koran.

Brad looked up at Amelia. She was still turned from him,
staring into the distance. "Amelia, did you read this?"

"No. He said it was for you."

Brad placed the sheets back into the envelope. The "Why" of
the whole mess had fallen into his lap. Two Vice Presidents confirmed
that the President was plotting to overthrow legitimate foreign governments. Pinthater would have his two sources—dead though they both
were—and the country would have a bigger story to mull.

"Do you mind, Amelia, if I mention that B. J. is his son and
that you two are now the new owners of Stratford Place?"

"No, Brad. We are proud of our heritage. Whatever Benjamin
did, you can be sure he did it because he thought it was the right thing
to do. He was not a coward."

AT NOON THE NEXT day, Brad's plane left from New Orleans. Shanker would meet with him in Tennessee for an hour or two.
He had called Brad after reading Monday's story. Then Brad would be
on to Washington to meet with George Garron. Garron didn't want to
talk, but Brad pledged to Pinthater that he would sit outside Garron's
door until Thursday's edition came out if necessary. They would give
Garron an opportunity to refute what Harrot and Ashford had written
about him, Steinheitz, and the President. It was only fair. It would
also protect them from a libel suit if it wasn't true. The President was
still too near death to speak with anyone.

Ashford's own pages were being photographed now to be run
in their entirety on the inside pages. The front page would tell the
story as Brad had learned it. But the linchpin would be the words of
two dead Vice Presidents—especially Ashford's.

THE ELDER SHANKER SAT on the porch in the same position as on Brad's first visit to the home.

"Out by the barn. Al's out by the barn!" he shouted when Brad
opened the rental car's door. The sun beat down in hotter rays than
it had the month before, but the old man still rocked and smoked his
pipe under the shade of the porch roof and his straw hat.

"Thanks!" Brad yelled and turned toward the barn.

"My son protects the President, you know. If he had to shoot
somebody, it was for the good of the country. He works at the White
House," Shanker's father said, his voice trailing off.

Al Shanker sat on the shady side of the barn looking toward
the bright green tobacco sprouts that had been recently transplanted.
He got up when Brad rounded the corner, wiped sweat from his fore-

head with a red handkerchief, and reached out his hand. He had returned to the farmer. Instead of the shiny suit that Brad had last seen him wearing in Louisville, he wore bib-overalls, a light shirt with sleeves rolled up to the elbows, and brown ankle-high boots. They both sat on a bale of hay and stared at the tobacco patch and the hills beyond.

"Brad, I've retired."

"Why? You should be given a medal. You did exactly what you were trained and sworn to do. You were protecting and defending the Constitution."

Shanker didn't look at the reporter. "I know. They were going to promote me and put me away at a desk job. I didn't want that. I wanted to be out protecting our leaders. I can't really blame them. What President or Vice President would fully trust me?

"I lost Harrot on New Year's Day. I shot his successor on Saturday. What kind of record is that for a Secret Service agent?"

Brad shook his head. "Al, you did what you had to do."

"Why? Why, Brad, did Ashford try to kill Teater? That puzzles me. I saw the flash of the barrel of his little gun. If I hadn't hesitated just a split second, Teater might not have been shot at all. But I did. My mind wasn't processing the information fast enough. Should I shoot the one I was supposed to guard? The question flashed through my mind. Then after he shot, I fired."

"Al, by this time tomorrow, some of the 'Why' will be answered. You saved the President, but Teater is going to fall. You did your job."

Finally, Shanker turned toward Brad. "You mean there's something out there that'll say Teater should have been killed? Did I shoot the wrong one?"

"No. Not at all. What both of them were planning isn't how we do things in this country. We have a Constitution and laws. You were the only one in Louisville that fired a gun for the right reason."

"I hope so."

They walked again, in silence, to the clear creek. Brad and Shanker took their shoes and boots off and waded like boys. With the cool water up to their ankles, they both scrunched their toes into the squishy mud.

Brad looked at his watch. "Al, I've got a plane to catch to Washington. I have one more stop to make before the story comes out tomorrow. I've got to try to talk to George Garron."

"Garron? Is Garron in on this too?"

Brad nodded his head. "Al, come to New Orleans for the wedding and be my best man. It's six weeks away. You have plenty of time now that you're retired. I'm counting on it."

BY SEVEN, BRAD WAS standing outside the west gate of the

White House asking to be let in to talk with George Garron. The officer looked at the guest list and did not find Brad's name. "You're not expected, Mr. Yeary. They don't have you on the approved entry list."

"Just call up his chief assistant and let me talk to him. I'm sure they'll want to see me after I tell them why I'm here."

Brad sat on a bench near the guard booth for the next half hour before anyone returned a call. The officer motioned him over to the phone. "This is Garron's executive secretary."

Brad took the phone and listened to the polite voice tell him that neither Mr. Garron nor anyone else wanted to speak with him. His trip was a waste. If he had called before flying up from New Orleans, they could have told him as much. He persisted. He told Garron's aide that there would be a big story in the morning edition pointing a finger of accusation at his boss. Surely, Garron would want to know about it and respond, he insisted. The voice on the other end finally consented to take it up with Garron. Brad could wait and if Garron wanted to see him, they would call the guard shack. Brad sat back down.

By eight Brad was sitting in the outer office of Garron in the executive branch off the side of the White House. Garron's door was closed. The young man sitting at the desk continued to answer the phone and tell those calling that Mr. Garron was unavailable and would not be able to talk with anyone until the next day.

For an hour Brad sat and wondered what he was really going to ask Garron. The words to the story were by this time making their way to the makeup room of the *Times-Gazette* and would be ready for the presses by midnight. While Teater lingered in the hospital fighting for his life, Garron would be the lightning rod for all the questioning in the morning once the words of Harrot and Ashford hit the streets. The chief political operative for the President had made no public statements since Saturday. He had stayed in Louisville, only returning to Washington this morning.

The young man's phone buzzed. He spoke into it and then went into Garron's office. A minute later he opened the door. "Mr. Garron will see you now, Mr. Yeary."

Garron's white shirt was rumpled and unbuttoned at the neck. His tie was pulled down and his sleeves rolled up. He rubbed his eyes and then ran his hand through his thinning hair. Without speaking, he motioned Brad to a chair in front of the desk. The aide left the room and closed the door behind him.

"Mr. Yeary, I'm an exhausted man. I haven't had more than three hours of sleep per night since the President was shot. I don't have much time to talk with you. What is it that you want? And what's this about some accusatory story that's to be in your little paper in the morning?"

Brad set his small recorder on the edge of Garron's desk. "Do you mind if I record our conversation, Mr. Garron?"

"Hell, yes, I mind. Put that damn thing away."

Brad retrieved the recorder, but as he slipped it into his shirt pocket, he pressed the record button anyway.

It took Brad but six minutes to tell Garron the whole of the story. He laid out before him the words of Harrot and Ashford. "We want your comment on it, Mr. Garron?"

Garron managed a wan little smile. "Not true. You couldn't have anything from Harrot's computer. Steinheitz checked that out. Ashford was obviously a crazy man. Who's going to believe someone who shot the President? It's all hearsay. We'll own you and your paper if you publish that. Here's a phone. You should call your publisher or whoever and tell them to pull that story." Garron pushed the phone console toward Brad who sat motionless.

"Mr. Garron, you can be sure that the October Fourteenth meeting of last year will be scrutinized very closely. There's probably photos of everyone coming into the White House that day. Harrot says you, Steinheitz, and Teater met with several Arabs. We don't have their names, but we will before it's over with."

Garron's face flushed. He brought his hands together in a double fist and pounded the desk in front of him. "I'm only the political operative, Mr. Yeary. Steinheitz and Teater could have been planning anything. That was not my bag. I don't know anything about it."

"You were at the meeting."

Garron sat silent for a minute. He looked at the clock on the side wall. "What day is this?"

"Wednesday."

"I mean what day of the month?"

"May Sixth."

Garron leaned back in his chair, placed his hands behind his head, and stared at the ceiling. "Five, six. That's May Sixth. If the year was Seventy-eight instead of Ninety-eight it would be perfect. I like numbers, Yeary. Seventy-eight was a lot better year for Teater, Steinheitz, and me. We were together a long time. You play poker, Yeary?"

Brad nodded.

"You know what a straight is then. Consecutive numbers. I see the clock says eight minutes after nine. In two minutes it will be nine, ten. So if this was Seventy-eight instead of Ninety-eight, in two minutes it would be five, six, seven, eight, nine, ten. I'm a numerologist. There's significance to numbers."

"Mr. Garron, do you have anything else to say."

Garron shook his head. "No."

Brad got up and left the room at nine, ten. Garron did not accompany him to the door.

Garron pressed the button for his aide on the telephone console. "John, I'm going to work a little longer. Buzz me at exactly twelve minutes past eleven, and then you can go home."

BRAD TOOK THE NEXT plane back to New Orleans. He wanted to see the papers come off the press. He arrived at one-thirty and went straight to his office. Danny Spurling sat at Brad's desk and already had him copies of the early press run laid out. Brad stepped into the office and glanced at the front page. They would be on the street in another hour and all hell would start breaking loose once again.

Danny handed him a piece of paper torn from one of the teletypes. "Did you see this, Brad?"

"No. What is it?"

"The AP is reporting that George Garron committed suicide a little before midnight. They quoted an aide who said he heard one shot shortly after he pressed a button on an intercom to tell Garron what time it was. He said Garron wanted to be notified at twelve minutes past eleven so he could go home."

Brad stared at the story. "Eleven, twelve." He laid the paper down on the early editions of the *Times-Gazette*. "All aces beat the straight."

# Forty–four

On June 19, the day before the wedding, Brad looked out over the railing of the balcony of his apartment on Burgundy. He was already dressed in suit and tie for their wedding eve dinner and party. The sun hung above the western horizon at eight in the evening, the summer solstice being only two days away.

"Jill, are you about ready? We told everyone eight-thirty."

"Just a minute, Brad. One more touch up." He could barely hear her voice through the open door.

He took a watering bucket and made a circuit of the plants and shrubs while he waited.

"How does this look?" Jill asked after she stepped into the doorway.

"Come on out in the light. Yes, yes, that's gorgeous," Brad said and admired the light blue satiny dress his bride-to-be wore. She had her hair pulled back and to the side. A simple strand of pearls encircled her neck. He took her into his arms and started to kiss her.

"No, no, you'll mess up my lipstick. There'll be time for that later on. Where's our cab?"

Brad shrugged his shoulders, went to the railing, and looked back up Burgundy. He heard him call out as soon as he turned the corner.

"Mr. Brad, Mr. Brad, don't you worry, I's here."

Brad brought Jill beneath the hanging baskets and to the railing. He pointed to the conveyance below. "See the cab I ordered."

It was the Cadillac of mule-drawn carriages. Brad had known the old black man for all his years in New Orleans. The clomp-clomp of the mule's hoofs settled to a rest directly beneath them. It was sparkling white with decorative fenders above the large-spoked wheels. The seating, which was designed to hold only two, was rolled and pleated red leather.

"A carriage suitable for Cinderella," Brad said and swept his arm downward.

"I don't think Cinderella was pulled to the ball by a mule," Jill said, smiled, and hugged Brad.

"Well, no. But she wasn't marrying a jackass tomorrow either."

The stout black man helped Brad and Jill into the carriage, encouraged the mule forward, turned the corner at Esplanade, and headed back toward the Quarter.

"You can skip the touristy guide monologue, Goose," Brad shouted over the sound of the traffic and the rhythmic hoof beats. The old man acknowledged with a wave of his hand. Jill and Brad joined hands and enjoyed the twilight pastels of the city.

"So, you're going to take a year off and write a book about it, huh, Brad?"

"Yeah, Shanker's going to help me with it. He knows the ins and outs of the Service and the Harrot investigation. He's retired and has plenty of time. The story's over since Teater resigned last week for 'health reasons.' You don't think those beginning impeachment proceedings had anything to do with his health do you, Jill?" He turned to her and smiled.

"I think it's wonderful. You can be a nice little house husband and write. You'll be at home every day when I get home from the Senate. I'm sure you can cook well."

"Yes. I'll probably have plenty of time to do that while I figure out how to write a book. I started to say we would write it as fiction. But no one would believe it."

"Are you going back to the *Times-Gazette* after the year?"

"Probably. I told Pinthater I would. He and Shanker are going to be at the dinner this evening. Ed's a little miffed that I chose Al to be my best man instead of him. Papa Legba and Danny will be my attendants."

Jill shook her head. "Oh, well. Shanker and you are closer after all you've been through."

The carriage turned from Esplanade onto Decatur. Jill pointed when they neared Jackson Square. The Mississippi was on their left and the St. Louis Cathedral on their right. "Look how beautiful the cathedral is in the evening light. We'll be there at two tomorrow."

Brad nodded his head.

A beeping sound came from the driver's seat. Goose picked up a mobile phone and put it to his ear. "Yes. Who? Yes, he's right here." He turned toward Brad. "Mr. Brad, it's for you."

Jill shook her head. "Can you believe it? A mule-drawn carriage has a high-tech mobile phone? And someone tracks you down?"

Brad reached and took the phone. "Yes, this is Brad Yeary. You're where? Great!" Brad turned toward Jill and put a hand over the phone. "It's the Reverend Hutteth. He's here for our wedding."

Jill rolled her eyes and turned toward the Mississippi.

"How did you find me, Reverend?"

"I have my ways."

"I want to thank you for your help. I guess the beast is gone, huh? Ashford and Teater are both out. Maybe the beast is within us. Wouldn't you say that, Reverend?"

"I don't know, Brad. When I first saw you, I just told you that 1998 would be the Year of the Beast and that he was behind the death of Harrot. I didn't say who he was."

"I know. But that all worked out. It's over."

There was a silence. "I'm sorry, Brad. One battle may be over. But the Year of the Beast, 1998, is not half over yet. Check your calendar."

## About the author:

**Chris Cawood** is a native of Tennessee. He is
a lawyer, journalist, and writer. He is a 1970 graduate of the
University of Tennessee College of Law. He served in the
Tennessee General Assembly from 1974 through 1978.

This is his fourth book, but the first of a series of general
fiction and mystery novels.